JEFF NOON

A MAN OF SHADOWS

A NYQUIST MYSTERY

ANGRY
ROBOT

ANGRY ROBOT
An imprint of Watkins Media Ltd

20 Fletcher Gate,
Nottingham,
NG1 2FZ
UK

angryrobotbooks.com
twitter.com/angryrobotbooks
Between dog and wolf

An Angry Robot paperback original 2017
1
.

Copyright © Jeff Noon 2017

Jeff Noon asserts the moral right to be identified as the author of this work.

A catalogue record for this book is available from the British Library.

ISBN 978 0 85766 669 7
EBook ISBN 978 0 85766 671 0

Set in Meridien and Refrigerator Deluxe by Epub Services.
Printed and bound in the UK by 4edge Ltd.

"Manchester's delirious prophet returns with scripture
written in shadow and light."

..., ...ced him more than ....

...inson, British Science Fiction Association
Award-winning author of the Europe series

"This superb novel of light, glass and blood proves again
that Jeff Noon is one of our few true visionaries."
Warren Ellis

"A disturbing and bizarre journey by one of the great
masters of weird fiction."
*Adrian Tchaikovsky, Arthur C Clarke Award-winning
author of* Children of Time

"One of sci-fi's leading prose artists."
SFX

"Startling, disturbing, original."
The Independent

"To say that Jeff Noon is a talented author is like saying that
Neil Armstrong has travelled a bit."
Starburst

"A literary maverick... Passionate, distinctive, demanding
and enthralling."
The Times

To Jack

QUICKSILVER

It was market time in Fahrenheit Court. Hundreds of people moved along the narrow aisles between the stalls, pressing against each other in their pursuit of bargains: silver cutlery, mirrors, glittering jewels, sequins, crystal jars, lanterns of every size and shape, decorative shards of coloured glass, flame burners, beads, baubles, shiny metal trinkets galore, with every object glittering under the powerful lamps that beamed down from the low ceiling. The temperature was rising steadily and a dense heat haze gathered in the roof space. Customers pushed and shoved. Flesh against flesh. Somebody fainted and was carried out: a common occurrence. A pair of buskers sang the latest street ballad "The Flames of Love", looking to put even more of a sparkle in the day. Hawkers yelled and cried, vying with each other to sell their wares: parasols, sunglasses, linen jackets and wide-brimmed hats, deodorant, perfumes. The noise was deafening around the stalls of the clocksmiths and horologists, a constant buzz of ticking, chiming and whirring. A recent report had stated that more than twenty million timepieces currently existed in the city, with more being designed, built and sold every day. People were obsessed. Members of the city's Guild of Chronologists handed out pamphlets detailing the latest timelines. A young man passed among the shoppers dressed as Apollo, the Sun God, and a mighty cry went up at the sight. For this was Dayzone. There was no other place like it, and the citizens were proud of being part of this overheated, overlit paradise.

One such was Jenny James. Her friends called her Jay Jay. She was twenty-six years old, a reporter for the *Beacon Fire*, the city's main newspaper. Married but without children as yet, as she worked hard at furthering her career.

Amid the noise and confusion, the light and the heat, the last few moments of her life ticked away, unseen, unheard.

Her husband Leon was by her side. They were shopping for a gift for her niece's birthday and had stopped at a stall selling kaleidoscopes. Jay Jay picked one up and raised it to her eye. She gazed first at the demonstration lamps on the stall itself, and then upwards towards the ceiling with its brightly lit neon signs and follow spots. The broken beads and fragments of coloured glass inside the tube shuffled into new patterns as she spun the instrument. The effect was hypnotic and she felt a little weak from a sudden intoxicating burst of yellow, red and orange. She lowered her sights onto a new target, a little boy who was carrying a battery-powered lantern in the shape of a star. He was so proud of his toy. The lantern glowed with a silver and blue prismatic light which, seen through the lens of the kaleidoscope, appeared to be a wheel of knives, ever turning.

Jay Jay felt strange. There was a pain in her side, and she could scarcely react before a similar pain struck her in the back.

Had she been attacked?

She couldn't work out what was happening to her.

The kaleidoscope fell to the ground. She tried to scream, but the sound caught in her throat. She could hardly breathe. Her stomach burned and when she put her hand to the pain her fingers came away smeared in blood. She stared at the redness, so bright under the myriad flickering lights and flames of the market hall. Her body jerked instinctively in order to escape her attacker. It was no good, there was no escape.

She collapsed to the ground.

Her husband stood there frozen for a few moments, still in shock at Jay Jay's sudden violent movement. Then he bent down to her. He saw the blood, the cuts in her flesh, and could hardly believe it. She was shaking badly. Her clothing was stained crimson in many places. She cried out for him, for his help, and her hands reached for him. Her fingers tightened around his. He felt he was holding onto everything that was dear and precious. And then Jay Jay's body convulsed one final time and lay still.

His wife was dead, Leon knew that. He could sense it.

The market hall was silent around him; nothing else existed. His entire world had closed down to this tiny space where the love of his life lay, unmoving. He touched her face gently. By some means he thought this would rouse her from sleep. The silence continued. And then a carriage clock chimed on a nearby stall, which set all the other timepieces in motion, and the noise of the market rushed into the vacuum.

People gasped and moved away a step or two. An older woman cried out in alarm. The little boy with the lantern hugged his father's legs in fright at the scene before him.

The word went out, whispered at first.

Quicksilver. Quicksilver.

And then louder, passing from person to person in the crowd, spoken in fear.

Quicksilver, Quicksilver, Quicksilver…

The autopsy revealed five separate stab wounds in the victim's flesh. And yet, out of the many people they interviewed, the police could not find a single person who had seen anything at all out of the ordinary. Leon James could only state that one moment his wife Jennifer was alive and well and laughing happily at his side, and the next she was lying on the ground, the blood flowing from her. No one had seen her being attacked. No one had seen her attacker. The weapon was never found: only its evidence, the wounds it had made. Here, in this city devoted to light and light only, where no shadows existed, no darkness, a murderer had struck in the middle of a crowded space and slipped away undetected. It didn't seem possible. Yet it wasn't the first such incident. *Quicksilver, Quicksilver!* The terrifying word travelled through the streets as the news spread. Another victim, another killing.

The city's clocks ticked on as ever.

PART ONE
DAYZONE

A STATION CALLED MORNING

Nyquist stepped down from the train. His fellow travellers either stared at him or avoided him completely as they hurried along the platform, leaving him there, a man alone in a crumpled blue suit and a slanted hat. Smoke from the steam engine filled his lungs. The sky burned fiercely, magnified by the glass panels of the station's roof. Close by, a team of workers were sluicing the carriages down with hosepipes, creating a rainbow effect as the water met the streams of light from above. The air sparkled and danced. Nyquist was feeling the heat already as he made his way to the ticket barrier. It had been a while since daylight had touched him. It was difficult to tell how long precisely, difficult to count the days and the nights because of the way he lived, the nature of the jobs he took on, the way that the city worked. It was easy to get confused.

A soft mechanical voice intoned from a nearby speaker column: "On your arrival in Dayzone please ensure that all necessary precautions are taken. We hope you..." Nyquist had heard it all too many times. He strode on, pausing only to look up at the large clock in the central dome of the concourse. It was twenty-five to nine. His own wristwatch read twenty-two minutes past eight. Thirteen minutes slow. He shivered a little before adjusting his watch. He felt better just doing this simple act. Fixed. In place.

Many people around him were doing exactly the same thing, changing their watches to the station's time: it looked like a ritual, so many fingers turning so many winders on so many dials, simultaneously.

Nyquist got himself cleaned up in the gentlemen's washroom. Braving the mirror, he pressed at the bruise on his face, causing the skin to move around the cut, a livid purple. He thought about covering it up with a sticking plaster but decided against it. The mark was all he had to show for the case: the only payment received. He walked back out onto the concourse and bought a three-shot coffee from a kiosk, most of which he had drunk by the time he got to the car park behind the station. It took him a while to remember where he had left his vehicle. A ticket for overdue stay was stuck under the windscreen wiper. He tore it loose and threw it on the backseat along with his jacket and his hat. The car was baking hot and even with the engine going and the fan sending out cool air, there was little relief. It was an old model in need of repair, or better still replacement. Nyquist felt the ache in his ribs where the punches had landed.

Day and night, it was getting worse.

The stale air inside the car started to move around a little. He looked at the dashboard; the dial read sixteen minutes past one. Nyquist groaned, wondering where all the hours kept going to. He checked his own watch again and used it to change the dashboard clock. Seven minutes to nine. That was better. Everything synchronised. Time to get the day started. He had one more job on the cards, searching for a missing teenager. He had to hope this one came good. The family had told him that the girl had lately become terribly afraid of the dark. Well, there were a lot of them around, these sufferers, and Dayzone was the place for them.

Nyquist drove out of the station's car park.

ROOM 347

The sky dazzled, alive with heat and light and colour, painful to look upon directly. Nyquist steered the car slowly along the dirt road. The radio churned out the latest dayside tunes, all major chords and bright sweet harmonies and lyrics about how the light of Apollo will shine on our love one day, one lovely day, one lovely dreamless day.

Ahead, the old hotel came into sight.

Really, he should've called in at his office on the way over, but the thought of that lonely place was too much to bear: dead messages, unpaid bills, and a lazy ceiling fan with a bullet hole in one blade. Earning some money was more important. So he'd spent the last couple of hours making calls, seeking out his usual contacts and checking out the known hideouts, hoping for a lead on the girl. He'd kept his eyes turned away from any clocks he passed on the streets, trying to keep to his own personal timeline. And coming up with zero hits, nothing, not until he'd spotted a gang of youths hanging around the doorway of a sunlamp emporium. One of them, Ricardo, responded to the photograph but said that he couldn't be sure: "Maybe yes, maybe no." The boy's eyes were hidden behind the purple lenses of a pair of swimming goggles, and his teeth shone a sparkling white against his vivid bronze skin. Money passed from hand to hand, information was exchanged. So Nyquist had driven further north towards Burn Out. Precinct Eleven. This was a shanty town situated on the far edge of the city, one of the hottest and brightest regions of Dayzone – and fear of the dark often led people to take refuge here.

Nyquist parked the car. He stepped out and looked across toward the rundown hotel. The old sign had been covered up with a large white banner and a new name given to the place, a single word written in red paint: *AMUSEMENTS*. Nyquist adjusted his shades and settled his fedora onto his head. A patchwork of avenues and courtyards lay on either side of the hotel: all these sales offices, car showrooms, workshops, moneylenders, all victims of the last time crash, their premises long abandoned and taken over by poorer, more persistent and less fearful inhabitants. Many people had erected tents between the low buildings. Plumes of smoke rose into the glare of the low-lying sky to show the places where the new tribes of the sun resided. The street was covered in dust, a cloud of which had already collected over his car. Nyquist felt his lungs start to ache after taking even a few steps. Colours fizzled and popped in his sight, while his body prickled all over with tiny electrical charges. He was hot, sweaty and uncomfortable. His shirt was clinging to him like a second layer of skin.

A gang of children were sitting on the steps of the former hotel playing a game, each of them attempting to do absolutely nothing at all for a longer time than any of the others. He threw them a coin. The kids watched it where it lay. The brass sparkled in the parched soil. The children's mouths hung open, their eyes blinking beneath the shade of their peaked caps. Not one of them moved.

Nyquist pushed through the revolving doorway. He was a big man, tough looking. There was a certain quality to his features, with so many raw edges; it gave the impression he wasn't quite completed. It was scary. He had been through some troubles, that was for certain, and you would think he was more than capable of handling himself. Until you got up close that is, too close, and maybe then you saw something different in his eyes, a giving away, a loneliness. But first you had to get close. And that wasn't easy.

The heat barely stirred inside the old hotel. Some years ago he had been here on a previous case; back then, this main room had been the lounge bar of a halfway decent establishment, where middle-aged executives sat together around polished tables. All of that was gone now, the furniture ripped out, the central bar turned into a food and drink counter, the entire surrounding floor space taken over by fruit machines and pinball games, hundreds of each. Colours blazed around the room, every bright shade seeming to melt around Nyquist's body as he moved along the main aisle. The arcade was crowded with players. There was a smeared quality to the air, a shimmering, a wetness. The noises made by the games sounded like so many hot glowing objects dropped into a pool of cold water. The silver balls zinged from post to post. Mechanical songs could be heard. Everything blurred together: the heat, the noise, the music, the machines and the kids working the levers and the light that pulsed between them, glistening, thick with moisture. Images of spaceships, ghosts, racing cars and tigers danced madly on the panels.

There was a large mechanical calendar on the far wall, another fixture from the hotel's glory days. The current year was 1959. This puzzled Nyquist; he'd had in mind that it was still 1958. He stared at the clock above the calendar. The time inside the building was exactly half past five. Now his head buzzed with irritation. He was suddenly hours out of step. There was no way to resist; his fingers automatically went to his wristwatch and he twirled the hands around the dial until they matched the arcade's timescale.

Reassured a little, he walked on, studying the clientele. The players were either locals, older kids from the families that had moved out this way, or else just middle-class boys and girls looking for a few hours of fun in a danger zone. A few had the look of longtime daylight fanatics: bleached hair, peeling skin, glazed eyes. Only their hands moved, fluttering like trapped birds on the flipper buttons or gripping the fruit machine levers in white-knuckled fever. Nyquist turned down another aisle, keeping his eyes open for trouble. The town of Burn Out was notorious for its carefree attitude to illegal activities, and he had no doubt at all that this place had its fair share on offer. Yet there appeared to be just two security guards on patrol, well-built specimens not that much older than the players themselves. In his early thirties, Nyquist was just about the oldest person in the room.

Ricardo had given him the name of this place, telling him to look out for a young man going by the name of Miles: greasy haired, tall and thin, distinguished by the burn marks on his face. Just such a figure was standing alone at a pinball game. Nyquist went up to him, trying to get his attention, but the player would not look away from the machine, his fingers working at the flippers continuously as they sent the silver balls into action, again and again. The bells and buzzers surrounded the machine in a halo of noise.

Nyquist peered around for sight of the guards, and then he pulled one of Miles's hands off a flipper button, followed by the other hand, and the young man let him do it easily, a mannequin being arranged into a new pose. Maybe there wasn't a single good solid muscle left in his body. The game died. Miles blinked a few times. His fingers trembled, caught in nervous patterns. Nyquist told him what he was after, pressing a couple of notes into a damp palm. The player's eyes caught a sparkle at the sight of the

money, more fuel for more games, and he had Nyquist
bend in close to hear a whispered message, a simple three-
digit affair.

"Are you sure?" Nyquist asked, displaying the girl's
photograph.

Miles smiled and shrugged, and he went back to his
beloved machine, his face covered in game glow.

It was enough. The room number. Nyquist made his
way over to the twin elevators at the rear of the arcade.
One of the guards had spotted him by now, so he carried
on past the elevator doors over to where a clutch of players
were bunched round a bright pinball adventure. He bent
down behind the machine, pulled the plug from the socket
and then walked right on. The kids started badmouthing
the establishment. One player banged his fist on the
glass cover of the machine, over and over, and the others
cheered him on. They tried to take over the next game
along, and a fight broke out. Nyquist glanced back to see
both of the guards moving in on the trouble. He took a
flight of stairs, climbing up three floors to a long, silent
corridor. He was exhausted, out of breath. The walls were
clammy, patterned by green mould. An electrical supply
box, fixed low on the wall, was patched with crocodile
clips and wires. Sparks flickered from bad contacts. Further
along, strands of a viscous white fluid dripped down from
an air vent. Nyquist took out a linen handkerchief to wipe
his brow. Tingles ran down his spine. He didn't like the feel
of this broken-down hotel. Most of the rooms were empty
as he passed, the doors hanging open to reveal one interior
after another. He felt he was viewing a series of abandoned
theatre sets where the despairing scenes of executive life
had once been played out. Nothing of that time remained,
but for the furniture and fittings, covered over now by
layers of dust. A number of the doors had actually been
smashed open, the wooden frames gouged out where the

locks had been torn away. Room 347 was halfway down the corridor, one of the few with its door still closed, still intact, a tray of uneaten food sitting on the carpet nearby. Voices could be heard from within, some kind of chanted refrain that stopped the moment Nyquist tried the door. It was locked. He banged a fist against the panelling.

"Let me in."

Silence. He knocked again, harder this time.

"Come on. Open up."

There was a scuffling sound and then the noise of breaking glass. Somebody screamed, a girl. Nyquist had to think. He had no way of knowing how many people were in the room, nor whether they would be friendly or otherwise. There were so many religious sects springing up, especially on the edges of the city, and tales were told of kids being held here against their will. He slipped off his sunglasses. Then he took a step back, coming forward again to kick hard at the door. A second time. The door started to give, and then it crashed open on the third attempt and he moved quickly into the room. It was like stepping into fire. His vision flared in a dazzle of gold and silver, with splashes of red. His eyes burned and closed involuntarily, the fiery shapes still throbbing inside his head. Again he heard the sound of glass breaking and he forced his eyes open to see a group of white figures standing amid all the colour and heat, their forms melting into view. Somebody pushed past him violently. It was a teenage boy, his shape vaguely human amid the pulsating light patterns. Nyquist could do nothing to stop him escaping. Instead, he had to turn his head away for a moment and back again, to find purchase on the room's confusion.

Well, he'd seen it bad before, but not this bad.

Violet fluorescent tubes closely lined the ceiling, with a tangle of bulbs hanging down between each tube, a countless number of them, all shining in different hues, all on different lengths of flex, naked, disturbed, swaying back and forth in curves of streaming light. The floor was covered in brightly-lit bedside lamps, their shades torn away. Many of these lamps had fallen over. Glass crunched underfoot as Nyquist took a step forward, his every move setting the hanging bulbs in motion. A globe of mirrored glass revolved at the ceiling's centre, stirring the lighted fragments into further confusion. Colours merged together and then broke apart. Strings of tiny bulbs flashed on and off in random sequences, flames danced from gas burners fixed to the walls.

Nyquist's vision settled. He stood tall and firm, blocking the doorway. Then he took in the room more clearly. The only window had been boarded up long ago, so the place was stifling; it stank of urine, body odour and fused wiring. The air crackled with noise. A threadbare mattress rested on the floor in one corner. A teenage girl was kneeling there, while another girl and a boy stood watching Nyquist. These last two looked scared, but the girl on the mattress seemed to be in some kind of stupor or daydream. Her eyes were closed and her upper body lolled against the wall. Dazzle junkies, they were called, hooked on soaking up whatever photons they could find, overdosing on the light. Nyquist glanced from face to face. The young man's mouth was stained orange, the colour extending beyond the lips in a clownlike grin. His eyes had no proper focus. He was jittery, unnerved. His hand came up to wipe at the substance, whatever it was. Some new drug, Nyquist surmised. The latest thrill powder.

"I'm looking for Eleanor Bale."

Nobody answered directly, but the pair standing looked at the third where she rested on the mattress. Nyquist nodded. "Now you two, get out of here." They followed his orders meekly, leaving the dazed-looking girl to whatever care she may find. Nyquist took out the photograph he had been given. It was all he had on her, apart from what little her father had managed to relate.

Eleanor Bale. Eighteen years old. Of a well-to-do family, and no doubt beautiful in that highly groomed way the rich seem to demand from their sons and daughters. Blonde hair, azure-blue eyes, well-shaped lips. It was all there in the photograph. But just now, in reality, there was little of this beauty on display. The girl was sprawled on the bed, wearing a vest, shorts and sandals. She was a mess: unwashed, dreadfully thin, hair dirty and bedraggled, her arms covered in scratches and her skin as pale and translucent as a moth's wing.

"Eleanor?"

The girl turned her face away, pressing herself against the wall.

"Come on. Stand up. Let's get your things together." Nyquist picked up a bag from the floor. "Is this yours?"

"Leave me alone!"

She had turned with a shocking violence, her whole body twisted up with hatred and fear. Fragments of light played over her skin, over the gaunt face and the sticklike arms. She looked ghastly. Nyquist stepped closer.

"Eleanor. Let's talk."

Without any warning the girl grabbed a light bulb from the mattress, flinging it wildly. Nyquist heard it smash into the wall behind him. He let the noise die away, and then held his hands open and wide apart. He stepped forward.

"Your family's concerned about you. They've employed me to bring you back home."

"What are you? Police?"

Nyquist shook his head. "Private investigator."

"Did *he* send you?"

"Your father? Yes."

The girl laughed bitterly. "I'm not going home."

Nyquist put on his sunglasses. "Some place you have

here," he said. "I know what it's like. You get scared of the dark. And what the darkness might hold. All of that. I know."

"I'm not scared of the dark. That's a lie."

"We're all scared of something."

Eleanor looked at him properly for the first time. "Is this the best he could do?" she asked.

Nyquist shrugged. "This is it."

"What happened to your face?"

"I was beaten up."

"Oh. Because... because of me?"

He grinned. "No. Another job. It turned nasty."

The girl shook her head in distaste.

"It was nothing glamorous, believe me. A mislaid import consignment. I was supposed to track it down, which I did well enough but it seems the whole thing was a scam, a dodgy insurance deal. I found out too much, and this is what I got for my trouble." He touched at the bruise below his eye. "Plus some wounds that don't show."

She seemed to take this in; evidently, there was still some kind of intelligence beneath the wreckage, however dimly lit. Then she turned it all round and swore and spat at him.

Nyquist sighed. "I know why you're here."

"Oh. Is that right?"

"Sure. It's all the rage. You're trying to burn away the pain."

The girl laughed at this. "Well, it's not working."

Nyquist could see that he'd struck a nerve. He took another step closer. "You can get help, you do know that? Proper help. Doctors, professionals–"

"No!" Eleanor grabbed a second light bulb, which she rammed against the wall next to her face, holding the splintered remains out in front of her. "Stay away from me."

Nyquist was calm now. He smiled. "That last job caused me problems. No result, no fee. So I really do need the money, girl. Times are hard."

Eleanor shook her head. Then she turned her hand around, pointing the broken part of the light bulb towards her own chest, repeating the same few phrases over and over: "I'm not going home. I'm not going home. He hates me. My father hates me!" She moved the jagged object closer, pressing it against the material of her vest, and closer still until a stain of blood appeared on the cloth. Her face was cold. She was holding herself tight against the pain, or what the pain might become.

"Don't do it, Eleanor."

Nyquist kept his voice steady. The girl looked at him. Blood ran down her hand, her body trembled. For one terrible moment Nyquist thought he had lost her, but then her eyes flickered with a different light and her fingers slowly opened, letting the broken bulb fall to the mattress. Nyquist knelt down next to her. He meant to pull her to her feet, but instead the young woman let herself be held; there was no fight left in her. He wasn't expecting the contact, and it felt strange. The girl was mumbling the whole time, words that he couldn't properly make out, a whispered prayer of some kind or other, to some god or other. And then she fell silent, but for the sobs and the harshly drawn breaths. Nyquist stayed where he was, half bent down, holding onto her hand. It was awkward, but there was nothing else he could do. And they stayed together like that for a time, these two lonely people, as the slowly turning lights of the room cast a spell of colours upon them.

HEATSTROKE

Nyquist led Eleanor from the room. She looked an even worse sight under the normal lighting of the corridor: stark white face smeared with blood, hair matted and falling long and ragged over her brow and eyes. She was clutching her only possession, a green tartan duffle bag. Nyquist wondered again how this well brought-up girl had fallen into such a state, but of course there were no rules or limits on pain.

"Keep moving," he said. "We'll get you sorted out."

A man was waiting for them just along from the doorway, a middle-aged man, thickset, dressed in a tailored, cream-coloured linen suit. He looked at Nyquist and the girl, the same time wiping his face with a red silk handkerchief.

"What are you doing?"

"I'm taking her home," Nyquist said.

"She owes me."

"For what?"

"Use of the premises. Rent thereof."

"I don't think so."

"I'm the manager. This is my place." He looked ill at ease, nervous even. His eyes closed momentarily, came open again. "Look at my door," he said. "Will you pay for this?"

"The kid's in trouble."

He smiled. "That's why they come to me."

"She needs help."

"Well yes, they have their needs."

Nyquist could see one of the security guards approaching along the corridor. "What's the problem?" this new arrival asked.

"No problem," the manager replied. "Not yet." He looked at Nyquist, then at the girl. "Let me talk to her. I know how to handle these young ones."

Nyquist felt Eleanor slip away from his hold. She backed up against the wall, inching along, with her mouth open and her eyes darting this way and that, and her hands bunched into fists, one of them still clenched tightly around the drawstring of her bag. And then her gaze fixed on the manager alone, her lips forming a single defiant word.

"No."

The manager pushed Nyquist aside, making to grab at Eleanor's arm. The barest touch shocked the girl, causing her to leap away and to cry out with such passion that Nyquist too was now trying to catch hold of her. His fingers closed around her wrist, just briefly, before she tore herself free, turning and falling back against the wall in panic and then taking off at speed down the corridor. The manager looked angry. Cursing, he gestured towards the guard, who came in heavy on Nyquist, swinging for a punch. But the guy had too few years in the game and Nyquist was on his mettle after last night's failure; he met the blow easily with his forearm, pushed it aside, and then brought his right hand in low, hard, fast, to the stomach. The guard was already moving into the punch, and this was too much for him. He doubled up against the wall, the wind knocked out of his chest. The manager started to say something nasty but Nyquist had already turned away, looking for Eleanor.

The corridor was empty.

He set off running. A turning led to a second corridor, the end of which was blocked by a metal fire door. Without missing a step, Nyquist hit the pushbar with both hands, forcing it open. He stepped through, and the sudden glare of the sky dazzled his eyes.

He was standing on the platform of a fire escape.

The shanty town of Burn Out was half visible below, clouded by haze. The buildings petered out as the tents and caravans took over, a great mass of them, a new conglomeration occupying the city's limits. Just visible beyond this sprawling encampment were the lands outside Dayzone: waste dumps, scrublands, barren pastures, villages, meadows, towns, and then other cities where time worked naturally, to one clock alone, and day followed night followed day followed night followed day followed night...

Nyquist clung to the rail for support. He felt dizzy. The ground below wavered in his sight and he felt that he might tumble and fall.

He concentrated, holding his gaze on one spot until the vertigo had passed. Eleanor could be seen through the gridwork below, more than halfway down already, a bright figure jumping from ledge to ledge with such desperate energy that the whole flimsy structure shook with her movement. What the hell was she running from? Nyquist took the stairs as fast as he could, but his extra weight and the dreadful humidity were holding his progress. His feet banged down on each step, and sweat dripped into his eyes. If he wasn't quick enough, the girl would easily become lost to him.

Nyquist reached the ground. The backyard of the hotel was littered with rubbish, but the wire fence surrounding it seemed to be intact, the only gate padlocked shut. He moved along the fence, finding a gap where the wires had been cut and folded back. Nyquist pushed through. A row of single-storey buildings faced him, the nearest two separated by a narrow alleyway. He hurried down it, coming out into a large courtyard area, from which another three exits gave way. A group of Burn Out residents were gathered here, below a low-hanging canopy of lanterns. The fierce light burned on every surface. Music could be heard, a high keening sound like an animal crying. Nyquist walked over to a ring of oil drums where most of the people were assembled. There was a smell of burning pitch, and flames were rising from each metal canister. The air trembled above the flames, the figures beyond seen as ghosts in the light, and the music flickered with the same heat, the same spirit.

There was no sign of Eleanor Bale.

Nyquist spoke to the nearest person. "Did anybody come through here, just now? A young woman? A teenager?" The man looked at him as though he were a visitor from another planet. Nyquist turned to the crowd at large. "Where is she? Which way did she go?" Nobody answered. Nyquist shook his head to clear it. He looked around at the three exits. The music was maddening, and he turned to see where it was coming from.

An old man was standing on the other side of the flames, balanced on a wooden crate. Nyquist walked over. The musician was dressed in a jacket far too small for him, with a lopsided hat perched on his head. The curved body of a fiddle was pressed against his chin. The bow moved across the neck at speed, back and forth, and the fingers of the man's right hand sometimes came in to pluck a few notes of their own, all these movements conjuring up the wild, exuberant music. A bowl was resting on the ground in front of the crate, hopefully to catch a few more coins than the two or three it already contained. Close by, a little girl was dancing to the beat. Likewise, Nyquist was fascinated by the music; the tune nagged at him, surely he had heard it before somewhere? If only the violinist would stop improvising, adding so many notes around the original melody. And then the old musician stopped playing and looked down, showing his eyes to be entirely black in their sockets. Black, staring, blind – his sightless gaze fixed upon Nyquist, who could give only one response: he threw a couple of coins in the tin bowl.

At that moment a small boy approached. He was carrying a green duffle bag, which he held out in front of him. Eleanor's bag.

"She dropped this."

Nyquist took it gratefully.

He made his way through the streets, back to the front of the hotel, to where his car was parked. His head throbbed with the glare, sweat clogged at his eyes. He was feeling faint. Clouds of dust were drifting along the road. A voice whispered inside his head, as though the dust were speaking to him: *Everything that does not move, we shall cover you, we shall bury you.* Nyquist spat to clear his mouth of it. He looked up at the sky, which hung suspended only a few yards above his head and was made up of thousands upon thousands of closely packed lamps. The light was everywhere flat and undiminished, without any direction, and no shadows were cast. The vehicle glowed with heat. He climbed inside, placing the girl's bag on the seat beside him and then waited for a while as the dashboard fan made its feeble effort. He had lost his hat at some point, he could not remember when or where. Out of habit he glanced at his wristwatch: he could make no sense at all of the time. And then he noticed the spots of blood on his palm. It made him think of the broken light bulb and the way in which the teenage girl had stabbed herself with it. The painful image fixed itself inside Nyquist's mind.

It would stay with him all the way back towards Precinct Two.

GUIDE BOOK:
THE CITY OF LIGHTS

AS THE TRAVELLER enters Dayzone, a constant haze
will be seen over the streets, caused by the many billions of
light sources the city uses in its tireless quest for brightness.
The sky, the real sky, which even the oldest residents cannot
remember seeing, is hidden behind a vast tangled web of
neon signs, fluorescent images, fiery lamps, gas flames,
polished steel struts, and decorative mosaics of glass.
Light cascades from this canopy, its radiant chaotic beams
caught, reflected, multiplied, back and forth between the
shining walls of the office blocks and municipal buildings.
Lower down, further sources of illumination are fixed to
every available surface, adding their own brilliance to the
city. Chinese lanterns swing from cables stretched across
the roads, floodlights bathe the scene, powerful spotlights
follow cars and pedestrians as they move along. At street
level, bare glittering bulbs dazzle in red, white, yellow,
orange; every shop front, bench, notice board and kiosk
dances with colour. Crystal chandeliers hang down from
traffic signs. Some of these lights are set in place by the
council of Dayzone in its official capacity, but many others
are added by the citizens themselves. The trees that line

the walkways are woven with strings of luminous globes, while from the pavements and tarmac a great sweep of cat's eyes sparkle like fallen stars. The air is heavy with gold and silver particles, adhering where they land, on the passing cars, the walls, the people themselves. And everywhere you look, around, above and below, tiny fragments of mirrored glass break and scatter the light. A constant buzzing noise is heard, the low-level hum of electricity. Strands of loose wiring will flash and fuse. The city crackles with heat. And whenever rain falls, making its slow way through the overhead canopy, showers of sparks fly from broken contacts; and then, like a series of colourful ghosts, numerous rainbows float above the streets. The people worship such sights, taking them as evidence of the God of Light and Heat looking upon them favourably. For darkness has been banished from Dayzone, sent into exile. This is the great achievement. The city pulses with a universal radiance. People talk of the sacrifices needed, by society, by the individual, in order to maintain the Glow, as they call it. Votive offerings are woven round lamp posts, or carefully arranged at junction boxes and electrical substations. Prayers are chanted. But despite these efforts on occasion a bulb will come loose from one of the high lamps. It will drop down from the neon sky, appearing to be just one more dash of colour in the spectrum, only to be noticed when the pavement suddenly explodes into a fountain of glass. And the people will look upwards then, suddenly fearful of night, that it might descend once more and smother their city in darkness.

CHRONOSTASIS

On his way back into the centre Nyquist stopped off in Shimmer Town, an area where many new arrivals to the city first find a home, and a job. Some of the latest arrivals could be seen, looking dazed and worried as they tried to throw off their old ideas of time and light. They looked out of step, pained even, adrift in the crosscurrents. It would take years for their body clocks to adjust fully to the new rhythms. He saw one older man almost fall over as his psyche attempted to keep up with his feverish watch-turning: he looked like a man teetering on a highwire. Whereas a younger couple nearby had recently made themselves at home in the city; this was obvious from way they were skipping lightly from one timescale to another, adjusting their wristwatches to match, broad smiles on their faces. Oh, it was such a wonderful feeling, to escape from the rigours of a universal clock!

Nyquist, like many native-born citizens, often used to ask newcomers about the world outside the city, desperate for knowledge. Not anymore. He was resigned to his place in the world, and now he walked down the main street scarcely noticing the different cultures on view. The constant buzz, crackle and hiss of electrical circuits and gas flames accompanied him. A chronologist was selling her wares from a shop doorway: *New timelines now available. Get yours here!* Above the street, giant billboards glowed with radiant light. The most prominent of them featured the image of the famous actress, Annabella Tempo, who held within her hands a clock face, the two hands of which revolved at speed around the dial, worked by a hidden mechanism. Annabella was advertising *Shiny Happy Daze*, one of the latest commercial timelines. Her teeth gleamed, as bright as arc lights.

Nyquist stepped inside a bar. He chose it purely because it looked emptier than any of the others. He ordered a sandwich and a beer. The barman was wiping the bar down with a towel and it took him a while to look up. "What time have you got?" he asked. Nyquist looked at his wristwatch in automatic response.

The dial was blurred.

"I'm... I'm not sure."

"You're not sure? What kind of answer is that?"

Nyquist concentrated on the dial. He felt faint, as though time was slipping away from him, but finally with relief he saw the numbers.

"It's six twenty-five," he answered.

But the stated time made no sense to him. He must have adjusted the hands at some point, surely? Why couldn't he remember?

"In the morning?" The barman looked incredulous.

"Yes, I think so..."

"Well, I can't serve you alcohol."

Nyquist was directed to a display hanging over the bar, upon which were painted two glasses of foaming beer and a slogan: *It's Drinking Time! Sponsored by the Whitsuntide Beer Company.* According to the clock below the slogan it was now twelve forty-six. The barman smiled. "Sorry bud, you're way too early."

Nyquist looked around. There were a couple of people

sitting at separate tables, and a guy perched on a stool further down the bar, a professional drinker by the look of him. His lips were held tight in a cruel grin. He was reading a copy of the *Beacon Fire*. Nyquist turned back to the barman. "Just give me a beer."

"No drinks before twelve. You want to get the place closed down?"

Nyquist held his anger in check. He pushed up his sleeve to get at his wristwatch, changing the time to match that of the bar's clock. At this, a glass of beer was banged down on the bar in front of him. And roused by the noise the old drunkard laughed, his mouth spraying foam. He said in a loud voice, "Another victim, have you seen?" Nyquist shook his head, not wanting to get involved. But the man brandished the newspaper. "Quicksilver has killed again. In Fahrenheit Market this time. Right there in the crowd." Nyquist had heard the news on his car radio: the latest in a series of killings, where a citizen had been attacked in a street or town square or even in a private home and yet neither the murderer nor his terrible act had been witnessed, only the immediate aftermath, the death of the victim. "Right smack bang in the middle of the crowd," the old man repeated with a foamy grin. "And then he's gone! Poof! Just slipped away. Unseen." He paused to take another drink and then prayed to his saviour with clasped hands: "Lord Apollo protect us from all darkness!" Nyquist nodded in agreement without saying anything. But the barman joined in, saying, "Aye that's right. I reckon Quicksilver moves so fast that no one can see him arrive, or kill, or depart." The drunkard grimaced at this opinion. He showed his teeth in an evil blackened grin from which one scarlet glass jewel shone like a car's brake indicator. "No, he's invisible, like a ghost." The barman cackled in response, which set the old man chanting. "Invisible, invisible!" The idea had taken him over completely:

"Invisible, invisible, invisible!"

Nyquist turned away from the argument, carrying his drink and the girl's bag over to a table. He passed a young woman whose body moved to a strange rhythm, while her eyes seemed incapable of fixing on any one object.

"Are you all right, miss?"

She turned to face him. There was a flicker of recognition and then her gaze quickly passed by, moving across to a poster on the wall. The barman came over, wiping the table. He said, "Don't bother with Maria. She's got no numbers left on her clock." He tapped the side of his head. "Midnight of the soul. Sad. But there it is." Nyquist nodded. Chronostasis. The syndrome was becoming more prevalent. Some Dayzone residents got so confused by all the different kinds of time on offer, their minds couldn't take it anymore. Time slowed down to zero, a space where nothing ever happened.

Nyquist looked at his watch again. The dial was still a little blurred. Were his eyes going? Yet he could see all other objects clearly.

Was this the start of the sickness, he wondered, of chronostasis?

He shuddered at the thought as he sat down to wait for his sandwich to arrive. The table was near a window, where a number of bluebottles were banging against the glass, enraged by the heat and the light. The same way madness pressed at his skull, the need to break free. To focus his mind he opened the green duffle bag and started to look through Eleanor Bale's possessions. First he pulled out a few items of clothing. Below these he found a leather purse. There was money inside, quite a lot of money, considering the girl was a runaway. In the purse's zipped pocket he found a slip of paper with a seven-digit number written on it, a telephone number probably. He put this aside and went back to the bag, where he next found a postcard addressed to Eleanor at the Bale family's Nocturna residence. The image showed a view of a beach in the south of France, and the message scrawled on the back read, "Amazing adventures! But missing you so much. Say hello to the Noonday Underground for me!" The card was signed by someone called *Abigail*. A girlfriend probably, travelling abroad while Eleanor stayed at home.

Nyquist moved on. He pulled out a white envelope with a single photograph inside it. It was a portrait of a man in his early twenties or so. Nyquist studied the man's face. He looked like he hadn't eaten in a while, but the sunken cheekbones only added to the intensity of his expression, framing his dark piercing eyes perfectly. Long black hair hung in curled folds down each side of the face. Two words were handwritten on the back of the photograph: *Angelcroft Silhouette*. Nyquist was thinking about what this could possibly mean as the barman brought over his food. Names, perhaps? Or one name? The name of the man in the photo?

He took a bite of sandwich, then went back to his survey of Eleanor's bag. He found a few more personal items but nothing of pressing interest until he pulled out a couple of small glass vials each decorated with a tiny crescent moon shape, and each filled with a bright orange liquid. He thought of the young man in Room 347, with his stained lips. Nyquist had lived through at least six different fashions in stimulants, and had taken most of them in his youth. He let the vials rest in his palm. He'd seen such objects before in his travels but didn't really have much knowledge of the drug they held.

There was one last item of interest in the bag, hidden right at the bottom: an object wrapped up inside a yellow dusting cloth. Nyquist unwrapped it carefully, revealing a figurine. It was a bizarre looking creature made of thin black leather. Long delicate jointed arms and legs were attached to the torso, and the face was viewed in profile, with a sharp snout and two horns protruding from a mass of hair on the domed head. Diamond-shaped holes had been punched into the leather all over the body, and these holes were covered with bits of transparent plastic of gold, red or sky blue. There was a primitive quality to the object, and yet the workmanship was skilfully rendered. More than anything, the creature looked demonic.

Nyquist put everything back into the bag. Here they were, the few precious belongings of Eleanor Bale, a puzzling collection. Where would they lead?

A cry from another table disturbed him. A glass shattered on the floor.

It was the chronostatic woman, Maria. She had risen to her feet. Her hands scrabbled at the air in front of her as though trying to grab at some elusive object. Her mouth opened and closed soundlessly, until at last she found her voice: "What time is it? What time is it?" Nyquist stood up to help her but the barman got there first. He took hold of her wrists, one in each hand, as he spoke firmly but kindly to her, urging her to quiet. But Maria had not yet finished her appeal for knowledge, her endless question.

What time is it? What time is it? What time is it?

SCATTERING DUST

Multiple beams of light cascaded down from the shining windows of the financial district, crisscrossing in the air, to be captured on the web of silver threads which stretched above the forecourt of the Ariadne Centre. The effect made the whole structure shimmer and sparkle with a life of its own. Nyquist walked through the main entrance. The reception area was dominated by a long line of wall clocks. He kept his eyes facing straight ahead. He had never been here before, preferring usually to meet his clients in the neutral ground of cafes and bars, and he looked out of place, scruffy and tired and poor compared to the brisk well-dressed men and women who passed by him, all moving in step to the shared rhythm of a corporate timeline. He felt like a dancer with a broken foot, ruining the performance for the rest of the company. The receptionist at the desk gave him a disdainful look as he stated his business.

"I'm afraid Mr Bale cannot see you just now. He's in a meeting."

Nyquist frowned. "When can he see me?"

"Would you like to make an appointment?"

"It's urgent."

"On what business?"

"On private business."

Nyquist could see that his attitude was getting to her. He had the feeling that she might well be pressing a hidden button beneath her desk.

"Would three-fifteen suit you?" she asked with a smile.

Nyquist looked at his wristwatch, holding his focus as the hands trembled in place. It read twenty-two, or twenty-five minutes past one. Or was it nearer to half past? Something like that.

"Three fifteen?" he repeated.

"That's right."

Nyquist stared at the side wall, where every clockface showed a different time. Each had a plaque beneath, announcing the varied timelines on offer: *Capital Business Time*; *International Communication Time*; *Executive Downtime*; *Financial Express Time*, and so on. The dials blurred in his sight, and he could feel a headache coming on. It had been a mistake, having that second drink. He could no longer remember just how many hours had passed since he had stepped off the train at Morning Station.

"What time do you have now, precisely?" he asked.

The receptionist pointed to the wall to the right of her desk. Nyquist followed her direction to see a clock marked *Ariadne Internal Time*, according to which it was two forty-five inside the building.

"Would you like to wait?"

Nyquist hardly heard the receptionist's voice. He had an overwhelming urge to change his watch to match the building's timeline. His hands clenched and unclenched as he managed to bring the desire under control.

"Are you all right, sir? You don't look well."

"It's about his daughter! Tell Mr Bale that. It's about Eleanor."

"I'm sorry. I don't–"

Nyquist grabbed the edge of the desk for support. A dizziness came over him, and he was about to make his way to the exit when an imposing, smartly suited woman appeared from the nearest corridor. She immediately took charge of the situation, greeting Nyquist as though he were an old friend. "There you are! I do hope we've been looking after you. Mr Bale will see you now."

Nyquist had never seen the woman before in his life.

They rode the elevator together. She introduced herself a as Pearce. No Mrs, no Miss, no first name. "Good news, I hope?" she said. "Mr Bale has been very troubled about this whole situation."

Nyquist kept quiet.

"Well, I can understand your reticence. It's a delicate matter."

Nyquist nodded. Behind the alabaster foundation and fierce lipstick, Pearce's face held not a shred of emotion. She had the confident shape and stance of somebody who spent more hours in the executive gym than she did at her desk, and her jacket and skirt was expertly tailored to display such a body. Her blonde hair was sculpted and lacquered into a precise style that reminded him of a warrior's helmet. In contrast, Nyquist took a look at himself in the mirrored wall of the elevator car. It wasn't a pretty sight.

A few minutes later he was standing in the office of Sir Patrick Bale, being cut down to size for letting Eleanor get away. "I can't believe this is happening," Bale said. "If I'd wanted a bad job doing, I'd have asked the police to find her."

Nyquist didn't feel like he should be apologising. "At least…"

"Yes?"

"At least we know Eleanor's alive. At least we've seen her."

"I'm not paying you to look at her, Nyquist. Where is she?"

Patrick Bale was a tall, handsome, somewhat artificially preserved man in his early forties. His hair was a little too dark and his facial expression had that slightly shocked look that comes from being stretched beyond its natural limits by a doctor's clamps and pulleys. His office was bland, corporate, showing little personality, whereas the man himself seemed to be filled with a pent-up anger, or a twisted desire, it was difficult to tell which.

Nyquist took Eleanor's purse from his pocket. "Your daughter left this behind."

Bale grabbed hold of it. He pulled out the bundle of notes, saying, "Well. She won't last long with no money. The girl is spoilt beyond measure."

"Were you aware of her taking drugs?"

Bale looked peeved at this proposition. "Drugs? No. No, she wouldn't..."

"She wouldn't?"

"She wouldn't dare."

It sounded to Nyquist's ears more like a threat than an observation. He handed Bale the photograph of the young longhaired man, while keeping the other contents of the bag to himself for now. "Do you know this man?" he asked.

The ceiling fans purred softly as Bale stared at the photograph. He took a while before answering. "No. Should I?"

"Your daughter carries his picture around with her."

"Will this help us find her?"

"Turn it over."

Bale did so. He stared at the two words written there. "What is this?"

"Mean anything to you?"

"Angelcroft. Silhouette... No. Nothing." He placed the photograph on the desk. "I don't care for these things, Nyquist. I just want my daughter back."

"That's in hand."

"Is there something you're not telling me?"

Nyquist looked at him. "That's funny. I could ask the same question."

Bale stood up from his desk. "I won't be made fun of."

Nyquist picked up the photograph. "I'll need to speak with her mother."

"That won't be necessary."

"Let me judge that."

"Now listen. Don't overstep the mark."

"Sometimes you have to, Mr Bale. If you want results."

"My wife Catherine... I'm afraid she rarely leaves Nocturna." He smiled. "And now, I have important matters to attend to."

Nyquist didn't move. He said, "You're not asking the right questions."

"What?"

"About Eleanor. You're not asking me how she is."

A moment went by. Bale stared at Nyquist, his eyes unblinking, his smoothed-out face held still. His lips hardly moved as he spoke.

"I've a good mind to have you–"

"Guess what? I'm not the problem."

Patrick Bale turned away. He moved over towards the office window and looked out at his view of the city. Nyquist followed him. Through the tinted glass they both gazed in silence at the vast network of lamps – all of different shapes, sizes and colours – that stretched outward from some upper floor, forming the neon sky. Four flights below, Nyquist could see the cars moving sluggishly along the street amid the constant sparkle of the city's lower levels.

Bale spoke firmly. "This city is a dynamo. It never stops turning, never stops working. And because of this, Dayzone constantly needs more glow, more heat, more power. But most of all it needs more *time*. Different kinds of time. A time for every single occasion, mood and desire. The people demand it. And we here at the Ariadne Centre have to administer that time as we see fit." It sounded like a well-designed machine was speaking. "We have two hundred and thirty-five new timelines coming up for purchase. Many parties are putting in their applications. Some of them are the usual options, but many are quite startling in their originality." He turned to face Nyquist, his voice growing more insistent; the machine in overdrive. "This is my chosen work. Until the city slows to a standstill, here I stand." His eyes glistened with love. "I will lead the people through the web of their own confusion, offering hope. Bringing a few more hours and minutes and seconds into their lives."

Nyquist smiled. "Nice speech. You're laying down the rules by which the city lives."

"We have to have rules."

"And you're making a lot of money from this."

"Where is this going, Nyquist?"

"Some people get messed up by time. Seriously damaged."

"Are you talking about Eleanor?"

"I'm seeing it more and more, lots of people. Chronostasis, they call it."

"We all have to make sacrifices."

Nyquist was taken aback by the statement. "What are you saying?"

"Our city is a very special place, an experiment in living, if you will. We are splitting time into its constituent pieces and rebuilding it from the ground up. That takes courage and skill, and great desire. The people's desire that the day might last forever."

"And nevermind who gets hurt?"

Bale blinked. "We take all necessary precautions. But you know, there are many pirates out there, bootleggers with their cheap homemade timelines. That's where the danger lies. Am I to blame if people misuse the products?"

Nyquist looked around the office. Smiling a little, he said, "People are predicting another time crash."

"These so-called experts–"

"We only just survived the last one."

Bale held his breath. "Do you think this job comes easily to me? Do you?"

Nyquist shrugged.

Bale's voice darkened. "The poet Tennyson described time as a 'maniac scattering dust'. But what else can I do? What else?" He turned to look directly at Nyquist, his eyes filling with an emotion so icy cold it was hardly comprehensible.

Then his gaze lowered as he noticed a few marks of dark red on Nyquist's shirtfront. "What is that? Blood? You have blood on your clothes…"

"That's right. Your daughter's blood."

"What? She's been injured?"

"She did it herself."

Bale's expression changed around the eyes; they creased at the corners, revealing a good few lines that the latest medical procedure had somehow missed. The first true emotion. Nyquist felt he was rubbing sandpaper on a wound when he pressed forward, saying, "Your daughter's suffering. She's not happy."

"Not happy?"

"I don't know what it is, Mr Bale, that's made her run away. But my god, that girl is running."

The chief executive shook his head a few times before locking his gaze onto Nyquist. The ever-changing colours of the city painted his face with flickering patterns. Seconds passed, one by one by one. Patrick Bale closed his eyes tight. When he opened them again a moment later, his face had gained full control of itself.

"I want my daughter found." The words came out in a steady rhythm, the machine back in charge. "Do this for me, if you will. Nothing else matters."

CLOCKS AND SHADOWS

Nyquist's office was situated in the area of Dayzone designated as Precinct Nine, otherwise known as Body Heat. Long ago it had been a thriving tourist spot for visitors from the outside world. From such heights it had drifted down-market to become the sex trade district. Later still, some of the artists had migrated over from their usual quarter to create this strange hybrid zone. Nyquist liked the feel of it, when he was out of the office anyway; the way the streets were flooded with various shades of red lighting effects, and the intense feeling of life such places can give off, human existence at the raw edges of the flesh. There were always rumours of the council wanting to clean the area up, but for now the artistic and the sexually bizarre mingled and prevailed.

After parking the car in his regular place Nyquist walked back along the high street. All the usual suspects were out and about: the street corner skin poets, alongside models and actresses specialising in the patterns of heat and light across the semi-naked human form. The avant-garde tanning merchants had set up shop on the paved boulevard, their mirrors, glass jars and pasting blades radiant with flashes of scarlet light. A little further along a troupe of actors showed off their illuminated scenes featuring the god Helios and his golden chariot. There was a scraping noise from above and Nyquist looked up to see a gang of bulb monkeys hard at work. In general, the poorer the district, the closer to the street the neon sky was; so here it was easy to make out the operatives. They were dressed in tight, heat-resistant outfits, with goggles to protect their eyes, and they carried their tools and a supply of new bulbs and other electrical parts in canvas bags strapped around their bodies. Their agility was always a pleasure to watch as they clung to the walls and the metalwork with their hooks, safety ropes and suckers, and then scrambled upside down across the canopy of lamps like restless spiders at their work.

Nyquist turned down an alleyway and entered a shop called Diverse Pleasures. Crystal chandeliers hung down from the ceiling and many objects of interest and curiosity were arranged on shelves: voodoo dolls, snake and bird skulls, old maps of the city showing the ever increasing spread of lights, crucifixes, antique gramophones, weird surgical instruments and the like. The sexual accessories for which the shop was most famous were hardly distinguishable from some of the other more innocent devices on display. A slatted blind covered the window and the beams of light that found their way inside patterned the dusty air into grey and white stripes. From every part of the store there came the sound of ticking, from wall clocks, from clockwork dolls and mechanical devices, from the many fob watches dangling by their gold and silver chains. Nyquist always felt that he was walking inside a machine designed only to tick and to chime.

The shop was run by the Lindseys, a married couple in their sixties.

"Johnny, my dear!" cried Alana Lindsey. "Where have you been hiding yourself for so long a time?"

Nyquist placed the green tartan bag on the counter.

"Nocturna," he answered.

"Oh, you stay too long nightside and it eats into your soul. We hardly go there at all these days."

Nyquist rubbed at his eyes in response.

"Have you been sleeping properly?"

"A few hours here and there." This was the truth.

She pursed her lips. "You should take more care of your days and your nights, Johnny. Make sure you know which is which, and where one ends and the other begins. And then make a choice!"

Nyquist nodded. "That's good advice." He reached into the bag to pull out the yellow cloth with its hidden contents. "Any idea what this is?"

Alana looked on as the strange figurine was revealed. She called for her husband from the back room and Jude Lindsey appeared instantly, dressed in his usual bright array of clothing. "Now let us see," he muttered, "what have we got here?" Carefully, he picked up the sculpted leather figure, turning it this way and that in the beam of an angled lamp.

"Any ideas?" Nyquist asked.

Jude nodded. "Of course. It's a *wayang kulit*."

"A what?"

"A shadow puppet. As used in the Javanese theatre."

Nyquist knew only a little about the subject. "This is from Java?"

"No, no," Jude answered. "This is not one of the traditional characters, not that I have ever seen. But well done, mind. Oh yes, nicely crafted. Usually they will have sticks attached here, and here, on the arms and neck, see, so the puppeteer can make them walk and run and leap and pray, as needed."

Alana pulled a small hardback book from a shelf, an old traveller's diary, which she opened out on the counter. She tapped one of her long red fingernails against a sepia photograph. Nyquist studied the image: a large sheet of white cloth strung on poles, with some kind of lighting source behind, and the mysterious puppets seen in action against the cloth, where they appeared as shadows. Two dark figures faced each other, either about to fight or to dance. It was a startling image but he couldn't work out why the missing girl should have such a puppet in her bag.

Jude offered to lend him the book. Nyquist thanked them both.

"Anything else, Johnny?" Alana asked.

"Yes." He took off his wristwatch and handed it to her. "Have a quick look at this, would you?"

"You really should have a new timepiece by now." She placed a watchmaker's eyeglass to her right eye, holding it in place with a practised squeeze of her brow and cheek muscles. "Well, it looks all right. It's ticking!"

"I'm having trouble with it."

"What kind of trouble?"

"It's losing time. Maybe the hands are loose."

"Yes, maybe. I can tighten them easily enough, but let me see…"

Alana prized off the back of the watch and peered inside. But as she did so a strange thing happened: a tiny, tiny grey cloud rose from the brass workings. It scattered in the air.

"What the hell was that?" Nyquist asked.

"Dust, perhaps."

"It looked more like smoke," her husband said. "Or mist, even."

"But I keep it clean. Sparkling."

"We know you do, Johnny."

"It was my father's."

"We know, we know. But still…" She held the wristwatch up in disgust. "Look at it! Tarnished, the strap almost broken, the face cracked, the minute hand slightly bent. And there are some very nice chronometers on sale, new ones just in."

It was suddenly too hot in the shop. "This is fine." Nyquist picked up the wristwatch, clicking the back in place himself.

Alana made one last sales pitch. "Fully adjustable, Johnny! Up to fifty different timelines."

"I'm fine. Really."

Again Nyquist thanked the Lindseys for their help and for the loan of the book, then made his way to the door. He paused outside to get his breath back, and to wipe the sweat away from his eyes. Thankfully, it was only a short distance to his office on Lower Flare Street. He walked up the steps of the crumbling apartment block. The manager, a little man called Queeps, was sitting in his booth on the ground floor. He was always there, nested in the glass chamber, watching a small rickety television set. He couldn't be avoided.

"Ah. Mr Nyquist! Yes? Come here, please. Thank you."

Nyquist moved to the cubicle. Animated clocks danced on the television's screen as a lovely voice soothed the viewer: *Where would we be without lovely* Old Mother's Time? *The family's favourite since way back when.* The clocks skipped across sunlit monochrome fields. Queeps cursed at the advert. "Such rubbish! Now this..." He pointed to a carriage clock on a shelf. "This is my only time. Every morning I set it, precisely, from the beeps on the radio. You see? Tick, tick, tick! And then I never change my time, not ever, not until I go home to Nocturna."

"I didn't know you had a home," Nyquist said. "I thought you lived here, in the booth."

Queeps waved the remark aside. "How it goes, one time for daylight, and one time for night. You should try the same, Mr Nyquist. Instead of all this hopping about from one line to another. And maybe you wouldn't look so tired then, no? Because you know what they say…"

"I don't, actually."

"…One of these days you're going to fall right off the edge of the clock. And then what, eh? Then what?"

Nyquist sighed. "What do you want?"

"Rent. Very much overdue."

"It's been a bad month."

"A bad month. A bad week, bad hour, bad minute, a bad second. Exactly the same for everybody. But you pay, soon please."

The clocks started to sing on the screen. Nyquist blinked and yawned.

"You know," Queeps continued, "you should leave this city, if it troubles you so very much."

"I can't. I can't do that."

"Well then. Yes. We will see what happens to you."

Nyquist made his usual promises and then took the creaking elevator up to the third floor. The wording on his office door read, *John Henry Nyquist, Discreet Investigations*. He'd debated over the extra cost of the word *Henry*, but decided it made him sound more reliable. Little good it did him. He clicked the room lights on as he entered the cramped space: a small couch bed, a desk, a typewriter, a couple of chairs, a rusty filing cabinet. The curtains were drawn across the one window, the heavy cloth coloured by slowly moving shapes. Over the years Nyquist had started to feel indifferent towards this place. Somewhere to rest, somewhere to change, to sleep if need be, a telephone line for any stray business. That was it. He picked up the collected mail of the last week or so. The usual bills and offers of "amazing timelines unlike any others ever experienced!" No cheques, no cash. He switched on the ceiling fan, for all the good the slowly moving blades did. Then he poured himself a shot of whisky, gazing at the map of the city as he took his first drink. The map was large scale, pinned to the wall opposite the window. He had bought it when he had first moved into the office. Such hopes. His mother had died when he was very young, and his father, beset by grief at his wife's death, had struggled to bring his son up alone. Nyquist wanted only to escape from such feelings, to find his own way in life. He had envisioned himself travelling around the city, this strange and beautiful metropolis, the whole vast array of it. He had spent too many years of his younger life drifting from job to lousy job, too long on the run. This new endeavour would give his life purpose, that was the plan: taking pictures of errant spouses, recovering stolen goods, digging the dirt, finding runaways, protecting the weak. Helping people out when the police had pulled up short or refused to even start looking. Nothing much, but he was out there on the streets anyway; he had the wherewithal and the muscle and the smarts, and over the years the city had entered his bloodstream, building a map inside his psyche. He might as well do some good by it. Sure, call it that: some *good*.

Life passes. Time passes. How long ago was it now, when he had first started out? Six years, seven years? More? No, he could not remember. Increasingly, the past was a nebulous substance, flowing and ebbing in his mind.

Such dreams, such desires...

He sat at the desk and slotted a sheet of paper into the typewriter and, one finger at a time, hit the keys:

```
THE ELEANOR BALE CASE
```

He stared at the blank space below the title, thinking he would make a list of everything he knew, all the pertinent facts. Instead, his mind wandered. His ex-wife had bought him this typewriter when he'd first started the business. He'd written his final letter to her on it: a long, rambling farewell.

He groaned in frustration and took another sip of whisky as he looked at the wall clock above the map. He looked from there to his wristwatch; thankfully, the hands were clearly seen now. But of course the two timepieces were out of sync. He picked up the telephone, dialling a three-letter code. The young woman's soothing voice spoke to him: "...it will be twelve minutes past nine, and twenty seconds. This week's time is brought to you courtesy of..." Nyquist replaced the receiver. He turned the winder of his watch, adjusting it to this new time. He couldn't tell if he was jumping forward or back, but that mattered little. It was good to get yourself fixed every so often to one of the official timelines. He walked over to the window, drawing back the curtain. The colours flooded his room.

Nyquist's office was situated above the skyline for this particular part of the city. This was the fate of the cheaper rents. Consequently, the view from the window was filled from frame to frame, top to bottom, with a complex jumble of lights. The bulbs pressed up against the glass. There were many colours on display, some of the expected red of the streets of Body Heat, others revealing the hues of a previous history: bright green, sizzling orange, pure white, sky blue, dazzling yellow. Some of the bulbs, a few, had burnt out already. He stared at the patches of darkness. He couldn't help thinking about what Queeps had said, about the dangers of adjusting his watch too many times.

It used to be, he could work this city with no trouble. He'd lived here for all of his life, learning to survive on his wits, walking confidently along the various interlocking timelines, jumping from one to the other with ease. He'd move through the web of the hours and the minutes, and still manage to be more or less where he wanted to be, at something like the correct time. His eyes and his feet, his body in general, had felt at one with the different chronologies, as though time itself was slowly infecting his flesh, possessing him. But increasingly these days he found himself lost in the moments. Bewildered, dazed. He was living on a series of shifting plates, each one corresponding to a certain idea of what time was, or might be. The plates kept slipping and sliding, and crashing against each other. Sometimes he would come out of a black void to find himself staring at a clock face, just staring, staring, willing the hands to keep still on the dial, to close their circles down to one final second. Where he could stay, stay forever. Clockbound, as they called it.

Bad timing. Wound up tight. That's what his wife had said: "You're all wound up, John. Your bloody spring's going to snap right in two. There's no excuse for it."

And she'd been right, of course. No excuses.

He lifted up the window, feeling the temperature rise by degrees. He searched in his filing cabinet until he found his collection of spare light bulbs, and then, using a rag to protect his hand, he replaced the broken bulbs one by one. He didn't really understand why he did this. Really, despite his best efforts and his moments of doubt, was he any different from near enough the whole population of Dayzone? Like them, he was obsessed with the light, the ever-burning flame.

Nyquist closed the window again and drew the curtain back across the scene. He emptied the contents of the girl's duffle bag on his desk. There were four items of prime interest: the telephone number on the slip of paper, the shadow puppet, the photograph of the young man, the vials of orange fluid. Also, he reached for the travelogue the Lindseys had lent him. He stared at these collected objects for a while. The wall clock ticked away the seconds. He picked up the telephone and dialled the number on the slip of paper. The ringing tone sounded distant. A faint hiss in the background. It rang on for a while, but nobody answered. Maybe it's not important, he thought: just the number of a relative, a shop, or a taxi company?

Nyquist studied the face of the longhaired man. He turned the photograph over: *Angelcroft Silhouette*. It was puzzling. He found his telephone directory and looked for each word, supposing them to be names. There was one Angelcroft listed: Edward Thomas, with an address in the Rosy Glow precinct, one of the more exclusive areas of Dayzone. There was no listing for anyone with the surname Silhouette, although a few businesses used the name, mostly located in Nocturna. He called the Angelcroft number and had a very brief and very irate conversation with a man who had obviously just been roused from sleep. Two people moving to their own timelines, arguing with each other: the usual cross-connections. It was predicted that eventually there would be a different highly personal timeline for every single Dayzone citizen. And what then? What kind of society would it lead to? Would it bring utter chaos, or a strange, unforeseen peace? Of course, it was too late to stop the process now, the twenty million clocks were ticking, ticking, ticking...

Nyquist stared at the items on his desk. These were the clues. If he could only place these few bits and pieces into some kind of pattern, perhaps he would find himself moving towards the missing girl. Nyquist felt certain that Eleanor Bale was in danger, either from herself or from some other party. It was a feeling, nothing more, but too powerful to be ignored. And the question remained: what was she running from?

He read through the relevant section of the old travelogue.

Finally, the evening of the performance arrived. What I saw absolutely fascinated me, and stays with me even now, years later, within the more general comforts of England. There was no theatre or building of any kind, no stage but for a patch of open ground between the trees.

The "dalang", the puppeteer, travelled the district, putting on these shows in each village he came to. He brought with him all that he needed: the white cloth screen, the oil lamp, the bamboo sticks, the various "wayang kulit", as they call the puppets, these last items safely bound in a wooden carrying case. The performance lasted all night, taking seven hours altogether, from dusk till dawn.

I learned from my enquiries that only a select few have the particular qualities needed to become a dalang. This particular one had learned the art from his father, and will pass it on to his son, who helped out with the night's performance. It is a serious undertaking, and a life's work; the dalang has to recite the story, manipulate the puppets, as well as speaking the dialogue for each character. Every so often his right foot will reach out to strike a kind of rattle, to mark off the different sections of the story. And all of this while sitting cross-legged for the full seven hours, never moving from the spot, and never daring to fall asleep.

The night that I attended, the puppeteer brought to life the old epic, the Ramayana, with its noble warriors, monstrous beasts, monkey kings, bawdy clowns, beautiful princesses, banished lovers, and great battles fought between the powers of darkness and light. The audience were gathered on both sides of the screen, some of them watching the puppets themselves, whilst many others, myself included, preferred to watch the shadows as they moved and danced and came to blows on the white cloth. I felt myself hypnotised by the artistry of the dalang, and by the puppets themselves in all their ghostly life. Insects flitted around the flame of the oil lamp, and the creatures of the night could be heard, calling from the forests that surrounded the village. I must admit that I lost all track of time, often coming to with a start, to realise that many minutes had passed without my noticing them.

The story continued in this way until dawn broke at last, in fiery streaks of orange light seen through the trees, and the performance came to an end. I later learned a curious fact from one of the older men: for the duration of the shadow play, it is commonly believed that the villagers are protected from evil.

Nyquist poured himself a second shot of whisky. It was deathly quiet in the room. All he could hear was the ticking of the wall clock. He really should get up and synchronise it with his wristwatch, but it seemed like too much of a task. He had the feeling that many more timelines would have to be crossed before the girl was brought to safety, if he ever managed it. Something was missing, a connection. He groaned and brought a hand up to his damp face. He was shivering despite the heat. The fan circled around overhead, hardly disturbing the air; the bullet hole in the blade a reoccurring stutter in the cycle. The lights pulsed behind the drawn curtain. The room appeared in a haze.

Clock lag. It was finally catching up with him: too long spent nightside, and then entering Dayzone, the sudden flood of light. The minutes slid and tumbled, slowly coming to a halt. He dozed. And dreamt of the fog, the dusk...

Closing in, writhing around him, touching at his body.

A figure in the grey light.

Approaching. The face. That look in his eyes.

It was his father, calling, calling from the mist.

Help me, Johnny Boy. Save me...

Nyquist woke up, cursing. The same every time. The same dream, as though dusk had found its way inside him.

He finished off the dregs of whisky in the glass and walked over to the wall map. Dayzone was spread over the whole northern part of the city, taking up more than half the total land space. To the south lay Nocturna, where the darkness lived. Between them was the swathe of grey that marked the narrow border zone between the two major parts of the city. There was no official name for this area but most people referred to it as Dusk, or the dusklands, or even Precinct Zero, and spoke of it in whispers as a place never to be visited. It was beyond explanation; Dusk had grown of its own accord over the passing years like a slowly spreading disease. A stain on the chart. The city council reassured everyone that Dusk was under control, that it posed no threat, its forward progress was infinitesimal. Yet people's minds dwelled on the subject, rumours spread that Dayzone would be misted over within one, two or three generations. It was said that ghosts and other strange beings lived there, in the mist, in the desolate fields and moonlit woodlands and the old abandoned villages. But the area was free of all detail on the map except for the few train lines, the only means, since all the roads had been closed, of getting from Night to Day and back again. Nyquist placed a hand on the narrow grey area and then moved upwards to trace the brightly lit streets of Dayzone. Faint black lines crisscrossed the map from top to bottom, left to right: the grid system. An idea came to him. He took his A-Z street atlas from a desk drawer and looked up Angelcroft. There was a single mention, a lane on the borderline of Dusk and Dayzone. Silhouette was more popular, all of them located in Nocturna: Silhouette Road, Silhouette Avenue, Silhouette Way, Silhouette Villas, and so on.

Could the two words refer to addresses?

He dialled the telephone number again, and this time made a different connection. Somebody had picked up the receiver at the other end. But there was no voice, only sounds down the line, strange noises, he could hardly make them out.

"Hello? Whose number is this?"

Nobody answered him at first. A faint rustling sound, and then at last: "You rang me." It was a man's voice, faraway, garbled.

"Yes, that's right–"

"You rang me! Why did you ring? What do you want?"

"My name's John Nyquist. I was hoping to speak with Eleanor. Eleanor Bale."

He thought he heard an intake of breath, but it might've been the static on the line.

The voice repeated the name in a surprised tone: "Eleanor?"

Nyquist squeezed the handset. "That's right. I've been employed to bring her home, by her family. I found your number among her things."

Silence. Steady breaths, one by one. And then: "I need you to help me." It was a desperate plea.

Nyquist was surprised. "In what way?" he asked.

"Don't let her find me." The voice was clearer this time.

"Who is this? Who's speaking?"

"Her father."

Nyquist froze. He could barely think. It didn't sound like Patrick Bale. "Look, is this some kind of joke–"

The voice squealed. "She mustn't come near me. Not anymore!"

Nyquist pressed the handset hard against the side of his head, desperate to hear more. Electrical hum, susurration, distant cries. "Talk to me. Who is this, really?"

The voice asked, "What time is it?"

Nyquist looked at his wristwatch, at the wall clock, trying to decide between them. "I don't know. I'm not sure."

"The girl. Keep her away, do you hear me! It's unsafe." A sudden gasp. "Listen! Can you hear?"

Nyquist listened. He heard music over the line, a melody being played. There was an odd quality to it, something artificial. A windup gramophone, perhaps? And then he heard a cuckoo calling softly over the line. Weird, mutated, mechanical. Once, twice. The caller counted along with the chimes, as they came. A third time. Another. "Three. Four..." The cuckoo sounded a final time. "Five. It's five o'clock. I don't know how long I can last, before..." The voice murmured. "I can't protect her for much longer."

Nyquist spoke quickly. "Where are you?"

"I'm afraid. I'm afraid of what might happen to her."

"To Eleanor?"

"Yes. Listen to me. She's in danger."

"You think she's heading for you?"

The man didn't answer directly, but he said, "I've warned her before, to stay away." It was enough to make Nyquist fear the worst.

"Tell me where you are!"

Only the noises continued over the line, a mixture of scrapes and wheezes and drawn breaths and almost silent animal cries. It was the sound of twilight, of the land called Dusk. *The Hiss*. His father's name for it, from all the recordings they had made together.

And the noise silenced Nyquist. It terrified him.

He could still hear the man's voice, but only just amid the static. These last few words: "Please. Don't let Eleanor find me." And then a clicking noise as the line went dead.

Nyquist snapped out of his fear. He flicked through the pages of the street atlas, finding the page with Angelcroft listed on it. Right there on Dusk's edge. Could it be? Was that the man's address in Dayzone? Angelcroft Lane?

He had to make a decision.

Was this really Eleanor's father? Was she looking for him?

I can't protect her for much longer. She's in danger...

That voice, that terrible voice; it had sounded so hopeless, so desperate.

Nyquist moved over to the wall map. His fingers traced the location. There it was, in a district called Fade Away, situated on the southeastern edge of Day, many miles from where he now was. He would have to hurry. He reset his wristwatch in accordance with the cuckoo clock he had heard. Then he grabbed his jacket and was almost out of the office door before he stopped himself on the threshold.

Was this something he really needed to do?

It was the fear, the shivers. The place he was going to...

The old nightmare.

He had to face it.

The time was six minutes past five.

ENTRE CHIEN ET LOUP

He was heading south away from the centre. The streets grew colder and darker as the car, by slow degrees, left behind the constant illuminations of Dayzone. It was barely noticeable in passing but Nyquist saw each dead bulb, each blown-out neon sign, each switched-off advertisement as a small part of the night seeping into day. The buildings became more rundown, many doors and windows were broken. A few shops were still open along the way, their displays exhibiting ever feebler displays of brightness and colour. Many other establishments were closed, seemingly forever, their windows dark. Wooden boards covered the glass. Men and women scurried between each small patch of light as though in danger of being caught out. They seemed dreadfully poor and desperate. Or else half-crazed.

Nyquist drove on. Hands tight on the wheel, eyes wide open for the next turning. The traffic signs were no longer working. He had to slow the car every so often to check the page torn from the street atlas. Twice already he had lost his way. He passed through the town of Last Exit. Here the streets emptied further. What few people he saw looked at the car as if it were some mysterious beast.

A few people. And then none.

The streets were deserted. There was a noticeable

change in the air quality, a slight thickening as though the atmosphere was smeared with an alien substance. One more turning and Nyquist noticed the first swirls of the grey mist. He drove on through a desolate industrial estate. Very few streetlamps were working. All the buildings were cast in shadow except for rare and intermittent lights flickering like lost spirits. Nyquist turned on the car's headlamps. The beams were affected by the dimming air, barely showing the way forward. The mist wreathed around the car. Nyquist could no longer see clearly. Everything beyond the headlamps' yellowing glow was lost to a murky grey world.

The car slowed to a halt.

He clicked on the interior light and picked up the single page of the map, finding the area he had marked with a red X. It seemed plain enough, the route he had to take, but when he looked out through the windscreen there was nothing to act as a landmark. He peered again through the car's windows, forward and to each side. There was nobody in sight, no sound of life. He was alone here, close to the threshold of the dusklands. He turned off the engine, opened the door and stepped out of the vehicle. He kept a torch in the glove compartment, which he used now to light up his wristwatch. A quarter past six. The drive had taken longer than expected. He turned the beam of the torch onto the road ahead of him and set off walking. This was the closest he had ever been to the dusklands in his adult life, outside of a car or a train carriage. And straight away he felt the dread building inside.

He hated with all his soul the dusk, the twilight and all that it held hidden.

The mist, as yet quite thin, seemed to reach out and touch at him as he walked on. This whole area was haunted. Unidentifiable noises sounded from the cold dark buildings as he passed. Disembodied shadows moved across the ground in front of him. More than once he wanted to run back to the car and give up on the girl, and the mysterious caller. Perhaps the whole thing was some kind of cruel joke. But the nagging impression remained, that he had in some way let Eleanor Bale down by allowing her to escape, back at the amusement arcade. Only these feelings kept Nyquist moving forward.

He approached a children's playground, a set of rusty swings and a roundabout that creaked slowly in the mist, although there was little breeze at this point. Seeing these things, Nyquist knew that he had moved beyond the old factories and industrial units and was now heading toward a group of houses, whose black shapes loomed out of the semidarkness ahead. He passed a car parked by the roadside and then another a little further on, their doors hanging open and their paintwork heavily scarred. All the houses were dark and empty along this derelict estate. A forsaken place. And not a person to be seen. Inexplicably, the air smelt of smoke, of dead leaves, of autumn. Nyquist's skin turned dry and tight against his bones. His mouth tasted of ashes. He had learned once of a French phrase for twilight: *entre chien et loup*, between the dog and the wolf, meaning that time of day when it's impossible to tell these two animals – one benign and the other wild – apart. A dangerous time, when the senses could not be trusted.

Nyquist walked on. His torch illuminated some items of clothing stuck on a wooden cross in a garden, making a crude effigy. It was a sign of more recent activity, perhaps of one of the weird religious cults that venerated the edges of Dusk as their sacred ground. The mist, which had been a dirty grey to start with, now took on a more crepuscular hue, silvery, and seemingly lit from within; tendrils of it wrapped around Nyquist as he walked along. The temperature dropped a few degrees. He turned a corner and there it was, the boundary of Dusk itself. A town called Fade Away.

In this city Dusk was a place, not a time: a wall of fog that the light of Dayzone faded into. A place of ghosts, of dead roads, unknown lives. Nyquist had been to most areas of the city, following leads on cases both in daylight and dark, but these twilit areas were personal no-go zones for him. He was fearful. Strange oblations had been found along these borders – at first the carefully prepared corpses of pets and other animals; later, tales of human beings, barely alive, their bodies staked out on the ground, left here to appease whatever gods or demons might rule these parts. Other victims had not been so lucky. Or so the stories told. The truth was difficult to find, but the reasons given for these ceremonies came down to one simple statement, often repeated: *The dusk will take its share of human life.* Nyquist shivered. The twilight beckoned. Directly ahead the moon was seen, hanging above the mist. Somebody or something was waiting for him out there, in the shrouded landscape, he was certain of this. He could sense it as he moved forward cautiously, the torch in his hand. He followed a railway track for a short distance and then cut to the left, over to where several bizarre metal objects were planted in the ground like pagan sculptures. Close up, these devices revealed themselves as the remains of a long abandoned weather station: thermometer, barometer, anemometer, rain gauge, sunlight recorder and the like. The torchlight sparkled on bits of broken mirror or strings of beads tied around the instruments. Again, evidence of a more recent human interference. A crow was perched on the arm of one device. It made a dreadful cawing sound as Nyquist approached. There was another noise, metal scraping against metal. Nyquist spun round, trying to locate the source. He glimpsed a figure dressed entirely in white.

Even the face was masked. This person, male or female, slipped through the shadows and then disappeared. A door banged shut.

"Eleanor? Are you there? Eleanor!"

The crow screeched again. The weather instruments creaked in the gloom. Nyquist pulled the map from his pocket and consulted it with the torch. He felt certain that the exact location was not far away now, if only he could orientate himself. The mist was affecting his vision. He walked on, trusting his instincts, and the very next turning in the road revealed a row of terraced houses, pitch black against the silvery mist. All looked to be empty of life. A few more abandoned cars were seen.

The last time he had been this close to the fogline was as a child of eight, when his poor addled father had dragged him along on various "scientific missions", as they were called. The city was not quite as brightly lit as it was nowadays, and the dusk didn't extend quite so far into daylight, but still the young Nyquist stood there scared out of his wits as his father set the recording device going. The large brass horn facing the mist, the sharp needle on its end scratching a spiral groove into a cylinder of wax, following and mapping the vibrations of sound. The boy's job was to keep the campfire next to the equipment going, so the wax would remain soft enough. By the light of the flames he watched the cylinder revolve. The needle almost jumped from the wax as a screech owl called out. The boy tried to hide his fright as his father spoke with wonder in his voice of Ghost Vapour Time, where the dead walk to strange rhythms, and the hours can never be counted. A faraway look came to his eyes as the moon shone through the fogbanks. He talked of his wife, Nyquist's mother, waiting for them in the fog. "She's out there, son." A whisper. "She'll speak to us one day, just you wait." Johnny could never reply. He lived in fear of something or someone coming out of the mist towards him. And he knew it would not be his mother. Rather, it would be some monster or a maddened beast, or a witch. It would drag him screaming to his doom.

And a few months later his father had walked alone into the grey zone, the fog of dusk pulling at his body. He'd never been seen or heard of again. "She's calling to me from the shadows." A father's final words to his son.

Nyquist heard a distant sound. The mist was cold against his face, like a mask pulled too tight. He shivered fiercely. He tried to subdue the memories of his childhood, to stay on track. Something was happening. The sound was getting louder, he was sure of it. Which direction was it coming from? He could not tell. The noise grew louder still. It sounded like some wounded beast crying out in the lost realms. His body could not move, not at all. The torch fell from his grip. And then he saw it, coming in fast from the heavy fogbanks of Dusk, its yellow eyes flashing in the mist and the sound screaming at him as it burst forth blazing with heat and colour and a shrieking rush of wind.

The express train thundered past Nyquist, just a few feet away, dense black smoke billowing from its funnel, the light from its windows pulsing across his fear-stricken face, its banshee whistle shrieking as it crossed the borderline, and then disappeared as fast as it came, heading for the lights of Dayzone. The sound of it was still present for a few moments, until that too faded. Silence. And barely heard: the Hiss. And there, deep within the mist itself, over the border of Dusk, a dark shape moved. He could not tell if it was human or animal but it was definitely alive, and standing on two legs, upright. For a moment it stood there, perfectly still, as though watching him. And then the mist covered it again. Nyquist was cold with sweat. His heart juddered. It took a good while to get himself steadied. Finally he bent down to retrieve the torch and then turned again toward the row of houses, concentrating on the task ahead to restore his nerves.

He saw the street sign: *Angelcroft Lane*.

This was it. A light glowed ahead, pale and flickering: the only visible illumination apart from the moon. The glow was coming from a window, the lower window of a house on the street. Nyquist moved towards it. The gate hung loose from its frame and he stepped through the gap into the garden. Immediately he was aware of the smell, the rank stench of rotting vegetation. He felt his stomach churn. The whole ground beneath his feet was wet and mulchy with fallen leaves and other dead or dying plant life. A stunted elm tree leaned its bare branches over the fence. Only a single type of flower had managed to find a hold in the muddy soil; its petals had a luminous quality as though designed by nature for these regions. Nyquist took another step and saw a torch lying in the weeds, its beam faintly stretching away into the grey air. A number of moths flitted back and forth in what little light it provided. Now he knew: someone else had been here recently, searching as he was.

There were many legends told of the dusklands, and Nyquist knew most of them by heart: how people were lost to this fog and never again found; that once breathed in, the mist infected the lungs, indeed the entire body, with a pestilence; that the dusk held secrets beyond what should really be known, a place of ghosts, of wandering spirits.

Stories. Just stories. He had to believe that. Despite everything he knew, despite his father's words, his father's disappearance.

The house beckoned. The light yellowed the window, and he saw that a wire led down from the nearest telephone pole to enter the house at the partially open casement. Nyquist took a few deep breaths to calm himself for the task. As he did so a noise called out from inside the house, a voice perhaps, a woman's voice. He couldn't be sure. Somebody crying in the half-light. The sound of it affected Nyquist deeply. It was a cry of despair. But muffled, drawn out, as though a cloth had been placed over a mouth as it spoke. The front door creaked on its hinges in answer, banging against the frame.

Nyquist tried to steady himself.

The dead tree whispered its branches together in the shadows.

He walked over towards the house.

A ROOM ON THE EDGE OF TWILIGHT

A cold silence settled as soon as Nyquist entered the hallway. Nothing moved within except for a few lines of mist crawling along the walls like ribbons of lace. The woman's voice could no longer be heard. The torch beam was considerably weaker now, the near presence of dusk stealing its power. The glow he had seen from the outside came from a room to the side where a standard lamp was placed in the centre of an otherwise bare space. The naked bulb burned brightly for a second and then dimmed once more, setting itself into a slow irregular pattern like the work of a drowsy Morse code operator. Nyquist entered the room. A little camping stove stood on a patch of mildewed carpet with some cups and a few tins of food set out around it. The only other object in the room was a telephone, the apparatus taken apart, the workings exposed. Thin strands of mist coiled snakelike around the telephone's flex as it stretched upwards towards the half-opened casement window. It reminded him of stories he'd read in the *Beacon Fire* of people who lived on the edge of Dusk making their own gadgets and devices: a whole other way of doing things, rather as certain drug addicts like to take apart and reassemble household appliances. Obviously, the man had set up some kind of home here.

Nyquist moved on along a short corridor. The whole place stank of damp, of things long abandoned. A dark green fungus was growing on the far wall. He stood near the foot of the stairs. From here he could see the kitchen. The views through both the kitchen window and the glass panelling of the back door were entirely obscured by fog. He was hypnotised by the sight of this strange vapour, which seemed to be the very colour of moonlight and was constantly shifting into newly formed shapes, while darker patches weaved about in their own patterns. The backdoor was partway open, allowing curls of mist to squeeze through. He turned to look up the staircase. Once again he seemed to hear the woman's cry, coming from the floor above. He dared to call out, "Who's there? Who is it?" There was no reply. Only echo. He climbed the stairs up to a landing. The voice was clear now, very low, but definitely that of a woman in anguish. Another sound joined it, that of the cuckoo clock he had heard over the telephone. He saw this object a few feet away, attached to the wall. It called to him once again, softly, eerily, the tiny yellow bird appearing from its hideaway. Nyquist walked up to it. The woman's voice had faded once more; he could imagine it seeping back into the patches of damp on the walls. After a pause the clock struck another three times. The wooden hands on the dial were in agreement with the cuckoo bird. It was still five o'clock, the same as it was during the telephone call. Time had not yet moved on here, in this household.

Nyquist looked at his wristwatch. The dial was misted over.

And then he heard Eleanor's voice clearly.

It was her. He was sure of it.

He followed the sound down the corridor and peered through an open doorway into a large bedroom at the rear of the house. The window here was fully ajar and the fog and the moonlight lingered at the opening. It gave an eerie silver glow to the scene.

Eleanor was standing to one side, perfectly still, with her back to him.

Another person, a man, sat upright on an ill-kempt single bed in the corner of the room nearest the window. His face was lost in the shadows. Eleanor was saying, "I don't believe you." Her voice was quiet. All the emotion had drained from the words. The man offered no reply, but he shifted slightly on the bed and Nyquist saw a glint of metal in the fog. The man was holding a knife. Its long thin blade shone dully as though touched by the moon.

Nyquist felt that he was watching a scene from a theatre play, with himself as the sole audience member. He had not yet been noticed.

He could not move, not a single step.

Time waited, for whatever the next moment might bring.

Eleanor breathed in deeply. Her mood shifted as her body seemed to weaken. "Please," she said. "Tell me it isn't true. Tell me!"

The man on the bed raised himself a little in response, and his face was revealed. It was the man seen in the photograph Nyquist had found in Eleanor's bag. But in that image, taken at a much earlier date, he had been young, in his early twenties; whereas the man that now confronted Eleanor was easily into his late thirties. The hair was still long, past shoulder length, but greying now with a slight recede at the temples. And the lined, pallid face was stricken, fear trapped in the features. He pleaded with her, his voice rising. "You have to understand, I acted out of love. Nothing more. Yet it bears too much cost, too much pain and loss." He moved the knife forward. It didn't seem a threatening gesture, yet the blade was pointed towards her. He spoke with yearning. "Please… Eleanor…

You have to stay away from me, stay away from Dusk."

Nyquist raised his torch so that the beam fell directly on the man's face. The eyes did not flicker in the light, nor did they shift their focus from Eleanor. The girl herself made no attempt to look towards the torch beam. Because of this, Nyquist felt he was hardly present at the scene. He was a silent, seemingly invisible watcher.

The mist was now entering the room through the window. It wreathed around Eleanor's body. Nyquist could feel his heart pounding. Damp heat prickled his skin. Droplets of sweat formed on his brow like dew, wetting his eyes. The fog billowed and thickened in the room, summoned here by some unknown atmospheric or magical process. It formed a moon-silvered curtain through which he could only stare in helpless wonder. Here and there darker elements took on a more deliberate form, creating shapes that suggested other shapes, with these in turn bringing their own suggestions. One of them seemed almost human, before it too dissolved into another pattern. Eleanor and the man on the bed remained in their fixed positions. The knife glinted. Nyquist tried to break free of the spell, but it was no good, the fog held him in its power. And he thought instantly and briefly of his own father standing on the dusk's edge, staring ahead with eyes that were already lost to daylight, and then stepping forward to meet whatever waited for him there.

The cuckoo clock called again from the corridor. Again: five times. The noise brought Nyquist to his senses, causing him to concentrate on the strange scene before him. The three people in the room stood as they had before: Eleanor, the man on the bed, Nyquist himself. Tendrils of mist were now reaching out for him like so many skeletal human arms seeking comfort or entreaty. They caressed him. He felt one of them curling itself around his wrist. He was possessed. He took a single step into the room. A moth batted at his face, its yellow wings fluttering. He raised his hand to shoo it away and suddenly felt faint. His vision blurred. The fog filled the room entirely. He could hardly see in front of his eyes. A noise lit his skull with a fierce white radiance; there was no other way to describe it. He was held in a trance. And then darkness. His eyes closed.

One moment passing. Another moment…

Eleanor was screaming.

Nyquist almost stumbled as though suddenly released from sleep.

He was now standing close to the bed, Eleanor next to him.

He couldn't remember moving.

The fog had cleared a little.

Nyquist stared ahead at the terrible sight before him.

The man on the bed had fallen back, his body collapsing against the pillow. Blood gurgled from the wound that had opened in the side of his neck. His poor eyes blinked as he reached out vainly toward the girl. "Eleanor, my child," he whispered. Again: "Eleanor, you have to get away, please, leave the city. They're looking for you!"

Nyquist realised with a shock that she was now holding the knife, the blade stained with red.

The man cried out: "Eleanor, run! Run! Get away!"

Nyquist's thoughts misted over. He could not make sense of the time, or the moments that had led to this. Only images. The knife in her hands, the blood, the wound in the man's neck. His mind reeled. And then the cuckoo clock chimed again, clearly this time, giving the signal for a quarter past the hour. Time rushed back into the room like breath into a drowning person's body after they've been dragged from the ocean.

Fifteen minutes past five.

Nyquist moved quickly, putting his hands on the man's wound, pressing down tightly to stop the blood from flowing. It was no good.

Eleanor came to his side. The dying man responded to her presence as to a last chance at life, a branch to hold onto before the final fall began. He called her name again softly: *Eleanor.* And then he fell, he fell sheer away in an instant.

The world had left his eyes.

Eleanor remained where she was. "Has he gone?" Her voice was hushed, almost in wonder. Her dress was red-spattered, and torn. She was still holding the knife.

He nodded. "He's dead. Did you... did you see what happened?"

She looked confused for a moment and then answered, "I think he killed himself."

Nyquist was suddenly fearful of what she might do, not to him, but to herself, that she might turn the knife on her own flesh. Her eyes stared ahead, almost sightless, and he remembered the jagged light bulb she had pressed against her chest, drawing blood. One bad thought might tip her over. He reached out and gently pulled the knife from her hold. He let it fall onto the bed. And by this simple act Eleanor's body was relieved of its power. She surrendered and stated simply, "This man. He was my father. My real father." Her eyes closed at the utterance. Nyquist took hold of her, held her back from whatever it was she planned to do. But she pushed him away. For a moment he thought she was going to break down, to scream in pain and grief. It never came. Instead they stood apart, far apart, and she spoke in a voice so quiet he could hardly hear the words.

"This is my fault. It's all my fault."

She spoke not to him, not to herself, but to the man lying motionless on the bed.

There was no answer beyond the wound, the blood.

Nyquist stood by the window. Looking out, he could see the mists of Dusk rolling in vast banks of cloud, and a milk-white moon hanging within them, bringing its deathly colour to the long-lost suburb of Fade Away.

GUIDE BOOK: BESMEARED
WITH SLUTTISH TIME

FIRST-TIME VISITORS to Dayzone are often confused by the problem of timekeeping. Mundane questions such as, "When are we having dinner?" seem difficult enough to answer, never mind more important matters reliant on punctuality.

Soon...

Many travellers and newcomers prefer to keep their clocks and watches set to the timescale of their hometowns, where the skies move through more natural periods of light and dark. However, only when such devices are put aside will the true Dayzone experience be fully appreciated. At first this letting go will invariably lead to feelings of disorientation. Originally conceived as a Glorious Realm of Eternal Pleasure, the city, with its perpetual daylight, seems to exist somewhere outside of normal time.

Soon. Soon...

More inexperienced visitors will often feel they are drifting through chaos. It is a pity that so many leave the city in fear at this point. They have failed to understand that Dayzone is not a time-free region; rather, it holds within its boundaries many different chronologies. The most popular of these, the one that most first-time visitors will choose to follow, is known as *Authorised Standard Time*. This scale, provided free of charge, divides the day into thirty-six equal units, each marked by a signal given out by Radio DZ1.

So soon...

After a while many people feel the urge to purchase one of the more exotic standards, such as *Artificial Real Time, Alternative Public Time, or even Independent Abstract Time*. In addition, separate scales are used by the different business communities, by political parties, by the police, the medical profession, and so on. Institutions, clubs, football teams and religious orders will have their own timelines. Television and radio programmes are listed under *Constructed Reality Time*. Families or groups of friends often find their own ways of dividing the day into suitable units. Meanwhile, those in love often move to a tangled chronology called *Florid Passion Time*, where the day consists of forty-nine unequal units, some of which move faster or slower than others, depending on the current level of ardour between the parties. An increasing number of companies are now sponsoring their own timelines. Other standards are created by local interest groups.

So very soon...

Dayzone has freed itself from the restrictive cycles of day and night, summer and winter. Because of this, time has evolved in many new ways, each with its own unique pathway. From the corporate down to the personal, across all scales in-between, these timelines coexist in the same moment, ever more numerous, covering the city's streets in a complex, invisible web. Long-term residents pride themselves on their ability to step from one scale to another, quickly and with little confusion. The transition gives them pleasure. Just remember to adjust your timepiece as you cross over, and to limit the number of timelines used in

any one period of waking. Also, please note that we have
listed here only scales of a legal nature. There are many
unlicensed chronologies. We advise that travellers avoid
such illicit products, no matter how tempting they may
appear; they have not been properly tested on the human
psyche, and may well produce undue effects on the body's
internal clock. In extreme cases such abuse can lead to
severe mental imbalance.

Soon. Soon. Soon...

Dayzone: the city of clocks, millions upon millions of
them, each ticking at a different rate. Where will you find
yourself? When will it happen?

Now...

LIMBO CASE

The Festival of the Sun God was in full swing on the streets. The district of Body Heat blazed with the light of a frozen noontime, creating such a mirage effect that the avenues and boulevards seemed to tremble with phantom figures. The latest songs of daylight could be heard, flowing in waves of heat from doorways and windows. Men, women and children were dressed up as Apollo, Helios, Hyperion, Chronos, Eos, or one of countless other such daytime deities, many of the celebrant's own invention. People worshipped below a giant suspended globe which burned with fierce orange light, the congregation's hands raised in supplication to this manmade sun. Each shop front, market stall, kiosk, office block, tower, church and department store had its own clock on display, illuminated with extra lighting just for the occasion, and all of them showing a different time. The crowds moved along beneath these displays, each person checking and then adjusting their wristwatch or pocket watch as they passed over from one timeline to the next, and laughing at their own audacity.

These were the streets of neon and glamour. These were the avenues and boulevards where all the citizens walked in a haze of colour, counting the seconds as though they were weighing particles of gold in their own possession.

The glorious buzzing sound of electricity followed their every move. Bulbs popped from the overload, and were quickly replaced by passersby, or by a bulb monkey. In this manner, the light would never die.

Nyquist took no part in these rituals. Instead he had shut himself up in his office, eating when he remembered to do so, and dozing for an hour on the couch bed whenever he got tired. He had no other schedule to live by. His wristwatch and the wall clock differed by many hours and minutes and he had no understanding of which held the correct time, the safest time, the best time. He couldn't remember how many days he'd been here like this, or even how those days might be measured out. Closing the curtain, drinking coffee or whisky, lying down again, burying his head under a pillow, opening the curtain, turning his face to the wall: anything to keep out the endless ticking of the clock. It was all to no avail. His body felt sticky, uncomfortable. Flashes of yellow and orange pulsed behind his eyelids. He feared the onset of chronostasis. If only he could get some proper sleep. Why was he suffering like this? The job was finished. One teenage runaway found and delivered, after a fashion. Really, he should head over to his place in Nocturna, to get some darkness around him. But the idea of making that train journey through the dusklands turned his stomach. But then his thoughts were roused and memories of the house on Angelcroft Lane would crawl into view once again. There was no escaping it.

The police had taken him in, first for a preliminary statement and then a day or so later to answer a further set of questions. He knew the commanding officer, Detective Inspector Gardner, well enough from when his previous cases had crossed paths with police business. But he'd kept his mouth shut as much as he could, saying just enough and no more. And pretty soon he'd worked out that the cops knew even less than he did about what had really taken place out there on the edge of twilight.

"So what happened, Nyquist? And no holding back this time."

"Like I said, the guy asked for help."

"Saying what, precisely?"

"He wanted me to keep Eleanor Bale away from him."

"He said that?"

"Something like that."

"And did he say why he wanted this?"

"It was dangerous for her. That's what he said."

"You're certain of that?"

"Yes. I think so. It was a bad line."

"Is that so?"

"You saw the state of his telephone. It was a pirate job."

"Sure."

"I heard noises."

"Noises?"

The interview room was small. The walls stank of all the sweat they had collected over the decades. Nyquist squinted at the overhead light with its bare bulb. "Noises on the line, you know. Spooky stuff. Breathing sounds, animal cries. That kind of thing."

"So you took off for this house in the dusklands, just like that?"

"I had the feeling that the girl might be heading there, and you know how it is..."

"Enlighten me."

"I was just doing my job, hoping to bring her back home."

"Sure, Nyquist, you're one of the good guys." The inspector studied his notes. "Tell me. How well do you know Eleanor Bale?"

"I don't. I was searching for her, that's all."

"A runaway?"

He nodded in response. "I tracked her down in Burn

Out, and then lost her. And I didn't see her again until I found her in the house on Angelcroft, talking with the victim."

"What were they talking about?"

"I don't know. Not for sure. He was trying to explain something to her, but I don't think she believed it, whatever it was. And then everything went..."

Gardner waited, tapping his pen against the desktop.

"Everything went strange around then. I'm not sure what happened. I think I blacked out."

"Christ, but you're a pile of help, Nyquist, you really are."

Silence settled back into the room. Gardner stared at him. Nyquist could feel his chest constricting. "Any idea who the victim is yet?" he asked.

"His name's Kinkaid. Mean anything to you?"

"No."

"What is it? Something on your mind?"

Nyquist thought for a moment. "No. Nothing." He felt tired, still deeply affected by his time in the house of dusk. He asked, "What about the relationship between the dead man and the girl?"

Gardner shook his head. "There is no relationship. Eleanor Bale's told us that."

Nyquist worried at the knowledge: she had told him that Kinkaid was her real father. True or not, he would keep the confession secret. For now.

"An old family friend, is what she said." Gardner turned serious. "So let me get this straight, you didn't see Eleanor Bale stabbing this Kinkaid fellow?"

"Of course not. No."

"You're certain?"

"Well..."

"You fainted, right? Like an old lady in a Victorian novel."

"I closed my eyes for a moment, that's all."

"That's unfortunate."

Nyquist rubbed at his face. "She didn't do it, Gardner."

"No?"

"She's not the type."

"Actually, I think I agree with you." The inspector's expression was set in stone. "There was a whole mess of prints on that knife, including yours."

Nyquist frowned. "I took the knife off her."

"So she was holding it?"

"Yes, I think she… she picked it up, after… after the man had…"

"You think he killed himself, is that it?"

Nyquist didn't know how to answer, not clearly. All he could see in his memory was a blank, a black hole, a few moments of darkness.

"Well?"

"Yes, he killed himself."

He couldn't tell if he was lying, or telling the truth. Both options existed in the same mental space, each one valid.

Gardner was shaking his head in despair. "Touching the knife like that…"

"I know. I wasn't thinking."

"Nyquist, it's rule number one: don't contaminate the crime scene."

The two men stared at each other, neither of them backing down.

Gardner sighed and threw a brass key down on the desk. "Does this mean anything to you?" It looked like a hotel room key with the symbol of a five-pointed star on the fob and the number 225. "We found it on Kinkaid's body."

Nyquist told him the truth: he'd never seen it before.

"What about the other person you saw…" The inspector consulted his notes. "Before you went inside. The blurred figure in grey?"

"It was a glimpse, that's all. I might've been mistaken. They were standing near the house, just beyond the duskline."

"Male or female?"

"I don't know. It was–"

"It was misty. Sure, I get it." Gardner banged the file down on the desktop. "Christ Almighty on his red and gold illuminated neon cross, I wish for the life of me I could get just one firm answer out of you."

"I don't think there is one…"

"One what?"

"One answer. It was a very confusing time."

Gardner pondered. "Time… yes. Of course. The great unknowable."

Nyquist needed a drink, badly. His throat was parched. Once again the memory of that strange room clouded his mind. The mist was still with him, that must be it. Still inside his skull. He had to stay focused.

"What will happen to Eleanor Bale now?" he asked.

"Don't worry about that. We have this under control."

"Really?"

Nyquist was beginning to see where this questioning was going: essentially, Gardner was checking to make sure that Eleanor Bale was removed from all suspicion. The police were under pressure, and it was easy to work out just where that pressure was coming from.

The inspector folded up his case notes.

"I think this is a safe call," he said. "This Kinkaid guy is a drifter, a dropout. He ends up living on the edge of Dusk. It all gets too much for him, and he takes his own life. And…"

"And that's it. Job done."

"What can I say, it's that kind of place, right?"

Nyquist closed his eyes. His thoughts revolved around one subject only, something he could barely bring into focus. Yet it plagued him. He had to let it free.

"Gardner?"

"What is it?"

He tried to speak clearly. "What happened to me in the room, with the girl, the knife, the man on the bed. With him dying like that, unseen. Unseen..."

"OK. Let's not go there."

"It was Quicksilver."

Gardner leaned back in his chair. A moment passed. It seemed that a third occupant had entered the room, a ghost.

"Now listen. This isn't–"

"Quicksilver. Another victim! What else can it be? Tell me."

"Jesus, Apollo and all the saints of daylight!"

"It was just like they've described it, the witnesses, in the newspapers, on the radio. The invisible killer–"

"That's bullshit, and you know it."

"The blackout, the sense of not knowing, of not seeing anything, confusion." Nyquist felt he was losing control, but he couldn't stop now. "It's the same goddamn feeling!"

Gardner raised his own voice in turn. "Quicksilver doesn't exist."

"What the hell is it with you cops? Are you scared? Scared that the people will panic?" Nyquist leaned forward. "Well guess what, they're already panicking."

For a moment it looked as though Gardner might explode into rage. Instead, with a great effort he calmed himself.

"I don't want you mentioning this idea to anyone, do you get me?"

Nyquist nodded. "Sure. I get it."

"Kinkaid stabbed himself. That's it." Gardner shrugged. "Dusk makes people go mad. All the crazies gather there. I mean, you should know that. With your old dad, and all that."

The inspector stared at him.

Nyquist wanted to answer clearly, and succinctly. His father was never like that, he wasn't crazy. His father was a scientist, an explorer...

But he stayed off the subject.

"The girl's family will be happy, anyway."

"Now look–"

"It's OK, Gardner. We've all got our job to do."

The inspector looked at him, his eyes steady on their target. Nyquist felt sure he'd hit a sore spot: Patrick Bale was powerful enough to bring his influence to bear on the police, and the courts. The case would be wrapped up as quickly as possible, with little knowledge reaching the press.

Gardner smiled at last. "Find yourself a nice cheating husband or wife case, Nyquist. This one's over with."

"I will. I'll do that."

"Don't make enemies."

The cops had finished up with some routine stuff and sent him on his way. Nyquist had headed straight back to his office, locked the door, opened the whisky. Every so often he'd send out for some food and more drink, and the latest copy of the *Beacon Fire*. The story started out on page three: "Dusk claims another victim." As suspected, there was no mention at all of Eleanor Bale's presence there. Or his own. And nobody speculated that this was another attack by Quicksilver. It's simple: suicide goes on daily, but when it happens in or near twilight, nobody cares, certainly not the police. If you live close to the dusklands, you're looking to die. Case closed. But Nyquist pieced together what he could from the news reports. The dead man was called Dominic Kinkaid. No fixed abode, no known employment, no next of kin coming forward to claim his body for burial. Nothing. The reporter, for want of a better or more truthful story, described the suicide victim as a typical example of the sort of person obsessively drawn to the edges of Dusk, and drew a fanciful picture of him staring with wild eyes into the mist as though looking for visions. More and more of these cults were springing up, the report stated, where strange desires were given a collective presence. They were known by the name *Tenebrae*, a term meaning a religious service or lesson from the shadows.

Nyquist knew only one thing for certain: something strange and unknowable had happened in that room. How had the knife ended up in Eleanor Bale's hands? What had really taken place in those few seconds of blackout? And he kept going back to the words Eleanor Bale had said over Kinkaid's body: *This is my fault, it's all my fault.* Just what did she mean by that? He could not tell.

Soon enough the story slipped to a mention on page seven, edged out by a middle-aged woman found dead in her own bathtub, her wrists slashed, her body clock completely destroyed. A psychiatrist stated that the poor woman had been living on sixty-four different timelines at once. Warnings were given, questions were being asked in high office. Sir Patrick Bale was quoted, the usual platitudes: "We're doing all we can to help the less fortunate. But really, you have to remember, the freedom of time is what makes this city of ours so great, and so very prosperous."

Nyquist studied his photograph of Eleanor. A cheque from Patrick Bale had arrived at the office a few days ago. Nyquist couldn't quite work out what he was being paid for, but the money was needed. And the girl was safe.

He kept telling himself to let it be, to let it go. But he couldn't.

He took the photograph of Dominic Kinkaid out of his desk drawer. He placed it next to the one of Eleanor. Was there a connection, a familial relation? Perhaps. They shared a certain look in and around the eyes: a darkness. A sadness, even.

Father and daughter?

Yet she had mentioned none of this to the police.

Family secrets, perhaps; the Bales keeping their public image firmly intact.

Nyquist tried to sleep, still sitting in his chair. He placed a cloth over his face, holding it there with one hand. Eventually, a small piece of the night laid its veil over him. And once again he was trapped in the room on the edge of twilight, with this time himself pushing the blade forward, right into Kinkaid's neck. Blood spurted onto his hand.

He woke up shaking. Only a short time had passed. A few moments. His eyes ached and would hardly open. He stood up and started to pace the room, end to end. He needed a shave, a shower. He needed release. Most of all he needed to get out of here, out of this space. It felt like his own shadow was creeping up in him. He switched off the desk lamp, switched it on again. Off again. On. Off. On. He was living to a timescale of his own mad creation, pure stretched-out body clock, moment to moment. It was a sickness. He was heading for breakdown, he could feel it. Time was fragmenting around him. He'd be one more statistic in the newspaper.

Lonely private eye found dead in office.

Maybe his ex-wife had been right all along: more and more his life was playing out like a character in a pulp crime magazine. Maybe he was heading for a lurid end, a madman raving in a padded cell in a hospital for the chronologically deranged.

The clock on the wall read six minutes to eleven. And his wristwatch read seventeen minutes past one, or twenty past. The hands flickered in his sight, back and forth; the dial was fuzzy, filled with smoke, with mist. Dusk had got in the workings: he still couldn't read it properly. Nyquist shook his head. His mind buzzed with images. A clock spinning round, too fast for the eye to register, ticking loudly. The cuckoo calling, once, twice, a third time. Four times, five. And suddenly he was back there again, inside the house, he saw the fog as it swirled, the man on the bed, the girl, himself. Time skipped. Eleanor was screaming. He couldn't make out the words. The knife flashed. But whose hand was wrapped around the handle? He couldn't be sure: Kinkaid's, or Eleanor's? Or his own. The fog closed over the memory.

A terrible knowledge flashed in his head: Eleanor Bale was still in peril.

Eleanor, my child. You have to leave the city. They're looking for you!

Kinkaid's final words to the girl, to his daughter, if that much was true. He was trying to protect her, to warn her, to make her run away. The danger still existed. But who was looking for her? Did they mean her harm? It certainly sounded that way.

He looked at the typewriter, the piece of paper still inserted in the roller:

```
THE ELEANOR BALE CASE
```

The blank space beneath.

On an impulse, he started to type, the keys clacking like bare bones against metal:

```
What the hell happened in that room?
```

That was all. Nothing else. He reached for the phone on his desk and rang the Ariadne Centre. A woman greeted him with a cheery message. He jumped in before she could finish.

"I need to speak with Patrick Bale."

"I'm afraid that's not possible."

"Listen to me, please. This is important. I need to get in touch with his daughter. It's urgent." Nyquist's voice was slurring. "Can you give me their home number?"

"Company policy dictates that–"

"Please. Listen–"

The call was cut off.

He looked at the clock on the wall, at the watch on his wrist. *Tick, tick, tick, tick, tick, tick, tick.* Somewhere between the two different times, he was caught, trapped.

Feeling like a dog locked in a cage, he strode to the window and wrenched back the curtain. The light and the heat poured in, the colours struck at his eyes. Electrical sparks jumped across his vision and he couldn't tell if they were coming from the lamps pressed up tight against the glass, or from inside his skull. His face was moist, his hair matted down flat to his brow. He could hear a hissing noise at the back of his head somewhere. It was too much. Too much light, too much heat, too many colours. Too many goddamn fragments of time circling around him. His senses fused together and his hands reached out to press themselves against the glass, the burning glass, and he kept them there as long as he could, palms flat and fingers outstretched, forgetting himself, forgetting, until the pain and the heat got too much, far too much, and he was shocked back to life.

He needed to escape.

A LADDER TO THE SKY

He came out of his office and turned to face the stairs leading upwards. Nyquist had visited the floor above a few times. Some time ago, there was a woman who worked up there, Janice, and a kind of relationship had taken place between them. He recalled the moments of pleasure as he started up the stairs. Maybe something could have been made from it on his part, but Janice had moved on to a new job in a different part of the city and, as the wise man once said, many bulbs had popped their filaments since then.

Nyquist started to climb. He had to get above the lamps if he could. He had to find out where the lamps ended and the normal sky began. Was such a thing possible? He didn't know; it was a need within him, a way to break loose, to break free. Upon reaching the landing above he turned around in a half circle and carried on upwards to the next floor. He had been here once, just once, when a cheque had been sent to the wrong office. He could not remember which office, or when this incident had taken place. It didn't matter. Nyquist reached the landing and turned onto another flight of stairs. He was now entering unknown territory. How many floors did the building contain? He didn't know. How many of them were occupied? He didn't know. The higher you reached, the fewer people you found; that was the ruling. Nyquist carried on and at the next landing he walked a little way along the corridor to the nearest open doorway and looked inside. The space was twice as big as his own, as though a wall had been knocked down and two offices joined together. The workers stared at him, this wild-eyed intruder. A woman asked him what he was looking for. He didn't answer. "Hey, buddy," one of the men said. "What's your problem?"

Nyquist walked over to the window. "This won't take a second," he said. "Just doing a test." The blind shot upwards as he jerked on the cord and the usual array of lamps came into view. Nyquist looked at the flashing colours and the dazzling, burning rays of light. He was feeling more than a little bewildered as he turned to face the workers in the office: all these people watching him, peering at him. Nyquist smiled weakly, then headed back to the stairway. Now he was taking the stairs two at a time. He was losing breath, his muscles started to ache. Footsteps sounded behind him but when he stopped to look, there was no one there. Just an echo. And so he carried on, climbing upwards. Every so often he would make a detour to glance through an office doorway, only to see the curtains drawn or the blinds pulled down. As he went higher he saw improvised protection: old blankets pinned up over the windows, or sheets of typing paper glued to the glass, layer upon layer. Still the lights outside could be seen, shining through the coverings. Only two or three workers manned these upper offices, pale silent figures, the ghosts of haunted business ventures. They stared at Nyquist blankly with their sunken eyes. Nobody spoke.

As he climbed higher the stairwell lights grew dark and he saw that many offices were now empty, sometimes completely stripped out, or still furnished with their work desks, chairs and filing cabinets. Sheaves of half-finished documents lay scattered on the desks next to rusting typewriters. In these offices the windows were often bereft of any covering. And yet even at this height the neon sky was still on display, albeit entirely neglected, the bulbs either dead or smashed into shards. Sometimes the window glass itself was shattered. It was easy to imagine people reaching the end of their tethers and taking up a paperweight or a typewriter to crack the glass and darken the lights outside forever.

Nyquist carried on, reaching each landing in turn and skidding around to climb the next flight, and so on, flight after flight, his pores flooding with sweat and his shirt clinging to his back. He was slipping, falling, righting himself again. He had set his mind on this task and would not stop now, and he tugged open his collar to get some air to his system. It was so humid up here, he was entering a different climate. Finally he had to stop for a moment, to rest, leaning against a banister. His body was overheating. His lungs wheezed, his heart pounded. He could smell the alcohol in his sweat. It made him feel nauseous.

All was quiet this high up. Nyquist imagined that the workers had long since fled to other office blocks in more downmarket parts of town, where the lower levels came at a cheaper price. Slowly, his breathing settled and the pain in his chest eased a little. He was all set to carry on climbing, when he heard a noise from the nearest corridor. A pale light was shining through one of the office doorways. Nyquist made his way towards it. The noise turned out to be a transistor radio or a gramophone; he vaguely recognised a tune in praise of the sun, popular a while ago. He entered the room unannounced. It was populated with a half dozen or so people, each of them intent on some task at hand. They were drawing or painting pictures at easels. Nyquist saw comic book images of the sun bursting over the city in a ball of flames, or of rain falling in great jagged lines, and countless lamps and bulbs exploding into fanned-out rays of colour. Nobody talked to him; some looked up at his passing and then went back to their work. The music played on. Nyquist went over to the window and pulled at the curtains so hard they tore free from the runner.

He stared out through the glass. All he could see were bulbs, more bulbs, lamps and flames and colours and all kinds of light-emitting devices. He turned to the artists. "Where does it end?" he cried. "Where the hell does it end?"

Nobody answered. One woman shook her head slowly from side to side. Her lips moved in silence. Nyquist banged a fist down on a desktop. He walked out of this last office, this final outpost, moving more slowly now. He was coldly determined in his heart, not wasting his energy, but simply taking each flight of steps in turn. Very soon he was moving through areas of complete darkness, the corridors gloomy and silent and dust filled, where every bulb had long since burned out and never been replaced. And then finally he reached the very top floor. One further door marked *Roof Access* led to a narrow flight of stairs. There were just six steps altogether, these leading upwards to a green metal fire door, which was propped open with a small length of timber. Nyquist opened the door fully and stepped through.

The vast dome of the neon sky stretched over the roof of the tower block, reaching down to touch the building on all four sides, but leaving a gap of some ten feet or so, between the roof itself and the dome's highest point. It was an irregular construction, made entirely of lamps, each of which was ablaze with colour. There was no glimpse of the real sky, of the sun and the clouds. Nyquist stood beneath this vault of lights. His hands reached up above his head and his mouth opened in a cry of abject despair. This cry was trapped beneath the neon sky like a bird in a coop, made frantic in its bid to escape, the sound merging with the constant buzz and pop of electricity. Nyquist was wondering why these bulbs were still alight, when he heard a voice.

"There's nothing else."

Nyquist turned. At first he could make out no human shape amid the fiery glow of the dome. And then the voice came again. "It's no good crying out or screaming, mister, there's nothing else." And now Nyquist could see the speaker more clearly. It was a woman sitting on an upturned crate. He guessed she was in her sixties, with skin the same colour and texture as brown leather. Her long greying hair was held back by a pair of designer goggles, which she had pushed up from her eyes, to her brow. She had the haunted look of a long-term photon addict, someone who had spent far too long in direct illumination. She was dressed in clothing made from many different patches of material, in all colours and shades; it was this outfit that made her almost invisible against the multicoloured complex of lights. Nyquist stepped closer. The woman's eyes were unlike any others he had ever seen, being a pair of overly large, pale, bloodshot orbs.

She stood up at his approach, saying, "It's just bulbs. All the way."

"There's no... there's... no..." Nyquist was having trouble speaking.

"There's no sky," the woman said for him. "Not here. Not in Dayzone. We don't believe in the sky. We believe in the Glow. The neon, the shimmer. The power and magic of heat and light."

Nyquist watched the woman as she bent down to choose a yellow bulb from a large cardboard box on the floor. He saw that her jerkin-style waistcoat had been fitted out with tools and gadgets, each assigned to its own specially sewn-on pocket or loop, and that her hands were protected by a pair of thin canvas gloves. "My name's Lucille," she said, as she walked over to where the neon sky came down towards the edge of the building. "Lucille Firstborn." She reached up to screw the yellow bulb into an empty socket. The light glowed evenly and she nodded in satisfaction. "Yes, I was a bulb monkey once. Over twenty-five years' service, mending the lights. Fixing the sky, we called it. Hanging on, clinging tight, swinging across upside down from hold to hold, from the ropes, the harness, the belts. Very often going 'pure' as we called it, with no safety gear. All the tricks and shortcuts, the technical knowhow, the snazzy uniform, the special glasses. The tools of the trade."

She smiled and then reached up to screw in a second bulb, this one shining with a bright red light. She stepped back to admire her work.

"There we are. That's much better."

"Stop doing it," Nyquist said. "Why are you doing it?"

"What?"

"Stop replacing the bulbs."

Lucille looked over towards him, before sitting herself back down on her crate. She reached into a shoulder bag, pulling out an electrical plug. A tiny screwdriver was extracted from one of her pockets, and with this she removed the top of the plug. Nyquist had never seen it done so quickly. She beckoned him forward.

"Do you see them? The wires?"

Nyquist nodded.

"One, two, three." Each wire was pointed out in turn. "Do you know what they mean, these connections? No? It's the Holy Trinity. Now, follow if you can. The neutral wire, here see, that's the Father, the circle that always returns upon itself. The earth wire, here, well that's the Son isn't it, the spirit made flesh, brought down to earth from the sky, so to speak. You see what I'm saying?"

"I'm not sure…"

"And here, the live wire? Well that's easy."

"It is?"

"Of course! The live wire is the Holy Ghost, the power itself that brings all to glorious existence."

Nyquist was confused. "What do you mean? I don't understand."

"I'm showing you the way, the Way of the Light."

A bulb blew out a little further across the roof top. It made a dull popping sound.

"Now! You see?" Lucille got to her feet. "Ablaze one second. And then darkness. Such is life." She walked over to the spot. "Help me. Quickly! The ladder."

Nyquist fetched the stepladder from where it was standing, already open. He set it in place for Lucille and she clambered up to remove the dead bulb. This she wrapped in a piece of newspaper, placing it in her shoulder bag. Then she pulled out a new bulb from a pocket. "The city wasn't always like this, you know?"

Nyquist did know, but he let her carry on.

"I was only fifteen years old when I first started out as an apprentice, and back then I often heard stories from the older bulb monkeys, the veterans. They said that the city was perfectly normal once, although it prided itself on being the ultimate twenty-four hour experience zone. This is what they called it. Later on, it became Dayzone. Well, it was just the city-centre at first, then it spread. And from that moment on, the lamps never went out." Lucille screwed in the new bulb and the light came on immediately with a lovely azure glow to it. "There were many benefits. Increased work time, without let up, because the machines need never rest, never go quiet, never stop turning. That was the promise. And therefore, increased profits. A better lifestyle all around, for rich and poor. Ha!" She let out a loud guffaw. "I'm still waiting." She climbed back down the ladder and Nyquist noticed for the first time the slight limp in her left leg.

"What happened to you?" he asked.

She shook her head as though to dismiss a troublesome thought.

"I fell."

And then she spat, aiming the large ball of phlegm upwards in a long arc so that it hit a naked bulb and sizzled like fat on a fire.

"Early retirement. Full pension. Such as it is."

She moved from side to side, to better admire the new light bulb she had fitted. But then, even as she smiled at her work, the bulb started flickering, and dying.

"Oh my. You see that? The wiring is shot. You see the trouble I have?"

The bulb flashed again, went dark once more, and then finally caught hold.

Lucille laughed. "It burns! Life itself."

Something happened. The woman's face changed. If there was a cloud in sight it would have passed over her features at that moment; but the artificial sky was bright, bright with the illuminated icons of the new electrical gods. "I'm only keeping the darkness at bay," she said, her voice quiet, directed inwards. "Truly, there is no greater process by which a human being can prove him or herself. None greater."

"So you do this just for fun, Lucille, is that it? For yourself?"

Her eyes squeezed shut at this. She grimaced.

"No. I do it for everyone. For the city." Then she breathed evenly and pronounced with deadly seriousness, "One bulb going out, is like all the bulbs going out."

"Just like in the war," Nyquist said. "During the blackout?"

"Oh, but those were frightening times! The whole city dark, every bulb turned off. Us bulb monkeys didn't know what to do with ourselves, I tell you truly."

Nyquist stepped closer to better hear her. He must have made a terrible sight after his drinking spree and the long exhausting climb up the stairs, and yet her eyes seemed to look upon him with compassion.

She said, "You were born here in Dayzone, weren't you? I can tell."

Nyquist wanted to turn away. "Yes," he answered. "I've never known anywhere else."

"So you've never seen the sky? The real sky, I mean?"

"Well..."

"Yes?"

Nyquist frowned. "Once... once I journeyed out, close to the city's edge."

"You were curious?"

"My marriage had just broken up, and I was at a loss, saddened beyond measure, cast adrift. The city disgusted me, everything about it: the light of Dayzone, the darkness of Nocturna. I had a sudden urge to leave, to find a new place elsewhere, a new start in life."

Lucille nodded. "Yes, I can understand that."

"I went east, to Precinct Ninety-Nine."

"That would be... let me remember... the town of Lambency?"

"That's right. I had heard a story that many people went there, when they wanted an easy way to leave the city."

Lucille nodded. "They have very few bulbs there, it's true. Silly people."

Nyquist looked into the distance. "I stayed there for a short while, in a small hotel close to the city limits. Then I set off walking, towards the border..."

He stopped talking. Lucille nudged his arm. "What happened? Come on, mister, did you reach the outside?"

He turned to look at her, his eyes fiery in the glow of the lamps.

"Yes. The bulbs ran out. Piece by piece, the neon sky fell away. My fingers kept fidgeting at my wristwatch, desperate to adjust it to a new timezone. Yet I knew, after this I would hardly need to change my watch again. One clock would rule me, one alone! I stopped and looked ahead. Beyond the final, dimly lit lamps I could see a field... farmland. A truck passed me on the road, carrying produce and foodstuffs into the city. A flock of starlings were also winging their way towards Dayzone. They flew above my head and I looked up and I saw... I saw..."

His brow furrowed and his eyes closed tight.

"You saw the sun! Is that it?"

"No..." He gazed at Lucille again, an infinite sadness in his expression. "No. It was cloudy. A cloudy day. The sun was just a soft yellow glow. It was enough... too much. I felt weak, dizzy. I dropped to my knees on the roadway and pressed my hands against my eyes."

His hands made the same movement now, following the memory. And his voice fell silent.

Lucille watched and waited for his story to continue.

Nothing more was said.

She touched his arm. "Mister? Are you all right?"

He nodded.

"You had to turn back, is that it? It was all you could do?"

He revealed his eyes once more. They glistened in the light. "I'm sorry," he said. "I haven't told that story before, not to anyone."

Lucille smiled. She tried to put him at ease. "You see, for me it's different. I came here when I was young, a child of six. The whole family. My parents were looking for work."

He wiped at his face. "So you've seen the sun? Really?"

"Indeed I have. Many a day."

Nyquist hesitated. "What's it like?"

She stared at him and then answered in a quiet voice: "I used to play on a sports field, just near to where we lived. The summer sky stretched overhead like a soft blue blanket. The sun warmed my skin. And then later it grew dark, as night fell."

Nyquist sighed. "It must be something to see, it really must."

She nodded. "A few years back, after my fall, I had the same idea as you, that I might build a new life elsewhere. So I went travelling."

"You left the city? How was it?"

Lucille gave out a gleeful laugh. "Bloody awful! All that space, that empty space. And the climate always creeping up on you, and the seasons changing before you know it. And just one clock, one timescale like an evil overseer. Everybody following the same patterns. Hell, no. It's a nightmare. It's a daymare. Now I understood why people are so reluctant to leave Dayzone, despite all the hassle and the heat and the constant ticking sound!" She scowled. "This is paradise! And I came running back, pronto. And here I'll stay, until I shuffle off the clock for the final time."

Nyquist thought for a moment. He realised this woman might have a great deal of knowledge about the city. "Tell me," he asked. "Have you ever been into the dusklands? Or to the edge of it? The very edge?"

Lucille screwed up her eyes. "What? No, I wouldn't go there. You don't go there. It's a bad place."

"But how do you know that?"

"Oh come on, mister. I tell you, it's a place of dangers."

"So you believe all the stories?"

"Of course I do. All the city's dead are living in there, in the dusk."

Nyquist nodded. "Yes. That's what my father believed."

"He was a wise man, then."

"Maybe… maybe it's just people talking. Rumours."

"You heard about that poor fellow, didn't you? The one they found dead out there, in a house on the borderline? Recently. You heard about him?"

Nyquist spoke more to himself. "I heard."

"They buried him in a pauper's grave. That's what happens, see, when you die in the dusk? You die alone, and then they stick you in the hardest, most desolate ground they can find. A dreadful fate. And the worst thing is, some horrible demon got hold of him. That's how he died."

"That's not true. He was stabbed."

"Oh, that's what they tell you in the *Beacon Fire*, sure. But listen, I have it on good authority. A demon got him!"

Nyquist saw again the dead man in his mind's eye. Kinkaid. He saw Eleanor standing near the bed, the knife in her hands. The memory plagued him.

Lucille checked the dome for anymore dead bulbs, then she said, "You've heard about Quicksilver, haven't you?"

"I have."

"Well you know he comes out of twilight every so often, to claim another sacrifice."

Nyquist didn't respond.

"It's why no one can see him. Because he's wrapped in a cloak of fog. It makes him invisible–"

Now he grabbed her by the upper arms. "Tell me about the twilight. What is the dusk, really? Why does it exist? What does it do to you? Lucille, you must know!" She looked back at him as though he were mad. But he carried on. "Tell me."

Lucille went limp in his hands, bringing him to his senses a little. He loosened his grip, enough for the woman to fix her eyes on him. "You be careful," she said. "You just be careful now."

Nyquist released her. He said quietly, "I think the dusk

has got inside me, somehow."

Lucille grimaced and moved a few steps away but then stopped. "Nobody gets free of it. You do know that? Once taken."

"What do you mean, taken?"

"People go missing, on the fogline. They get taken over. And even if they come back, which is rare, they're never the same."

He looked at Lucille, shaking his head slowly. "How can you know that?"

She didn't answer directly. Instead she said, "Do you want to know the truth about Dusk? The worst thing of all?"

Nyquist nodded.

"Time is a fluid substance in there, not a solid. It moves back and forth, back and forth like the tide. There's no *when*. There's no now, no then, no if, no was, no past, present or future." Her voice rose in pitch. "There's no waiting, no expectations, no chance of change. It's a limbo state. And all you can do is wander around twilight forever. Half dead, half alive. Now that's the truth." The woman started to laugh at her own words. It was a horrible sound that scratched at his nerves like a scalpel.

Nyquist looked away, towards the overarching dome of lamps. He was thinking of his father: the sight of him walking off into the mist, the young boy watching scared from the edge of Dusk, never daring to follow. Was his father still alive in there, or half alive? A ghost in the mist. It was too much to hope for. Or to fear.

The sizzle of the electrical circuits joined in with Lucille's manic laughter. And the dazzling colours of the neon sky bled into each other, dissolving in Nyquist's sight.

HERE LIES A STRANGER

Nobody wanted to bury their dead in the dark. Because of this fact, almost all of the city's cemeteries were located in Dayzone. One such was Cotton Springs Remembrance Garden. The attendant showed him the way, past the formal tombs and the well-tended plots, over to the dry, cracked, weed-strewn ground where those who had died unknown or unloved were laid to rest. The stone was simply made, standard issue, carved with the name of Dominic Kinkaid and the year of his death: 1959. That was all. No date of birth, and no message of any kind. Nyquist looked down at the small bunch of withered flowers that had been placed in a tin vase. It wasn't much to show for a life, especially one that had ended in such sorry circumstances.

"Were you here for the ceremony?" he asked.

The attendant nodded. "Such as it was."

"Why do you say that? Not many turned up?"

"Nobody. Nobody turned up."

Nyquist felt his head throb with the heat, the unremitting glare. The lamps were very low here, just a few feet above his head, and the buzz and hum of the electrical circuits was almost deafening. If he reached up, his hands would make contact with the sky. Why had he come to this place, what was he hoping to find? He looked around at the other graves in the area, hardly any of which had flowers laid upon them. The attendant seemed to understand his reasoning, saying, "I need to throw these away now," and he bent down to remove the dead flowers.

"Did you put them here?"

"No. The woman did."

"The woman?" Nyquist immediately thought of Eleanor. "I thought you said nobody attended the funeral?"

"She came later."

"Tell me about her."

"Why should I do that?"

Nyquist looked at the man. He was thin and tall and wrinkled, nearing retirement age. He had probably spent most of his life in such surroundings; and whatever it was that he was seeking in recompense for knowledge, almost certainly it wasn't money.

"What do they call you?"

"Usually? The man with the spade."

"Otherwise?"

"Delamonte."

"That's a good name."

"Aye, it is. I stole it off a dead man." He squinted in the harsh light. "We're being watched."

Nyquist followed the attendant's gaze over to the iron fence that edged this part of the cemetery. An indistinct figure was standing near the gate, his or her body the only dark object in the surrounding lampscape.

"We get all sorts here. Drunks, tramps, courting couples, grief junkies, hooligans. Bloody flower stealers as well, can you believe it?"

"I can." Nyquist turned back to view the headstone, saying, "I was with Mr Kinkaid, the day he died."

"Is that so?"

"We spoke together. He asked me for help, and I did what I could. But it was too little, and too late."

Delamonte bowed his head. He held some private thoughts to himself for a moment, then he looked up. "It was quite a shock seeing her here."

"Why?"

Delamonte smiled. "Oh, she was celebrated in her day, and very beautiful. I remember her well, from the photographs in the newspapers. Of course, she's not quite so beautiful now. But then again, who is?"

So it wasn't Eleanor then. "Who was it?"

"Catherine Bale."

Nyquist thought about this. Catherine was Eleanor's mother, the wife of Patrick Bale. She had been the young heir to a business fortune, once high society's favourite darling, but now rumoured to be a virtual recluse. Indeed, even Patrick had said that his wife hardly ever left Nocturna. Well, this grave had obviously drawn her forth, out of the darkness.

Could it be true, that Dominic Kinkaid was Eleanor's real father, not Patrick Bale? In which case, Catherine Bale was paying her final respects to an old lover.

"When did she visit?" he asked.

"Mrs Bale came after the service had finished," the attendant said. "Much later. After the priest had said his few words, and the body was lowered into the ground."

"Was she alone?"

"No. She had a maid with her, and a chauffeur. She was well looked after, protected, if you like. Hat and veil, dark glasses, long black gloves, the whole rigmarole. She stood at the graveside and lifted the veil away from her face and I recognised her straight away."

Nyquist brought out his photograph of Eleanor Bale. "Tell me, have you ever seen this girl?"

Delamonte shook his head. "Not that I recall, no."

"Well, thank you. You've been very helpful."

"A dreadful business, though. Being killed like that,

right on the edge of Dusk. The worst place to die, don't you think?"

"You could be right."

"But somebody loved him at least."

"Why do you say that?"

"Here. See?" Delamonte knelt down and started to stir up the soil on the grave, revealing a few sparkling objects buried just below the surface. Nyquist bent down next to the aging man, who continued, "Nothing of value, just these little trinkets. Mrs Bale left them here. Buried them herself. Kneeling down just like we are now, and taking her time about it, a good fifteen minutes or more. Amazing. That such a woman..."

His voice trailed off.

"Sure." Nyquist picked up a tiny necklace of coloured gems, a length of scarlet ribbon, a miniature doll. He dug further, unearthing coloured marbles, beads, sparkling bangles, a fairy light, feathers, a toy watch, glass jewels and crystals.

"Children's playthings," said Delamonte. "A little girl's possessions."

"Looks like it." Nyquist felt strange: he was examining the toys and precious items from Eleanor's early years. But then he found something that made him hold still. It wasn't much, and his reaction had hardly anything to do with the teenage girl, but more to do with himself and his own childhood. It was a music box. Small, intricately made, no more than three inches square. He lifted the lid to reveal a tiny ballerina who revolved slowly as the music started playing. The melody was slow and tender, with a beauty all its own, spiky as the notes started, and soft as the notes died away.

He stood up and looked over towards the fence. The figure at the gate had vanished. Only the fierce glow of light remained, under a barrage of bulbs. Everything blurred. He suddenly felt weak on his feet. It was the lack of sleep, the overpowering heat of the day, and the melody from the music box. His eyes misted over as he stared once more at the simple gravestone.

"Is that the current year?" he asked. "1959. Definitely?"

"It is. I think."

"By whose calendar?"

Delamonte shrugged. "Who knows? I try my best to keep track, but whenever there's an election and a new council come in, they insist in bringing their own timescales with them. Left wing time, right wing time, left of centre time, right of centre. I've lived through them all."

Nyquist nodded in reply. The lamplight shone down fiercely on his head. He wiped the sweat from his brow with his handkerchief, and said, "Sometimes I wake up and it feels like whole years have been taken away from me."

The attendant smiled. "You and me both."

The conversation was over. Nyquist walked back to his car. The dashboard fan had breathed its last, and so all the windows were wide open. A faint breeze touched at his face, like the whisper of a spirit only recently deceased. He examined the music box more closely, noting the engraved writing that spelled out the name of the melody, Beethoven's "Für Elise". He had had such a toy himself when he was small, of more or less the same design. The melody itself was different but of a similar quality, enough to suddenly transport him back there, to his younger realm, the council house in New Lantern Town. Artificial sunlight streaming in through the living room window, his mother bending down to present the gift to him. And hearing this similar tune, being drawn back like this, Nyquist had the uncomfortable feeling that time, like the music, like the Eleanor Bale case, was either slipping away from him, or creeping ever closer; he could not tell which.

NEGATIVE HALO

As Nyquist started his car and made for the exit, another vehicle suddenly pulled over and halted, blocking his way. He waited, but the other car didn't move. He tried honking the horn. It had no effect. With a sigh, he got out and walked over. The other vehicle had blacked-out windows, a sight that was hardly ever seen in Dayzone. It puzzled him. Who would want to keep out the light? He tapped on the glass, but then stopped at a noise to one side, as the air close by seemed to darken suddenly. Had a bulb gone out overhead, or a number of them at the same time? Such a thing could happen, he knew that, a chain reaction. But no, all the bulbs looked to be brightly lit. Yet a shadow moved. And again, a fleeting presence. Here in this illuminated realm, an area of gloom was visible. Nyquist shivered. And then his eyes adjusted and he saw a slowly moving figure, a tall, well-set male figure. It looked more like a body of gloom than a body of flesh. The darkness covered it entirely from head to foot in a uniform of dark grey. Even the facial features were hidden behind a smoky mask.

Nyquist stayed where he was, a few feet from his car.

The shadow man stopped at the same time.

Was he being looked at, examined? Nyquist could not

tell; the other man's features were too well veiled.

"Can I help you?"

The shadow did not respond. Nyquist took a step forward. The shadow waited. The darkness glowed around it like a negative full-body halo. Perhaps the man was wearing some kind of light-cancelling suit; Nyquist had heard of such fashions among the young, especially in Nocturna. But here, in the daylit side of the city? No. It was unheard of.

And still the shadow did not move.

"I don't know what you're playing at, but you're starting to royally piss me off."

Intimidation had no effect.

Nyquist moved back towards his parked car. There was a strange noise behind him, a dry crackling sound. He turned back.

"Where is she?" The shadow man's voice was as grey and indistinct as his body and face; a hissing sound surrounded each word.

Nyquist narrowed his eyes. "What's that?"

"Where is she? The girl?"

"I don't know what you mean–"

"Eleanor Bale. Where is she?"

"Who wants her?"

The face shook behind its mask of fog. Nyquist could imagine it was grimacing.

"She must be taken. She will be ours."

Nyquist had the idea the shadow man was speaking on someone else's behalf: he was some kind of agent sent here on one purpose.

He kept his voice steady: "Show yourself."

The figure stepped forward and made a mistake; he moved into a powerful, focused beam of light. He trembled, suddenly distressed. Wisps of fog slipped away from the body.

"What's wrong? Don't you like the idea of light, of heat?"

The figure shook with fear. "I don't want to hurt you. Just tell me where the girl is hidden. She belongs! She belongs to us."

Nyquist realised: this man was connected in some way with Dusk. "You're a long way from home. You poor bastard."

This triggered something in the shadow man, a bare nerve. He moved swiftly and silently in anger, gliding across the concrete. He was upon Nyquist without warning, without mercy. The darkened figure towered over him. Whatever orders he might've been given were now cast aside. The hands of smoke circled around Nyquist's neck and took hold. They closed tight, pressing against the larynx. He coughed and spluttered. His mouth struggled open. His assailant's hands opened as well, just slightly, enough to let the smoke enter. It seeped in. Nyquist could feel it in his throat, his lungs. It moved like a snake through his chest. He was choking.

His back was up against his car, there was nowhere else to go. His arms came up blindly to push against his assailant; they pressed on cloth, and muscle beneath that was unyielding. It was useless. No breath. No breath! None. His eyes were filled with haze, with flashes of red light.

The last few gasps of air.

Soon, soon, it will be over…

He welcomed it. And that thought, that moment of surrender: it disgusted him. It gave him strength. His own disgust. He fought back. He jammed the heel of his shoe against the car's bodywork and pushed with all his might. The figure was taken by surprise. They tumbled forward together and fell to the ground, where Nyquist was once more easily overpowered. The man pinned him down, grabbed him by the hair and bashed the back of his head against the gravel. He was blacking out. He swung wildly with his right hand and hit at the hidden face and he felt the contact of his bunched fist on softer flesh. In desperation he reached up and tore at the cloth mask with its garlands of mist; he dug his nails in and pulled the mask loose. His attacker's face was exposed, and the rest of the mist dissipated from his clothing like a ghost escaping flesh. Nyquist pushed the man away. He scrambled to his feet and stepped back so the harsh rays of light fell directly on the prone figure. Immediately the man tried to escape the glare. He was in agony.

Nyquist let him suffer.

A pale face, washed-out eyes, a shaved skull. He shook his head from side to side and started to shriek.

Nyquist stood over him, offering a little shade. "Who are you? What do you want from Eleanor?" He bent closer, grabbing the attacker by the lapels. "Tell me." He was about to apply more pressure when another darkness closed in from the side, another agent.

Time slowed down.

Mist curled around Nyquist's face and head.

And in the mist, a voice.

It whispered close and he was back once more at the fogline, twilight was calling to him and he gave in, he couldn't help himself. All thoughts of daylight vanished.

The voice whispered again.

Quicksilver awaits you.

It was the last thing he heard before the mist covered him completely.

HANGING BY A THREAD

One of the entranceway's door panels had been smashed in, probably the result of a brick or some other object thrown in anger. The web of cracks in the glass mirrored the tangle of shining wires above the forecourt of the Ariadne Centre. People came and went. Nyquist had been waiting across the street for some time, his body clock itching with need as he stared at the broken window, wondering about who might have done such an act: drunken hooligan, disgruntled ex-employee, or a protester against the company's promotion of excessive or dangerous timelines? Perhaps the mother or father of some poor chronostatic victim.

He took a sip from his flask, feeling the delicious burn of cheap blended whisky in his throat. Events had led him here; they would lead him away. Time wrapped itself around him in one thousand binding cords, ever tightening. There was no wiggle room. He felt that he might burst apart at any moment, and he no longer cared. He'd had all good sense beaten out of him. Only the case mattered.

Nyquist checked his watch. Was it really twenty-five past three? If so, which timeline was he on? When had he last made an adjustment? He couldn't remember, and his fingers ached to grab hold of the winder, to twist and turn and change the time, over and over again.

But then he spotted a lone woman coming out of the doorway. She walked across the street, towards where Nyquist was standing. He stepped out from the bus shelter, startling her a little. "Excuse me," he said.

"Yes?"

"I was wondering, do you have the right time?"

The woman looked confused. "What do you mean?"

Nyquist guessed she was a senior administrator or a low-level manager of some kind. He nodded over to the centre. "*Business Time.*"

She looked at him with disdain, at his damaged face, his shoddy suit and his greasy self-cut hair. At the driven look in his eyes.

Nyquist waved his hands about, dismissing his own image. "I know what you're thinking," he said. "I'm not executive material. But listen, there's many different kinds of business. Isn't that right?"

"I guess so."

"I'm just trying to make my way in the world, to get back on the right track."

She looked at her wrist, which held two watches, one next to the other. "Well, let's see. Inside the centre, it's ten past six." She spoke the words as though throwing a coin to a beggar.

"Thank you. Thank you very much!"

The woman hurried away. Nyquist adjusted his wristwatch with a deft but frantic hand. Then he returned to the bus shelter. He'd found a tiny spot of shade where a broken bulb had not yet been replaced. Nyquist's head fitted the small area of darkness precisely, as though it were made for him especially by a bespoke shadow designer. Yet the act made him think of the man who'd attacked him in the cemetery car park, a man who carried his own shadow with him. And the second person who had hit him on the head from behind. Old Delamonte had seen all this from Kinkaid's graveside, and had coming running up to help. By the time he got there, the two assailants had left in the vehicle with the blacked-out windows. Delamonte described this second figure. "Just a shadow. Only a shadow."

Nyquist reached up to touch the tender bruise on the back of his head. It felt like a crowbar had been used, or some such.

Well then: one more wound to add to the list.

But it was the second attacker's final words that he remembered most, the man leaning down to whisper in his ear as he slipped into unconsciousness.

Quicksilver awaits you.

It sent shivers through him, even now as the minutes ticked by, as people walked by, living their gilded lives in this well-to-do area of the city, unaware of the darker forces that gathered.

He kept his attention on the Ariadne Centre. More and more people were coming out, others arriving in groups; a shift had ended. Half past six. End of the day for one half of the work force; the beginning for another set of workers. The ones leaving were all adjusting their wristwatches to personal time zones, just as the arriving workers synchronised themselves to the collective office time. This was the real advantage of Dayzone: work never stopped. The profits soared far and above other cities around the country. And sure enough, about ten minutes later Patrick Bale strode out of the building. He was accompanied by Pearce, whose role seemed to hover something between personal assistant, second-in-command and female bodyguard. They turned down a narrow side street. Nyquist followed them. A private car park was situated around the corner, where a chauffeur was already opening the door of a highly polished limousine. The surrounding lamps were reflected in the paintwork, their many colours blurring together, transforming the entire vehicle into an abstract picture show.

Nyquist approached. "Mr Bale!"

Pearce made a threatening gesture but Nyquist shouted, "It's about Eleanor."

This simple statement caused Pearce to hesitate.

Bale came forward, his voice cold, emotionless: "All that business is done, Nyquist, as you know."

"Is it?"

"Certainly. I believe you have received payment already?"

Behind the cool, expensively modelled exterior, Nyquist could sense the pressure this man was under. His skin was mottled with red and his eyes were slightly off focus.

He asked, "Have you been in a fight?"

Nyquist ignored the question. "I need to speak with Eleanor. She's in danger."

"How do you mean?"

"I'm not sure. I can't say as yet, not precisely. I was attacked..."

Bale squinted at him. "Really?"

"I don't know who they are, or what their goal is. But they're looking for Eleanor. That's a fact."

"I really don't understand."

He didn't dare mention the Quicksilver threat. Instead he said simply, "They're going to harm your daughter. And they might well... they might come after you, in order to find her. Or your wife. They're desperate."

Bale shook his head in response. His eyes blinked as sweat dripped into them. He looked furious. "Thank you for your services, Mr Nyquist. But my poor little girl has been through enough already. Now, I have a train to catch." He turned to the car, indicating for Pearce and the chauffeur to get ready to leave.

"Are you her real father?"

Bale stopped dead. His body shook for a moment.

Pearce stepped forward. "Are you all right, Mr Bale?"

Her boss gestured angrily at her to back off. "Keep away from me!"

She moved off to stand next to the chauffeur. And only when they were safely out of hearing, did Bale speak. His voice was hushed, tight, filled with disbelief.

"What in Apollo's name are you talking about?"

"Eleanor claims that another man is her father. The dead man. Kinkaid."

Bale moved quickly. He grabbed Nyquist by the arm, pulling him even further from the car. "That… that girl!"

Nyquist kept his cool. "Yes?"

"She does not respect me. I've given her everything. Everything!"

"Have you?"

"I'm warning you, Nyquist. Don't mess with me."

The two men faced each other, until finally Bale pushed Nyquist away.

Nyquist shouted, "Look after her, Bale. Don't let her get hurt!"

The chief executive ignored him. He walked over to the limousine where he spoke to Pearce in a low voice. His assistant nodded before shooting a glance of pure hatred over at Nyquist. Then she followed her boss into the back of the vehicle and the doors closed.

Nyquist tipped his flask until the last dregs of alcohol soothed his tongue.

The limousine drove away, a silver chariot under the lamplight. It seemed to vanish amid the haze, as though swallowed up by a mirage.

Damn it. He needed a drink, a proper one.

Something to make him forget.

Or rather, to remember. Because always at the edge of his vision, those lost moments in the twilit room hovered… just out of reach.

MISTER TICK-TOCK IS DANCING

He sought oblivion in No Sleep precinct, the entertainment sector. In these streets a constant parade of dancers, singers and musicians plied their trade for both tourists and long-term residents. This flashing neon jungle excited the revelling tribes beyond measure. Granted, the more chronologically challenged were left with serious clocklag, but it was all worth it for the joy of a sleepless, overheated adventure. And then it was back to the quieter, more sedate precincts of Dayzone, or the servitude of a single time stream somewhere outside the city.

But Nyquist didn't want to return anywhere, only to keep moving forward. He pushed his way along the crowded boulevard.

Animated chatter mixed in with music streaming out of club doorways, while street singers caressed the ears with hot jazz rhythms. Circuits crackled in the power surges and brightness flared from lamps on the edge of burnout above the radiant streets, above the blazing stores and the fiery windows, amid the glow and the gleam of daylife. Neon gods and goddesses were hanging from the hoardings, all dazzle and golden hair. These deities of light were clutching tantalizing products in filamented fingers, while down below, far below, a raconteur stood on a small makeshift stage reciting a story to the throng of listeners gathered around her. "Once there was a little boy," she began. "A mere child, his name now lost to us, even though he is well known as the first creator of our beloved city of light." The crowd responded with excitement. The raconteur held her arms aloft, calling for silence before carrying on with her tale. "One day the child climbed up onto the roof of the apartment block where he lived. He was hoping to see if the sun ever closed its eye. This is how he saw it, the sun was a giant eye that looked down upon the city, keeping the streets alive with its fiery gaze. The boy was just six years old. Six years old, ladies and gentlemen! But such vision! He stood there on the roof, waiting, as his parents worried and searched for him. The child settled down to eat his bread, to drink his water. Many hours went by until a cloud passed over the sun. And he wept bitterly at seeing this. Oh, how the poor boy, our founder, wept. And he promised himself: one day soon, darkness will be forever exiled from this city!" The listeners murmured their approval at the story.

Nyquist hurried on. He was more than halfway to being seriously drunk and so it was uncomfortable being in such a crowd. A circle of light seemed to be following him wherever he moved. Looking upwards, squinting his eyes, he located a theatrical spotlight fixed to a second floor balcony. Somebody, a half seen figure, was working the spot, keeping it on Nyquist even as he dodged through the crowd. This was a common pursuit in these parts, but why was he being singled out? He turned onto a side street to escape its attention, only to run into a circle of people gathered around a musician. With a start he realised it was the blind fiddle player he'd seen in Burn Out precinct. The old man was playing the same melody as before, but speeded up now, even more frantic. The notes rang in

Nyquist's skull like a mantra. The listeners pressed in on him from all sides. There was no way through, and no way back. And then a vision materialised in front of him, two words shimmering, words that meant something. He forced his eyes to focus: *Noonday Underground*. It was a dayclub, with a human face of bright neon flames dancing above the doorway. He managed to make his way to the entrance. The doorman gave Nyquist the once over and then let him through without any trouble. Obviously, a place without taste or care.

It was a cellar dive, the walls damp and the dancers' bodies dripping with sweat. The music was all loud, ragged, broken beats and high-pitched wailing. Electrical fire elements glowed red and yellow from the walls. Gas jets shot upwards from funnels, each singular burn in time with the music's rhythm. Nyquist could only liken it to being trapped, willingly, inside an oven. He felt out of place. The more serious clientele wore smart clothing in the Neo-Modernist style, incorporating swirling patterns and mismatched colours. Others wore very little. These were the young at play in the heat of the day.

The Noonday Underground. He'd seen the name on the postcard in Eleanor's bag. Was this place a frequent haunt of hers?

Nyquist took a seat at the bar and ordered a whisky, and downed it in one. He saw himself in a mirror, a desperate individual, completely alone, no matter how crowded the club was. There was a space around him, an emptiness. His reflection mocked him. The barman refilled his glass without a word. This time he savoured it. He turned to watch the dancers making their moves. Half naked bodies pulsed and whirled, emitting dots and flecks of iridescent colour as the lightshow bathed them in ever-changing patterns. And through all this chaos and noise Nyquist spotted a clock on the wall. But he couldn't tell the time by it: the hands blurred on the dial. It must be the sweat in his eyes. He stood up, setting off across the dance floor. The dancers melted around him, pure movement, colour, body heat. The clock moved closer, away, closer. It was ten minutes to twelve. No. A quarter past two. It was no good: time flowed away from him like water seeping through the closed fingers of a dying man in the desert.

Nyquist finished his second drink in one gulp. Moving further into the club, he passed from this room to another. Quieter music played here. People were sitting or lying around in cushioned alcoves. He was drawn to the sight of two teenage girls sharing something between them. It sparkled in a see-through container. One of the girls passed the object under the nose of the other, who swooned in response, her eyes closing in pleasure. Nyquist wandered over. "What's happening here?" he asked.

The other girl answered him lazily. "Zero, old man. The big nothing."

"I'm looking at your friend there."

This second girl was by now lost to the world. Her face had already taken on an orange tint around the lips. Her friend smiled. "Oh yeah. Daisy's zoomed ahead."

Nyquist picked up a small object from the cushion. It was a glass vial, the same size and shape as he had found in Eleanor's possessions. He was curious.

"What's your name?" he asked.

"Sadie."

"You take this stuff, too?"

A look came in her eyes, a yearning. "I've tried it a few times, but nothing happened. And yet I waited and waited and waited." Her mouth was set in a pained line, her teeth barely showing, as she pondered on her loss. "But all I saw was darkness. No knowledge, no looking ahead. No zoom, old man. No bloody zoom! Not for sad little Sadie." Her hands clutched at the cushions she was perched upon.

"It's like that for some people, see, they just don't get the privilege."

"What does it do, when it works? Has Daisy told you?"

"Oh, she tells me all the time." Bitterness crossed Sadie's face. "It lets you see what lies between every single second." Her eyes longed for distant places. "You can see things there, hidden away. Can you imagine?"

"I don't think I can."

Her voice dropped to a fearful whisper. "You know, some people inject it direct to a vein."

Nyquist moved closer. "Sadie, do you know a girl called Eleanor. Eleanor Bale?"

She nodded. "I do. But she hasn't been around for a while."

"She takes this stuff as well?"

"Sure, a little." Her eyes wandered.

Nyquist leaned closer. "I need to try some."

"You want some kiaro?"

"That's what you call it?"

"Mostly kia. Sometimes kiaro. It's short for chiaroscuro. The play of light and shade in a painting." She was proud of the knowledge.

"Sure," Nyquist replied. "Rembrandt and all that. I've seen the pictures in my dentist's waiting room."

The music suddenly increased in intensity and the dancers moved in step.

"Sadie, do you have some kia to sell me?"

"Ah. No. No, no. Not me. No way! No. What is this? No. Not me. No."

"Look. I'm not a cop. Look at me."

The girl looked him over. "What are you then?"

"I'm a wreck. Natural born."

"I don't know. I mean... I'm not sure."

Nyquist opened his wallet and handed over a couple of notes to the girl. There was no hesitation. Sadie took the money.

"Just your dealer's name," he asked. "And maybe where I can find him or her. That's all."

"Right over there."

"What?"

"There he is. That's him."

She was pointing over to a young man standing beneath an archway. He looked to be late twenties. Slick and dark, halfway handsome, bejewelled, bone thin, dark hair greased back from a low brow. He was dressed in an electric pink suit which shimmered under the lights as he walked under the arch into another part of the club.

"What's his name?"

"Sumak."

"Sumak? I've got it."

"He's one of the few. This stuff is rare, you follow me? Special delivery."

"Thank you, Sadie."

Nyquist followed the young man down a short flight of steps into a third room at an even lower level. A vast fiery globe was suspended in the space, an artificial sun glowing orange at the centre and flickering with gold flames all around. Here, the people swayed back and forth to music that was more nebulous, a mirage of sound. Nyquist felt his old skills taking over, the alcohol lying low in his veins. Sumak was standing near a doorway, watching the girls on the dance floor. Nyquist approached him, leaning in close to whisper some words. Sumak gave him the one-two, grinned, nodded, and then gestured towards the doorway.

"My private office," he said. "Come through."

The room beyond was a kind of bower. Nyquist felt clean air on his face and he looked up to see that the space was entirely open to the lamps of the neon sky far above. The bower held a number of wooden tables, each surrounded by exotic plants and tropical leaves. Two men were drinking and chatting at one table and Sumak nodded to them, saying, "Gentlemen, a new customer". The two men smiled politely and turned back to their conversation. Sumak lit a cigarette. "So then? What's your desire?"

Nyquist studied the dealer before answering. Away from the fierce lights of the club, he was much less of a character. There was an odd feeling about him, a slightly mannered attitude; maybe he hadn't been in this business for too long.

"Kia."

Sumak nodded. He took out a leather pouch, which he opened to reveal a half dozen or so of the orange vials. He handed one of them to Nyquist, saying, "Be careful, my friend. The good Lady Kia does not welcome everyone."

"What do you mean?"

The dealer smiled. "Lady Kia rules over a realm of fog and sorrow. She will elaborate your vision, and pull your eyes open to more freely see the shaded road ahead."

"And what then?"

"Time itself is revealed to you, the very essence thereof. Past, present, and future: all rolled into one."

"That's some sales pitch."

"Alas, our petty minds cannot take such knowledge in abundance. And so we receive glimpses only. What follows, of course, is entirely up to the user."

"So you've taken it yourself?"

Sumak shrugged. "I have. But only the once."

"Once only? What happened? Didn't it work for you?"

"Oh it worked. It worked too damn well." The dealer shook his head, side to side. "I learned enough."

Nyquist leaned in, saying, "I'm interested."

"How many?"

"First of all, have you seen this girl?"

He was holding out the photograph of Eleanor. Sumak looked at it, licked his lips.

"You know her?"

"I've seen her around. The Bale kid. She's famous on the scene. And rich as all hell."

"She buys from you?"

"Once or twice, but to be honest…"

"Go on."

"That girl doesn't need any nasties. She's the thing itself."

"How do you mean?"

"Time, man. Time! She's got it at her fingertips." He laughed. His eyes flickered with lust. "Man, that chick can slow your clock right down. Just with a kiss, a glance. A single touch."

The remark pushed Nyquist over the edge. He moved fast and sure, grabbing Sumak by the bunched lapels of his tailored jacket. He pushed him backwards into a bunch of potted plants, and then went on further, harder, until he had the young man up tight against the inner wall of the bower. The two men at the table jumped to their feet. One of them shouted out, "Leave him alone." There was fear in the voice. Nyquist ignored it. He put the squeeze on Sumak, demanding, "What do you know about her? Come on!"

"Like I said–"

"What?"

"She's the real thing."

The other two men hurried from the bower. Nyquist knew he was still uptight from the beating in the cemetery. His edge was blistered. Anger was taking over. It felt good. But seriously twisted. A ticking sound came and went inside his head. He laughed as he let up the pressure on Sumak a little, allowing the dealer to catch a few breaths.

"Tell me more. Why should anyone want to harm her?"

"How would I know?"

Nyquist tightened his grip.

"Hey! Come on, man. I'm just the dealer."

"You're lying."

"Right, right. Believe what you want. But that girl…"

"What about her?"

Sumak's eyes darkened. "She's from the dusk. That's where she was born."

Nyquist stepped back in surprise. The words seeped into him.

His clock was being wound up, tighter, tighter…

Sumak struggled free. He danced and howled. "Oh man! You've creased my suit!"

Time was passing. Nyquist could hear it now, like a lover's breath in his ear. *Tick, tick, tick, tick, tick.* His mind buzzed. The noise, the heat, the dazzle of lamplight. There were too many seconds, minutes and hours in his head, that was the trouble, all of them moving at once along different pathways.

He turned away.

A bouncer was standing in the doorway.

Nyquist pushed past him.

From room to room to room. Time followed along, closing in. The cuckoo called to him. *Once, twice.* Eleanor's face wreathed in shadow. *Three times. Cuckoo!* The knife in her hand, thrusting forward, again and again, the blood flowing freely. *Four, five times. Cuckoo, cuckoo!* He stumbled onto the dance floor. The giant golden orange sun above his head radiated fire. Slow flashes of red and gold were turning, turning in rhythm, as the dancers moved away from his flight, his sudden fall. A teenager screamed at him, but Nyquist heard only the rush of his own blood and the dull pounding of music like a stunted heartbeat. He tried to get up but somebody's boot came down on his chest, pinning him to the floor. The electric sun was in his eyes, making a liquid haze of sweat through which he saw some other men standing nearby, maybe three or four of them, a regular gang, one with the booted foot in place, the others taking up their chosen positions, and Sumak doing a rock and roll stroll over to the spot of bother. "Tut, tut. Really." He leaned in close, his breath tinted with cigarette smoke and lavender.

Nyquist rocked his head from side to side. The boot had by now moved down to his stomach, and then lower still, and was pressing down heavily there, making him stutter some words, he could hardly tell what, just babble. It made Sumak smile. He removed himself from Nyquist's immediate vision. And then laughed out loud. "Oh dear. I do believe he's saying sorry to me. Do you hear that, boys?"

Laughter all round. "It's a disgrace," one partner said.

"Truly," answered another.

Sumak came down a second time, even closer. "You must never apologise, my friend. It's a sign of weakness."

Nyquist closed his eyes. He lay there expecting some kind of blow, a slicing away of flesh, but neither came. The music screamed louder, the floor beneath him pumping his veins full of noise, and when he finally got his eyes open all he could see were the dancers around him, a circle of staring faces, and the artificial sun above, pulsating with light.

His mind buzzed in painful sympathy.

The orange of the globe was splashed with blood-red streaks. And then the club itself appeared to bleed with fierce heat, the music singing at fever pitch, pure light, pure vibration of sound. His vision smeared, the monstrous ticking sound filled his head. There was no escaping it. He felt himself being lifted up, to his feet, by one of the club's bouncers. He was led away with no struggle on his part, no protest. His thoughts were taken over by the fact that, no matter how hot the daylight, and no matter how bright the ten billion lamps of the city, all the time he would keep returning to that strange fog-wrapped vision witnessed on the edge of twilight, the death of Kinkaid.

He covered his ears with his hands, pressing his palms hard against his skin. It was no use. He could still hear a clock, a single timepiece now. *Tick, tick, tick, tick, tick.* The sound of it rose up from the regular beat of the club's music, louder, faster, more insistent, and even when Nyquist hit the pavement outside and the rogue spotlight picked him out once again in its cruel and radiant circle, still he could hear the death clock ticking.

PREPARATIONS FOR TRAVEL

He managed to get back to the office in more or less one piece, travelling on instinct through the static and blur of the crowded streets. Back to base. He asked Queeps if anyone had come calling for him. No one had. That was good. But he couldn't imagine the shadow men showing themselves in such a public place as the city centre.

Another session at another mirror, patching himself up. Coffee, soap, sugar and painkillers. Getting his things together. Nyquist took the *wayang kulit* puppet from his desk drawer, wrapping it carefully in the yellow dusting cloth, and then placed it inside Eleanor's bag. He found her other belongings. The teenager's face stared at him from the photograph, seemingly innocent. There was so much he hadn't noticed, and so much he still didn't know.

He sat down for a moment, tempted by the whisky bottle, but denied himself the pleasure. The piece of paper was still inserted in the typewriter: one simple question still unanswered, still tormenting him. He took his handkerchief from his pocket: it was sopping wet, so he opened a desk drawer and took another from the pile of six neatly folded inside. Another present from his wife: each square of linen, blue and white in colour, was decorated at the corner with an embroidered eye design. "For my big brave private eye," she had said with a knowing smile. In truth, she knew how easily he broke out into a sweat, often during important meetings. Nyquist dwelled on the memory for a moment, a pleasant thought amid the chaos. He took a second handkerchief from the pile. Next he bent down to the bottom drawer of his filing cabinet and pulled out a locked metal box. Inside was a small hand gun. He'd fired it only once in anger, managing to take a bite out of his ceiling fan, yet now he felt it might offer protection. He took a handful of bullets, loaded the chamber, and then strapped a holster around his chest and placed the gun in it. His jacket hid the weapon completely. He changed his wristwatch to correspond to the time shown on the wall clock. This was done without thinking, without knowing the reason why. Ten to nine. Last of all he picked up the postcard sent to Eleanor from abroad. He turned it over, reading the address: *Eleanor Bale, 5 Beckett Drive, Darkness Falls, Precinct Forty-One, Nocturna.* All was set. He thought about what he was planning. His part in the case was over, but since being attacked by the shadow men he had felt only a piercing rage: they wanted Eleanor as their own, for whatever vile purpose. His job was to stop them. It was that simple.

The name of the serial killer buzzed in his head, the great unseen murderer. The attack that came from nowhere, and faded back into nowhere, leaving only the mark, the wounds, blood and death. The killer's name was spoken often by so many people, living in fear. When would the next attack happen?

Quicksilver awaits you.

Those words whispered in his ear. Lord Apollo! Was he a victim, marked out, waiting to be killed? Nyquist couldn't be sure of anything. Too much alcohol, too much fear, too many regrets, wasted chances, too many timelines crossed and recrossed, the proximity of twilight, the fog, too many bad memories of his own: his father walking away, his mother's death when he was only seven years old. But he couldn't take the chance of being wrong. He would have to go and see the girl, make sure she was all right. He would do what he could to help her, to protect her if need be. And that meant travelling back into Nocturna.

But first there was one other place he had to visit, if he could stand it, and one other person he had to find.

THE METEOROLOGIST

Nyquist walked away from the parked car. He had brought along a more powerful torch this time, and he had no intention of getting too close to the fogline, but still, icy fingers started up his spine as the first swirls of dusk appeared in the air. The evening sky was painted in many different shades of grey except for where the yellow moon floated half seen in the distance. There was much speculation about this moon, one of many that occupied different areas of Dusk. It was common knowledge that this particular orb was the giant neon logo atop the old Luna Insurance office tower, a building long since given up to the dusk. But who or what was it that kept the moon aglow all these years? It was just one more mystery of the twilight.

Nyquist stopped. He had reached the Fade Away weather station with its weird-looking instruments and measuring devices. Close up, he found the instruments to be even stranger than he remembered; the spindly elongated structures looked more like abstract sculptures, or primitive totems. His torch beam flickered across the various decorations that had been added to the poles and collecting dishes: mirror shards, lenses taken from cameras and sunglasses, polished shapes cut from aluminium foil, fragments of coloured glass. Fine sparkling chains hung from steel rods, each one strung with silver cogs and springs taken from the movements of clocks and pocket watches. Numerous cobwebs were strung between the struts, each dotted with dew, and each containing its own guardian, a bulbous orange-bellied spider unlike any other that Nyquist had ever seen. The whole station glittered with light in ever-transforming patterns, a magical effect; and yet, when the torch beam moved away, all of this splendour was lost to the gloom.

Nyquist cast his attention to the darkened street in the near distance, the row of houses where he had found Eleanor and the man she claimed was her father. The mist clung to the buildings. The whole scene seemed to be melting away, into memory, into the past. And then some further movement caught his attention. A crow had landed on one of the twisted metal struts of the weather station. One crow, and then another. Three more. Half a dozen. He lost count. They stabbed at the orange spiders with their beaks, gobbling them down with glee. Nyquist didn't know how many crows it took to make a murder, but this seemed sufficient. And still they came, one by one landing on the instruments. Their croaks and wing rustles made an eerie sound. The birds' eyes flashed brightly as the torch beam passed over them. Nyquist shuddered. A louder noise attracted him, and he turned to catch a glimpse of a figure in white moving in the shadows some few yards away.

"Hey! Who's there?"

The crows answered him, screeching maniacally for a moment before settling back into their usual sound. The rusty scientific instruments creaked in harmony. Nyquist walked over to where the pale form had moved through the half-darkness. He had seen just such a figure on the night of Kinkaid's death, and was hoping that the person was still around. This was why Nyquist had come back here. He moved ahead cautiously, until a small wooden hut emerged from the gloom; closer still, and he could see and hear an open door knocking gently against its frame. He looked inside the hut, seeing a few personal odds and ends, nothing of interest. He stepped back out and turned, and again he saw the figure. Nyquist flashed his torch, catching a glimpse of a body clothed in white, a hood, and a stark face. The apparition retreated, falling backwards over a pile of old gardening utensils. Nyquist moved quickly now, reaching out to try and catch hold of a sleeve. But the person turned and showed his hand, the knife in the grip. A broad blade, dirty and nasty looking.

"OK, OK," Nyquist whispered. "I'm not–"

"Keep off me!" It was a man's voice.

Nyquist thought for a moment if this person was connected in some way to Kinkaid's murder, but then he noticed that the knife was in fact a rusty old garden trowel. It was comical. He lurched forward, knocking the thrust-out implement to the side and then moved in fast, wrestling the man to the ground.

"No, no! It wasn't me. It wasn't me. It wasn't!"

The stranger was babbling. Nyquist got him to hold still as he shone the torch on target, revealing a startled face.

"It wasn't me!"

Nyquist gritted his teeth. "Keep quiet. I'm not hurting you."

The man calmed down a little, more from the exhaustion of fear than anything else.

"Get up."

The stranger did so. Nyquist took a good look at him.

He was a middle-aged man, dressed from head to foot in ragged white overalls, with a woollen hood of the same colour hanging down his back. His clothing made it seem that he properly belonged to the silver-misted landscape of the duskline. An unruly mop of greying hair fell over his brow, the strands stained at the tips in nicotine yellow. Only the man's face was fully visible, and this was almost as white as his clothes, covered in some kind of make-up, and set with a pair of eyes that had a washed-out, albino cast to them.

"What were you doing?" Nyquist asked. "Spying on me?"

"No! No, I was…"

"What?"

"I was scared!"

Nyquist realised the man was a scavenger of the outskirts, that was all. "What's your name?"

"George Frederick Carlisle. At your service, sir."

Nyquist shone the torch onto the ground, until the trowel was caught in the beam. He bent down to pick it up.

Carlisle wailed. "No, no! Don't kill me!"

"You were going to use this?"

"No, sir. Only for protection."

Nyquist threw the makeshift weapon away. He asked, "Do you live round here?"

"Yes. In the hut there. I keep charge of the instruments." He pointed to the weather station where the crows were still sitting, their wings gently rising and falling as though in preparation for takeoff.

"Show me," Nyquist said.

Carlisle responded with glee. "This way, sir. Right this way. Follow me." He moved quickly, obviously well accustomed to the rough ground and the dismal air. The crows seemed glad of his company, some of them raising their wings in full salute, others hopping to new perches, their beaks clacking against the steel supports. "For years now I've been on duty." He moved from instrument to instrument, checking the panels. "Every day. Day to day.

Day in, day out. Daily. Taking the measurements."

Nyquist couldn't see how any of the instruments could still be working. "Why are you doing this?"

Carlisle raised a hand. "It's getting closer."

"What is?"

"This is what I've found, by the measurements. It's getting nearer, every day."

"You mean the dusk?"

"Yes, sir." Carlisle ducked under a swinging steel beam. "Moment by moment, and shade by shade. The dusk is creeping forward. Towards us. Towards the light of day. Do you understand me? Do you? It's a consequence of the city, and all this experimenting with time. It's not natural, is it? And this is why people gather here, you see, at the edges. With their magic spells, and the witchcraft. And the ritual killings of chickens and rats. It's to keep the dead at bay, sir."

"What are you saying?"

The meteorologist stared at Nyquist. "The dusk has jaws made of mist, it has needs. It must be fed. Or else it will creep upon us entirely." He chanted a phrase: "The dead need the living. They do. They need the living. They feed on breath and blood and the vital energies." His pink eyes danced in their sockets. "It keeps them alive!"

Nyquist shook his head. He walked past the weather station and then hesitated. The old fear trembled at the back of his neck like a crouched spider. "Did you know the man?" he asked. "The one who died in the house over there?"

"What's it to you?"

"Just tell me the truth, did you know him?"

Carlisle started babbling once again. "It wasn't me! It wasn't me that killed him. No. Not me."

"You're talking about Kinkaid?"

"I didn't know his name. The poor sufferer." Carlisle

pointed to billows of fog just over the borderline. "He came from the dusk. But the dusk pulled him back."

Nyquist tried to keep things clear. He was getting caught up in the tangles of Carlisle's wounded psyche. "But you talked to Kinkaid?"

"A little. Yes. Of course. A tiny little."

"What was he doing there, in the house?"

Instead of answering, Carlisle busied himself with the instruments. His gloved fingers set the decorations jangling. The crows hopped from strut to strut, calling to their master, or their servant, whichever it was. Colours twinkled in the torchlight. Nyquist was dazzled by the shivering movements. He blinked a few times and then focused his mind afresh, asking once again, "What was Kinkaid doing here?"

Carlisle's face tightened. "Waiting, sir."

"Waiting?"

"Yes, sir."

"For what?"

"Ah well. We spoke only once or twice, sir. And even then, not properly."

"Still, you must know something."

Carlisle opened and closed his eyes rapidly. "He was a magician, a conjurer. He travelled into the dusk, over the line."

"He walked there?"

"That he did. To mingle with the spirits of twilight. Crazy! I told him. No good would come of such ventures."

Nyquist could see that the man was getting more and more overtaken by his own obsessions. He asked, "Did you see him talk to anyone else?"

"The girl. She came a few times."

"More than once?"

"A beauty. I watched her. I watched her carefully, hidden away."

Nyquist thought about this: so Eleanor had visited Kinkaid before.

Carlisle clapped his hands. "Be careful, sir. The idolaters will get you. Verily, they will stake you out, and bind thy person hand and foot."

"Really? You believe this?"

"They will leave you here, to appease the spirits of the dusk. The hungry ghosts. They will eat you!"

"Ghosts?"

"Yes sir. Oh, the noises I have heard. The words, without mouths to speak them. The whisperings. The screaming. And the shapes that move in the fog. Oh, I have been a witness, truly!" Carlisle made a series of elaborate gestures towards the fogline. The crows responded with their own cries and rustlings.

Nyquist moved closer. "Carlisle! Tell me what you've seen."

"Hush now! The hour is almost upon us."

A sudden and unexpected silence gathered. All the birds clung to their perches, their beaks quiet at last, their wings carefully folded.

Nyquist was worried. He could feel a tension in the air. "What is it?" He spoke in a hush. "What's happening?"

"Only the birds can tell the true time." Carlisle too was whispering. "Only they know when the night truly begins, when it is time to move on, towards the sleeping grounds. Wait now! Wait…"

Nyquist held his breath; the landscape all around did the same.

Silence, stillness.

And then, as one and entirely without warning, the entire flock of crows took off from the weather station. They made a dreadful noise, a mass beating of wings, and a raucous cawing sound. And other similar clouds of ragged black birds rose up from other parts of Fade Away, all of them conjoining in the murky air. Carlisle was going crazy at this, flapping his arms in imitation of wings, and making his own discordant calls. "Caw! Caw! Caw!" And with that he ran off into the surrounding gloom, his tatty white clothes giving him the look of a runaway spirit. Nyquist let him go. His whole attention was fixed upon the crows as they flew away into the misted lands of Dusk. The yellow face of the moon was speckled by them, wave after wave.

WAITING ON SUNSET

The nearest train station was a small tumbledown affair some way off either of the main lines. Nyquist found an empty space in the long-stay car park. He bought a ticket from a machine on the concourse and then walked out onto the platform, taking a spot some distance from the few other people waiting there. This side of the station, where the tracks led into the mist towards Nocturna, was called Sunset. The platform clock showed the time to be ten minutes to four. Nyquist adjusted his wristwatch to match. The train would be here soon. He could feel the uneasiness starting already, bringing up the memory of his last journey across the dusklands, from Night to Day, at the start of this case. He had almost lost control on the way over, and his fellow passengers had moved away from him in disgust, or in fear. They must have thought he was crazy. And now he would have to do the same thing again. And he felt worse this time, far worse.

He kept glancing at the platform clock. One moment the hands seemed to be stuck on the dial; then they jumped forward, or else moved backwards a minute or so. Nyquist felt that he was losing little pockets of time. He could only hope he wasn't becoming seriously time sick. He turned away deliberately, setting his eyes on the opposite platform whose sign read "Sunrise". He looked down the track in that direction towards the city, towards the light. How comforting it looked, how he longed to go back that way. It was not to be.

Just then a couple of people came close to where he was standing, to buy items from a vending machine. He went over to have a look. The machine was selling Cronopax tablets, specially designed "to ease your travels along the timelines". Nyquist usually avoided such artificial preparations, preferring alcohol and brute will; trouble was, he had none of the former on his person, and as for his will power, well that was at an all-time low. He saw that the train was pulling in, so he placed the required number of coins in the slot, pressing the lever. Nothing happened. Nyquist couldn't believe how angry he felt. He had really set his mind on getting this comfort inside his body before the journey started. This solace, this blissful relief, whatever the hell they called it on the advertisements. He jabbed at the lever again and again, he banged a fist against the side of the machine. Nothing. And yet he was certain it had worked fine for the other people. The tablets glistened within the little display window, so enticing in their foil wraps.

The steam train had stopped, the doors were opening. Smoke from the funnel settled around the engine.

Nyquist hit the vending machine a few more times. "Come on!" Glancing round he could see people entering the carriages. "Open up!" It was no good, the machine wasn't working. He would have to look after himself.

He ran over to the nearest train door and climbed on board.

CROSSING THE LINE

It must've been rush hour on one of the city's more more popular timelines because the train was crowded, end to end. It was one of the cheaply built, post-war models, with seats down the sides and standing room in the middle. Nyquist made his way to the emptiest carriage, the one closest to the engine, where he managed to find a vacant seat. He pressed his shoulders and back against the hard cushioning. Eleanor's green tartan duffle bag was nestled between his legs, the strap wound loosely around one of his hands. The train rocked along with an unsteady movement. The overhead lights spluttered fitfully, and most of the fixtures and fittings were in need of repair.

He turned to gaze through the window. They had not yet reached the borderline, and he could see the blasted remains of factories and warehouses. The whole area was lit by arc lamps which gave off an ultraviolet glow. Another much smaller train chugged slowly past, moving in the opposite direction, away from Dusk. It was a maintenance wagon, piled high with tools, old track and replacement sleepers. Rough-looking, dirt-covered men and women hung onto the wagon as it powered towards a train shed. They were caged in, held behind wires. The job of linesman was seen as just about the worst thing that could happen to a person. Prisoners used to do the work, until a major protest at the creation of modern day chain gangs brought the practice to an end. Nowadays the job was taken up by ex-criminals, failed soldiers, burnt-out cops, terminal drunks and addicts and other such outcasts. Nyquist had read a magazine article once, which included photographs of one team in action; the wagon had stopped somewhere in the middle of the dusklands, spotlights penetrating the fogbanks a little way as the workers mended the track, while armed guards kept their rifles trained at all times on the dismal mist-filled fields to either side of the railway line. It was a dangerous job. The next three pages showed close-up portraits of the workers. Their faces were prematurely creased, scarred, and their bones pressed tightly against their skin. But the eyes were the worst; you could not look upon such haunted stares without wondering about the things they must have seen and experienced in the mist, in the half-light. A low-hanging moon so cold as to freeze the blood, and then some nebulous shape moving through the fog...

Nyquist had torn the magazine into shreds.

The train moved on. He was tired suddenly, the pains and turmoils catching up with him. He let his head bow down and his eyes close. With luck, he might be able to sleep out the entire journey. He had managed it before. But a noise disturbed him, as more passengers entered the carriage, seeking empty seats, amongst them a number of children who were overly excited at the prospect of travelling through Dusk. Their cries and shrieks of fearful delight made it impossible for Nyquist to find rest. People were standing in the aisle, strap-hanging. He felt a quickening anger at being trapped here in the carriage. All he wanted was to get this over with and to arrive in Nocturna without any trouble, or as little as possible. Most of all he could sense the fear building, and he looked around anxiously.

Didn't any of these passengers feel as he did? He studied the faces of those closest to him; their gazes were bleary-eyed from lack of sleep or red raw from clocklag, or else jammed wide open courtesy of one or other of the branded wake-up tablets. Nyquist turned away from each person just as the carriage lights blinked on and off. Moments later the whistle of the engine made its mournful call as the train passed over the boundary. It was a sound that Nyquist sometimes heard in his sleep, the crossing whistle. They were now in the dusklands. A hush fell over the carriage. Nyquist was glad about this, to know he wasn't the only one living in fear. But the silence lasted for a few seconds only, and then people starting chatting again, quietly at first, and then louder as the journey progressed.

The carriage windows were now misted over. Nyquist imagined the train's progress through the semi-darkness, the long caress of day turning into night. He could picture the clouds drifting away from the face of the nearest moon, the pale light falling on the gloom-laden landscape beneath, where the train moved through the grey air, through the shadows. To a creature out there, a wild dog or a rat, the carriage windows would be bright yellow squares, each one blurring as it passed. The passengers would seem like lost souls on their way to hell: adults, children, workers, strangers, wanderers, loners, saints and sinners, himself.

Nyquist forced his eyelids shut. It was all he could do.

Darkness, specks of colour, vibrations.

Now the voices made their plea. The passengers were talking; they were speaking of night-time things, of the darkness and what the darkness promised; they were sighing and breathing and whispering. A young couple could be heard, murmuring their dear sweet little endearments to each other. The group of children were giggling amongst themselves. How could they chatter so? This creaking metal box on its flimsy wheels could so easily fall apart, crash and crumble, the skin cracking open. Nyquist had heard stories of trains breaking down halfway across, and the problems that followed. People disappearing, almost certainly being killed, their bodies never found. And dreadful reasons and rumours were given for the stoppages: the mist clinging to the carriages, dragging the train to a standstill, the embrace of twilight.

Nyquist could feel sweat prickling his skin. He could hear the noise of the wheels as they hit the joints and the gaps between. The trapped air was sticky against his face, it was too warm, he could hardly breathe. His eyes opened and immediately darted across the gaudy images and slogans of the advertisements above the seats opposite, each with its own unique offer of time and how to spend it: *Free time, work time, playtime, finding time, losing time, a loving time, endless time, easy time, overtime, borrowed time, accelerated time, out of time, slow time, a time for oneself, a time for others, a few brief moments of pleasure can be yours today! Send off now for Instant Gratification! Time waits for no one! Seize the day!* One poster praised the latest kind of chronometer: "More than one hundred different timescales preloaded for easy lifestyle choice". Nyquist started to read the advert a second time, to keep himself distracted, when he realised he was being stared at by a young boy sitting across the aisle. He was about six years old, his eyes carrying a sullen expression as they peered at Nyquist. A woman, presumably the boy's mother, was sitting next to him, her face entirely hidden by the pages of the *Beacon Fire*. The headline on the front page read, *Police No Nearer to Catching Quicksilver*. Nyquist returned the boy's stare but found that after only a few seconds he had to turn away. On this side of the carriage, in the seat to the right of him, a man in a business suit sat in silence. Every so often he would take a sip or two from a hip flask. Nyquist's lips went dry at the sight. On his other side a young woman was humming a melody to herself. Her sleeves were rolled up above the elbow, and around each arm a series of watches had been fixed, each slightly higher than the last, the straps at different lengths to allow passage over the thin muscles. There must have been five or six watches on each arm, and no doubt each one was set to a different scale. Seeing this, Nyquist found himself settling into a rhythm of his own, that of the train mixed with his own body clock, tick tick ticking away. And once again his head lowered and his eyes closed.

The train moved slowly on, its rhythm more lulling now. Nyquist was neither asleep nor awake, but in some place halfway between. His mind flitted here and there across an array of memories, some good, and many not so good; his thoughts were a series of tiny lamps, each one being lit in turn, lit and then extinguished until he felt his mind settling upon one particular memory, entirely unbidden. It was an incident he hadn't thought of in such a long while. His mother's death.

Fragments, splinters of light, a young boy cowering in fear on the pavement.

Seven years old, by the family's chosen timescale.

Helpless.

His mother's stricken face as she went into a sudden spasm.

He could not move, yet neither could he take his eyes away from the sight.

Her body convulsing, those last gasps for strangled breath.

Somebody rushing up to help her.

Too late, far too late…

The train moved over a cracked rail and he woke up. The lights flickered. How long had he been asleep? He couldn't tell. He looked at his watch but the numbers meant nothing to him. It was an alien language. Perhaps by now they had left the dusklands behind; but no, when he lifted his head to look out through the windows, he saw the silvered mist lingering there. The train seemed to be moving even more slowly than before. He pressed at his eyes with the fingers and thumb of one hand. As he did so, the man in the business suit moved in closer, leaning against him from the side. Nyquist shifted his body away, as far as it could in the tight space.

"Look at that for a sight," the neighbour said.

"What do you want?"

"It's pathetic, isn't it? Don't you think?" He was nodding over to the young woman with the ten or so watches strapped around her wrists and arms. "All the energy these people waste, trying to keep track of things. You don't mind me talking?"

"I just want to rest, that's all."

"I know the feeling. It's been a hell of a day, I can tell you. A day and a half of hell."

Nyquist didn't respond.

"Are you tired? You look tired. I'm just asking. Because you see, what you really need is one of these." The businessman rolled up his sleeve to show off his watch, a monster of a timepiece even more elaborate than the one advertised on the poster opposite. "You see this? Bold, alluring, and dare I say it, more than a little avant-garde! Quartz crystal with sapphire movement. One hundred and fifty official timescales. Another fifty completely user-definable. Any which way you want it. Fully programmable. Look here. Click, click, click!" The man was pressing buttons on his chronometer. Nyquist could see the hands on the dial changing positions. The man kept on pressing and the hands speeded up, becoming a blur of movement. "Click, click! You need never be late again." Nyquist's hand shot out to grasp the man's wrist, covering up the watch face. "Hey! That... that hurts. Let go of me! Let go." The grip tightened. Nyquist could feel the watch digging into his palm, bringing a pain of its own, but no matter: this would happen, he would break this thing, he would tear it clear off the stupid man's fragile wrist, he would break the hand itself, if need be.

The victim cried out in pain.

Other passengers were looking over. The young boy was shrieking with laughter. His mother tried to make him turn away.

Fear had spread all over the businessman's face. "Please. Let me go. Please!"

Nyquist was blanked out to all other feelings but for the power in his hand, the fingers tightening, twisting. And then somebody tapped him on the shoulder, another passenger, and Nyquist saw clearly what he was doing, how far he had gone. He stood up, releasing the businessman's wrist. He muttered some words of apology and then tried to get away, to find a space of his own. The air was suffocating. He felt faint. It was the gathered heat of the carriage, that was all, the flickering overhead lights, the brightly coloured adverts, the shapes in the fog at the windows, the constant rattle and groan of the train, the closeness of other people's flesh. That was all! A woman's gaze met his own and then jerked away as though ashamed of what she saw in Nyquist's face.

This was crazy. He had to stay calm. His hand reached up to grab a vacant strap. The train moved on its way down the track and his body swayed with the rhythm.

Nyquist closed his eyes once more. And now the varied sounds of the carriage melted away, until only one remained. *Tick tick tick tick.* It was the sound of his own wristwatch, and the watch of the man standing next to him, also ticking. The sounds rose up. *Tick tick tick tick tick tick tick tick.* And now other tiny mechanisms were joining in, until every wristwatch in that long carriage could be heard clearly. Together, they made the sound of a giant clock, a funeral clock. Tolling, tolling. But not for himself, not for Nyquist. But for Eleanor. Death had marked her out. And he was suddenly back in that terrible room, in that house in Angelcroft Lane. Kinkaid died again.

The murderer a shape in the fog...

Nyquist forced his eyes open. The ticking sound remained, even though nobody else seemed to notice it; louder now, more insistent, a tinny beat, blurring the air, glittering, the sound of it. It worked upon his senses like a swarm of hyperactive insects. All the people nearby were staring at him like he was some kind of animal; not clean, not bathed and not sweetly smelling, not smart, not suitably dressed for the night to come. None of those things. Not on time. No. He would be late, too late, always late. Or else too early, far too early. No time. None at all! The young woman to his left moved away from him, as far as she could manage in the crowded space. Voices were raised, hands pushing at him. The clock, the clock: turning, ticking, the hands, turning, the chimes, turning, whirring, measuring, alerting, reminding, alarming. He found himself alone near a window. People had squeezed even more tightly together, to make this space for him. The children were staring, a little scared, thrilled even. The madman, the crazy man. Oh, look at him. Look!

Tick tick tick tick tick tick tick tick tick...

Nyquist put his hands to his ears. He pressed hard. It was no good. The sound could still be heard. The sweat dripped from his face, his hair; his hands were wet. He would have to make a noise, that was it, any noise, anything louder than the ticking sound, nothing else would make it go away. He would have to scream out loud. Which he did, but the terrible screeching came not only from his mouth but from the train itself. The two sounds joined together. The carriage rocked a little more than usual, and then a little less. The screeching noise continued. People had shifted their attention away from Nyquist. They were worried, their voices rising up in dread.

"What is it? What's happening?"

"We're slowing down."

"No!"

"I can feel it. Can't you feel it?"

"No. This can't happen. It can't!"

Voices bitten by fear. The train was definitely losing speed, the sound of the wheels lowering in pitch, growing quieter, the carriage settling down on the tracks as the train pulled up to a slow, slow standstill.

The lights fluttered.

Not a single movement could be felt.

Nyquist's eyes darted to the window opposite, where the shapes of mist were sticking to the glass. Somebody started to pray out loud. The young boy was looking terrified now, all the moodiness gone out of him. His mother drew him to her. "It's all right, Billy. Don't worry now. Don't worry."

The businessman said, "We've stopped. Why? What is it? Why have we stopped?"

Nyquist told him to be quiet.

"What—"

"Shut up!"

The whole carriage obeyed him. A tomblike silence followed. Only a teenager dared to speak. "What's going on?" Nobody answered, and then she too fell silent.

Quiet. Deathly quiet.

Nyquist listened.

Even the ticking noise had faded away.

The mist brushing against the glass; the low sound of breathing; that was all.

And then the lights went out completely.

Panic flared. People were crying out, screaming, moving around and banging into each other, fear taking charge of them. Nyquist could feel his heart trying to crawl out of his chest. Now the lights flickered overhead, bright, then faint, then dark, failing to catch. And then clicking on and staying on, but low level, dim, so the carriage was painted in a ghastly yellow glow. All the windows were now covered in the thickness of mist, so that not one inch of glass remained untouched. It seemed that the glass itself was made out of fog.

Nyquist couldn't stop shaking.

A voice came over the loudspeaker system. "This is your guard speaking. We are experiencing a small engineering difficulty. Please. Do not be alarmed." The voice crackled and died.

The businessman stood up. "What the hell is that supposed to mean?" He shouted towards the loudspeaker, as though he might be heard: "What kind of trouble is this? Speak to me! Help me!"

Others joined in. "Help us! Help!"

The young mother looked petrified. She couldn't move. Her son, Billy, slipped away from her grasp. The guard's voice spoke again: "We are endeavouring to resolve the situation."

"There, see," said one passenger, a well-dressed woman in her forties. "They will send for help."

"How will they do that?" asked the businessman. "We're in the middle of Dusk! You know the radio doesn't work out here. The signal gets messed up."

"They have... they have cables. They've laid cables."

"Yeah, and they get destroyed. I read about it."

"Who does that?" asked Billy's mother. "Who destroys them?"

The businessman shook his head. "Nobody knows."

"Lord Apollo protect us!" The mother looked about her, desperate for somebody to offer comfort, anything, but then her gaze fell on a sight that disturbed her even more, and she called out, "Billy! Come here! Come back here."

The boy had squeezed through to the nearest door. He was knocking against the panelling, trying to get it to come open. The door wouldn't budge. His mother cried out to him, "Billy. Don't do that!" She couldn't reach him. There were too many passengers in the way. "Billy!" And then...

Thump. Something landed on the roof of the carriage. Something big, heavy. The lights flickered and died which set the people screaming once more.

"Sweet Helios! What was that?"

The thing, whatever it was, could be heard moving about on the roof, shifting about with a dull, dragging motion. It was scraping at the metal of the carriage. Every single passenger conjured up their own worst imaginings.

And then silence once again.

The mist that pressed itself against the window brought the only light, a silvery tint. It clung to the glass in patterns that seemed to be forming and reforming. Again the high-pitched scraping noises were heard through the ceiling, like sharpened claws on metal. Somebody flicked on a hand torch. The beam skidded about, finding a man's face, a stark white expression of fear.

It was Nyquist, caught in the glow.

Somebody dared to whisper: "What is it? What's out there?"

Nobody answered. Nobody. Until...

"The dead."

It was said in a hushed tone. And really, what else could it be?

There was a gasp of shock, and another.

The lights came back on, gloomier than before, a murky red colour. Young Billy had found the emergency door release panel. He lifted up the glass cover, exposing the handle. Nyquist saw this, but was unable to move; he witnessed the sight as a distant event, unconnected to his present life.

The loudspeaker crackled. The guard's voice started a sentence, the first few words chopped off. "Don't try to–" People listened, waiting, cowering in corners, holding onto themselves, each other, their neighbours, strangers, anybody. Again, the scratching sound. And then something slid down one of the windows, a presence in the mist, made of mist, but more viscous, alive almost. It was a darker shade of grey, streaked with thin swirls of orange. It seemed to have a face, a face that might once have been human.

"Oh my god, save me! Save me!"

A single voice. A trigger. Everybody moved at once, trying to get away, bunching together. All except Nyquist. He was standing apart, hypnotised, his eyes moving from the beast, the ghost, the monster, the demon at the window, whatever it was, and, over to the young kid at the door. He could see the boy's hand wrapped around the release lever.

The mother shouted out, "Billy! Don't."

The boy was aware of his own need to escape, nothing more. He yanked at the lever. His face screwed tight, his hands gripped and pulled a second time. The handle dropped down at last. It made a creaking, tearing sound, and expelled air hissed from the mechanism. The door remained closed, the two halves pressed together at the rubber lip.

Something else hit the roof, a second monster. It scuttled and scraped.

The passengers clung even more tightly to each other, crawling as one away from the new fear.

Somebody gasped, trying to speak. "He's got..."

Another person finished the sentence: "He's got a gun!"

Everybody turned to look. It was Nyquist. He was standing there, with the gun pulled swift and clear from the holster, and directed straight and true towards the thing that clung to the glass.

Somebody said to him, "Shoot it! Go on."

Another voice: "No. Don't break the glass."

Another: "You'll let them all in."

Now the gun trembled in his hands. Sweat stung his eyes. The target blurred. He could hear the boy working at the door, and the sounds of the carriage cut into the tender part of Nyquist's brain.

He turned to face the boy, saying in a calm voice, "Don't do that."

Billy carried on. He was pressing against one half of the door, forcing a gap to open, a small gap. He was sobbing. "Let me out... please... let me out!"

The gap opened up a little more. Mist seeped inside.

Nyquist turned the gun towards the child. He spoke again, louder this time. "Kid, don't do it."

Billy could feel that something was wrong. His hands were still pressed against the rubber lip, but without moving. His body quivered.

Everybody was staring at Nyquist in disbelief.

Nyquist felt his body coming alive like a charge of pure hot electricity had travelled through him.

"Don't open the door!"

Billy ignored the call. He pushed again, further, using all of his might. His mother looked terrified. She could hardly speak: "You can't... you can't!" This said to Nyquist, as he glanced back to the window. The thing was still clinging there, moving along as though seeking entrance. The glass appeared to be melting. Nyquist turned back to the boy.

"Step away!"

"No!" the mother wailed. And now she did find her strength, pushing aside all in her way, positioning herself between the boy and the gun. "Leave him alone! He's my... he's my child! You can't do this!"

Nyquist took a step forward. Everybody had moved

out of his way and now only the mother stood between himself and the boy at the door. He spoke again, more quietly now, coldly; it put the shivers in all who could hear.

"Let go of the door. Let go."

The voice was deadly enough to cause an effect. The boy's fingers uncurled from their grip, and the two halves of the door closed upon each other tightly. His mother immediately turned and gathered the child up in her arms. She screamed at Nyquist in wordless rage.

The carriage lamps flickered again. The sound of the train's engine could be heard, straining for movement.

Nyquist's face was a terrible sight to behold. Pain and doubt were twisted in his skin, in his eyes. He seemed to be coming out of a place of shadows, all of his own making. And realising what he'd done or was about to do, he slowly lowered his hands, taking the gun down from its target.

The light sputtered for one last time and the train started to move, jerking into motion. A woman cried out, "We're moving!" It was the voice of somebody brought back to life, and all in the carriage heard it gratefully. The lights returned to full brightness as the train picked up speed, the carriage rocking as before. The thing at the window clung on for a moment longer and was then sucked away by the rushing back draft, lost to the mist. Some people were crying, or even laughing, shot with nerves. Others could not speak, and would not speak, not for a good long while.

Nyquist had not moved from the spot. The gun was still in his hand, but lowered to his side. In a quiet voice he said, "I'm sorry. I'm sorry." Nobody responded to his words. His fellow passengers only stared at him in horror and distaste. His own sight was locked on the window and whatever it was he saw there; his own reflection, the mist and what lay beyond, the dead land itself, the dusk unfolding as the train surged on and on towards the safety of night.

PART TWO
NOCTURNA

GUIDE BOOK:
THE NEW CONSTELLATIONS

THE CITY HAS closed its weary light-drenched eyes and found some rest here, in the southern precincts. In the dark, in the shadows; in the soft black cloudfall of the sky, beneath the gentle sparks and flashes of the stars.

Many citizens use Nocturna simply as their home base, travelling back here once their work or play in Dayzone is finished. Others partake of the darkness in a more symbolic manner. Lullabies sound from bedrooms, old blues songs issue quietly from open windows, and many people speak in whispers, if at all. This desire is easily understood; there are certain human activities both good and bad, joyous and wretched, that demand the cover of night.

First-time visitors often wonder how to find their way around, seeing that the street names and signposts are either cast in shadow or hidden completely by the pitch-black atmosphere. Only a few sources of light are visible. People do carry torches or lanterns, but this scarcely explains how long-term inhabitants so easily find their pathway from A to B to C and back again. The secret can best be explained by first of all offering a contrast with Dayzone, where people often walk along with their heads bowed. In the dark half of the city the opposite effect can be seen, for here people are constantly looking upwards to view the sky. They are in fact navigating by the map of the stars; it is the only sure way of orientating oneself in Nocturna.

Be warned that all normal expectations need to be set aside. It is always bewildering to the tourist that the night sky seems so very different from that seen outside the city, for not a single constellation relates in any way or form to those normally seen in the cosmos. The constellations of Nocturna are manmade. Also, the stars are fixed in their positions, making no progress at all across the sky. Here they rest above the buildings and avenues, ready to guide us. Each square, each street, each precinct has its own unique set of patterns, and local residents will have given names to these shapes.

Some of the more famous and easily spotted of the constellations and other heavenly bodies include: the Tiger's Claw, the Broken Web, the Crashed Motor Vehicle, the Blot of Ink, the Peppered Moth, the Devil's Mask, the Tie and Handkerchief, the Little Beetle, the Giant Beetle, the Swan with Two Necks, the Bride of Morpheus, the Pinpricks, the Wash of Milk, the Mad Hatter, the Last Leaf on the Tree, the Wound in the Night Sky, the Beggar Child, the Ghost of Tears, the Long Lost Dream, the Black Snow, the Wires, the Door in the Lion's Face, the Stolen Kiss, the Hand with Six Fingers, a Melody of Jewels, a Sigh, a Gunshot.

These and other deities of the sky are soon picked out by careful study of the star maps, available from most of the local all-night stores, and from every coach and railway station. Please be aware that various parties offer their own alternative constellations; these should be avoided, at least until visitors feel more at home in the darkness. By these and other means, may you walk safely beneath the heavens.

NOCTURNE IN YELLOW, SILVER AND COBALT BLUE

The train pulled into a station called Cloudtown Hollow. The travellers moved in a daze as they stepped down from the carriage doorways, many of them being helped by station officials. Only Nyquist marched ahead, reaching the ticket barrier first. The concourse was lit by a few dim and shaded bulbs hanging down from the ceiling; between these scattered pools of light the place shaded into grey and then to black. Two police officers were standing beneath one of the lamps. Nyquist would have to pass them to get to the exit. He knew that it wouldn't be long before someone complained about the gun incident, so he couldn't take any risks. And then he saw a lamp vendor wandering across the concourse, his body so entirely covered in torches, lanterns and other light-giving devices that his shape was three times the size it would have been shorn of the goods. He kept one or two of these lamps alight in order to advertise his wares; otherwise he moved in darkness. Nyquist made a gesture, and the lamp vendor came over.

"What will it be?"

"One of those hand torches."

"Good choice, excellent choice. Batteries included."

Nyquist handed the seller some money, more than was needed, and said, "Keep the change."

The seller nodded.

"Now, let's walk together nice and easily, towards the exit over there."

"I was going that way, as it happens."

They set off together, Nyquist keeping himself well hidden behind the seller's bulbous and irregular shape, until they came to the arched doorway. Outside, the darkness was more or less total, broken only by the crisscrossing of the pedestrians' torch beams as they made their way to and from the train station entrance. Nyquist had been in this area of the city a few times before and so he knew his way around. He looked up at the sky, noting the fixed stars of this precinct in their various patterns, and he opened his mouth wide to breathe in the clean sharp air. It always took the body a while to adjust to Nocturna's temperature and climate. He shivered in the cold for a moment, and then followed his beam out along the exit ramp and into the main street.

Half an hour later he was driving along through the dark roads behind the wheel of a hire car. It was a good-looking, midnight blue saloon model, the windows made of tinted glass. Nyquist was tired but he had to keep moving. He had to find the girl. Keep her safe. This was his task. If only he could keep his mind clear of all the chatter, back and forth. The image of the kid on the train wouldn't leave him alone. Why the hell had he taken the gun out like that, in a crowded space? He could've just gone over and pulled the kid's hands loose from the door handle, it would've been easy. All the time he felt himself moving closer and closer to the dial's edge. What would happen if he fell over, with the numbers one to twelve tumbling alongside?

Out of nowhere a thought came to him. Out of the

night's darkness a terrible thought that shocked him: how he wished that Quicksilver really did exist, that the invisible serial killer was in some way to blame for Kinkaid's death. Because that would free both Eleanor Bale and himself from the murder, it would remove the knife from both their hands, it would wipe the blood from their fingers once and for all.

As it was, only the moment of blackout remained, the lost memories.

Nyquist glanced at the dashboard clock, which was still set to the scale used by the hire company. The time was thirteen past five. He turned on the radio, flipping through stations until he found something to keep the bad thoughts at bay. This was good: a minor key guitar melody, slow and weird, that crawled its way through the chord changes, setting a pattern for the singer to come dancing in on, off the beat, her voice bending low in the old style, like the nighthawk blues that Nyquist used to listen to in the Broken Filament club a few years back, when he used to go out at night for purposes other than chasing down losers and freaks. The blues of loss, the cold cold sky, unrequited love. *Every night when the stars come shining, I lay down my weary bones and cry.* The lyrics matched his mood perfectly as he drove on through the town's outlying streets. The blocks of shadow, the shop windows with their faintly lit displays, the muted hoardings, the intermittent signals of torch beams moving along the pavement, the song, the loneliness; Nocturna welcomed him.

A short time later he left the built-up area behind and the darkness intensified, with fewer streetlamps to guide him and fewer lighted windows shining from houses along the way. Every so often he would pass another car, but even these fell away the deeper into Night he travelled. What people there were on the streets – their forms caught momentarily in the yellow of the headlamp beams – appeared as pale apparitions in the darkness, nothing more. They walked along slowly like benign creatures seeking their nests, or windup dolls winding down. Moths fluttered ahead of the car, their wings scattering a fine powder that sparkled in the headlights.

A sudden lantern flash, a slow fade; the face of a small child, startled.

And then darkness once more.

Nyquist worked the steering wheel with a lazy focus, his gaze hardly taking in the road ahead. The dial of the radio was glowing a shiny cobalt blue, currently the brightest thing in his universe. It was hypnotic: the road, the music, the pulse of blue light.

The shadow man's hands around his neck, tightening.

The whispering, hissing voice.

Quicksilver awaits you...

Nyquist gripped the wheel in panic. He felt the rush of white-hot adrenalin as his eyes popped open and the night swerved towards him and he reacted instantly, as though on the edge of crashing.

No. No, it was all right. Breathe again. The car was still under control. He'd dozed off. A few seconds, if that.

He pulled to a halt as an old lady crossed the road, her body preceded by a wavering, hesitant torch beam like a groping antenna, until she reached the other side and the night engulfed her. More slowly now, aware of his growing tiredness, Nyquist drove on. His face was illuminated by the blue light of the radio; a ghost himself, drifting into danger.

A little later the last house went dark, a solitary window shuttered. The yellow light blinked momentarily as though the person within had tensed with a sudden fear. The road signs all but disappeared, their bulbs long since removed, or broken. Now the darkness was complete. Only a scattering of artificial stars remained in the sky. Nyquist worked the dial to find another station, one playing louder, more insistent music. He had to stay awake, to keep watching the road. And then he saw the seven well-known stars of the Dark-Eyed Venus in the sky. Because of her distinctive shape she was amongst the most easily recognised of the constellations. On a more personal level Nyquist had always seen her as the guardian deity of his home precinct, her silvery body held aloft almost directly above his apartment, his few small rooms, his bed, as he slept, as he slept, as he slept, as he…

Something was wrong. His brain flashed with images, colours, a woman's cry. His mother calling to him. And then he could feel his hands moving, sliding, the wheel turning. The wheel, what was this? The steering wheel? Another sound then: piercing, wailing. What was happening? *You're asleep.* His own voice talking to him, loud, insistent. *Wake up. Wake up!* Nyquist forced his eyes open. He was blinded by lights ahead of him, twin beams, another car fast approaching, its horn screeching like some terrified night creature.

He jerked the wheel around as hard as he could.

The two vehicles passed within bare inches of each other.

The whole movement happened slowly in Nyquist's sight: the touch of his fingers on the wheel trim; the cold air whispering on his skin; his eyes fixed on some distant point ahead, far ahead, where he could be alive once more, totally alive.

The passing car's horn drifted away, deepening as it faded.

Nyquist pulled over to the side of the road.

He waited, willing his body to relax. A song was just coming to an end and the deep resonant voice of the radio presenter came in on the cross fade: "These are the Songs of the Night, with your favourite nocturnal host, Jeremiah

Owl. Soothing your grooves with the smoothest of moves. And now let us check the time, my friends. The hands of the studio clock are slowly approaching half past ten."

Nyquist looked at the dashboard clock. It was only a quarter to six.

"Now you know that's the real time," the presenter continued. "Brought to you courtesy of *Easy Time*, the city's favourite chrono-palliative preparation. *Easy Time...* the only time."

Another melody started, the first movement of Beethoven's "Moonlight Sonata". The music affected Nyquist deeply, seeming to carry some emotional weight beyond the notes, powerful as they were. Then he recognised it as the tune he had listened to incessantly as a child, the one released from the little music box whenever he lifted the lid. He thought of the grave of Dominic Kinkaid, the tiny objects left there by Eleanor's mother.

"Für Elise". For Elisa.

He tried to remember who Elisa was, the woman or child to whom Beethoven had dedicated the piece of music. He had read about it once, he was certain of that, but like so many other things the knowledge had faded with the years.

He stared at the dashboard clock, and then at his wristwatch.

More than anything he wanted to change the both of them to the new time given out by the radio. His fingers twitched. But no. No. He would control himself, he would fight this. He would stick to one timescale only, for as long as possible, the one on his wrist. That was his promise to himself. The music played on, the rhythm so languorous; it held such a dreamlike quality that the hands of the pianist seemed barely capable of lifting themselves from the keyboard.

Nyquist started the car once more. He looked ahead,

to where the Dark-Eyed Venus beckoned. He had meant to journey directly to the Bale household; instead, this goddess of the night sky had drawn him along some hidden pathway of her own choosing.

She was pointing the way home.

WAKE-UP CALL

Like many people Nyquist kept two places where he could sleep, one in daylight and one in the dark. His Nocturna apartment was situated in Widow's Veil, a low-rent area to the east of the Central Darkness. Living room, tiny bedroom, even tinier kitchen, a bathroom the size of a wardrobe. Returning here after a period in Dayzone, he always felt like he was visiting a small, out-of-season boarding house. The air of loneliness was palpable. On top of which, invariably he left the place in some kind of mess, forced away suddenly by work, or more likely by an urgent need for daylight, and heat.

He knew something was wrong as soon as he walked down the alleyway that led to his front door. The lock had been broken, the door hung partway open. He pulled the gun from its holster, checked the chamber. And then pushed open the door fully.

Moving quietly down the short hallway, he checked each room in turn.

There was no one to be seen.

But his living room and bedroom had both been ransacked, the furniture turned over, drawers pulled out, papers and books scattered everywhere.

He made a second check of each room.

He was alone. His breath steadied. He placed the gun on the coffee table, turned on a single lamp, heavily shaded, and then went in search of alcohol. He found a dirty tumbler and a bottle of whisky containing more air than liquid. He poured himself a drink and tried to relax. The wreckage lay around him. It could've been burglars, of course. But what did he have to steal? No, they were looking for Eleanor Bale, that was his first thought: or if not her, then an address, a location, a clue pointing towards her whereabouts.

If this was the work of the shadow men, of course. He had made a few other enemies these last days and nights.

His eyes lighted on the small carriage clock perched on top of the bookcase, according to which it was nine minutes to midnight. He walked over and turned the clock round, so the dial was turned to the wall. Next he went to the front door and dragged a chest of drawers into place, jamming the door shut. This would have to do for now until he could get a new lock fitted. It felt secure enough. In the bathroom he took a good long look at himself in the mirror over the basin. There was a single low-wattage bulb situated above, the only light Nyquist allowed himself in the room. Still, the sight that greeted him was quite shocking. He looked ghastly, a wasted spirit clinging on somehow or other inside the flesh. He said to himself, "Look at you. Who are you? What are you doing?" It was strange, but he only ever spoke to himself like this in Nocturna, never in the Day. And only ever in this particular room. Only here would his eyes lock on themselves, almost daring him to see the worst, the shadows inside that seemed to be rising ever closer to the surface.

A stray thought came to him, and his hands gripped the edge of the basin in fear. But once there, it would not go away. He could feel himself weakening, his curiosity taking over. And something else. A need. A giving in.

Back in the living room he emptied out Eleanor's duffle bag and picked up one of the two vials of kia. He unscrewed the top. Strangely, the scent of flowers came to him. He tried to remember what he'd learned about the drug in the Noonday Underground club; the teenage girl, Sadie, had talked about being able to see what lies hidden inside every second, something like that. She'd said that her friend, Daisy, was "zooming ahead", and the dealer Sumak had also implied that the drug offered some kind of vision, or even a premonition. Nyquist remembered the way Sadie's eyes darkened as she talked about her own inability to experience its pleasures.

Now he raised the vial to his face and moved it back and forth under his nose. He lifted it a little higher. It was a sweet aroma, cloying and overpowering. Words came to him, a distant cry, calling from the shadows of a hotel room…

Immediately he dropped the vial, spilling the contents. He felt sick from what little he'd taken. Damn it! He needed to keep straight, clean, lined up directly on target. He went back into the bathroom and washed his face and stared at his reflection. Already his lips were taking on an orange tinge, he was sure of it. He kept washing; it had no effect. The colour remained. He breathed out deeply a good few times, as though he could somehow dispel the chemicals from his system. A wave of tiredness came over him, so intense he could hardly stand upright. He headed for the bedroom, and sitting on the crumpled sheets he tried to empty his mind of all worry. A little rest would cure him. He would wake up refreshed and then get himself clean, a shower and a shave. He would dress up smartly, maybe even wear his one good tie, the blue and yellow one. Yes, that would do it. The colours of daylight, set against night-time's dark. And then he would go out, visit the Bale homestead. Perfect. The alarm clock at his bedside told him it was ten to one. He fought back the urge to change it. Instead he dropped the alarm clock into the top drawer of the bedside cabinet. The drawers had all been pulled open by the intruders, the few things inside rifled through. He saw the photograph. It was a picture of himself and his parents, when Nyquist was young, the age of five. Just a few years before his mother's death. He searched for more images, one of them showing his mother alone, her face in closeup. She was, he guessed, about thirty years old. That face, those eyes. It wasn't just shyness that caused her to look away from the camera's gaze; rather, there was another world to look upon, one of her own desiring. Nyquist turned the photograph over and saw written on the back, *Darla, 1934*. His father's handwriting: Darling Darla, he had called her. But the stated year made his mind race. 1934? What did it mean? How could he possibly measure the time from then to now? The passing years opened like a chasm.

Overcome with remorse he put the photographs back in the cabinet, closing the drawer on them. He stretched out fully clothed on the bed, letting his eyes close. Within a moment he was asleep.

She stood with her back to him, the young woman.

He wanted to warn her, that it wasn't safe here, in the hotel room. They had to move on, keep moving. Something bad was going to happen. If he only knew what the danger was, he'd be able to fight against it.

He turned and looked out through the window. The street below was empty, barely lit, and covered in mist. Only the neon sign of the cinema opposite could be seen clearly. He couldn't make out the name of the movie written on the marquee.

Now the woman called out his name, a call that transformed into a scream. It was terrifying. But then the scream was cut off, suddenly, as though by a switch. He turned to see her. His eye passed over a clock mounted above a mirror on the wall.

It was seven minutes past seven.

Everything moved slowly in his sight, in a dreamlike fashion. Strands of mist drifted around the room. A shadow stirred, a man, his face obscured by smoke.

Again, the young woman tried to scream, but her mouth would not open. Her hands waved in helpless gestures.

Nyquist could not work out what she was saying to him.

But now he recognised her: Eleanor. Her mouth was clamped shut. He knew that he had to help her, but could not see how.

She fell back onto the bed.

To all the world, she looked like she was drowning, drowning in the mist and the air.

A flutter of hands, helpless, helpless...

Nyquist could not take a step.

Between one second and the next, an eternity stretched out.

The shadowy figure moved to the bed, it covered Eleanor in its form, enveloping her completely, suffocating her. Within its deathly embrace she struggled, and then fell still, fell silent. Not even a breath was heard.

Nyquist moved at last, calling out to her...

He woke up with the girl's name on his lips. *Eleanor*. Something had startled him, a noise of some kind. Where had it come from? He listened. Only silence. And then it came again, the tiny sound of breaking glass.

They've come back, he thought. The shadow men.

He tried to remember where he had put his gun. He must have left it on the coffee table, that was it, near the girl's bag. He had to get to it. He stood up, trying not to make a sound of his own, and crept out into the corridor. He peeked in at the living room doorway. There was no one there. Empty, quiet. He moved quickly, snatching the gun up from the table. He clicked off the safety catch, at the same time scanning the room. Something was wrong, he could not place it yet. His eyes scanned the bookcase. There it was: the carriage clock – the one he had turned to face the wall earlier – was now facing outwards again. Had he done this himself, without knowing it? Perhaps in his sleep, or in some half-waking, drugged-up state? Nyquist moved closer. The clock's dial had been smashed. Tiny pieces of glass littered the top of the bookcase. And then he noticed that the two hands of the clock had changed position, either losing or gaining time. They were now pointing at seven minutes past seven. The numbers meant something to him, the particular time, but he couldn't think why it was so important.

He spun round, the gun moving with him. "Who's there? Who is it?" His voice came louder. "Who's doing this?"

No answer. He rushed to the front door, only to see that the chest of drawers was still in place. No one had forced their way in. Moving quickly, he went back to the corridor. Holding the gun with both hands, outstretched, he moved into the bathroom. Empty. But he had to check everywhere. A shadow crossed the wall. Nyquist swung round.

"Who's there? Come on! Come on!"

Silence. And then once again the faraway sound of breaking glass. It was coming from across the corridor, from his bedroom. He moved back along the corridor, more cautious now, the gun swinging in a wide arc to take it all in.

Nyquist was alone. Only his breathing could be heard, coarsely drawn. His heart was beating far too quickly. He moved to the bedroom window, to see that it too was locked tight. And then a noise. Not breaking glass this time, but loud, high pitched, continuous. Nyquist jumped and cried out at hearing it, the shock of it. It was coming from his bedside cabinet, from the drawer. It was the sound of his alarm clock, calling out to him to wake up. The sound was piercing and shrill. Was he dreaming? No. No, this was real. He pulled the drawer open and, immediately, the alarm stopped ringing. He picked up the clock. The glass on the dial had been broken. The hands were frozen in place, exactly at seven minutes past seven. The clock fell from his hand.

Seven past seven, seven past seven…

Memories stirred. This was the time he'd seen in the dream, when Eleanor Bale had been attacked. Yes, he remembered it now, as the poor girl suffered, being suffocated, and her eyes closing in death.

Yet he'd seen no attacker in the dream, only a moving shadow.

What did it mean? Had the drug spoken to him?

Nyquist couldn't think clearly anymore. There was another ringing sound, quieter this time, a melody of some kind, made of tiny bells and chimes. He walked back into the living room. The sound was coming from somewhere in there.

The music box.

It was sitting on the coffee table, the lid opened up, the ballerina dancing around and around. The melody played on. But the tune was different, slower than usual, darkened with too many minor notes. Had he done all this himself ⊠ moved the hands on the clocks, smashed the dials, activated the music box ⊠ all while under the influence of kia? He could not remember.

Nyquist snapped the lid shut. The music died.

He looked at his watch, his father's watch, still attached to his wrist.

It read seven minutes past seven.

THE GATES

The rain falls sparsely in Nocturna. It is said that only one in ten droplets manage to make their way between the tightly packed, broken lamps of the night sky down to ground level. The plants and flowers have adapted over the years, sucking up the moisture with extra tubers and roots. The people make similar adaptations, finding ways to live in such limited circumstances, indeed they learn to love the conditions of their lives. To view such a place as paradise.

The car sped along through the dark, headlamp beams flickering. Nyquist gripped the steering wheel tightly, his upper body pushed forward to better see what lay ahead. The road blurred as the wipers smudged the raindrops across the windscreen. He passed a few other vehicles, not many; this was one of the most exclusive areas of Nocturna. People tended to stay indoors.

The car pulled up at a junction, where a traffic sign was lit up with a soft, eerie glow. Four directions were offered. Rain slanted through the small patch of light. Nyquist dragged the girl's bag from the passenger seat, revealing a road atlas beneath. He checked the sign and then drove on, taking the next turning on the right, towards Darkness Falls.

His mind played over the vision he'd had under the influence of kia.

Eleanor being attacked. Murdered. The event happening at seven minutes past seven. But on which of the many thousand timelines, and measured by whose clock?

It felt like a future event waiting to happen. But surely such thoughts led to madness? And then he remembered what the retired bulb monkey had told him on the roof of his office block: in this city time is a fluid, not a solid substance. It moves forward and back like the tide.

How far could he trust the vision? Just what was being revealed?

Did it hold any kind of truth, symbolic or otherwise?

Was Eleanor really in danger?

If such a tiny amount of the drug had given him that much access to the hidden part of his mind, what would a full dosage bring into the light?

Questions, questions. Secrets gathering at every twist and turn.

A short while later he was travelling along a narrow country lane lined with trees. There were no streetlamps, no light at all except for the headlights of the car. He glanced from side to side, looking for signs of life, noise, radiance, anything. The black night closed in around him. He had the feeling of being lost, of the night playing tricks on him. Still, he kept going, taking each winding bend at a slow pace, hoping that his map-reading was up to scratch. And then he saw something through the trees; a flame of some kind, another, two flickering lanterns perhaps? The car slowed further as it turned off the road. A pair of ironwork gates were set across the entrance to a driveway. The two lanterns were fixed to the upper parts of the gate, one on each side, and the address *Number 5 Beckett Drive* was plainly seen, the letters made out of a luminous material.

Nyquist brought the car to a halt.

Only the sound of the rain could be heard.

He glanced at his watch; it had not moved on since the episode in his apartment, and was still stuck on seven past seven.

The dashboard clock read twenty-five to eleven.

Which one should he believe?

He got out of the car and walked up to the gates. Looking through he could see the driveway continuing until it vanished into the gloom a little further on. He pressed a button at the side of the gate and seconds later a pale light came on in a nearby window. A small outbuilding nestled in the trees. A door opened and the beam of a torch emerged, followed by a dark bulky figure. Nyquist waited, shivering from the cold. The approaching person was dressed in a shiny black waterproof coat. He had some weight about him. His face was only partially visible under the coat's hood, as he stared at Nyquist through the gateposts.

"What do you want?"

"Let me in."

The gatekeeper grimaced. "Do you know what the time is?"

"The time?"

"It's gone two o'clock."

"I need to speak with Eleanor."

"Two in the morning, mind. It's late."

The torch beam dazzled Nyquist's eyes. "Please. I need to see her."

"Miss Bale is away just now."

"Away? Where?"

"Do you think they tell me everything?"

"What about... what about Eleanor's father?"

"No. Sorry." The gatekeeper shook his head. Drops of rain fell from his hood. "Only Mrs Bale is present at this moment."

"Eleanor's mother?" Nyquist grabbed hold of the bars. "Tell her I'm here. Wake her up."

"Oh. Mrs Bale will still be awake. She does not sleep. Well, not often."

"Tell her it's Nyquist. John Nyquist."

"I'm afraid that won't be possible."

"It's about her daughter, Eleanor. She's in danger."

The gatekeeper frowned. He looked suspicious. "What kind of danger?"

Nyquist shook his head. "I don't know."

"You don't know?"

"I'm not sure. I just need to see Eleanor, or anybody, the family. Anybody!"

"I can't–"

Nyquist thrust both of his hands through the bars, grabbing the gatekeeper by the collar, making him cry out in alarm. The torch fell to the ground. The gatekeeper's face was pulled up tight against the bars, distorting his features. He couldn't speak, he was making rude babbling sounds. Nyquist relaxed his grip just a little, allowing the man to get his words out. "I can't let you in," he cried. "I can't."

"Tell her!"

"I have my… my orders."

Nyquist pulled the gatekeeper forward once more, harder this time, mashing his face up against the railings. "Listen to me. Eleanor Bale is going to be killed." He spoke coldly and plainly. "She's going to die." The gatekeeper looked scared. Nyquist pushed him away, so that he stumbled and fell to the ground. The man lay there for a moment and then scrambled to his feet, setting off immediately for his hut. He vanished inside. Nyquist wiped the rainwater from his face with his sleeve and waited. He was aware of his own smell, the caked-on dirt, the sweat. He hadn't changed his clothes, nor had he got round to that shower and shave, too scared, petrified at what was happening to him. In the distance, further up the drive, a dog barked. Probably more guards were on the way. They would force him to leave and that would be that.

And then, without any further word from the gatekeeper, the gates clicked open and started to move slowly apart.

A WOMAN OF UNUSUAL HABIT

Pinpricks of light ahead turned out to be strings of multicoloured bulbs arranged on the branches of the trees. These provided the only illumination as Nyquist's car edged along the driveway. He peered out through the windscreen as the final bend took him into a cleared area and the Bale residence appeared before him, a large mansion house with a well-tended night garden extending to one side. A number of ornamental lamps cast a muted glow onto the scene, each yellow bulb cast in vapour by the rain.

Nyquist parked the car in the shadows. He got out and immediately a muscle-bound security guard approached him. The guard was dressed in black, a nocturnal creature with glittering red eyes, a result of the special night-viewing goggles he was wearing. A snarling dog moved at his side. Nyquist walked to the front door under the guard's silent inspection. The door opened as he approached and a maid greeted him by name. She led the way into the hall.

The house was filled with antiques, their beauty barely seen in the low-level lighting. Nyquist, for his part, looked terrible. He was wet through, bone-frozen, and shaking still with the nerves that had driven him here. The young maid took an intense interest in his appearance, moving closer to him. Nyquist felt nervous and he wiped at his face with a handkerchief. The maid smiled. "You are very lucky, Mr Nyquist. We sleep only when Mrs Bale sleeps." She spoke quietly, almost in a whisper. "This way, please." They walked through into an antechamber, whose walls were hung with oil paintings, some of them very large and imposing. Each of the larger paintings had its own discreet lighting; apart from these faint dustings of colour, the room was dark.

The maid paused. "It's not often that she agrees to see anyone. Although, I must warn you..."

"Go on."

"Don't expect too much of her."

The maid turned to set off again but Nyquist gently caught hold of her arm. "Tell me..."

"Melissa."

"Melissa, do you know Mrs Bale's daughter well?"

"Eleanor? Yes. I would like to think that we are friends. Well, as much as two people can be, in this sort of relationship."

"Relationship?"

"I'm an employee. A servant."

Nyquist gripped the maid's arm a little tighter. "I'm on Eleanor's side. You have to believe me."

Melissa looked worried. She glanced back, over to where another security guard was standing, watching them closely. She said to this character, "It's all right, Jacob. I'll be fine here." The guard stood to attention, silent and unmoving.

Nyquist leaned into the maid once again, whispering himself now. "Just tell me where Eleanor is. That's all."

"I cannot say."

"But you do know?"

Melissa's voice changed tone, becoming businesslike. "Wait here please." She hurried away through a doorway.

Nyquist looked at the security guard, nodded, but got no response. The pendulum of a grandfather clock swung slowly back and forth, producing a deeply resonant sound. According to the antique's dial the time was approaching twenty past two, which seemed to fit with the time the gatekeeper had given him. The house was working to its own chronology. Nyquist felt the usual overwhelming need to change his own wristwatch in accordance, but resisted it. He glanced at the dial: it was still fixed on seven minutes past seven. Just then the security guard coughed and stared at him intently. Nyquist walked over to the nearest work of art, a large oil painting depicting an eerie twilit landscape where the shadows of unseen people lay frozen on the ground between strange-looking towers and archways. It was signed *de Chirico*. Nyquist had the feeling the painting might well be an original. He was examining an abstract marble sculpture when the inner doorway opened once again and Melissa appeared.

"Mrs Bale will see you now."

"Thank you."

She held the door wide for him and Nyquist entered the room.

It was the sound he noticed first. The room was as dimly lit as all the others, but the sound of ticking, of chiming, filled the shadowed air so completely it seemed as though he had stepped inside a machine. His eyes slowly adjusted to the gloom and he looked around in astonishment, for every single wall and shelving space was fitted with a timepiece of some kind, all of a different design and age. Pendulums swung to and fro, hands turned around dials, mechanisms whirred and clicked. He noted that the clock nearest to him read twenty minutes to four, completely out of step with the timescale he thought the house was running to. Obviously, in this room the clocks moved to a different instruction. And then moving on he saw that every single dial showed approximately the same time: twenty minutes to four.

He became aware of a voice, a woman's soft voice saying over and over the single repeated word: "Time, time, time. Time, time, time, time, time. Time, time. Time, time, time." The voice lowered to nothing more than a whisper, at one with the constant ticking sound of the room. "Time. Time, time, time. Time, time…"

The mother of Eleanor Bale was a living ghost of a once startlingly beautiful woman. She was in her late forties, but her skin had the pale drawn-out quality of somebody who has never seen the daylight, not in many years, whilst the look in her eyes reminded Nyquist of his own mother in the photographs, fixed as they were upon some other realm just slightly askew to the present-day world.

"Oh, just look at the time, will you. You're late! I don't know. A dreadful affair." She was moving from clock to clock, adjusting the hands of each in turn. "No matter how I try, there's always something wrong. The time is wrong. There now!" She turned the hands of a large clock on the mantelpiece, appeared to be satisfied for a second, but then noticed some other timepiece nearby had already moved on. She rushed over to it. "Oh my. Look at the time. Is that the time?" She started to adjust the hands of this new instrument. Nyquist realised that she was trying to make sure that every clock in the room always registered the exact same time: twenty to four.

It was an impossible task.

"Mrs Bale?"

The woman stopped, her body suddenly tense. For a moment she looked like a young girl caught performing some naughty deed, and then she turned to look at Nyquist, evidently seeing him clearly for the first time. "What are you doing here?" she asked, her voice on the edge of breakdown. Now she fumbled with a desk drawer, pulling it open. "What are you doing in my room? Get out of my room!"

"I'm trying to find..."

She pulled something from the drawer, a small metal object. Nyquist saw what it was. He stopped moving.

"My father gave this pistol to me," she said, "for my sixteenth birthday. He knew that many people, many men, would take an unhealthy interest in me, in both my body and my fortune. It's a lovely thing, don't you agree? Do you see the handle, here, decorated with jewels?"

"Yes."

"You don't wish me any harm, do you?"

"None at all–"

"Leave me alone!" Her voice broke in fear and the pistol trembled in her grip.

"I'm trying to..."

"Get out of my sight! Can't you... can't you... can't you see I'm busy?"

"Mrs Bale. I'm trying to find your daughter."

The woman cringed at the statement. Both of her hands wound themselves tightly around the pistol's stock. Her mouth set itself in a grim line and her eyes blazed with fear. Then, finally, she let the weapon fall back onto the desktop. Her whole demeanour changed, growing softer. "My daughter? My daughter, sadly, has been taken away from me."

"Taken where?"

"Taken from me. Passed over. Sadly."

"I don't know what you mean."

"All is gone. Gone."

"I'm trying to find Eleanor."

"Ah. Yes. Eleanor. That is her name. Now I remember."

Nyquist shook his head in despair. The woman's mind was so conflicted with itself that any conversation would be broken at best; and at worst, of little or no use to him.

He moved to her. "Mrs Bale. Please. I need to speak with Eleanor. It's urgent."

The woman gathered herself together, standing tall and proud, seemingly more in charge of herself. She said, "Oh, but you must call me Catherine."

"Catherine." He tried to smile. "My name is John Nyquist."

"I know who you are."

"You do?"

Nyquist was startled. Eleanor's mother had lost all sense of being disturbed. She appeared now to be perfectly normal. "I believe that my husband employed you to find my child, isn't that so?"

"That's correct."

"And you did find her. My dear Eleanor came home a short while ago. But now she has gone again. I don't know where she is, I'm afraid. I really don't."

Nyquist steeled himself. He said, "I think she's in trouble. She's in danger."

Catherine grimaced. She seemed to be struggling, trying to decide which of several worlds to focus on. Her eyes ranged over a line of clocks on the mantelpiece, and then found Nyquist once again. "How do you know this?"

"I was attacked, by people who were searching for her."

"People?"

"Men. Two men. They wore... they wore masks of shadow." Even as he said the words, he could hear how absurd they sounded.

But the statement obviously meant something to Mrs Bale. She was tipped back over the edge. Her entire body shuddered.

"Oh, my dear little child. In danger!"

Nyquist's head was filled with strange music, generated by the complex pattern of ticking sounds, each mechanism slightly out of sync with its neighbours.

He tried to concentrate. "Do you know who those men might be?"

Catherine Bale stared at him without speaking.

He carried on: "I believe these same men will stop at nothing until they find your daughter. I believe... I believe they want to kidnap her. Or worse."

He had hoped that such words would instil fear, and make her tell him where Eleanor was; but instead her eyes started to lose focus. "No. No," she said. "Look at this now! It's all wrong." She broke away from Nyquist, moving quickly to a clock far across the room, adjusting it feverishly. "Wrong! All wrong. Look at the time. Time, time, time. I'm late! I really am so very, very late."

Nyquist followed her. "Mrs Bale..."

"I am so very sorry. I simply haven't got a moment to spare."

"But you asked to see me. You let me through, the gate was opened."

"Ah..."

"Yes?"

"Mr Nyquist. Now I understand." And once again, she seemed to re-enter the real world. "You were looking for Eleanor. Yes, that's right. My husband employed you. Did you find her?"

Nyquist felt exhausted.

"Well? Did you?"

"Yes."

"Yes. Of course. And you were well paid, I hope?"

"I just need to speak with Eleanor. That's all. That's all I ask."

Now Catherine looked nervous. She would look anywhere but into Nyquist's eyes. "This is my home," she said.

"I know that–"

"I was born here, in this house, on the dark side of the

city." She moved on to another clock, adjusting the hands. "They say it's a curse, being born in the night. But those born in daylight would say that. They are jealous of our knowledge." She picked up the next clock. "My husband was a dayside birth. He married me for the company's fortunes, of course. You do understand, the business was created by my family?"

"And what about Eleanor's real father?"

Catherine froze, and Nyquist saw that he had got to her now, shocked her into some kind of reality.

"Dominic Kinkaid," he said.

"Dominic…" She was trying to locate a memory. "Dominic?"

"Tell me about him. What does he mean to you?"

"Ah yes. The lovely Dominic." Her voice softened. "My beau. My handsome young lover. Oh, but I haven't seen him, no, not for a long while now. Not for such a long, long time."

"Tell me about him."

Her hands paused in the winding of a clock, and she nodded eagerly, smiling, catching hold of a sudden memory. "We would meet in secret, in secret places, in little pockets of shared darkness. He was a painter, a sculptor, a maker of things. A magician. Oh, he kissed me! How he kissed me. Dominic took me to the edge of Dusk, where his lips first met mine; and then we walked further on, into the mist itself, the moon-white lands." The story had taken her over completely. "The mist was cold against my face and my hands. Dew clung to my hair, making it sticky. I could hear voices in the fog. Such cries of pain. But we kept on walking. He seemed to have no fear of the dusk, no fear at all, and I felt quite safe by his side. Along the way we talked of art and lost time and the world of spirits." Now she looked directly at Nyquist, her eyes taking on a young woman's brilliance. "And still we kept on, entering a circle of strange wooden figures, like… like sculptures."

"Effigies?"

"Yes! That is the word. And there, and there we made love, we made our love together, oh, with the fog rolling over our naked forms and the blue sparkle of Venus low in the sky like a guardian angel. I could hear voices in the gloom, a chanting sound. I felt I was being watched. I was part of something at last, a ritual. A spell. It was very exciting. Ever so! And this is where my dear sweet Eleanor was conceived; conjured from the dusk, a child of the fog and the moon and the shadows."

At last her voice slowed and came to silence. She turned her face away from Nyquist, suddenly embarrassed. Nyquist let her be for a moment. He remembered what the dealer Sumak had told him, about Eleanor being born in the dusk. But he'd got the story slightly wrong: not born, but conceived there.

Catherine Bale spoke in a whisper. "Tell me, have you seen Dominic lately?"

"I'm afraid…"

"Yes? What is it?" Her face was still hidden.

"I'm afraid Dominic Kinkaid is dead."

"He's dead."

The clock fell from her hands, smashing on the floor, and it seemed that all the other clocks in the room stopped their ticking for a long drawn-out moment, as though in shock or sympathy. Catherine shuddered. She picked up another timepiece, hardly aware of what she was doing, and began to turn the winding mechanism. The room started ticking again.

Nyquist brought out the music box. He said, "You placed this on Kinkaid's grave." Catherine glanced over, as he lifted the lid to allow the music to start, the ballerina to dance. "You were seen, at the graveside."

"Well then. I suppose I must've done. Yes, I remember

now. Melissa came with me. She looked after me."

Nyquist felt a sudden compassion for this strangely damaged woman. He asked gently, "What's the significance of twenty minutes to four?"

Catherine hesitated. Then she said, "There are certain times of the day and night that must never be forgotten. Never! Do you believe that to be true, Mr Nyquist?"

"I used to think that only the present moment counted for anything real. But now, I'm not so sure."

"My daughter was taken from me at twenty minutes to four."

Nyquist thought she was referring to Eleanor and her current disappearance, but then he glimpsed a more disturbing reason for Catherine Bale's behaviour. He could think of no easy way to express it without opening a wound, and bringing further pain to this woman. He kept his council, and his silence infected Catherine as well, and the two of them stood in the room of ticking clocks for a few moments. Then she shook her head, saying, "I don't know where she is, can you imagine that? My husband has hidden Eleanor away."

Nyquist touched her on the arm. "I'll find her for you," he said.

"You will?"

Nyquist nodded. Catherine held his gaze. Her face took on the most serious aspect she had yet managed, her fragmented mind in control of itself, for this brief period at least. "Be careful," she said. "There are forces at play in this city, they are not to be trifled with. We are reaching the limits of time itself."

"What do you mean?"

"You will find out."

Nyquist drew in a breath. The conversation was coming to an end, and yet the difficult question remained. "Mrs Bale, tell me..." He paused, nervous of her reaction, before asking: "How many children do you have?"

A shadow passed over the woman's face, a shadow generated from within by some terrible thought or memory which had risen to the surface, to her pale and drawn skin, entirely unbidden. "I have... I have..." The words struggled in a dry throat. Nyquist felt he had gone too far. He could see the hurt he had caused and was all set to apologise when Catherine's eyes widened with knowledge and her mouth moved to speak, this time with a sudden, fierce determination: "I have two children!"

"What happened to the other child?"

"Passed over."

The same phrase she'd used before.

"You mean she died?"

Catherine nodded, a barely noticeable movement. Her mouth opened to speak, but then she stuttered once more as she looked across from Nyquist over to the doorway where Patrick Bale now stood.

"Nyquist!" Bale strode into the room, followed by the security guard. "What are you doing in my house?" He was livid with anger.

Nyquist stood his ground. "Looking for Eleanor."

"You're upsetting my wife."

"Yes. I'm sorry. I didn't mean to..."

"If you would step into the other room. Please."

The guard came nearer. Nyquist felt himself tighten up, ready for a fight, but then he heard Catherine's voice softly murmuring. She had retreated once again, her hands working and twisting at a clock's mechanisms as though to wind up the world itself and hold it tight, forever held in that one precious moment.

PRIVATE AFFAIRS

Nyquist was standing in front of the large oil painting of figures lost to twilight, with the security guard Jacob close at hand. Patrick Bale stood a few feet away, rubbing his brow with his fingers. "I don't understand you," he said. Nyquist kept silent, forcing Bale to look up at him. "I've paid you. I've paid you for work that strictly speaking you didn't even do, that is, find my daughter for me and bring her safely home. Instead, a police car brought her home to me, from a murder scene!"

Nyquist started to speak, but stopped himself.

Bale carried straight on: "I've given you every warning. What do I have to do?"

"Beat me up. Kill me. I don't know."

This statement angered Bale even further. He looked around the room before settling on the guard, who was trying to suppress a grin. "Jacob!" he shouted at the employee. "Get out of my sight. Now!"

The guard left the room.

Bale waited until the door was closed before he walked over to a cabinet and poured himself a drink. He didn't offer one to Nyquist. He said, "You don't know me. I don't think anybody knows me. Not truly."

"Maybe not. But I'd like to understand."

"Why?"

"Because of Eleanor."

"What of her?"

"Is there anybody you know that might want to harm her in any way?"

"No."

"You're the head of the most important company in Dayzone. You must have enemies."

"Yes, but–"

"What drives you, Bale? Tell me that."

"I don't know what you mean."

"I don't think it's just greed…"

"Of course not. I have made my fortune ten times over and feel hardly better for it."

"Well then?"

Bale looked to be on the edge of admitting something, but then he pulled back and said, "The family business was in the doldrums when I took over its running. They made clocks, wristwatches, fancy timepieces. A few rudimentary timelines. The monetary value was fine but it lacked, shall we say, imagination. No, what fascinated me, was *time* itself, our ability to capture it, and manipulate it. To no longer be its slave. And that has always been my driving force."

Nyquist stepped a little closer. "I was talking to your wife earlier, and she mentioned something strange; that we're reaching the limits of time."

"Ah well, Catherine says many odd things."

"The limits of time. I wonder what she meant by that? And what happens to us, to the city, once we step beyond that point?"

"We have everything under control."

"And if we have another time crash, what then?"

"We have been working extensively to ensure that such an event does not happen again."

"I hope you're right."

Nyquist remembered the last two crashes, when the city's carefully constructed web of timelines had suddenly overloaded and collapsed into chaos. He shuddered at the thought: many people were frozen in place, incapable of moving from the spot; others could move but only at a dreadfully slowed rate. Nyquist had been affected in the opposite manner: his body clock had speeded up so that whole days would seem to pass in a few seconds. In the end he'd retreated to his Nocturnal home and stayed in bed, in the dark, until the nausea had passed and the city's system had regained its equilibrium.

"And what about those being damaged by all this?" he now asked. "That woman I read about in the newspaper, for instance. Over seventy different timelines coursing through her psyche."

"And each of them individually tested. What can we do—"

"The poor woman sliced her wrists."

Bale faltered slightly. "Yes."

Nyquist moved in. "I hear that questions are being asked in parliament. What are you going to do? Buy them off?"

"This has nothing to do with you. Nothing at all!"

"I believe Eleanor is tied up in your struggles."

"My struggles?"

"Your battle. Against time. And I think the death of Dominic Kinkaid is connected to all this. I just don't know how yet."

Bale's whole body shook fiercely, as though experiencing physical pain.

Nyquist softened his voice. "You have to believe me, Eleanor is being targeted. I just need to find out why this is happening, and who's seeking her. And then I can... and then *we* can make sure that she's safe."

The approach had no good effect. Instead, Bale's eyes

filled with a cold anger. "I will ask you one final time to leave my family alone. Leave my daughter alone."

Nyquist let a few seconds pass, before he spoke: "But Eleanor's not your daughter, is she?"

Bale swallowed the last of his drink in one gulp. For a moment, Nyquist thought the empty glass was going to break in the man's hand. But he drew in a few breaths and then smiled. It was like watching an ice shard snap in two. "You're right. You're right, Nyquist. She's not my daughter."

Nyquist was surprised by the sudden admission, but he resisted the urge to follow up the questioning. Instead, he watched as Bale put down his glass and walked over to examine one of the oil paintings. The room was so dimly lit, his figure seemed to merge with the surreal landscape. "It was a tawdry affair," he began. "That's all. I don't know the details. I don't want to know. Some kind of artist. My wife was always attracted to such sensitive types. Of course, he was much younger than her."

"And this was Dominic Kinkaid?"

Bale turned away from the painting. "Yes." His face gave nothing away saying this, not a trace of pain or loss.

Nyquist pressed on with the story. "So your wife starts seeing this guy, and then what, she falls pregnant?"

A nod in reply.

"And so Eleanor was born?"

Bale smiled briefly. "All that matters is that I've brought her up as my own. My own child. How many men would do such a thing? Yes, I've given Eleanor everything she could possibly want from life. I'm speaking in purely material terms, of course. Whatever else she might need, well, I don't know. I can't be the judge of my own ability to love. Can anyone?"

"I guess not. No."

The two men stood in silence. The room seemed to

echo with sound where none was made, and the frozen landscapes on the walls offered glimpses of other worlds, as though through a series of moonlit doorways. The subtle lighting devices hummed with carefully controlled power. For the first time Nyquist felt a connection with the other man. He asked, "What happened?"

Bale murmured, awoken from some dream or other. "I'm sorry?"

"What made Eleanor leave home?"

"She found out about Kinkaid."

"You never told her?"

He shook his head. "She has taken me as her father, all these years. As I have viewed her as my daughter." Bale looked pained. "Of course, she was upset when she found out. Well, you can imagine."

Nyquist paused. He had to ask the question, the difficult one. He said, "What about your other child?"

"My what? I don't have another child."

Nyquist tried another guess. "Really? I thought she was called Elisa?"

Bale's face was cast in shadow. He said, quite calmly, "I have one child only. Her name is Eleanor."

"It was something your wife said, about her daughter having died. Passed over..."

"Elisa? It does ring a bell. Ah yes. That was the name we had first chosen for Eleanor, before she was born. Later, we changed our minds."

"I see," said Nyquist. "That might explain it."

"A woman's ravaged mind playing tricks upon itself." Bale stepped forward slightly, allowing his face to be seen. "I'm sure you have realised by now, Nyquist, that our family has been through great pain in its time, and a good part of that was caused by a problem of my own."

"Which is?"

Without hesitation Bale said, "I'm sterile."

Nyquist was taken aback. He was still trying to find a word to say in reply when Bale continued: "My dear wife could hardly bear such a thing. Perhaps it drove her into the arms of another man, who can say? And who can say what demons still arise from all this?"

"In whose mind?"

Bale didn't answer. He closed his eyes momentarily. "There. Now you have it. I have admitted to being less of a man. Are you happy with such knowledge?"

Nyquist nodded. "I was curious. It goes with the job."

"I suppose it does."

"Where is Eleanor?"

"My daughter... and I make no apologies for the word; my daughter has been deeply disturbed by the events of the last few weeks or so. But rest assured, she's being well looked after."

"I have some things of hers."

"Leave them with me."

"I can't do that. I have to see her."

The steel came back into Bale's voice. "That's not going to happen." But it was only momentary, as though the very act of putting on the armour had weighed his soul down, and a sadness came over his features. He came towards Nyquist, reaching out a hand. He said, "I don't know what to do for the best. I love my wife dearly, but... well, you have seen how she is. Really, Eleanor is all that I have now."

"Yes. I can see that."

"I'm doing the best I can, Nyquist. But you know, I'm alone in this." He shook his head. "I'm alone." Just then the grandfather clock that stood against the far wall began to chime; once, twice, a third time, the toll of the bell seeming far too loud for the size of the room. Yet Bale was lulled by the sound of it. His eyes took on a sleepy cast. He said, "When all is said and done, we all want one thing only. To escape from time, and to live. To live forever. On such dreams are fortunes made, my own included." Then he made a little bow, a kind of signing off ritual. "And now I really must see if Catherine is all right. Goodbye, Mr Nyquist. I trust our paths will not cross again. You will take this I hope in the spirit it's intended."

These were the last words spoken.

ONE RULE ONLY

A few minutes later Nyquist walked out to his car. He was watched by the same or another security guard, completely unidentifiable behind the night-vision mask, whose vicious-looking dog strained at the leash. Patrick Bale's limousine was parked nearby, its silver paintwork sparkling under the patio lamps. Nyquist looked back at the house. Above, at a dimly lit window, the lonely figure of Catherine Bale could be seen. He remembered what she had said: *There are certain times of the day and night that must never be forgotten...*

The rain fell more gently now, as the hire car moved slowly down the drive. The trees were dark on both sides, the colourful bulbs having been turned off. As he drove along, Nyquist thought about the case, or rather, the jigsaw puzzle, as he now considered it. He felt he had a few more pieces in place, with many others still missing. There was a hidden shape, a form in the dusk just out of reach.

The last drops of rain fell through the headlamp beams. Nyquist was lost in thought, his eyes scarcely aware of the road ahead. Patrick Bale had opened up, a little way at least, and there was an air of truth around his words. But he still didn't trust him, not fully, especially when it came to Eleanor.

If only he could find the girl! That was still his number one task.

A small flicker of colour shone in the trees near the roadside. The yellow light moved, faded, came back again, brighter now. It looked like some kind of deliberate signal. Or a warning. Nyquist stopped the car. He pulled the gun from beneath the driver's seat, and then got out and moved towards the trees; as he did so, the light went out. He looked up and down the driveway, seeing only darkness. Nyquist turned to the trees again. The huge leaves were curled at the edges to form a series of green funnels, specially designed to channel all of the meagre rainwater down into the earth and the roots below.

"Who's there?"

There was no answer to his call. But then somebody moved among the branches. Nyquist stepped closer, and the person came forward to meet him. It was the maid, Melissa. She said, "I have to be quick. They'll notice I'm gone."

"What do you want?"

"To help Eleanor. Here..." She handed Nyquist a small object. "Do your best for her."

"I will do."

"Let me see your face. Because you let her down last time."

Nyquist moved closer. Melissa held up her lantern and searched his face for clues. "This time, I need to know for sure that you'll do your very best for her."

"I'll do that."

"Good."

Melissa's eyes were filled with the same loneliness he had seen in Eleanor's. Despite their differing positions in life, they were two of a kind.

"Be careful. Mr Bale is not to be trusted, not when it comes to Eleanor."

"What do you mean?"

"He's scared of her. Petrified."

She gave a tight smile, a nod. Then she stepped back.

"Wait. I need more information."

It was no use. The young woman moved away into the trees, becoming just another dark shape in the undergrowth. Nyquist took a step or two after her. The leaves were cold and wet around his face. Rain dripped down from the branches above.

Melissa had vanished.

He went back to the car, clicking on the interior light in order to examine the object she had given him. It was a business card, with a logo depicting the sun and moon joined together in harmony. Finally, Nyquist felt that he might be getting somewhere, closer to the source. And then his eye fell on the dashboard clock. With a shock he saw that the glass was broken in a single diagonal crack from top to bottom. The hands were frozen in place. Once again he thought of Catherine Bale and how one particular moment of time had caught her in its trap. Perhaps he was as much a victim as she was.

The time shown on the dashboard clock was seven minutes past seven.

He was still under the drug's spell in some way.

Nyquist started the engine and drove on toward the gateway. When he got there, he saw that another car was entering the Bale estate. He slowed down as the two vehicles passed each other. The light from the gatekeeper's hut shone directly on this new arrival, a large estate model. Nyquist saw the driver in his uniform, and then the passenger sitting alone in the rear. The man's face was familiar – gaunt, a dark complexion, his hair pushed back from the forehead – but there was little enough time to make a recognition. Another of Bale's associates, no doubt, legitimate or otherwise. Nyquist watched in the rear-view mirror as the other car vanished into the gloom of the driveway, then he made his own way through the gates and back onto the country road. He drove on a little way, until he came to a corner with a telephone box. He dialled the number on the business card that Melissa had given him.

A woman's voice answered. "Hello. How may I help you?"

"Is that the Aeon Institute?"

"It is, yes."

"I was hoping to come and see Eleanor Bale."

"One moment... Ah, yes. I'm afraid Ms Bale is on our restricted access list."

"I know that. I'm a close associate of her father, Sir Patrick Bale."

"You would have to bring proof of your connection."

Nyquist turned over the business card, looking at the single word handwritten there. "I'll do that. It's good that you're taking so much care of Eleanor."

"Of course, sir. That's our job. Visiting hours end at nine o'clock."

"Nine. OK. What time do you have now?"

"A quarter to eight."

"Right. I can make it. I'll be there."

"I must inform you, sir. We only have one rule for visitors."

"Go on?"

"No timepieces of any kind are allowed within the public areas of the institute. Will that be a problem?"

"No, of course not. Thank you."

Nyquist left the phone box. He needed to adjust his wristwatch in order to arrive at the institute on time. He looked at the dial through half-closed eyes. Thankfully, the glass was in one piece, but the hands were still fixed on seven past seven. He pressed it to his ear; the instrument was ticking away with such a vigorous and beautiful sound he felt his heart beating faster to keep in step. He wound the hands into a new position and they moved easily enough. Thirteen minutes to eight. His mind took charge of a new determination.

He would not fail the girl this time.

The car was back on the road and heading towards the Central Darkness before he got to thinking about the estate car he had just seen arriving at Bale's house; and with a shock Nyquist remembered where he had seen the passenger before. It was the dealer from the Noonday Underground club, Sumak, the man who supplied people with the kia drug.

Now what business did such a lowlife have with the man in charge of the city's timelines?

A SHADOW PASSES OVER

Bibleblack was a small town located some few miles to the southwest of Nocturna. Nyquist drove through the outskirts until he found the overly large, rambling building that housed the Aeon Institute. He found a parking space in the area provided near the main entrance. He took one last look at his watch and then unwrapped it from his wrist, placing it in the glove compartment. The time was eight fifteen. He would have forty minutes or so in which to see and talk to Eleanor Bale, and to make sure she was all right. He stashed the gun back under the driving seat, along with the one remaining vial of kia. He would play by the rules, until the rules started playing against him.

At the reception desk, Nyquist was asked to write the password on a piece of card. He wrote the six-letter word that Melissa had written on the back of the business card. The card was then placed in a brass canister and sent on a journey along a series of pneumatic tubes that shot up through the ceiling above the reception desk. He pictured a dusty old man or woman in a dusty room on the dusty top floor checking the passwords against a ledger. As they waited for confirmation, Nyquist was searched by a member of staff. The duffle bag was emptied out, each item examined and then returned. The person in charge

wanted to know what the leather figurine was. Nyquist
told her it was a puppet, an item of personal value to
Eleanor. All this was fine. But the metal canister had not
yet returned. He started to panic. Perhaps the password had
been changed? Or Melissa had got it wrong. He imagined
somebody ringing Eleanor's home at this very moment,
asking to speak with Patrick Bale.

Nyquist smiled at the receptionist. He noticed a shelving
unit behind the desk where a good number of wristwatches
had been placed, each with a name tag attached. Visitors
had left their time here, to be picked up later.

At last the canister arrived back, falling out of the tube
into a wire basket. The card it contained was examined,
and the receptionist smiled back at him.

"Have a pleasant visit, Mr Nyquist."

A middle-aged gentleman in an ill-fitting suit met
with him, introducing himself as Doctor Shapiro. Side by
side they walked along a dimly-lit corridor. Shapiro was
interested in Eleanor's case, and he explained a little about
the work they were doing, saying, "Aeon is a charitable
foundation, dedicated to looking after people who suffer
from temporal disorders."

Two orderlies passed by, dressed in grey uniforms.

"Are you certain Eleanor has such problems," Nyquist
asked.

"They can be difficult to spot, if the sufferer is clever
enough. But rest assured, we do know our job."

They reached a locked, iron-barred gateway. This was
opened by a guard, allowing Nyquist and the doctor to
pass through and continue down another corridor. Shapiro
continued with his spiel. "We offer our patients a more
comforting cycle of night and day."

"It's a lock up?"

The doctor sighed at this. "We are governed by
chronology. All of us. Reason itself is closely tied to our

basic understanding of time. We make value judgments by comparing that which has passed, with that which might come to pass. If this understanding should fail, if the body's clock gets sufficiently knocked out of joint, well then…"

"Go on."

"Let us say that some of our more extreme patients have violent tendencies. Of course, Eleanor Bale is not in this category."

A few discreet lamps cast their gentle balm over the corridor. "What's she doing here?" Nyquist asked. "This doesn't seem right."

"Her father took the precaution of–"

"Patrick Bale?"

"Yes. A very generous, kind man."

"Generous. I see."

"Oh yes. Now…"

Howling sounds were heard in the distance. A number of orderlies hurried by, along an adjacent corridor.

Nyquist stopped. "What's happening?"

"It is unfortunate. Some people are so ravaged by time, they lose all grip on reality."

The cries of anguish drifted through the building.

Nyquist walked on, following the doctor. He said, "Personally, I don't think there's anything wrong with Eleanor."

Shapiro smiled. "Really? But you are hardly in any fit state to make that judgment."

"What do you mean by that?"

"Well. Your own sense of time is out of balance. Severely so, if you don't mind me saying. You have four of the five classic telltale signs."

"Now listen–"

"Ah. Here we are." The doctor gestured towards an open doorway. "I shall leave you now, Mr Nyquist. But please be aware, Eleanor has been through a lot of pain lately."

"I know."

Shapiro nodded politely. "And remember, if you should ever decide to do something about your problem, we provide a free consultation service."

"I'll survive."

"I don't doubt it. In some form or other."

The doctor moved off down the corridor. Nyquist was alone. He looked through the open doorway. All was dim and shady within the building, as it should be in Nocturna. But the space beyond the door was brightly lit in warm colours. He walked through and immediately felt himself overwhelmed. A golden haze of artificial sunlight streamed down through the high glass roof of a circular courtyard, and a beautiful, lush and extensive inner garden occupied the space within, complete with ornamental plants, goldfish ponds, benches and wire sculptures.

Nyquist was stunned by the vision.

He wandered through the garden along a gently twisting pathway. The atmosphere was humid. Many kinds of birds could be heard, whistling and singing from the trees and bushes. Insects buzzed amid tropical flowers and the calming sound of trickling water accompanied his every turn. Here and there he came across little groups of people, some of them obviously patients or clients or inmates or whatever they were called, all of them wearing the same outfit of a crisp blue smock over linen trousers. Their faces were dulled, their expressions betraying a soft and perhaps chemically induced smile. Other people, fewer in number, were visitors like himself, looking hot and uncomfortable in their darker, heavier clothing. There was a certain mood to these groupings, a sense of discomfort, as though everything of any use had been said and done already, and now the empty minutes of the rest of visiting time were to be somehow endured.

Nyquist found Eleanor sitting alone on a bench, gazing

into a pool of water. His first thoughts were spoken out loud, entirely unbidden: "Thank Apollo, you're all right. You're alive." But there was no active response to this. He carried on watching for a moment, unseen as yet. The girl looked different, healthier, with more weight to her body; but older too, sadder, subdued almost. She was dressed in the standard light blue tunic and was holding a closed paperback book in one hand.

"Eleanor?"

The girl murmured in reply, nothing that could be heard. She had not yet looked up from the pool, where red and gold coloured fish swam lazily through the shallows. Nyquist took a step closer, careful not to make any sudden moves.

"I've brought your belongings. Your clothes."

Eleanor looked up for the first time. Her eyes were lifeless, glazed over, and it seemed that she didn't recognise her visitor at all. But then she moved her head slightly and said, "Nyquist? The private eye?"

"Yes, it's me."

He handed her the green duffle bag. Eleanor took hold of it as though it were some strange, alien object. A slight smile came to her lips. "What do you mean?" she said. "I'm alive? Of course I'm alive."

So then, she had been listening. There was still a mind at work, somewhere in there.

"That's good," he replied. "Alive is good."

She started to look through the bag.

Nyquist glanced over at a young couple on a bench not too far away. They looked for all the world like two lovers who have just had their first real argument and were shocked into silence by its burning message that perhaps love is not forever. A bird twittered away in a nearby tree.

"What is this place, Eleanor?"

"Day and night. Night and day. The one following the

other. As it should be. As nature intended it."

Nyquist looked up at the artificial sun, seen through the glass roof. He could almost believe it was real, the light was so perfect, so unlike the fake suns of Dayzone. Reaching out to the nearest tree he parted the leaves, revealing a small mechanical canary fixed to a branch. It chirped merrily.

"They lock the doors," the girl said.

"Sure. It's a prison. And don't tell me, Patrick Bale is one of the benefactors."

There was no reply to this. The girl's attention had wandered.

"Eleanor? Are you on medication?"

"Little white pills. Happy pills. But shhh…"

"What?"

She lowered her voice. "I've thrown mine in the water. Well half of them, anyway. Do you see how slowly the fish are swimming?" She laughed at this.

Nyquist didn't know whether to believe her or not. He watched now as she pulled the bundle of yellow cloth from the bag. This was unwrapped with a careful hand, revealing the *wayang kulit* puppet within. Her fingers moved over the delicate leatherwork.

"He made this. My father."

"Dominic Kinkaid?"

"Of course." Eleanor smiled again. "He was very skilful. A very creative person." And then the joy left her face as quickly as it had come. "They wouldn't let me go to the funeral. That's one reason why Patrick put me in here, to keep control of me."

"And what else?"

"Because of my power. My power over time."

"Now what the hell does that mean?"

She looked at him. Her eyes were brighter than before, and more intense. He felt unnerved under their stare.

"He's scared of me."

"Bale?"

"He hates me. He thinks I'll destroy his little world, his pathetic little city with its ever-growing tangle of timescales, that I'll make it disappear." Her voice rose in anger. "All he cares about is his wealth, and his stupid position in the world."

He was worried her outburst might bring an orderly along, but she immediately quietened and fell into a reverie. "Why have you come here, Nyquist? You hardly know me."

He told her straight. "I think somebody's trying to hurt you. They wish you harm."

She shook her head and stared into the water. A goldfish rose to the surface, caught a tiny insect, and dived back down again.

"You mean Patrick Bale?" she asked.

"No. Not him."

"Who then?"

Nyquist couldn't bring himself to tell Eleanor of the two shadow men who had attacked him, demanding her whereabouts.

"I want to help you, Eleanor. That's all."

"Why?"

He closed his eyes against the brightness of the garden. "Because I let you escape, and because I let your father – your real father – die in front of your eyes."

Now she was silent. Moments passed. The artificial birds sang their artificial songs in the trees.

"Tell me what happened, Eleanor. Why did you run away from home?"

She looked at the puppet in her hands and said, "I never got on with my father, with Patrick I mean, not really. And then one night I found some letters of my mother's, love letters, all from a man called Dominic. And that's where I found his photograph, with the letters."

"Were they dated?"

"Yes. But in some invented, romantic timeline. I couldn't work it out. But they were obviously old, years old. The later ones mentioned a child, a girl child." She was speaking quickly now, carried along by the story. "One thing was obvious. This was a man desperate to see his child. It was all there in the letters, all of it, handwritten on beautiful paper. I read and I read. And… and suddenly it all made sense. This was me, I was this man's child."

"What did you do?"

"I spoke to my mother. But she just started babbling away, even crazier than usual. Then I asked Patrick."

"And?"

"Well, he admitted it. It took him a while to do so, and he was very upset by it all, but finally he told me the truth. I wasn't his daughter. I was the child of Dominic Kinkaid. But he forbade me from seeing him. Of course, that just made me more determined."

Eleanor stopped speaking. Her eyes had drifted back to the pool.

Nyquist prompted her. "So you went in search of him, your real father?"

"Yes. I found out that he was working in a puppet theatre. Living and working there. A tiny place in Precinct Thirteen, in a town called Vespers. Do you know it?"

"No."

"It's in Nocturna, but right on the edge of twilight. So only a very few people dared go there." She smiled at the memories. "It was a rundown theatre right on the fogline, where night faded into grey. He'd discovered the place when he was young and taken it over, teaching himself the puppeteer's craft." Her head tilted slightly. "I can remember first arriving there. I was really scared. But also excited. I've always been attracted towards dusk."

Nyquist found the idea incomprehensible. "Why?"

"I can't explain it. Everybody was always talking about how dangerous it was, but whenever the train passed over the borderline I would be drawn to the windows. I liked the shapes the mist made against the glass. When I was young I saw faces there, animals, all kinds of things conjured up by my imagination. And my body would shiver with excitement. It's not the kind of thing you admit to, right?"

Nyquist shook his head.

Eleanor smiled and continued. "Of course when I met Dominic Kinkaid, all of this... all of this yearning started to make sense."

"Tell me about the theatre."

"The building had no name, no sign out front, no official address in any brochure or anything like that. It was the kind of place you had to discover for yourself. But later on I found out it was called the Silhouette Theatre."

Nyquist remembered the photograph of Kinkaid with the two words written on the back: Angelcroft and Silhouette. Kinkaid's two residences, one on each edge of Dusk, dayside and nightside.

He sat down on the bench next to Eleanor, the better to hear. "So you went inside?"

"Yes. I went inside to meet with my father, my true father, for the first time in my life."

"How was it?"

"Awkward at first. Well, more than that. He wouldn't accept me. Not after all these years. But I kept on at him. And then it became a little better. And after a few visits, it was really good, very natural." She smiled to herself. "We got on. We really got on well together. Better, I guess, than if I'd known him all my life. But things happen in strange ways, and you have to take advantage of them no matter, don't you?"

"You do, yes."

"I would leave the house as though on my way to

college; instead I would go to meet him. Sometimes we'd visit his house on the dayside border, on Angelcroft Lane, but mostly we stayed in the theatre. I would help out there, cleaning and tidying, reading scripts for him, things like that. And then Dominic started to teach me the basics of puppetry, how to make the shadows dance in the light." Saying this, Eleanor moved the puppet she was holding from side to side, lifting it up into the air and down again in a wavelike motion, as though on a journey. Her eyes brightened. "It was just the best time for me. The very best. I had found my place in the world at last." The puppet collapsed, dying in her lap. "After I'd been there a few times, he told me a little about his upbringing."

"Go on."

"He was born in Nocturna, but abandoned as a baby, left right on the fogline. And taken in by a woman who lived there, over the border."

"In the dusk?"

She nodded. "That's right. Does that scare you?"

Nyquist looked away from her gaze.

She continued, "This was his adopted mother. Aisha, he called her. Right there in the mist, in twilight. He spent his childhood days in there, never seeing a bright light, or true darkness."

"Nobody lives inside Dusk, Eleanor. It's not possible."

"Believe what you like. I know what I've seen. I've stood on the edge with my father, even taken a few steps into the mist. People do live in there." She screwed her eyes half shut. "They have faces made of fog."

Nyquist came alert, hearing this. "I've seen such people," he said.

"You have?"

"Yes, but outside of Dusk, they came to find me. They wanted…"

"What?"

He didn't answer her. Instead he asked her to carry on.

"And once I saw Aisha herself. Just the once. She came very close to me, right to the edge of Dusk. She was a bit scary, to be honest. An old, old woman, staring at me with these really intense yellow eyes. She was close enough to breathe on me, and fog came out from her mouth, it wrapped itself around my face." Eleanor shuddered. "Apollo knows what she did to Dominic when he was a child, but she changed him, I know that. He was half in love with her, and half terrified."

Nyquist asked, "You didn't mention any of this to Patrick? Or to your mother?"

Her reply to this surprised him. She said, "We're all corrupt, you do know that? The whole family."

"Why do you say that?"

"It's the truth." She stared at Nyquist. "We're cursed. I saw it all around me. The way Patrick conducted his business, motivated by his own desires alone. So then, no, I didn't mention anything to him. How could I? He would ban me from seeing Dominic, that was obvious. And well, with my mother... it's difficult."

"Yes. I've talked to her."

Eleanor nodded. "You'll know what I mean then."

"You like your mother, don't you?"

"Yes, I do. Of course I do. But she's been terribly damaged."

"By what?"

"By life." The girl closed up a little. "You know how it gets sometimes."

"Tell me."

"My mother would sometimes disappear. This is when I was younger, nine or ten. She would get in the car and drive away, herself driving, no chauffeur. Oh, she was quite lucid at times, back then, perfectly capable of looking after herself. For a time at least."

"Where did she go?"

"I used to think outside the city. Now, I'm not so sure. There was… there was such a blank despair in her eyes, whenever she came back, such distance. I believe now…" She blinked back tears. "I believe she was going to visit Kinkaid on the edge of Dusk, or even further. I imagined her walking over the edge, following her lover, the mist swirling around them as they embraced."

"What about Patrick? He didn't mind her going off like this?"

"He would never admit to such feelings, no."

"You've had a strange upbringing, Eleanor. You do know that?"

She gave him a deep, intense look. "Ever since I was a little girl, I've had the feeling that something was missing from my life. Something taken away from me. I can't explain it."

By now her arms were clasped around her chest, as a shiver ran through her. Nyquist was feeling a little cooler himself. The quality of the air seemed to be changing; he couldn't work it out at first, and then he understood. The garden was slowly becoming darker. They were turning the lights down, degree by degree. Soon, the staff would be asking him to leave. He needed to find out as much as he could, before then. He said, "What happened next, with Dominic?"

Eleanor rubbed at her eyes to clear them. "The next time I went round to see him, the theatre was closed up, locked. Nobody answered. But I had the sense that he was inside, hiding from me."

"What did you do?"

"I broke in, of course."

Nyquist smiled. "Of course."

"It was an old place, like I said, and the windows were rotten anyway."

"And was he there?"

"He was." She looked saddened.

Nyquist kept his voice as quiet as hers. "Go on."

She took a deep breath and said, "I found him cowering in a corner of his workshop. There were half-finished puppets hanging all around in the dim light. And he looked the same, himself. Half-finished, I mean. In a terrible state. It frightened me."

"What was wrong with him?"

"His eyes stared at me out of the shadows, and yet I felt that they looked through me. Right *through* me. It gave me the shivers. And then... and then he told me the truth. The terrible truth, of what he was."

Eleanor fell quiet. She folded the puppet into its cloth, placing it back inside the duffle bag. Nyquist let her be for a moment. He reckoned he had about ten minutes before visiting hours ended. He was about to ask her to carry on, when she began again of her own accord, the words tumbling out now.

"I ran. It was all I could think to do. I ran away from there, from him. From everything. From my home, my college, my life." Her hands clenched and unclenched on her lap. "I was in despair. I stopped eating. I stopped caring about myself."

"So you ended up in Burn Out, in the room of lights."

She nodded. "I needed to get clean, to be cleansed of what Dominic had revealed to me. To get it all *burned* away, in the heat. And the other kids there were as troubled as I was, in their differing ways. They welcomed me."

"Sure. And then I kicked down the door and messed up everything."

Eleanor slipped her paperback book into the duffle bag and tightened the drawstrings. "Something like that."

"This is very important, Eleanor. Look at me." She did so. "What did Kinkaid tell you that was so bad?"

She hesitated. Nyquist could tell she was on the edge of confession. He repeated his question, as quietly as he could.

"What was so bad, Eleanor?"

She was whispering to herself. He leaned in to hear her.

"I had to kill him. I had to. I had to kill him." Her body had tensed up as she repeated the phrase. "I had to kill him. I had to."

"You've killed somebody?"

She looked at him, her face stricken. "Didn't you see me?"

"No."

"I killed him. I stabbed him in the neck. My own father. I had to."

"You mean Kinkaid?"

"He told me to do it. He pleaded with me, and he handed me the knife. I'm certain of it. I murdered him."

"Eleanor. Believe me, that didn't happen. I was there. I never saw that."

"What did you see?"

"I... I don't know."

She laughed bitterly. "But I had to do it, don't you see. I had to stop him from killing again. Because of who he was."

"I don't understand. Who was he?"

Her eyes were pierced with daylight as she revealed her secret.

"Quicksilver."

Nyquist felt his heart grow cold.

A bell started to ring out amongst the trees. Eleanor said, "There's the signal. It's the end of visiting hours."

A nurse walked by, saying, "It's time to leave now, sir."

Nyquist stood up. He shook his head. "I need to stay a little longer."

"That's not possible, I'm afraid. We close at seven."

"Seven o'clock?"

"Yes, sir. And we're running late, as it is."

"What time is it now?"

"It's five past."

The nurse walked on. Nyquist turned to Eleanor. "There's something wrong."

"What is it?" she asked.

"It's wrong. It's the wrong time. I thought this place closed at nine."

"It does."

"But the nurse said it was gone seven."

"I didn't hear her."

Nyquist looked back along the path, but the nurse he had spoken to was not to be seen. The clockwork birds fell silent in the trees, as the glass roof overhead started to darken. A line of shadow was crossing the courtyard. Nyquist watched it approach in fear.

Eleanor said, "Night is falling."

The golden fish in the pool were slowing to a halt as their mechanisms shut down. Nyquist backed away, but could not move quickly enough. He cried out, "I can't do this... No! Don't let it touch me." The leading edge of the shadow crossed his face, painting his skin with dusk's silvery grey colours. He closed his eyes, opened them again, and now the garden was filled with mist. Eleanor rose up before him from the bench, a ghostly form. One of the male orderlies was approaching. Nyquist felt strange, unearthed from himself, as he watched the orderly bend down to pick up a silk scarf that one of the other visitors had dropped. Nyquist could not see the man's face properly, it seemed to be covered in a mist of its own. A shadow man. He was standing behind Eleanor now, his hand coming up holding the scarf. Nyquist saw the hands loop over the girl's head, bringing the scarf into position against her face; he saw the orderly pulling the scarf tight so that Eleanor's face was outlined beneath; he saw the girl's mouth open wide beneath the cloth, desperate to suck in air, failing, her hands coming up to try and pull the scarf away, clawing at it, but it was no good, she was suffocating...

"What is it? Nyquist, what's wrong?"

It was Eleanor, talking to him. Alone, untouched. He heard her voice from far away, like a caller from another land, and then the line of dusk passed over him entirely and he was returned once again to the garden, to the Aeon Institute.

It had lasted a few moments only, this slow sweep of twilight across the garden, but during this whole passage his face had turned stark with fear. Now darkness had fallen over the flowers and trees. Artificial stars had taken the place of the fake sun, and wailing sounds could be heard coming from the upper galleries of the building.

Eleanor said, "Nyquist, wake up."

There was no sign of the shadow man. Had it all been a vision? Orderlies were urging visitors to make their way out. "It's nine o'clock," one of them shouted. "Please vacate the garden." Torch beams moved back and forth through the dark. Nyquist was forced into action by the sight.

"Come on." He grabbed hold of Eleanor's arm.

"Hey!"

"It could happen anywhere. Anywhere!"

"What can?"

"Never mind. We're getting out of here. Just do what I say."

He pulled her along, towards the garden's nearest exit door.

THE MINUTE HAND

Nyquist didn't know how he was going to find a way out of the place, just that he had to do it. This girl had taken over his life, just as the case had infiltrated his everyday purpose. He moved quickly down an ill-lit corridor, pulling Eleanor behind him. She had the green duffle bag with her, which she clung onto like a sacred object. Two orderlies entered the corridor some way ahead and started walking down it. They looked to be big guys, the sort who might take charge of the heavier, more violent patients. Nyquist dragged Eleanor around a corner, into a second corridor. Here another member of staff was seen, a doctor. Nyquist tried the nearest door. It was locked. He tried the next and this opened at his touch and he pushed Eleanor through, followed her and then pulled the door shut.

It was dark inside. Nyquist held the girl close to him, his hand over her mouth to keep her from making a sound.

He listened.

All was quiet outside, but a noise was heard from further inside the room. It was a small cry of pain. Nyquist turned to the sound. Artificial moonlight had crept in through a grilled window, but hardly enough to see by. And then a small desk lamp clicked on and a young man's face appeared in the glow. He was sitting at a table, staring intently at the items that lay before him: the many pieces of an antique clock – the large dial, a pendulum, the hour and minute hands removed and separated, hundreds of cogs and jewels and springs and wheels. He picked up two of the cogs and tried to fit them together. Then he looked up.

Nyquist put his finger to his lips, to urge the young man into silence.

The patient obeyed his order.

Footsteps were heard as the doctor passed by outside.

The girl struggled. Nyquist held her more tightly.

He whispered, "Keep still. Shhh!"

Without warning the young patient swept the wooden casing of the clock off the table. It clattered on the hard floor. He started to howl, a long continuous sound that rose in pitch. There was no stopping him. Nyquist looked on in horror.

A knock came at the door.

Nyquist could hardly think straight. He had to do something. He had to move fast.

The doctor entered the room.

He looked at the young man at the table, who was now merely staring into space, his hands linked together on the tabletop amid the scattered clock parts.

"What is it, Anthony? Are you sickening–"

The words were cut off as Nyquist pressed the long brass minute hand of the clock against the doctor's neck. The sharpened tip dug into flesh. The man froze. His voice stuttered.

"Uh, uh, ugh!"

"Do you feel that?" Nyquist said, close to the man's ear. "Do you feel it? Cold and sharp and painful?"

The man nodded as best he could.

"It's a knife. The shiniest knife you've ever seen. You got that?"

"Yuh!" The doctor was terrified.

"What's your name?"

"Leonard."

"OK, Leonard, let's take this nice and slowly..."

Moments later the doctor was being force-marched down the corridor, Nyquist behind him, holding the clock's hand tight against the small of his captive's back. Eleanor followed. She was fearful herself, too scared to be left behind, too scared to go forward. Nyquist urged her on. An orderly was approaching, leading a couple of female patients, both of whom appeared to be half asleep. Nyquist dug the metal point a little deeper into the doctor's back, tearing the cloth of his jacket. Metal touched flesh. He whispered, "Be nice." The orderly and the two patients were nearly upon them. The doctor grimaced and the orderly was obviously confused by this signal. But all seemed fine, and they were safely passing along. Nyquist felt he might be getting away with it when one of the patients suddenly lurched out of her sleepwalking state. She reached out with both hands toward the doctor.

Nyquist lost his nerve. He reached up and pulled back on the doctor's neck with his free arm. The doctor managed to blurt out, "He's got a knife!" And then the arm lock tightened. The little group was held motionless for a few seconds, until Nyquist pushed the doctor on violently, saying, "Keep moving!" They turned a corner. He could feel Eleanor hanging onto his jacket from behind. She had fallen in step with the plan, whatever it might be.

An alarm bell rang out, piercing the shadow-lit corridor.

The locked gateway could be seen ahead, with a number of security guards waiting there. Doctor Shapiro was standing close by.

Nyquist pushed the captive doctor forward a few more steps and then pulled him up short. "We're going through," he called out.

Shapiro looked at Nyquist through the bars. "Now then. Let's not–"

"Open the gate."

"Don't do anything stupid–"

"Open the gate! Come on. I'll knife him!"

Nyquist pressed the metal in, hard. The doctor shrieked in pain and fear. He cried out to the guards, "Do it. Do it!"

Shapiro looked confused. He said, "Eleanor can't leave. Her father specifically asked that we–"

Nyquist cut him off, saying, "Patrick Bale is not her father."

"What?"

Nyquist nodded towards Eleanor. "Tell him. Tell him!"

The girl hesitated for a second, before calling out, "It's the truth. Bale isn't my father."

"Her real father's dead," Nyquist added. "Murdered. Now open the bloody gate!"

Nothing happened. Nyquist felt something flash inside his head. Anger lit a bulb in the night. It made him pull back with all his strength on the doctor's neck, bending him over, and at the same time digging the sharp metal into his flesh, drawing blood. The doctor cried out, "Ah! No. No!"

"One more chance. Open the gate!"

Shapiro waited for a moment. Then he stepped back a little, nodding to one of the guards. This person unlocked the gate. The door opened.

Nyquist pushed his captive forward. He turned to the girl, saying, "Come on, keep up," and they moved off together, the three of them, along the main corridor. The front doorway lay ahead and they passed through safely. Some of the visitors were chatting to each other outside, near their cars, and they looked on in surprise as Nyquist bundled the doctor down the steps to the pavement.

The air was dark. A single arc light shone down from a pole.

Nyquist let go of the doctor's neck, while still keeping the clock's minute hand in place. He used his free hand to pull the car keys from his pocket. He threw these to Eleanor, yelling at her to get inside. She did so with no hesitation.

Members of staff were standing at the top of the steps, watching all this. Two security guards were marching forward, batons in their hands.

Nyquist forced the doctor to his knees, saying, "Stay there."

"I'm doing it. I'm doing it!"

The clock's hand fell to the floor.

Nyquist ran to the car. He got in behind the wheel, fumbling with the ignition key. But then the engine started and the car moved off, clipping the side of another vehicle before he got control and they drove away at speed.

The girl was screaming madly beside him. Yet when he glanced over, he saw that her face was lit up with joy.

EXTRA SPECIAL FOR FUGITIVES

These were the back streets of a rundown part of town. Nyquist turned the steering wheel to the left and right as needed, working on autopilot. His face was set hard, his bones and skin unmoving. So many thoughts were flickering through his mind. He dwelt more than once on the image of the front door of his apartment still being smashed in, left unlocked. It seemed to symbolise the fact that his life had swerved off its usual pathways. He stopped at a set of muted traffic lights and turned to look at Eleanor.

The girl was sitting there, hugging the duffle bag to her stomach like a comforter. All of her previous excitement had left her. Nothing was said.

He thought back to the vision he'd received in the garden of Aeon. Again, Eleanor Bale was being killed, by a scarf this time, strangulation. Perhaps the future wasn't fixed in place, perhaps several futures were fighting for position? Maybe, just maybe a future existed in which she didn't die, in which he saved her…

The very thought of it made his heart glow.

Could he dare to believe such a thing?

The road unravelled in the dipped headlights. He'd lost all sense of how long they'd been travelling for, but felt they'd gone far enough. He turned into an alleyway, where he brought the car to a halt. The place was thick with darkness, so the midnight blue vehicle practically disappeared.

The noise of the engine died. Silence.

Eleanor frowned. "What now? You're not taking me home, are you? Because I really don't want to go home."

He reached under the seat, pulling out the gun. The girl's eyes widened at the sight.

"Out. Now."

She did as she was told. Nyquist got his various things together and followed her. They started to walk down the alleyway, away from the vehicle.

"Keep up," he said.

"Where are we going then? Your place?"

"No. They'll be looking for us there."

"Will they get the police onto us? I mean, have we broken the law? Lord Apollo, this is incredible."

"Bale is powerful enough. He doesn't need the police."

"Just how many laws have we broken?"

"Quit talking. You're giving me a headache."

They came to an avenue where dead neon signs hung over closed-down cinemas, casinos and theatres. Once an area of lavish entertainments, now a zone of deserted dreams. The people on the streets were desolate types in the main, who turned away hastily from Nyquist's hard stare.

A little later Eleanor said, "I'm hungry. I'm tired. Please let's stop somewhere. Let's eat. My feet ache."

They were walking down a narrow side street.

"Here, this will do it."

Nyquist went up to the front door of a small, dark, pitiful building called the Starblind Hotel. The foyer was smelly and gloomy, but this would do them just fine. He handed over some cash to the person behind the desk, a dirty looking man with untidy hair and pocked skin. "The two of you, is it?" he asked. "Just the one room?" He gave Eleanor a salacious look. His tongue licked at his thick wet lips.

"Just the one," Nyquist told him. "That's right."

"Nice. Very nice."

Eleanor made a face. "Ugh. Disgusting."

"Ah! Spirit. I like that in a woman."

"Just give us the key," Nyquist said.

"Surely. I can see that you're keen. But you know, we're very crowded at the moment. We have a convention going on. See there?"

Nyquist turned to look at a poster board announcing the Third Annual International Convention of Whispering Poets.

Nyquist shook his head at this.

"But don't worry too much," the man behind the desk continued. "They won't disturb you much. Quiet souls, really. You'll hardly know they're here."

The keys were handed over.

"One more thing," Nyquist said.

"Ask away."

"We never stopped here. Right?"

The man sneered. "Of course not. We're very discreet, when needed." He laughed and then he mumbled something under his breath. Nyquist came in close.

"What was that?"

"I said: May the night gently enfold the both of you in her arms."

"What are you talking about?"

"Poetry, sir. Extra special. No charge for fugitives."

He bowed deeply.

Nyquist followed Eleanor to the stairs.

A FEW SECONDS OF LIFE

It was a small room near the top of the hotel. A three-quarter bed, a wooden chair, a basin. That was it. A ten-watt bulb whose light died within inches of its shade. No clocks, no radio, no telephone. The only window was covered with slats, and every so often a train would pass by on an elevated track outside, close up and very loud. The two people occupied this tiny space as best they could. Eleanor Bale was sitting on the bed, finishing off a surprisingly tasty room-service meal. Nyquist was leaning against the wall, drinking from a half bottle of whisky. He'd had a wash and combed his hair. He felt little better for it, but it was all he could do to keep his mind at bay.

"You like to drink, don't you?" Eleanor said. "What are you doing, numbing the pain?"

"Just finish your meal."

"I'm done. What now? What are we doing here? Why did you kidnap me?"

"You think that's what I did?"

"What else can it be?"

"I rescued you."

The girl laughed. "You rescued me?"

"That's what I did." He took another drink.

"Oh. Right. So let me go then."

"I can't."

"Why not?"

"It's too dangerous."

"And how exactly are you going to help me? By drinking too much and waving that stupid gun around. Is that it?"

He didn't answer.

"I saw a movie once, with a guy just like you in it, a man who was constantly running from one threat or another." She paused. "He died at the end. Shot down in a hail of bullets." She imitated the noise of a gun firing. "Bam! Bam, bam, bam!"

"What time is it?" he asked.

She smiled at this. "You do realise the absurdity of that question?"

"I've left my watch in the car."

"Let's go and get it–"

"No! No, we stay here. Tell me about Quicksilver."

She sighed. "What's to say? He killed some people. So I killed him."

He recalled his attacker's message: *Quicksilver awaits you.* Which implied not only that Nyquist was targeted as a victim, but that Quicksilver was still alive.

He said, "Eleanor, what if you've got it wrong? What if Kinkaid wasn't Quicksilver? Then you've killed an innocent man."

"He confessed."

"And you believed him?"

"Why would he lie to me?" She hesitated, and then continued, "That's why I went back to see him, at Angelcroft, to confront, to see if it really was true. Well... he told me it was. He insisted. And that's when you arrived."

"I heard you say, 'It's my fault. It's all my fault.' You were looking down at your father's body."

"Well there it is. Actually, I wasn't sure at the time. But now I know."

"Do you think it's your right to kill a man like that, to be judge and jury?"

"No."

"So you're saying–"

"Oh for heaven's sake! No one else could've done it. No one! Kinkaid would never have been caught. He'd just slip back into Dusk."

"I didn't see it happen. That's the trouble I have with your story. I didn't see you kill him."

"Well that just frightens me."

"Why?"

"I don't think you'd understand, a man like you…"

Nyquist looked at her. Tiredness caught up with him. He took another drink. Then he sat down on the chair and lowered his head into his big, scarred hands, and he stayed like that for a good while. Neither of them spoke a word. A train moved past outside the window, casting its flickering black and white patterns over the hunched figure, the noise of the engine and the carriages deafening. And then the silence and the barred shadows closed in once again. The shadows held Nyquist within them like a man in a cage.

Eleanor said quietly, "You're scared, I can see that."

He didn't look up.

"I saw your face in the garden, Nyquist, as twilight fell. You're terrified of the dusk."

"Why don't you keep quiet? Let me think."

"Sure. You do that."

Eleanor upended the duffle bag and started to go through her belongings, the bunched-up clothing and the shadow puppet, the postcard from her friend holidaying on the French coast. She gazed at the image of the beach and smiled to herself. Then she found the photograph of Kinkaid and her expression changed utterly, becoming a strange mixture of loss and disgust as though she couldn't decide on which emotion to go with.

"What was Kinkaid's power?" Nyquist asked.

She didn't answer.

"Eleanor? You have to start helping me. You have to believe me, your life's in danger."

Now she looked at him, disgust having won its place. "What the hell do you know? I mean, really? You don't know anything about me, or my life."

Nyquist held his hands up in surrender. But she wasn't taking it.

"You're a sad and lonely little guy, aren't you? Behind the muscle and the scars."

He shrugged in response.

"Were you ever married?"

"Once upon a time."

"Children?"

"It didn't last long enough for all that."

"I'm not surprised."

He kept the hurt hidden, as best he could manage. He walked over to the window, looked out at the dark streets below, the few lights on display in the buildings on the other side of the train track. Life went on behind the shades and drawn curtains: people in love, families, eating, chatting, listening to the radio, playing board games.

"What's this?"

Nyquist looked over. She had pulled the music box from her bag.

"Your mother, Catherine, she placed it on Kinkaid's grave. You have to lift up the lid."

She did so and the melody rose into the air. It sounded very ordinary now, a few brittle notes plucked by a metal plectrum, almost pitiful. Had he read too much into it?

"I thought it belonged to you, as a toy."

"No."

"From your childhood..."

"I've never seen it before." She closed the lid. "Another mistake."

"Give it to me."

She handed it to him. He lifted the lid and listened, searching for a memory, something from his own childhood.

It wasn't there. It was dead. Dead and buried.

He threw the box to the floor and brought his boot heel down on it, breaking it in two.

"Oh my god!" cried Eleanor. "What is wrong with you?"

Nyquist stared at her. Her hands punched the air.

"You're crazy," she yelled. "I actually think you're halfway disturbed."

"I'm doing what needs to be done." He wiped at his face with his hand. "What does the time seven past seven mean to you?"

"Nothing. Why?"

"Think! Seven minutes past seven. It must mean something."

Eleanor ignored the question. Instead she started to push her belongings back in the bag. She stood up.

"Where are you going?" he asked.

"I need to get out of here."

"That's not going to happen."

"This is ridiculous. I'm leaving. Open the door."

"Sit down."

"Give me the key."

"Sit the hell down!"

Nyquist's face had a brutal look, there was no arguing with it. Eleanor sat down on the edge of the bed. She said, "You're as bad as they are, as bad as Kinkaid and Bale."

"Yes. I'm sorry."

"What is it?" she asked. "What's wrong with you?"

Nyquist took a breath. His eyes held too much darkness. And then he said, "I have no parents. None. My mother died when I was young, a boy. My father left me shortly afterwards. I was eight years old. He walked off into the dusk."

"Oh."

"There it is."

"You poor man. How on earth did you manage?"

All emotion had left his face. "I got by. I'm still doing it." The bare code of living. "It drives me forward. It pulls me back."

"How did she... how did your mother die?"

"Run over. I was there with her, standing on the pavement. My father was coming to pick us up, but he was late. He drove a red saloon. I'll always remember that car. He'd been drinking with his friends. As always. Mother bent down to wipe dirt off my face, then turned and stepped out into the road. Without looking. He didn't stop. He did not stop. My father..."

Nyquist stared into space, his face and eyes taken over by the memories. The old traffic lights and road signs flickered over his features, his mother's hand in his for that last moment, the speeding red car still swerving, the cry, the noise her body made when it broke, when it broke apart. His father's face behind the wheel, the look of utter despair...

The girl stared at him without speaking.

"It was an accident," he said. "He never meant to..."

He couldn't finish the sentence. The shadows grew along the walls and ceiling like a sickness.

He felt at his throat. "I need a drink."

"There's no more."

"I need something."

"Let's ring down, we'll get you some–"

"No." His head shook violently. "I have to... I have to keep..."

"You don't look too good, Nyquist."

Another train passed the window. It was so loud, it sounded like it was almost inside the room with them. Lines of shadow and light crossed Nyquist's face. His parents stood in opposite corners of the room, staring at him.

He waited until the sound had fallen away and the vision had faded. Then he said, simply, "That's how it is. One moment. That's how we lose people."

Eleanor whispered, "I'm so sorry."

Nyquist grunted. His eyes narrowed. "Tell me. Have you heard of a girl called Elise?"

"Why do you ask?"

"Or Eliza. Or Liz. Elizabeth?"

"My mother used to mention that name sometimes. Eliza."

"Eliza. Right."

"I thought she was an old childhood friend of my mother's, or a distant relative."

"You don't know?"

"It's difficult to unravel the truth from what she says."

Nyquist kept his voice level as he said, "I think she had another child."

Eleanor was shocked. "What?"

"Your mother. She had a second child. Another girl."

"That's not true. That can't be true."

"Are you sure?"

Her eyes lit up. "Lord Apollo. So they did have a child, Patrick and my mother." Her voice sped along, excited by the revelations. "Eliza. I wonder where she is. Do you know? This could explain a lot, about their relationship, I mean."

"It's not that easy. Patrick told me he was shooting blanks."

"What?"

"He's sterile."

"But that means…"

"It means your mother had two children by Kinkaid."

Her eyes screwed shut, as though to hide the truth from herself.

Nyquist asked, "Was your name mentioned in the letters you found, the ones Kinkaid sent to your mother?"

"My name? No, just… the girl. The girl. That's all it said."

"So it could be…"

"I've got a sister?"

"Maybe. I don't know. It might be…"

"What?"

"I think she died."

"No… don't say that."

"Your mother said as much. But of course…"

"How can we trust anything she says? We can't."

Nyquist shrugged.

Eleanor looked at him, her face beset with worry. "I can't take this in."

"It all depends. I might be wrong about Eliza. And Patrick might not be telling the truth about being sterile."

"Why would he lie about that?"

"I don't know. But this whole case was suspect, right from the very beginning, when Bale first employed me to find you."

"Yes. I know."

"People are keeping secrets, burying things. And you, Eleanor, you're tied up in it somehow."

"How?"

"I'm still figuring that out." He pulled the last of the orange vials from his pocket. "Have you ever taken this?"

She nodded. "Kia? Yeah, a few times."

"Why? What does it do to you?"

Instead of answering the question she looked at him and said, "Have you tried it?"

Something in his eyes or his gesture gave him away.

"I thought so. What was shown to you?"

"Nothing," he lied. "I fell asleep."

"Of course you did." She smiled. "Did it scare you? Or did it thrill you?"

He moved back to the window and its view of the nightbound city. Another train passed along the elevated track, right at his eye level. He could see the passengers – black shapeless figures in the barely lit carriages. A cargo of shadows.

The train vanished. He was aware that the girl was standing close behind him.

He didn't turn to her.

Quietly she said, "Can you hear them?"

He listened.

Yes, there they were...

Voices.

Many of them.

All murmuring through the walls.

He lowered his own voice as well. "Who are they?"

"The whisper poets. Shhh. They're reciting..."

Together they listened. No words were discernible, no lines of verse, only a soft hissing sound; and no meaning, only the sound itself, searching for meaning in the night, in the ill-lit realms of Nocturna.

She said, "I gave up on kia. I was getting addicted to it."

"What did you see?"

Her voice was still quiet, the speech split into fragments. "Myself. In dusk. Dancing. With a young woman. Under moonlight. It was... it was the most beautiful feeling I've ever known."

He waited a moment. The whisper poets continued.

He asked, "Do you think it's true, Eleanor, that kia reveals the future?"

"I don't know."

"Someone told me that you don't need the drug,

anyway. That you have control over time."

"They were lying."

"So you have no power…"

"Not power, no. Not control. But some small effect. It's chaotic. Watches, clocks, they might speed up or slow down in my presence. It started when I was young, a little girl. It happened only occasionally, and without my knowing when or how."

Nyquist thought back to the confusion he'd felt whenever he looked at his wristwatch, the hands slipping this way and that, the blurring of the dial; yes, the trouble had begun after his first meeting with Eleanor, after he'd held her hand in the room of lights.

"Is this why Bale tries to protect you so much?"

"Maybe. But I think the effect scares him, more than anything, because it can't be explained. Maybe he sees it as a random element that threatens to destroy all his carefully managed timelines. He's petrified there might be another time crash."

"His worst nightmare."

"Exactly."

He moved away from the window. "Tell me what you know about the kia drug."

"Kinkaid told me it came from the dusklands, from a flower that grows there."

"So Kinkaid was a dealer?"

"Yes. He admitted as such."

"And Bale?"

"He's in the chain as well. He's making a profit from it."

"Kinkaid told you this?"

She nodded. "But Dominic hated the drug himself. He said it was dangerous, and warned me off it. In fact…"

"Yes?"

Eleanor screwed up her face. "He told me that he regretted going into the business now. He'd made a mistake."

Nyquist sneered. "It's too goddamn late for regrets."

She turned away from the remark.

He watched her as she returned to the bed, to take her seat once more. Sometimes she was a teenager, a girl; while at other times she appeared older, beyond her age. He couldn't help feeling sorry for her. The poor kid had two fathers, and both of them were scum. Her life was a tragedy waiting to happen. And for some reason his life had joined with hers: two timelines crisscrossing in the night, under a scattering of stars, fusing for a while. And there seemed little way of escaping the pathway.

He spoke sharply to get her attention. "Eleanor. How did Quicksilver commit the murders without being seen? Did Kinkaid tell you?"

"He did."

"And?"

She looked down at her own hands where they rested in her lap. He waited. The room held them both in its bare, cold, dingy embrace.

Far off a train whistle called, a lost animal in the night.

Then silence.

Eleanor spoke at last. "He stole time."

Nyquist wasn't sure what he'd heard. "How do you mean?"

She sat up on the bed and told him what she knew.

"It's something Kinkaid was born with, something to do with the city, and with dusk in particular. And it only happened when he was in a certain mood, whether disturbed or fearful, or angry, and overtaken by emotions. He told me it first happened when he was a youth, around puberty." She paused. "He could never go far from Dusk without feeling weak. He said it was a bit like being a vampire in the daylight." She grinned at this memory, as Nyquist did a quick calculation in his head: yes, every Quicksilver killing had taken place in those populated areas that were closest to the fogline: Moonstruck, Fahrenheit, Glareville, Penumbra. In itself it meant little, but it added substance to Eleanor's claim. She carried on. "He was always being bullied, beaten up, especially by a gang of lads that used to hang around the dusk edge. They caught him spying on them one time and the leader made a big show of it, he really laid into Dominic. The others held him down as the leader punched at my father's face, over and over."

Nyquist watched her. She was telling the story from the inside out, as though she herself were the subject.

"He was helpless. In great pain. There was blood everywhere. In his eyes, his mouth. And the gang leader wouldn't stop. He just kept hammering him. And then it happened."

She stopped for a moment as she sought to get the details right.

"This is how he told it to me. He felt that he'd passed out. Or fainted. A blackout, he called it. In fact, a few seconds of his life had been taken away. One moment he was getting beaten to a pulp, and the next he was the one on top. There was no inbetween. And suddenly he had the advantage. His attacker was reeling backwards, as though he'd been punched. It was all Dominic needed, those few seconds. He managed to get to his feet and start to run. He escaped. And he didn't even know how it had happened. He didn't have a clue. Not until later, when it happened a second time. And then again, a third time."

"So this only happened when he was in danger?"

"In danger. In a rage. In pain. Or close to someone else's pain. And the more disturbed he was, the more terrible or dangerous the situation, the more time he could steal. When someone died, for instance, or was killed. Murdered. Then he might steal a minute or even more from everyone in the vicinity. But he didn't really have that much control over it, not to begin with. In fact the moment disappeared for him as well. Because he was also bound up in time, just as much as the victim was."

"So he couldn't remember what had happened during the blackouts?"

"No, only that something had taken place, usually to his advantage."

Nyquist looked at the broken pieces of the music box on the floor.

Eleanor carried on. "It's why nobody ever saw Quicksilver commit his crimes. One or two minutes of time had just *disappeared*. For everyone concerned. And all the witnesses saw was the beginning and the end of the sequence." Her eyes looked up as she remembered. "He told me it was like being on your own personal timeline, one that no one else can ever travel on, and when you're on it, it's like you're invisible. Time is still passing for you, and you can act within it; but you're *outside* of other people's time frame, don't you see? And then you strike!"

"And afterwards..."

"And afterwards, you're back in normal time. And the memory disappears."

Nyquist thought back to the news reports he'd read, and also to the room on the edge of twilight, to the moment of his own blackout, how events seemed to go missing from his sight, and from his memory.

"But why can't you remember what happened?"

"I don't know," she answered. "I really don't. I think Dominic knew, but he wouldn't tell me for some reason. But I see it as a scene cut out of a movie. Or like a tape recorder edit. The missing portion still exists, but separately from the rest of the film or the tape."

Yes, Nyquist could see that. The jump cut. It corresponded to what he'd experienced. Yet he found it so hard to comprehend.

"And you think you stabbed your father in that missing minute?"

"What else could have happened?"

"And what, Kinkaid's anguish, his pain, his body's final torment in some way activated the process?" She didn't answer. He carried on: "But how can you know for certain, Eleanor, if your own time was stolen as well?"

"I can't. All I see is darkness, like you. But I can feel the knife in my hand, I can almost see it there…"

"You were holding the knife, I saw that."

"Yes. Exactly."

They both fell silent.

"I don't know if I can believe this," he said. "Whole minutes can't just be taken away like that. Not from a person's life."

Eleanor nodded. "I know. It's difficult. But if there's one place on Earth where such a thing could happen, it's here, in Dayzone, or Nocturna. Here, where we've broken the hours down into fragments, into dust."

"And you're sure of all this?"

"Believe me, I know. Because…"

He waited. "Yes?"

"Because it wasn't Dominic that stole the time, not when he died. It was me. Because I can do it as well. He's passed it on to me." Her eyes blazed. "I'm Quicksilver."

ONE BY ONE, THE STARS

A little later he was standing at the window, looking out to where the stars flickered in the sky. It was a tempting illusion and like many citizens, Nyquist had easily fallen into the spell. But really he knew the truth, that the entire sky of Nocturna was made from old burnt-out lights. Only a certain number were still working, and these were the current stars. They fizzed and sparked. Perhaps it was raining, up above, in the real sky, in the real world, where time behaved normally.

He shivered. He knew none of the constellations in this area, not one. He was lost. And then he noticed a small, black-draped figure moving across the sky, not too far above the window. A lamp was being repaired.

Only a select band of bulb monkeys worked the darkness. It was seen as being one of the most revered and the most mysterious of all jobs in the city; but despite the workers' best and bravest efforts, he suspected that fewer and fewer of the bulbs were being replaced. One by one, the stars were going out. The night was growing darker.

And somewhere out there in the city...

Nyquist wondered about Patrick Bale, and what he must be thinking right now, the anger he would feel when he learned of Eleanor's escape from the Aeon Institute. It was easy to imagine the chief executive closing in, using his power and his money to seek out this damp, crumbling hideaway and the two people that occupied it.

Nyquist turned back to the room.

Eleanor was asleep on the bed, still fully clothed. A blanket had fallen off onto the floor. He pulled it back over her, and as he did so she murmured and her eyes fluttered. Her voice rose out of sleep. "I stole your time, Nyquist. I think I did. I'm so sorry. I couldn't help it." He made no reply and in a moment she was slumbering once more. It made him think back again to the room on the edge of twilight.

The death.

The knife entering Kinkaid's neck.

But whose hand had wielded the weapon, whose anguish had stolen the time away? Who was to blame, Kinkaid or his daughter? Nyquist couldn't tell. And neither could Eleanor. That was the problem; everyone contained within the moment of time was equally affected, equally lost. There was no way of knowing.

And yet if Dominic Kinkaid really was Quicksilver, then why would he commit a series of murders that he had no later knowledge of? To what end? No, it didn't make sense. There was something else going on that Nyquist could not yet understand. And the most disturbing question remained: if Eleanor Bale had really taken over the mantle of Quicksilver, if she'd inherited that terrible power in some way, as she claimed, then where would that lead? Would there be further victims?

Quicksilver awaits you…

One thing was certain: if Nyquist could only find out what had happened in the room on the edge of twilight, this case would be solved. Yet it seemed an impossible task, despite the fact that the answer lay somewhere inside his own head, painted over by darkness.

He sat in the wooden chair.

He was tired, and lonely. The girl had yelled at him, called him crazy. What was the phrase she'd used? *Halfway disturbed*. And maybe he was. But he had tried so hard. Nyquist had grown into adulthood determined to be a different kind of man than his father was, to be someone who didn't drink, who didn't hurt the ones he loved, didn't run away. And he shuddered as he recalled how he'd behaved with his wife, towards the end of their marriage, how he'd increasingly taken refuge in the bottle as the troubles set in.

He should've told Eleanor about the vision he'd received. But how can you reveal to somebody that you've seen them being killed? The moment of their death. Even if it was only imagined. No. It can't be done.

Nyquist looked at his wrist and cursed. He kept forgetting that he'd left his watch in the glove compartment of the hire car, parked in the alleyway.

His father's wristwatch. Would he ever see it again?

Well then. Let it be. Good riddance. He'd carried that old thing around for too many years now.

The spell was tightening.

Seven past seven... seven minutes past seven...

His mind drifted as his eyes closed.

The girl had confessed to murder. If he found out that she was speaking the truth, he would have to report the crime, he had no choice.

These were his last thoughts before sleep took him away.

He lay back in the wooden chair, his head resting against the grimy wall behind him. Bars of light patterned the room, moving across his body and then across Eleanor's form on the bed in fluid parallel lines, although the train's passage made no sound this time.

His mother was sitting in the bedroom alone, at her dressing table. She was brushing her hair one hundred times precisely, her lips mouthing the numbers as always, every night the same. The brush moved slowly but firmly through the dark locks. The young boy liked to watch from the doorway. But now he was no longer young, no longer innocent; but he was still there at the bedroom door, fully grown, watching, hoping, praying that the brushing of the hair would never end, that his mother would never rise, never leave the house, never stand at the pavement's edge, never step out into the road...

Nyquist couldn't work out where he was when he first woke up. He felt terrible, aching from the awkward sleeping position, his joints painful. He thought he'd only slept for a moment or two, but how could he tell? It might've been an hour or more.

And then he noticed that the bed was empty.

The girl was gone.

His immediate thought was that she'd been taken, kidnapped while he slept. No. The room was too tidy. He reached inside his jacket pocket, searching in vain for the door key. He stood up and went to the door. It was open, just slightly, the key in the lock. He looked back into the room. Eleanor had taken all of her things.

"Damn it."

Then he heard noises from the landing. Voices. Loud. Angry. He got to the door, closed it and turned the key in the lock. Just as he did so, somebody tried turning the handle from the outside, trying to get in. The lock held. A fist banged against the panelling.

Then: "Nyquist! Open up!" A woman's voice.

It was Pearce. Bale's assistant. Nyquist held his breath.

"Come on. We only want the girl, nothing else."

He heard talking: Pearce and someone else, a man's voice. But it didn't sound like Bale. Probably one or more of the company's bodyguards. Now the fist banged again on the door, more insistent. The door rattled in the frame.

Somebody was trying to fit a second key into the lock, but the key on this side was preventing access. Pearce made a brutal curse, which was closely followed by renewed violence against the door.

"I've got a gun," Nyquist shouted.

"We just want Eleanor, that's all, no trouble."

He pulled the gun from its holster, slipped off the safety catch and fired it, all in one nervous action, so that the bullet hit the wall above the door, tearing a hole in the cheap plaster: a warning shot. The noise was deafening.

Screaming, shouts from the corridor. Smoke from the barrel, white dust floating down. The smell of it inside Nyquist's mouth and nostrils.

He hoped the shot would buy him enough time. He slipped the gun back into the holster and then rushed to the window. He tore aside the slatted blind and tried to lift up the sash. It was nailed shut, it wouldn't budge. He grabbed the wooden chair and swung it around in a wide arc to smash against the window, shattering the glass. There were still jagged edges in the frame; he knocked a few of them out and then climbed up, over the sill. He scrambled through.

Outside.

He was standing on a narrow window ledge, three storeys above the street. It was pitch black except for a line of small red lights which lined the elevated train track. The lights blinked on and off. Nyquist peered into the darkness. Blood dripped from his left hand, where he had cut it on the glass. He felt no pain. His body trembled on the very edge of falling, the sickening drop, the street far below, passing cars, concrete. Ahead, he could just about make out the steel and wood structure of the train line's platform, stretching out to either side. But how far away was it exactly? Three feet? Or four, or five or six? More than that, even? His vision was hazy. He could not judge distance correctly. What was he doing up here, what was he thinking? And then he heard the hotel room door splintering open. There were no choices left to him, none at all, and so he pressed his hands against the window frame as hard as he could on both sides, he bent his knees and then leaped out into space.

The sudden cold rush of air.

The red lights.

Emptiness.

The night, the night's breath on his face and the cold stars looking down, looking out for him, lighting his way in the darkness.

BLACKOUT

It was too far. His lower body missed the edge of the platform by inches, and he fell. His arms flailed in the void, managing to grab hold of a wooden strut. His fingers dug in tight, his wounded fingers, and he clung on above the street, above the people walking by down there, the good citizens of Nocturna. He felt that all his bodily knowledge rested in those fingers alone, those hands, these arms, the muscles, his chest, and then his legs and his feet as they found purchase on a steel girder. With an almighty effort he pulled himself up onto the wooden boards that skirted the train line. He was winded, out of breath. But there was no respite. He heard voices from the hotel's window, shouting at him, and he ran from them, along the platform, following the red marker lights as they pulsed in front of him. The metal tracks were vibrating, taking on a spirit. A train was speeding toward him. Time slowed down. For once time was on his side as he moved across one track, across the other. He could do this! His body knew precisely how long it would take, precisely where to place his feet, each step, each moment, and then the train's whistle blew and the passing locomotive sucked every last particle of air from his lungs, and he was over, he was across, clouded in smoke from the engine's funnel. He moved on a little further until he came to a ladder set in the structure's side, which he climbed down, sliding down the last few yards to the street.

Immediately, Nyquist set off running. He had to get away, to keep moving. He took the first turning he came to and then the next, through the narrow gloom-filled alleyways, along shaded underpasses, beneath the elevated streets. Around the next corner, keeping the trail cold, cold and complicated. The streets were empty to begin with, and then dotted with a few stragglers, and then more, until the entire way forward was crowded with people. A huge outdoor market bustled with life as hundreds of customers and revellers milled around stalls and kiosks. Here they gathered like candle-moths for their dark-eyed entertainments, and Nyquist welcomed their embrace. The stalls were selling torches, designer body-lamps, vampire lingerie and accessories, and a whole array of dolls and play figures representing famous Night Stalker ballad singers. Just about everyone was dressed in dark clothing with here and there dots and splashes of colour. Many of the shoppers had small lights attached to their outfits, and some of them sported paper lanterns dangling from antennae-like wires strapped to their heads. They looked like bizarre hybrid creatures, half human and half insect. A pair of buskers were singing melancholic nocturnes together. Their harmonies seemed to come to earth from some region of further darkness.

Nyquist walked along in a daze. He had slowed down, moving at the crowd's steady pace. He could feel the pain in his hand now, and he looked down to see the cut in the palm. It wasn't too bad, not too deep. He pulled out a piece of glass and wrapped his handkerchief around the wounded part, holding it tight against the cut to stop the blood. To stop the pain. The doubt. The case was unravelling, coming apart in his grasp. Once again, he'd lost Eleanor. She could be anywhere by now. But at least she had escaped Bale's heavies. He had to give thanks for that small mercy.

Before him stood the portable wagon of an itinerant clock-seller, where a vast mixture of illuminated wristwatches burned at the eyes, their iridescent dials glowing like sexually aroused beetles. Nyquist was pressed in on all sides by eager customers. The clock seller showed him a fake designer watch, which he bought without thinking. It cost next to nothing, a cheap plastic affair. The trader demonstrated the mechanism; by pressing on the dial, just so, the watch would light up in luminous green. Nyquist strapped the timepiece around his wrist and then activated the special feature. The dial shone with its own radiance.

It was twelve minutes to ten.

Oh, that felt good! The second hand moved around in its balanced rhythm, and his body responded; he could feel it, his heart, his blood. Time had hold of him once again, however gentle it might be, however crazed.

He moved on a little through the crowd.

And then he heard the voice.

It was a whisper at first, spoken by one person only.

Then another picked it up and passed it on.

Quietly.

Whisper upon whisper.

A single word passed from one person to another, gathering, growing louder.

Louder. More insistent.

Every mouth the same, the same word, the same emotion.

Fear.

Quicksilver.

Quicksilver. Quicksilver.

Quicksilver. Quicksilver. Quicksilver. Quicksilver…
Quicksilver!

Nyquist forced his way through a throng of people around a stall where a transistor radio was playing. He heard someone ask his neighbour: "What is it? What happened?"

"Another killing. A young man this time."

"Helios save me! Is it Quicksilver?"

"That's what they're saying."

And then the stallholder's voice rose about the tumult. "Quiet! Listen!"

They listened, huddled in a semicircle, as the news announcer spoke to them from the radio's speaker grille.

"…this time in Nocturna. Nobody saw anything…"

That was enough to set everyone chattering.

Nocturna

Whereabouts? Which precinct?

He could be anywhere, he could be among us!

But all Nyquist could think about was Eleanor Bale, the fact that she was out here in the streets. Had she told the truth about her powers? Had she left the hotel room, left him sleeping there for hours, and gone out, driven mad by her blood, by the force within, seeking her prey? Had she killed someone, a helpless victim?

Once the thought was in his mind, he couldn't get rid of it.

He escaped the crowd of listeners and walked onto a boulevard of shadows, a long wide street lined with night clubs and occupied by a tribe of Night Stalkers. Dark complex music sounded from the club doorways. Nyquist realised that he must have entered the Shadeville precinct, where tribes of Gothic persuasion lived. They were easily recognised, with their purple clothing, cobwebby hair, and their stark white faces offset by violet lipstick. They glanced at each other in a disaffected manner, their kohl-lined eyes turning away almost immediately. Evidently, the news of the latest Quicksilver killing hadn't reached them yet. Or else they were too caught up in their own fantasies to care.

Nyquist stumbled on. He'd seen a young woman ahead, moving away from him. It looked a little like Eleanor, but the figure vanished into the crowd almost immediately. He tried to push through, causing several people to hiss at him, like snakes. *Sssss!* Their tongues were dyed black or mauve and tipped with silver metal extensions. The music grew louder, more hypnotic. And then the woman came back into sight just as she turned off the boulevard, entering a side alley. Nyquist followed her.

Shadows moved in the darkness of the passage, set in motion by naked gas flames that flickered from high on the walls. A voice was booming out from a public address system: "Amidst grief and torment! Amidst grief and torment!" The passageway led to a small makeshift church where a preacher worked his congregation into a frenzy. "Verily, amidst grief and torment I did wander, alone, trembling beneath Dayzone's unforgiving glare. The artificial sun punished me. And though I tried to escape my suffering, I could never be free of myself, or my own torments." Nyquist moved through the gathering, searching for one face alone. The preacher roared on: "Only when I let myself fall into night's sweet embrace did I find my release. Therefore, in the soft darkness let us walk, all of us, seeking our salvation." A low rumbling drumbeat could be heard. And then Nyquist saw her once again, Eleanor Bale; she was walking through an open doorway at the back of the church. The drums pounded out as Nyquist followed her, onto open ground. The night air blossomed with sparks. A great line of people were carrying large illuminated lanterns up a hill, to where a bonfire blazed. The lanterns were designed to look like clocks of various types, shapes and sizes: hourglasses, sundials, giant pocket watches, old-fashioned alarm clocks, grandfather and grandmother clocks, traveller's clocks, carriage clocks. They were made of transparent materials stretched over wooden frames, and were lit from within by brightly coloured bulbs, in green, blue, orange, yellow and red. The parade moved up the hill like a long tail of daylight caught in night's grasp. Nyquist's face danced in the light. The music pulsed. He looked around, dodging between the procession, calling out, "Eleanor! Wait!" But the young woman carried on walking, away from the crowd and down the gentle slope of the hill. She passed beneath a streetlamp, just as Nyquist caught up with her and grabbed her by the shoulder, pulling her round to face him.

"Eleanor!"

"What is it?" The woman looked at Nyquist. "What do you want?"

"I... I'm sorry. I thought you were..."

The young woman's face was powdered to make her look like a ghost; her violet-coloured lips parted to form a smile.

Nyquist felt embarrassed. "I thought you were somebody else."

"I am," the stranger said, "every time I visit here."

And then she turned from him, walking quickly down the hill and disappearing into the shadows. Nyquist shook his head to clear it. His eyes were hurting. He was feeling sick, both exhausted and manic at the same time. At the top of the hill, the clocks were being thrown to the flames, as though time itself was being set on fire. The words of the preacher rang in his ears like a mantra. *Amidst grief and torment I did wander, alone, trembling. Amidst grief, torment, alone, trembling...* He pulled the square of linen off his hand and stared at the blood on his palm. It was useless. The handkerchief fluttered to the ground, a scrap torn from a shroud. As he turned to get back to the main road he bumped into somebody. He started to apologise, when the person's face moved into the light.

It was Pearce.

Nyquist had one split second of recognition, and then shock. And then a hand came round from behind, holding a cloth. This was clamped hard over Nyquist's mouth. The smell of petrol. And something else. A doctor's surgery, when he was a child. He couldn't process it. His heart was racing, the lights going out in his eyes, getting smaller and smaller, until a deeper shade of the night veiled him, like a mist that he fell into endlessly.

Blackout.

A TALK AMONGST FRIENDS

All was darkness, and in the darkness a woman singing.

La le laa la lele la…

Nyquist was roused slightly by the sound and his eyes came open, tiny slits, just enough to let him know he was slumped in the backseat of a car.

A moving car.

A neon sign shimmered in the night sky. Colours melting into other colours. Passing by. Sounds from an open window: laughter, cries of delight, car horns.

The world was blurred, at a distance.

Le lea la le la le laa…

The woman's voice came from the dashboard radio.

Nyquist was aware of a figure up front, driving, and somebody sitting to his side on the backseat. Now he could hear a voice, voices, the words muted.

"Take his gun off him."

"I am doing."

And then a hand covered Nyquist's face, closing his eyes once more and returning him to darkness. Where the song lived.

La le laa le lela le laa…

"Wake up. There's a good boy."

Nyquist's eyes came open a second time. He was sitting

in a wooden chair, that much he knew. His mind raced: I should most probably move on now, make a start on whatever it is I'm supposed to be doing, if I could only remember what that was exactly…

A man lurched into view, just for a second, before a cold weight of water hit Nyquist in the upper body and face, rousing him, almost knocking him back, drenching him. He heard the sound of a metal bucket being thrown away, tumbling over. Hard echoes on a concrete floor.

Silence. Water dripping from his body, his clothes.

Somebody slapped Nyquist on the side of the face, and then again, on the other side. He slumped down, his head falling into his chest. He could not move his arms.

Now he realised: his arms were tied to the chair behind his back.

He was helpless, trapped.

Nyquist tried to focus, to get a grip on the situation he was in, seeing dust in the air, and spotlights working in one corner, the rest in gloom. Hearing: what was that noise? Generator hum? Think. Where are you? Some kind of workplace, or a warehouse, something like that. Two figures moved by, their shapes indistinct. Another lamp came on, casting a circle of light over Nyquist.

And then the two people moved forward.

One of them was Pearce.

She walked up close to Nyquist, bending down to his level. "You little prick. Where is she?"

Nyquist could hardly move his lips. "Uh…"

"Where's the girl? Eleanor?"

"Don't…"

"Speak up."

"I don't…"

Nyquist couldn't hear himself properly, so the words had to be trusted from their feel in his mouth.

"I don't know."

The other person came into view suddenly, and carried the movement straight on to hit Nyquist hard around the face with a bunched fist. He was knocked to the side, the chair falling with him, his right shoulder smashing against the floor.

Sudden taste of blood in the mouth.

Pearce saying, "Go easy on him, Jacob. We need answers."

Jacob? Where had he heard that before? Memories pulled up: the Bale household, the maid Melissa speaking to one of the security guards. *It's all right, Jacob. I'll be fine here.*

Pearce was lighting a cigarette. "That's all we want, one little answer."

Nyquist spat out the blood, saying, "Go to hell."

"Now let's be reasonable. Just tell us where Eleanor is, and then we're done."

"I don't know. I really don't know."

Nyquist was wet and shivery, in pain, lying on his side on a hard stone floor. The chair was still attached to him by the ropes, making his position even more painful and awkward. It was humiliating. He was ashamed.

Pearce knelt down to his level, saying, "How much does the girl know?"

"About what?"

"About the drug supply."

"Kia?"

"What does she know?"

"Nothing. She's innocent."

Pearce sighed, her cigarette tip glowing. She stood up again, walked away. There was some kind of commotion, people talking. Nyquist turned his head to see the powerfully built Jacob dragging a large object across the floor, a dead weight of some kind, a human form. The body was dumped directly where Nyquist could see the face.

It was Sumak, the drug dealer from the Noonday Underground club. His pink suit was torn and dirty and his black hair had fallen forward over his gaunt features. At first, Nyquist thought he was dead, but then he saw that the man was breathing, only just. There were no obvious injuries, although his eyes were open wide and filled with a dreadful fear. He looked like a man who had seen a ghost, and found the ghost to be himself. His mouth was stained with the bright orange colour of the kia drug.

Pearce nodded. "One more application, and this man's dead meat." She bent down beside the dealer's limp form. "You see how it is, people are given jobs to do, and they don't do them. Instead, they steal the product off you. Now that's just not right. It's bad business practice." Grinning, she stubbed her cigarette out against Sumak's cheek. "Salesmen, eh? They can't be trusted."

The dealer hardly responded at all to the burn.

So Bale was involved in the drug trafficking: that part of Eleanor's story was true, at least. Behind the executive suit and the title, he was just a grubby little criminal in hiding.

Pearce came over to him. "You see what we do to those who betray us?"

Whispered: "I see it."

His interrogator smiled. "That's good."

Nyquist could feel Pearce's breath on his face and he cringed, expecting his skin to be burned. Instead, he felt himself being lifted up by Jacob, as Pearce said, "Now let's get you more comfortable." Lifted, chair and all, until he was sitting upright once more. And then Pearce reached down to lay a gentle hand beneath Nyquist's chin, to raise the half-broken face directly into the thin beam of light. Now the voice had a measured lilt to it. "You're in a right old state, aren't you? You look a mess, Nyquist. Dirty, filthy. And that's because you're going around sticking your face in other people's excrement. You have been warned all along that these were private matters."

Nyquist was confused. He murmured some words.

"What's that? Speak up."

"Patrick Bale employed me."

"That's right. We had it on good authority that you were good for a simple task, and nothing more. Boozed up, living in fear of yourself. This is what we heard. Perfect for the job in hand. To find Eleanor. That's all. No police involved. Nothing. Just you. The poor burnt-out, no-good, junked-up failure of a man."

Pearce moved away slightly.

Nyquist's head fell back into his chest. He was moving in and out of awareness, his skull still fuzzy from whatever he'd been given to make him blackout, and his arms and legs ached from where he had fallen. He groaned.

"What's wrong?" Pearce asked. "Don't tell me you're scared? Here, look. Look at me!" This last was shouted out with such vehemence that Nyquist had to respond, to turn his face towards his interrogator, to listen to Pearce's tirade: "I know you by now, Nyquist, I know the kind of man you are. Creepy, uh? You wake up, what's that in the mirror? Is that really me, you ask? This face, this body, how the hell did I get like this? How did I get so ugly? So corrupted? How come I'm so twisted and bitter all the time? Why can't I look myself in the eye anymore?"

"I'm not like that." It hurt to speak; his lips were cut open.

Pearce laughed. "You're amongst friends here. How long are you going to deny your own true nature?"

Nyquist felt alone, alone in the world, abandoned. He was angry at himself, that he'd lost control and fallen into this trap. Angry. And weak. At the very end of all that he could do. Was he going to die here, in this place, in this cold and lonely place? He screamed out for help, for anybody anywhere to help him but the sound coming from his lips was a wordless noise to which only his own echoes made reply, his own voice coming back to haunt him with his helplessness.

Eealaaaleiiiialaaaeia…

"That's right," Pearce said. "Let it all out. Here, maybe this will help." She threw down a few small objects which landed around Nyquist's legs, some of them falling onto his lap. He made them out as capsules of the drug, kia. The liquid sparkled with glints of orange and gold. Pearce held one vial in her hand. "I hear the kids are taking this in ever stronger doses. They're actually injecting it. When we fed it to Sumak here, I swear I could hear his brain explode. Can you imagine that, Nyquist, having such an intimate, physical knowledge of your own future? It must seem like the days to come are rushing through your veins, as though death itself were accelerating towards you. Like a steam train hurtling through the night. Can you dodge it, can you escape? No, I don't think so." Here, she kicked idly at the drug dealer's body. "Oh my, what a feeling that must be! What a thrill." She raised the glass vial higher, into the beam of the light. "And then *bam*, there's your head smashed up against the brick wall of tomorrow. And all the time you know precisely what's going to happen. Bang! No wonder your body gives up on you."

"Let me go." Nyquist spat out blood from his mouth. A tooth moved in its socket. "Please. Just let me go."

Pearce turned to face him. "I can't do that. I've got my orders."

Nyquist found a voice that burned directly from his anger. "Pearce, you bitch. Bale is stringing you along. He's playing you."

"Really?"

"He'll use you. He'll set you up."

"I don't think so."

"You do know Eleanor isn't his daughter."

"What do I care? The boss wants her back, and that's it."

"He doesn't love her. It's because of what she knows, about Kinkaid, and the drug deal. I swear, he'd kill her if he could get away with it. Instead, he's trying to control her."

Pearce grinned. "You poor sod. You couldn't be more wrong."

A noise then. A door opening.

"Now what?" Pearce moved aside.

Nyquist looked over, seeing the light that came through an open doorway, and a figure standing there.

Voices. Pearce talking to the new arrival.

Nyquist could not hear properly.

The voice again, louder now, familiar. "See to it."

It was Bale.

The door closing once again, as Pearce walked back into the circle of light. She leaned in close and said, "Last chance. Tell me where precious little Eleanor is."

Nyquist rocked on the chair. He felt all his bile rising, his eyes glinted with spots of red light. He'd had enough. "Keep your hands off her."

"Tell me!"

Nyquist held his interrogator's stare. He kept his breath steady, controlled, the one word coming out clean and cold: "No."

And suddenly it was all too much for Pearce; she nodded, and Jacob instantly appeared at her side. Without warning, he smashed his fist against the side of Nyquist's head with a hard vicious blow, worse than before. Again, the chair was knocked over, taking Nyquist with it. He felt his lights go out, blood bursting inside his skull, down his face. He hit the concrete floor, crying out in pain. Pearce followed him down. She grabbed hold, one hand around his shirt collar, the other wrapping itself around his face, pressing tight.

Nyquist had one chance left.

He sank his teeth deep into whatever flesh he could find.

Pearce leapt back in shock, screaming, grabbing her injured hand with the other. Blood had splattered onto her blouse, her jacket.

Jacob moved in.

A boot came down on Nyquist's shoulder.

There was a cracking sound.

Then darkness.

He lay there for a time, drifting in and out of consciousness. He heard a chair scraping, a door opening. Footsteps. Pearce was speaking, and then Jacob replying, but nothing was coming through clearly, nothing solid. Only mumbles, the rustle of clothing.

"He's a wreck."

Was that Bale speaking?

Pearce laughed. She said, "Let's tidy up."

"Yes. Good. You know the drill." Yes, definitely Bale speaking now. "As though no one's to blame, only himself."

"Sure. Just like the dealer. We'll handle it."

Nyquist tried desperately to make his eyes come open, to stay open.

Pain, somewhere distant in his body.

And then a white lamp shining, hot against his skin. Nyquist squinted, moving his head aside, but the harsh beam followed him. Pearce was seen as a shadowy form. One of her manicured hands entered the lamplight, holding a vial of kia. She said, "I really don't want to do this, you know?"

Jacob sniggered.

The liquid glistened in the light. Pearce's other hand appeared, holding a syringe. She slowly inserted this into the top of the vial.

The syringe filled up with orange fluid.

Nyquist tried to back away, but there was nowhere else to go. He was lying on the floor, his wrists still knotted tight behind his back. And then Jacob grabbed him by the shoulders, holding him tight, as Pearce bent down close. She pushed Nyquist's head to one side and pressed the tip of the syringe against the clammy, exposed neck.

Pearce whispered, "This is the kind of thing makes a man go crazy."

Nyquist struggled against the hold, against the ropes. It was no good. He cried, "I don't know! I don't know where she is! She ran off. I was looking for her!"

"It's too late, my friend. Your time's up."

The needle entered flesh, finding a vein, and within seconds the mists of dusk were travelling through Nyquist's body. His vision clouded over and he groaned one last time. And then he was slipping away from the warehouse, from his bonds, his captors, from the night, the city, and finally from himself. Until he was aware of only thing: a clock ticking. The slow, steady noise came from inside his skull, deep inside.

Tick tick tick tick tick...

SHADOWPLAY

...Tick, tick, tick, tick, tick, tick.

There is only the present moment in time, and then the next, one moment following on from another, all in darkness.

No past, no future, only this...

One tiny pinprick of light, flickering.

He tries to concentrate on it.

Where is he?

Focus!

A medium-sized hotel room, blandly furnished, the walls and bed linen coloured in the same washed-out shade of grey. He can't remember how he got here. Everything seems distant from his touch. A pale beam of neon light shines through the only window. It stutters like a cheap, faulty lamp. Shadows dance. He looks around, noting the mirror on the adjacent wall, a clock just above it. He can hear the mechanism ticking, the sound of it far too loud. His face in the mirror is wreathed in smoke.

He turns again at the sound of a voice and sees a teenage girl moving swiftly across the room. Her name is Eleanor Bale. He knows that, yes, he remembers that.

He tries to call her name out but only silence leaves his lips.

Yet she answers him. "You're scaring me," she says. "Leave me alone."

He walks towards her. Eleanor backs away, terrified, until she bumps into the bed and falls down onto it.

"Keep away. Keep away from me!"

Now he sees her face in closeup, framed against the sheets. He's caught in a task he cannot escape from, no matter what he does. And so he picks up a pillow, soft and grey, one hand on each end, tightly held, and he presses it down on the girl's face, causing her to struggle, to snatch at whatever breath she can find. He imagines a mouth filled with mud, with soil, with feathers, with salt, with dust. She's choking. The pillow presses down, harder now, harder, holding the head of the girl in place until, until...

Stillness. The body lies at rest.

She's dead. Hollow flesh. The spirit has departed.

Yes. It's done.

The murderer steps away. The pillow falls to the floor. The room is cold, distant. He looks at the wall clock, noting the time. It's seven minutes past seven. Good. That's correct. Yes, he's done well. The mirror beckons and now he sees himself as he really is, as the smoke clears from his features at last.

His name is John Nyquist. John Henry Nyquist. He knows that now.

His face is devoid of any real feeling, yet his body is tense. He's shivering.

And his hands are trembling still, from the crime.

In sudden fear and disgust he turns away from his own reflection...

FULL DARK

He could not see properly, he could not open his eyes. All was darkness. Silence. His own breath, nothing more. And then his mouth was opening, closing, the tongue moving, words being formed, broken, mumbled and then lost in the cold, cold air.

Uh. No. No. Ah no. Please. No, no, no…

Nyquist reached out, touching flesh. His eyes opening just enough.

Cold, shivering.

Here in the dark with him, another person. A face next to his. Dead eyes, hollow mouth, orange stained. Freezing skin, unshaven.

Recognition.

The drug dealer. Sumak. Once a dandy king ruling his realm in the daytime club full of light and heat and music, now a corpse: a stilled heart and lonely flesh and matted hair and the devil's bright lipstick.

And Nyquist thought he too had died here, and been left to rot. But he flinched away from the idea of his own demise; he clambered to his feet somehow and set off walking, his feet dragging along, moving, moving without thought or direction, his lungs dragging in harsh breaths. His head throbbed with pain. He could feel the poison inside his body, in his blood, still moving through him. It scared him. He wanted to run, to outrun death.

His eyes stared ahead, seeking direction.

Everything was pitch black. In front, behind, to all sides. Black. No light. None.

The night had no exit, no doors at all, no windows, not a crack of light.

Where could he go?

Darkness, only darkness.

He spat out dust and soot and ash and blood and slivers of flesh torn from his own lips, and grit and soil and bits of enamel from his teeth; he spat out cheap beer and bad whisky and stale air and bile and hatred of all known people; and he spat out last of all the prospect of ever being anything different than what he was, a bad of the lowest degree, a damaged soul adrift in the night and the day, afraid of shadows, made of shadows.

Black air, black earth, all around.

He was blind.

Now he started to run in panic and after only a few strides smashed into a wall, or a concrete post, a parked car, something, he could not see what it was.

He fell. In pain. Sticky blood on his face when he pulled his hand away from the cut where he'd cracked his head. His body folded, curling up tightly for protection, for comfort, to hide himself away from himself and from whatever awaited him here, in the darkness.

It was no good; it could not be hidden away.

The vision came back to him. The girl Eleanor in the grey hotel room, the pillow in his hands, *his* hands, *these* hands, these aching, scuffed, bloody hands, the way he felt when the pillow pressed down upon her face. That young life, extinguished. The exultation of the act passing through him like desire, his body sparked with need. The clock ticking. And then his own face in the mirror, and the way he had looked then, without feeling, with no trace of compassion.

No, no! Please. No…

He had killed. He was a killer.

No, not yet, but soon: he *would* be a killer.

Nuh…

Crying, mumbling, the words just pure sound, pure gibberish.

Nu ah plu ne ahh shh…

His body was shaking a little less, growing quiet, until he was lying still at last, and his eyes slowly opened. His vision was saturated with light, with a strange green light, close up, touching his face, pulsating in time with his own blood beat.

Luminous, blurred, filling his world entirely.

The light moved away slightly, melting from view.

Then back again.

Nyquist held the sight in place, concentrating, until he understood what he was seeing.

The watch.

His new wristwatch, the one he had bought from the street trader. His face was pressing down on the dial, activating the green luminous light.

He concentrated as best he could, willing the time to come into focus.

There it was. A few minutes to twelve. Almost midnight.

Taking great care now, one planned action after another, he got to his feet again and set off walking.

How long had he been knocked out for? He could not tell. All he could remember was the dream, the vision, the girl being killed…

He walked on and on until he felt a little more clearheaded, willing his eyes to adjust themselves to the dark. But the darkness never faded, and when he looked up, the sky was empty of all stars. There was nothing to offer guidance. And Nyquist realised then, that he had entered the region known as Full Dark, the furthest edge of the night, where even the artificial stars and the planets were invisible. It was an area of the city that many feared, and very few visited. Sight was useless. Instead, he stretched out both hands in front of him and shuffled on until his fingers touched at something: rough, crumbling, powdery on top, hard beneath, sharp against the flesh. A wall, a brick wall. He listened, hearing tiny scratching sounds, and the murmur of human voices. He edged along the wall step by step until he saw specks of light somewhere ahead, appearing and disappearing like glow worms. Fluttering colours, sudden flashes, slow fades like a retinal burnout. And somewhere within them, the vision of the girl being murdered, smothered. He waved his hands around frantically, trying to wipe the pictures away. The side of his head ached, the bone tender.

Nyquist moved on through the darkness. Progress was difficult, his legs were too tired, too heavy. Again he looked at his watch, pressing the button to illuminate the dial. It was one minute to midnight. Yet surely many more minutes had passed since he'd last checked? He raised the watch to his face, to his ear, pressing it close, listening: *tick tick tick...* It was still working, but the mechanism was turning too slowly, the ticks sounding like the heartbeat of a dying animal. Time was moving along as thickly as black sludge here, in this place where the night coagulated. Yet he kept on walking, desperate to escape the feeling of stasis. Seconds going by, a minute, one more. He counted the passage of time in his head, and then he looked again at his watch.

It was ten seconds to twelve.

He carried on, until his fingers lost contact with the wall. He made a few more tentative steps, arms outstretched, fearful of what he might find.

Stop. Stop here.

A movement ahead, black against black.

Nyquist stepped forward.

Another movement. People. Living human beings, those who embraced the darkness completely.

Each one was dressed entirely in black, with no skin visible at any point. Even their faces were covered, their eyes hidden behind strips of cloth. They moved slowly, slowly, one breath at a time. Nyquist stared ahead, where the night seemed darker than it ever was, a deeper shade of black his eyes could not register. Total blindness. He looked away from the darkness. His watch barely glowed, the time a faint smear of colour.

Midnight.

The two main hands meeting at the top of the dial.

The realm of zero. This was a polar region, he realised, where time slowed to a stop. The mechanism of the city revolved around this one point, this singularity. Nyquist cried out to the people closest to him, "Help me please. I can't... I can't find my way back. Back to the city. Help me." They turned to see the stranger. None of them spoke, none replied. They had given up entirely on time, on any notion of moving forward or back. Nyquist could not tell where each person ended and the night began; they were blurred creations, emerging, dissolving, from the darkness, into darkness. "Help me," he said again, quieter now. He was too weak. The face of the girl loomed before him, his victim, his chosen one. The future had taken over his flesh, his veins, and was seeping through him like a slow river. The night wavered, the people before him seemingly made from vapour, of no substance. They spoke in whispers, the words indecipherable.

If he could only get through to them.

Midnight beckoned. Here. Now. This moment...

...Here... now... shadows across a wall... tick... where

the clock and the mirror hang, waiting... the girl moves... fearful... No, keep away! Keep away from me... tick... the killer draws near, holding the pillow... tick... pressing, pressing down... tick, tick... the girl's face... her breath, fading... tick... the hands clutching at the sheets... until, tick, until...

Nyquist moved forward one more step and then looked at his watch, the only lighted object for miles around. The second hand trembled on the very edge of the figure twelve. One more step and the cloak of midnight surrounded him completely.

Tick...

Tick...

Tick...

Tic...

tic...

ti...

t...

His watch stopped.

Neverness.

His body froze. His heart murmured. His blood slowed. His eyelids barely fluttered. His breath would not have stirred a piece of cotton, nor a moth's wing. His vision stood still. Nothing moved. Only one thing remained in all this darkness and that was a voice, this voice. Now. Speaking this. This word. Another. One by one by one. These words, this story. His story. Only this: that he was aware of himself as a voice, a mind thinking, an entity. A story. A goddamn story! Somebody alive. A man. A man of shadows. Somebody who deserved to be alive for whatever reasons, good or bad. Somebody with a purpose in life, whatever that purpose might be.

The girl's face appeared to him. Eleanor's face.

He had to kill her.

Somebody with a purpose in life...

Of course. It was his destiny, a force that took possession of him.

It was simple; in order to escape – from fear, from his past, his troubles, from himself, from stasis, from darkness – Nyquist had to murder the girl. Only this gave him any reason to move on from this frozen moment. And stirred by this one terrible notion, this task, at last he took a single tiny shuffling step forward, moving out of midnight's embrace.

Tick…

The people of Full Dark looked to him as he reappeared. One of them came up close; he could not tell for sure, but he imagined that the person was female. Gloved hands hovered around Nyquist's face, the fingers passing before his eyes gently, gently, slowly, closing them, closing his eyes with a gesture and then letting them come open again. This done, the woman moved off to rejoin her companions; not a word was passed from one to the other. Nyquist looked up at the blank vista of the midnight sky; without any stars to give direction, how could he find his way back to the city? But something happened then; he could barely understand how or why but a calmness came over him, and he brought his left hand up to his temple, pressing his wristwatch against his ear. *Tick*. It was working again, and he listened carefully to the mechanism as he set off walking. *Tick*. He took tentative steps in different directions, gauging the liveliness of the ticking sound. *Tick, tick*. He was thinking: the livelier his wristwatch sounded, the faster the workings ticked, the further he must be from Midnight, and the closer he would be to the city, where the timescales beckoned like the pull of gravity. It took him many wrong turnings before his ears became used to the sound, to the tiny differences that each new direction brought, but soon enough the darkness started to take on a slightly different hue, to become a little less dark. Slowly,

slowly, slowly time came back to him, the brain being wound up by some deft, invisible key. His eyes retuned themselves to the dark, allowing a little vision. Now he could actually see the hands of his watch moving. *Tick, tick, tick.* He could see the second hand in its quickening sweep around the dial. And now the night sky shone with a soft emerald light. When he looked upwards, Nyquist could make out the stars, just faintly. Pinpricks of light, nothing more. It was enough.

There she was, the Swan with Two Necks. It was a well-known constellation, because of its beauty. He had learned the shape by heart at school, as the teacher intoned the famous passage from Lady Margaret Asquith's "A Children's Ballad of Stars".

O swan with two necks,

Most beguiling of patterns,

eleven stars all told, most precious

shining over night's black lake.

Yes, he was now heading northwards. He knew where he was, at least vaguely. It was enough of a direction. Something to head for, if nothing more. Yet, he still felt strange, washed out, empty, as though all potential but one had trickled away from his body, and when he looked ahead all he could see was the next moment, the next moment after that, the next, and beyond that, the girl dying, dying by his own hand. His eyes closed and he stopped for a moment, until the feelings of dizziness had left him. Then he walked on, and on, and on until his feet stumbled over some obstruction. He looked down to see a road sign, uprooted, and fallen to the ground. The long pole was covered in weeds and the sign itself eaten away by rust, but the sight of something so familiar brought a flood of joy, and recognition; here was his way of escape, surely, back through the night, back towards day. His eyes sparkled with tears.

He knelt down and scraped away the dirt, brambles and slugs from the sign. He had to bend down close to read the several destinations on offer, and to work out as best he could which way the sign would be facing when upright. And then Nyquist set off once more through the darkness, following this new direction along a narrow roadway, one eager step after another until he could see a few welcoming lights ahead, red and green and yellow.

It was a train station.

THE DOWNSHADOW TRAIN

He stood alone on the platform, waiting. The stars were shivering in the sky. The signalling lamps glowed red then green down the track, and the cold air blowing across the telephone lines made a desolate music, the night playing a tune to itself. Nyquist blew on his hands. He was listening to the sound of the wind, watching as the breeze carried pieces of litter down the track, back towards the pitch black regions, where the train line petered out.

The station was called Starlight's Edge.

Nyquist searched through his pockets. His wallet was gone, taken by Pearce most probably, along with all his personal effects. He had a few coins, not enough to buy a ticket with.

But he was still alive. Alive! How could that be? He should've overdosed, like Sumak. Had Pearce made a mistake, given him too little of the kia? Or had he built up a resistance over the years of abuse? He only knew that his body had fought back for some reason, and was still fighting, still clinging to the shreds of life. He had fallen deep into Midnight, fallen into Neverness and been cleansed, perhaps that was it: something had happened to him, something strange and unknowable and he was alive, set on a course, the future pulling him forwards, forwards,

forwards, stronger than the drug, dragging him along a straight and narrow track as surely as a locomotive moves to its next destination. Time itself was catching hold of his body and spirit, carrying him along.

His fingers touched at the empty gun holster, strapped around his chest and stomach. He was unarmed. But what did he care for such things now? There are many different ways of killing people. He removed the holster and threw it over the fence, into the bushes that lined the rear of the platform.

Again, the teenage girl's stricken face hovered in his sight.

He shook the vision away, looking instead to the station clock. The dial glimmered under a pale lamp, the only light. It was twenty-five past nine. Without any real conscious thought of what he was doing, he adjusted his watch to the same measure.

Something nagged at him, something Pearce had said during the interrogation: *You poor sod. You couldn't be more wrong.*

Now what did she mean by that? It worried him. He tried to think, what had led to the remark? Something about Bale, about Patrick Bale's purpose in all this...

No, he couldn't remember, not properly.

The train drew up at the platform.

Nyquist chose an empty carriage. A few people got on at subsequent stops, but not many. These were the lonely night passengers, making their way from the dark sky's lost and lonely perimeter, back to the Central Darkness, or onwards from there, towards daylight. Once he heard a young couple talk to each other of the latest Quicksilver murder.

The darkness of a tunnel silenced them.

Nyquist touched at his injuries, his shoulder, the side of his head, all over his face. Only now was he becoming aware of the damage he had received.

He must look like something evil, bloodied and bruised. He took a clean handkerchief from his pocket and wiped his face with it. He stared at the embroidered eye on the linen and thought of love lost, in time, in space. And he was suddenly glad that he'd taken two with him, two handkerchiefs. It was a ridiculous thing to be happy about, but there it was: a small human act of self-kindness in the long desolate night, it was enough to get him smiling and sobbing at the same time.

A family group got on the train at the next station, two adults, two kids. People kept their distance. The children looked at him; they whispered together.

Nyquist didn't care. He hardly heard them.

He felt that his life had been covered in darkness more or less completely, until one light alone gleamed inside, like the coloured signal at the end of a train line. This light took on shape as he closed his eyes: the room, the hotel room, the clock above the mirror, the girl…

Nyquist trembled. He felt a tingle at the back of his neck. It felt like two bits of loose wire sparking against each other, creating a different kind of light. That was it! He had to kill Eleanor because she was now Quicksilver. In some way she had taken over her father's role. He remembered her claim, that she could manipulate time, and had done ever since she was a child. If she could cause a clock to move backwards a few minutes, could she also steal time in some way? In this city of warped chronologies, it was definitely a possibility. And she'd already started on this mission: her first victim had already been chosen, and murdered, right here in Nocturna after she'd escaped from the hotel room. He'd heard it on the radio. And she would carry on. Further victims…

He felt the truth move through him. Killing Eleanor wasn't a future event.

It was future desire.

This is what kia had revealed to him. The drug didn't predict the future, it predicted a future compulsion of the user. An urge, a need. An impulse strong enough even to allow him to escape from midnight's clutches.

But what if he escaped the city?

Yes, of course! He would stay on the train, get back to Dayzone, pick up some cash from his office and then catch another train, or a motor coach. Go elsewhere. Anywhere, the furthest distance he could afford. Cross the borderline, find a place to settle down, another city. A place where the clocks moved at one tempo only. Leave this world of distorted time behind him, once and for all. By doing this, he would remove himself from the murderous task, no matter how necessary it might be.

It was simple. He would run away.

This would be his journey.

He settled back in his seat. The train had been travelling for quite a while now and people had got on and off, on and off, at the small towns and villages along the way, and currently only about half a dozen people occupied the carriage.

The train stopped at another station.

The darkness had taken on a lighter hue, signalling the edge of dusk. Usually he would be worried by the prospect of crossing over, but now all he wanted was to return to Dayzone: he would endure it.

Nyquist waited for the train to start up again.

It didn't happen. And one by one these remaining passengers got up from their seats and exited through the doors.

Nyquist was alone.

The train remained where it was, perfectly still.

He waited.

A few minutes later the guard came through. Absurdly,

Nyquist thought he was going to be told off for not having a ticket; instead the guard told him that the train terminated here. Nyquist said, "But I need to get into daylight."

"I'm sorry, sir. There's been some trouble in Dusk, a train derailed. Nothing's going through tonight, not on this line."

He couldn't believe it. "But I need to get to Dayzone. It's urgent."

The guard shook his head. "You'll have to change, before travelling on."

Nyquist stood up and walked to the carriage door. He stepped down onto the platform and saw for the first time the name of the station.

Vespers. Precinct Thirteen.

He remembered the name from somewhere.

A whistle blew, low and mournful, and the train reversed away from the platform, moving off into the darkness of Night. It left behind silence. A few stars were seen above, especially that strange constellation known as the Wound, which hung over the station like a necklace of jewels embedded in a scar. Nyquist looked around. A single lamp cast a yellow circle onto the concrete platform and a lone figure could be seen, standing just beyond the light. Music drifted through the air. Nyquist moved towards the sound. The figure was an old man playing the violin, the very same blind musician he had seen twice before. The same wooden box on which the player stood, the same tin bowl with a few coins already lying within; the same battered instrument, the same lopsided hat, the same black sightless look in the man's eyes. Only the music was different. Not in its melody, which seemed to be essentially the same; but in Dayzone the tune had been played as a wild dance, whereas now it was slowly drawn and surrounded with otherworldly harmonies. It sounded as though it were being spun from the twilit air itself, each note, each melodic phrase made of mist. And then Nyquist realised that the tune was none other than "Für Elise". The notes were well hidden, but there they were at the centre of the web.

Dusk music. A lesson from the shadows.

He felt himself utterly possessed by it, so much so that he hardly noticed the single coin dropping from his hand, into the bowl. The old man nodded at this payment, his music never missing a beat.

Nyquist walked down the platform towards the station's exit gate.

CREPUSCULIA

The silver mists of dusk swirled around at ground level, touching the night here and there. Nyquist moved as one drawn forward by the spell of somnambulism, his mind hardly registering his surroundings. On occasion he would see another person in the distance, someone walking slowly along in a similar manner to himself, the feet dragging, head slightly bowed, hands held loosely at their sides. Otherwise, the streets were his alone. Soon he came to a large open square surrounded by tall buildings, all of them dark. A number of fetish objects were strung on a series of poles in the centre of the square. These objects were made from human hair, feathers, rusty machine parts, broken knife blades, bullet casings, animal skulls, piano keys. Nyquist saw them as appeasements to the spirits of twilight. A cloud of yellow moths danced around the only streetlamp still working. Beyond this sodium glow, the evening star glittered cold and blue and lonely above the dusklands.

Nyquist walked parallel to the fogline, towards a tiny flickering light some way ahead. A few other people were making their way there as well, a small gathering. Coming up close he saw that the light was a single gas flame attached to the wall of a building; it might have been a small factory, or a church, or a library. The structure was rundown, crumbling, the rear half of it already belonging to the fog, to the folds of dusk. The outside walls were covered in old peeling posters for theatrical events. There was no name above the doorway, no signage, no indication of what might be happening within; only the half-open doorway offered any welcome. Nyquist entered.

A woman was sitting in a little glass booth in the foyer. He bought a ticket from her with the last few coins remaining in his trouser pocket. It seemed to be the exact amount required. She smiled at Nyquist, as though she knew him, or knew his purpose here. Her voice was gentle: "Welcome to the Silhouette Theatre."

The auditorium was a tiny space, with five rows of banked seats arranged before a raised stage area. Nyquist joined the other spectators already seated, each one sitting alone, isolated. The lighting was subdued. Soft music could be heard, produced by metallic percussion instruments. A large sheet of white cloth was stretched across the darkened stage, from left to right, and floor to ceiling.

He waited. Nobody spoke a word. A few minutes later the houselights went down and the white cloth shimmered, becoming semitransparent: through it the wall of dusk could just about be discerned where it had penetrated the rear of the building, the fog billowing, lit by its own spectral glow. The stage lights came up slowly, bringing the sheet of cloth to life and, as the music grew louder and more dramatic, a large shadow appeared on the screen. The puppeteer herself could be vaguely made out, a blurred figure only, but Nyquist could tell it was the girl, Eleanor Bale. Now the shadow form had taken on a human shape as it moved about in a dancing motion. In time, other puppets joined the dance. On occasion, Eleanor spoke aloud through a crackly loudspeaker, adding details where needed.

Between the shadows and the puppeteer and the audience, a story was shared.

In the beginning there was only darkness.

The night sky ruled the darkness with his various companions, the moon and the planets and the stars. One such was called Hesperus. She was also known as Venus, the evening star, the most beautiful. The night sky loved her deeply. The moon was jealous of this fact, so jealous that she sliced a hole in the night sky and daylight poured through the wound, from the inside of night's body.

In this way, sunlight was born.

Eleanor worked the puppets with skill, each new character born out of a blurry realm, coming to stark black life suddenly as the puppets touched the white cloth, their temporary kingdom in the light.

Now the universe was shared equally between night and day. All was well until the sunlight grew tired of the night sky encroaching upon her realm every evening. The daylight was cunning however, she knew that she could not contest the night sky with brute strength; instead she seduced him, in the guise of a comet. From this union came forth the dusk. This offspring of daylight and the night sky was always placed between the two parents, so that one could not directly affect the other without the child's agency.

A kind of peace ensued, until the dusk child started to desire her own kingdom, and so she stole from both night and day; she stole the moon and the evening star, she stole a dozen sunbeams; she stole sparkles of light from the day, and a few smudges of darkness from night. From these she made the mist, with which she covered her world for protection. Flowers grew in the once barren soil, pollinated by a family of giant moths. Finally, within this fogbound land the city of Crepusculia was built, a magical place that held the future within its walls of grey vapour.

And the people of twilight rejoiced and prayed to their gods, saying: "Into the dusk I have wandered, in the pale fog I have fallen and become lost, both lost and found."

Hearing of this great city within the confines of Dusk, both night and day grew envious. A great war took place, during which the dark and the light joined forces to gain control of Crepusculia. Battle ensued, a battle that is still being fought. As the evening star hovers in the sky, the People of the Dusk celebrate not victory, not defeat, but the edifying nature of their continuous struggle. They pray to the moon and make sacrifices to her, this goddess who floats on a cloud of fog, looking out across the twilight world. Her soft yellow light hangs like a balm over the city. The struggle goes on.

The shadow play came to an end and the stage lights dimmed. Nyquist sat upright, as if from a deep sleep. He felt he had been placed under some kind of charm. The other members of the audience were in a similar state, moaning to themselves softly, shaking their heads, barely able to get to their feet. The vibrant beat of the metal gongs and rattles was still ringing in their ears. There was no applause. How could there be? This story belonged to them, these few people in awe of twilight's edge for all their strange and varied reasons. Indeed, Nyquist could only think of the story as being his own: the wound in the night sky his own wound, the evening star his own love, the sunlight and the darkness his enemies, the moon his cruel and jealous mistress, and the dusk his rightful place upon the world.

ACCUSATIONS

Later, when the tiny audience and the few members of staff had left the building, Nyquist pushed through a side door and walked through into a short corridor leading backstage. He found Eleanor in the wings. She was packing away the puppets from the night's performance, folding the leather figurines into a wooden box decorated with jewels and carvings. The mist could be seen, seeping in through open doorways and broken windows to billow across the further reaches of the stage area. Nyquist could smell dead leaves and taste flakes of ash in his mouth, his body reacting spontaneously to the nearness of dusk.

Without glancing up, Eleanor said, "At least tell me you enjoyed the show."

He made no reply.

Eleanor looked at him, only to meet his hard stare. She saw the state of his face. "Another fight?" she asked.

Again, no reply.

"Look," she said. "I'm nearly done here. Then we can talk. You do want to talk?"

"As you wish."

The girl smiled weakly. "I know I keep running away from you, but what else am I supposed to do? I have to live."

"Do you?"

"You really are behaving very weirdly, Nyquist. Has something happened?"

"Bale tried to kill me." He felt his skin tighten in memory. "And his crony, Pearce. They injected me with kia, an overdose."

"But that's terrible... the man's crazier than I thought. "

"I don't know how I survived. I almost didn't."

"What did it feel like?"

Nyquist's eyes stared ahead. "I stepped right off the clock's edge and kept on falling. All was dark. And still. Nothing moved. Only myself falling away from time. And then... and then I thought about you..."

"About me? Why? Why would you do that?"

"A light shone in the darkness. And I moved towards it."

He didn't tell her what the light was, how terrifying it was, or how it pointed the way to her death at his own hands. Instead he said, "I have the feeling this city isn't finished with me yet. I have things to do."

Eleanor stood up, saying, "I know what you mean."

He spoke coldly, mechanically. "Eleanor, I want those minutes of my life back. The minutes you stole from me." Anger took over. "I *want* them back."

"So you believe I killed Dominic?"

"Yes."

Eleanor nodded, thinking to herself for a moment. Then she reached out her hand to touch his damaged face and she said, "I'll get you cleaned up, come on." She led him up a spiral flight of stairs, into a room in the upper reaches of the theatre. "This is where my father lived, most of the time." Nyquist looked around. Half-finished puppets hung from the ceiling. Piles of books were balanced on the chairs and on the floor, manuscript papers were piled high on a desktop, on the single bed were heaped even more sheets of paper, all of them covered in handwriting.

A single framed photograph on the wall showed a lush blue sky, a green field and the sun, the real sun.

Eleanor pulled him away from the sight of the world outside the city.

"Come on, sit down. That's it…"

He sat on the bed as she looked at his injuries. There was blood matted in his hair, and the skin was broken and bruised on his face.

"You never get any prettier, that's a fact."

She wet a cloth at the room's tiny basin and started to wash the wounds. Nyquist let her do it, while inside his head a voice whispered: *This is your target. This is the person you have to kill.*

"Leave me alone." He pushed her away.

Eleanor looked upset. "I was only trying to–"

"What is all this?" Nyquist grabbed up a sheaf of papers from the bed. He waved them at the girl. "All this! What does it mean?"

"I don't know. I'm–"

"What?"

"I'm still going through it all."

"There must be something here, some clue."

"To what?"

"To stop it happening."

"What do you mean? What's going to happen?"

He didn't answer her. Something had clicked inside him, another tip of the scales, back towards humanity, towards compassion, and he felt himself once again a man caught in a trap. This might be his last chance; he had to understand the case, the secret history behind it, the hidden motives. Only then might he escape his designated fate. He started to read through the papers on the bed, trying to decipher Kinkaid's scrawled words.

He said, "Eleanor, did you kill again, tonight?"

"What? No, of course not."

"After you left me there, in that cheap hotel?"

"No! I came straight here–"

"You didn't black out?"

"Of course not. Nyquist, what are you talking about?"

"Quicksilver has struck again."

She was shocked at the news, shocked enough to convince Nyquist of her innocence. Not that it did him any good.

"I don't understand," she said. "You mean my father wasn't the murderer?"

"Maybe."

"But that means…"

"It means you've killed the wrong person."

He watched her face, looking for clues. She was defiant at first and then the signs of a more stricken nature showed through.

"But he told me he was… He confessed to me!"

She turned away in despair and moved over to a small desk in the corner of the room where she sat down with her head in her hands. He was about to offer some words of comfort, but stopped himself. He would let her be, for now.

His eyes scanned the page he was holding, finding a few readable sentences amid the chaotic scrawl.

Every time I look at her I feel my heart about to burst apart. How can I protect my daughter? It doesn't seem possible. And yet I have to keep doing it. There's no alternative. Or she will die. That's obvious now.

Nyquist jumped to another passage.

I'm frightened. I can't carry on like this. I don't want to hurt people, I don't want to kill anyone. It's too high a price to pay. Yet if I don't do it, what will happen to her?

Here the writing broke down.

Nyquist grabbed another paper, one that seemed to deal with kia and its properties. He homed in on a legible passage that had been underlined.

Or else consider it this way: Dayzone is the mind of the city, Nocturna the body, and Dusk the subconscious. Mind, body, spirit. The things people see in the flower's heart are really their hidden fears. And terrible desires. But how can they be conquered?

Nyquist felt he was reading a journal of his own madness.

In many ways it's worse; the future can be viewed as a fixed property of time, whereas human fear is ever-changing.

Words were scrubbed out here, only becoming clear again with:

It's not so much what will happen, but what might happen. No. Worse even. What the user might allow to happen. Or worst of all, what they might make happen. But how can a person fight such a thing? They would easier catch the mist in their hands.

Nyquist felt terrible. His temples throbbed with a dull ache. He read on:

You can walk away from events, but not from your own darkness.

Eleanor interrupted his reading. "What have you found?"

Nyquist frowned. "Well, he admits to killing people, or at least wanting to. It's not quite clear."

"I know. All these messages to himself. Look..." She opened a cupboard and showed him the hoard of paper and journals stuffed inside. "Where do we start?"

"We?"

She started to pull papers from the cupboards, scattering them everywhere. "We have to find out what happened in that room, when he was killed. We're in this together." Then she sat on the floor and started to read.

He watched her for a while, a lonely teenage girl reading her dead father's letters. Then he saw something of more interest: a bottle of gin on a shelf. There was enough for one good mouthful but that was sufficient: immediately he felt more alive.

Eleanor gasped.

"What is it?" He knelt down next to her.

"Look." She handed him a single piece of paper, pointing to a certain passage. "Read it. The underlined bit."

He started to read the words to himself.

I have committed terrible crimes, I have taken lives, all for the sake of love...

He stopped. "So that's his confession?"

"Carry on," she said. "A few more lines down. Where it's indicated."

Nyquist saw the line she meant. As he read it, a cold shiver went through him. He could hardly speak, hardly find the words, not at first. He read the line again, saying. "This doesn't necessarily mean–"

"Read it to me," she said. "I need to hear it from another person's lips."

Nyquist stared at her.

"Read it."

He looked back to the paper in his hands, saying the line out loud this time: "Now I see it clearly. I have to kill my daughter. I have to kill Eleanor."

"Again."

"Eleanor, you don't need–"

"Again!"

Nyquist repeated the line. "Now I see it clearly. I have to kill my daughter. I have to kill Eleanor."

The room was quiet around them.

He was aware suddenly of the close proximity of dusk.

Just beyond the wall, it lies. In wait.

His eyes glimpsed his own father's last few steps over the fogline.

Eleanor spoke at last. "Don't you see, if Dominic was

going to kill me, then I must've fought back against him, in the moment. And that's when I stabbed him. It was self-defence."

"Keep quiet. Let me think."

She was upset by his tone. He didn't care. He held the piece of paper between his two hands. The line plagued him, it circled around inside his head.

I have to kill my daughter. I have to kill Eleanor.

I have to kill my daughter…

Something troubled him, something out of place. Why would a father have to do that? What could be stronger than the bond between parent and child? Had Nyquist in some way inherited the job of killing her? He felt his anger building, that he'd been dragged into this pitiful situation against his wishes. He couldn't stand it any longer, and shaking at his own helplessness, at his own preordained part in the story, he tore the paper in two, in two again, again, again, letting the shreds fall to the floor. He was trapped in this tiny space with his intended victim; and trapped in time, moving to one conclusion.

Eleanor was making a noise. He focused on her.

She was sobbing quietly.

"Look at me," she said, anguish growing in her voice. "Look at me! Look at what I am. Look closely. Look!"

Nyquist couldn't do it, he could no longer stare Eleanor Bale in the face. He was scared himself. He was torn in two, pulled one way then another, back and forth. He got up from the bed, looking around in panic. His mind was racing: *How can I escape this. Where can I go?* Even if he stepped out of the door and walked away, far away, he knew that somehow or other he would find himself in that hotel room, with Eleanor before him, the pillow in his hands. For the first time he felt a real sense of his own violence, building inside. He banged a fist against the wall. The cheap plaster shattered around his hand.

"Nyquist…"

The tiny room seemed to shake under his presence, his rage. Even his own shadow angered him.

"Nyquist, you're scaring me."

He turned on her. "By all the power of Lord Apollo, I wish I'd never set eyes on you. Not once!"

She stared at him, trembling.

He cried out in utter despair, "Give me back my time! Give it back to me!"

"I swear, I can't remember what happened. I can't."

He moved towards her. Compulsion took him over.

"Nyquist! What're you doing?" She cowered.

He came to a stop.

"I don't know." It was spoken simply, from the depths of his being. "I can't escape myself."

They stared at each other, victim and killer, as preordained.

He moved again.

A sudden noise was heard. A tearing sound.

It held the two of them.

Eleanor whispered, "What was that?"

"I don't know. Let me–"

"Listen!"

Again, louder this time. It sounded like wood cracking in two, into splinters.

The girl looked fearful. "Somebody's breaking in."

"Wait here."

Nyquist moved to the staircase. Slowly, silently, he descended to the corridor below and craned his head around the side door. The auditorium was dark, with only a few of the houselights still turned on. The noises had ceased, but something stirred in the shadows at the rear of the seating area. Nyquist was fearful it was the shadow men, with their masks of smoke, come out of the dusk to find Eleanor. But the figure stepped closer: a man, and his face was clear, on view.

It was Patrick Bale.

He walked down the centre aisle towards the stage, looking to be unsteady on his feet. He was muttering to himself, out of breath.

Nyquist watched for a moment and then stepped through the doorway.

Bale was shocked, seeing him. "Nyquist? You... what are you... I thought..."

"That's right." There wasn't a trace of goodwill in Nyquist's smile. "I'm a ghost."

Bale tried to compose himself. "Where is she? Where's Eleanor?"

"I don't know."

"You're lying. I knew she'd come to this place, eventually."

"She's safe now."

"Safe? What do you mean? Safe from whom?"

"From you."

"Nyquist, you really don't understand what's going on here."

"Enlighten me."

Bale frowned. "Why aren't you dead? You should be dead?"

"It's a mystery, isn't it?"

Nyquist moved forward quickly, grabbing the other man by the lapels of his tailored suit. The cloth tore.

"What are you doing?" Bale's voice pitched upwards. "Get off me!"

Nyquist pulled him closer. They were face to face, a breath apart. "You tried to kill me."

"No, no. That was–"

"Where is she? Where's Pearce?"

"I don't know. Really..."

Bale looked terrified as Nyquist pushed on. "Maybe I should haul you back to Dayzone. Tell the police–"

He quit the sentence halfway. Something had pressed itself against his lower chest.

Bale's voice: "Ah. Now we feel it. Now we see it."

Nyquist backed away.

"This is your own gun. How do you like that for a turn?" Bale was giggling, suddenly triumphant: "It's your weapon."

Nyquist saw that Bale's obsession with controlling time had tipped over into madness. The chief executive's eyes blinked repeatedly, two cameras clicking on one second after another, seeking to put the world together in the correct order.

"You're losing it, Bale."

"Yes, I've messed up. I know that. I've let things get out of hand."

"Give up. Surrender."

Bale shook his head. The gun jabbed forward. "That can't happen. I've come too far, and the police don't know the half of what I've done in my life."

"Sure. Rules are for the little people, right?"

Bale screamed. The cameras clicked away madly, even faster now. He shouted, "Get down! Go on. Down on your knees."

"Go to hell."

"You think I wouldn't do it?"

"You know what, Bale? I had you down as more than a lousy drugs man."

"That's Pearce's business, not mine. I stepped away."

"Really? That's not how it looked when you ordered me killed."

He dismissed this with a wave of the gun. "I only wanted the knowledge the drug could bring me, that's all." His eyes blazed with the thought. "Imagine it, Nyquist, having such awareness of the future? If we could only learn to control it, the power it would give us then."

"And what if you don't like what you see there?"

Bale trembled. He pressed the gun hard against Nyquist's face.

"Get down on your knees!"

The barrel ground into flesh, then bone. For a moment the man's finger pressed at the trigger, but then stopped at the sound of a voice.

"Please. Please don't…"

It was Eleanor. Bale's eyes darted over to where she stood, framed by the doorway.

"Please don't hurt him, Daddy."

And that last word was the release button. *Daddy.* His face creased with pain, and love, a desperate love, and his hand moved on, with the gun still in it. He looked around nervously, as though he might yet find a suitable target. But there was none, only himself.

"Eleanor…"

She came forward and reached out to take the weapon from his hand. He let it happen without a word, without a struggle.

"Why have you come here?" she asked.

Bale seemed incapable of answering. Nyquist used the opportunity to take the gun from Eleanor's hand; quickly he emptied the chamber, making it safe.

Eleanor repeated her question and this time Bale found his voice. "To take you away."

"To hide me away. To keep me locked up, and silent. To stop me from messing with time, your precious commodity."

"You don't understand, Eleanor. I want… I only want to love you."

That was the spark. Eleanor went for him, her hands flailing at his face, his chest. Bale stood there and took it, took the pain, letting the pain get through, letting it hurt him.

Nyquist watched from the sidelines.

It was a one-sided fight.

Still the blows came, although weakening now, and all Bale could do was mumble over and over, "I'm sorry. I'm so sorry. Please forgive me. I'm sorry."

Eleanor grew tired. Her arms dropped to her sides, both fists clenched.

Bale looked defeated. Yet he had one thing to say. "I'm trying to protect you. That's all."

She sighed deeply. "From what?"

"From the person who wants to kill you."

The statement stunned Nyquist. He couldn't help but think once more of the terrible visions he'd been given, of himself killing Eleanor.

What did Bale know of this?

And once again Nyquist thought back to Pearce's statement: *You couldn't be more wrong.* About what? About Eleanor and Bale? Yes, they'd been talking about her.

Could that really be it? Bale wasn't trying to hurt Eleanor, at all. He really was trying to find her, to protect her. But from what? Or whom?

In confirmation, Bale said to Eleanor, "I found out that your life was in danger. It's why I stepped away from the drug deal, and why I didn't want you to see Kinkaid, or to come to this place. Eleanor, it's why I locked you away in the Aeon Institute. Everything… everything was for your own protection."

But Eleanor dismissed Bale's words. "I don't want your protection. I want to be free."

"But what else can a father do for his child? What else?"

She answered, "I'm not in danger. I don't believe your story."

"You *have* to. Leave it at that."

"You're lying–"

Bale screamed. "No! Leave it at that!" It was a burst of

pure rage, driven by fear, and his body was drained by it. All the life he had built for himself, all the work and the planning and the distrust and the greed and the coldness and the fear and the sheer obsessive desire, all came down to this moment, all broke apart in this one moment of time and Patrick Bale collapsed onto his knees, looking up at Eleanor, pleading with her, his hands held forward, fingers entwined. He might have been praying, praying for the safe return of what used to be; but his daughter turned away from him and he was left there alone, a pitiful sight.

Nyquist walked over to him.

"Get up."

He did so without a word.

"Talk."

Bale's eyes were half dead. "What do you want to know?"

"The truth. About Eliza, about Kinkaid. About Dusk, and what's really going on here, in this city."

"It's to do with–"

"Not to me." Nyquist dragged him over to face Eleanor. "To her. Now. Speak."

Bale said, "Eleanor, you are my child, in spirit if not in flesh." He paused for breath, and then added, "I ask only that you understand that."

"From the beginning," Nyquist said. "Everything."

THE WHITE CURTAIN

Patrick Bale began slowly. "There was trouble between us, between your mother and me, right from the start. We were... we were trying to start a family together. Trying, and failing. And failing, over and over. Our business would lack an heir, it seemed. This was of vital importance to her family. Catherine took to her night-time wanderings, her charity affairs and artistic gatherings, and I threw myself into the company. Our lives settled into this routine. Until that night when she told me that she was pregnant. It felt like a miracle, I could scarcely believe it." He kept his eyes on Eleanor as he spoke. "Our two daughters were born. Yes, twins. Yourself, Eleanor. And then Elizabeth. Eliza, for short. A few minutes later."

Nyquist heard Eleanor gasp with shock, but he calmed her with a gesture.

Bale smiled at her. He seemed to relax a little, now the story was begun and that first revelation was over with.

"Catherine and I were so happy then, our love grew strong again. It was a blessing, you see? A double blessing. I would often come into the nursery to watch my two children sleeping. Sweet Ellie and dear Eliza. Sisters. It was a joy to see."

His voice dropped to a whisper.

"You, Eleanor, you grew up strong and healthy. But poor Eliza was ill. She became terribly sick within the first few months of her life. Her skin turned pale, her weight dropped, she was wasting away. The doctors could offer little or no help. It was a mystery. I would hold her in my arms to make her warm, to urge her back to health." He paused, bringing to mind the feelings. And then his tone changed again, becoming more agitated. "Shortly after this, about five months into the child's life, I realised that my wife Catherine was troubled in some way. Of course I thought it a result of the child's illness, but there was more to it than that, something beyond the illness. I tried my best to comfort her. It was little use. And then I received a letter."

"From Dominic?" asked Eleanor.

"Yes. It was plainly written. He told me that he was the real father of the twins, and he asked that Eliza, the sickening daughter, be handed over to him. Kinkaid explained that Eliza was different from Eleanor, a different kind of child; and he claimed that only he could cure her before it was too late. He seemed to have superior knowledge. He said that the child would surely die if she wasn't properly treated."

"Did you know who Kinkaid was at this point?" Nyquist asked.

"I remembered him, vaguely. The company had sponsored an exhibition of his work some years before. For a while he'd become something of a friend, to Catherine. But I had no suspicions. Out of arrogance, I could not believe that a woman would cheat on me. And, frankly, he looked so odd, and so weak. What would she see in him?"

"What did you do, when you found out?"

"I went crazy. I was mad, I was angry. Humiliated, incredulous. I went through every painful emotion a man can possibly experience. I insisted that Catherine tell me the truth, which she did." Bale shook his head. "Can you imagine what it's like, to discover that the two daughters you've loved since their birth turn out to be another man's progeny? I had the urge to go and kill somebody. Her, or him, or both of them. Or myself. Or some random stranger. Anything! Anything to purge the feelings. Instead, I had a paternity test done."

"Which came out negative?"

Bale nodded. "I wasn't the father. And I also learnt that I would never be a father."

He was lost in his own thoughts for a moment, until Nyquist gave him a nudge. "Keep talking, Bale."

"Please. This is not easy." He took a deep, almost painful breath. "Catherine told me everything: the details of the affair; and how she had been exchanging letters with Kinkaid; and more recently telephone calls, during which she had told him of Eliza's illness."

Bale sat down in one of the theatre seats. He looked at Eleanor, hoping for some kind of response. She nodded slightly. And he went on with his story.

"I didn't tell Catherine about Kinkaid's offer. Instead, I went to see him on my own, here in this place." He waved a hand lazily to indicate the auditorium. "He was a strange man, I felt, a lonely man, an outcast. He persuaded me that Eliza was a child of Dusk, she had been conceived there, and would only survive within the region's particular atmosphere."

Nyquist asked, "Did you believe him?"

"I had little choice. The doctors had predicted two years of life, that was all. Eliza was living on borrowed time. She was in and out of hospital, the poor thing." He paused. "It seemed a chance worth taking."

"And your wife agreed to this?"

He looked at Nyquist and then at Eleanor, with a nervous expression in his eyes.

"I never told her. Not until the night it happened."

Eleanor frowned, hearing this. "You mean... you took the child from her?"

Bale nodded, a birdlike peck of the head.

"Against her wishes?"

He leaned forward in the seat, holding both hands out towards her. "Eleanor, I had to do it, don't you see, I had to save Eliza, your sister! Your twin! I had to save her."

Nyquist remembered the room full of clocks, and the woman who worked so hard to keep them from moving on.

He said, "And this took place at twenty minutes to four, is that right?"

Bale settled back. "Yes. My dear, sweet Catherine. When I first met her she was a lively, beautiful young woman who loved to dance along the different timelines of her life, jumping from one to another merrily, laughing as she did so. But now... now, her time came to a halt, a dead stop."

Nyquist understood what Catherine had meant when she'd stated that her daughter had been passed over. She meant taken from her, given away. Stolen.

Bale stood up. He said to Eleanor, "There is one thing you must never underestimate, and that is my love for your mother."

It was evident that Eleanor didn't know how to respond; the emotions were too far away from her version of reality.

Bale took a careful step towards her. He spoke softly: "I followed Kinkaid's wishes exactly. I took the child from her cradle, while Catherine screamed at me. It took two of my security guards to hold her back. I met up with Kinkaid at a house near the fogline. The child was crying incessantly. But he took her into his arms, and immediately..." Bale's voice broke. "Immediately, she stopped crying. In some way Kinkaid had lulled her, and I knew then that I'd made the right decision, no matter how painful it might be." Bale's eyes brimmed with tears as he found the strength to continue. "And then Kinkaid turned away and walked inside the house with her. And so it was done."

A moment passed in the small, silent theatre.

Nyquist said, "But you can't just give a child away like that. What did the authorities say?"

"I directed them to the house where Kinkaid lived, saying that the baby was staying with him for a while, because of the illness of my wife. I can only assume that he appeased the authorities in whatever way he could. Perhaps he was good for one thing. After all, he was the real father, and the mother was obviously in no fit state to bring up two children. Not now. And I did my own share of persuading."

Nyquist nodded. "I can imagine the pressure you brought to bear."

"I did everything in my power. I pulled every goddamn string in town, I brought home favours. I greased every palm. Yes, *whatever* it takes!"

He looked to both Nyquist and Eleanor for understanding. Met with silence, he cried out, "I was saving a child's life!"

Eleanor moved away, towards the stage.

Nyquist thought about what he'd heard up to now. "So, what happened next? You started to work with Kinkaid?"

"That came later, much later. When news of the drug kia reached me. But it was Pearce who took charge of the project. She does get excited by such things."

Nyquist put it together. "Pearce was in charge. While Kinkaid helped to ship the kia out of Dusk. So what was your role?"

"I wanted only knowledge. Of the future. The things unseen, just out of reach." A glimpse of his old power was returning, and his ego. "Surely, that would give me dominion over time itself."

"I don't think kia works like that, Bale. It's not that easy."

"No. I guess not."

Something in the chief executive's face made Nyquist hesitate. A deep yearning in the eyes, the pained line of the mouth. He had seen that look before somewhere. And then he remembered: young Sadie, in the Noonday Underground club.

He said, "But you can't see anything, is that right? Inside kia?"

Bale nodded. His eyes blinked rapidly and started to water.

"You're blind to it, to the future?"

A quick jerk of the head. His mouth opened and closed, seeking a word, a phrase, a scream, anything that would alleviate the hurt. Nyquist, in all his years, had never seen such a wretched expression of loss in a person. In the end, Bale could only murmur to himself:

"Nothing. Nothing there. Nothing at all. Nothing…"

And upon seeing such a pitiful sight in the man who had brought her up as his own, a strange emotion welled up within Eleanor. Her voice caught on a word and a spasm of pain shot through her. "No," she said. "No. This is wrong. Everything about you is wrong! You don't–"

"Eleanor…"

"You love me by locking me up. You love my sister by giving her away. What kind of behaviour is that?"

Bale pleaded with her. "Please, Eleanor…"

"It's wrong!"

"I had no choice in the matter."

"You let my sister go."

"I saved her."

"How can you know that? How can you know what happened to her, out there!" Her hand swept towards the shadow curtain and the rear of the theatre, towards the direction of the fogline. "Eliza probably died, in the mist, in the cold grey air."

"No. I saw her again."

This stopped Eleanor. "When?"

Bale's face lit up. "A short while ago, when Pearce first started to work with Kinkaid on the drug deal. I met with them both one night, and having a moment alone with Kinkaid I dared to ask about Eliza, expecting silence, or some vague news, possibly a lie. Instead, the next time we met he brought Eliza with him, to the fogline." His eyes widened in delight. "Oh, she wouldn't come near me. Instead, she stood some way off, shrouded in mist like a queen with her cape about her. Her body seemed to be lit from within like some strangely beautiful deep sea creature. She was her own lantern! And she looked at me." The words trembled on the edge of his tongue. "She gazed at me from out of the dusk."

Eleanor approached him warily. "What did she look like?"

"She looked like you, Eleanor. Like you."

Nyquist watched as the girl brought a hand to her mouth, and held it there.

Bale stated his case: "I saved her. I *did* save her." He believed utterly in his own act, his own deeds. He took a step towards Eleanor, holding out his hands for her to take.

But Eleanor trembled. "Stay away from me. Stay away…"

She backed off, stopping only when she bumped against the edge of the stage. The white curtain stirred behind her, a home for ghosts.

Bale, for his part, could not move any further than a single step.

Nyquist took over. "You said that you were protecting Eleanor from the person who wants to kill her. Who would that be?"

It was a vital subject, one that Nyquist needed desperately to understand, but Patrick Bale hardly even heard the question. Instead, he was staring at Eleanor, who had by now climbed up onto the stage.

Nyquist followed his gaze.

Eleanor was moving in a slow circle with an invisible partner. "I danced with her. I danced with my sister in the dream." Her voice was melodious, lilting. "I saw it all, the two of us. Inside the kia. Music was playing, a slow waltz, and there she was, in my arms, Eliza, in the circle we had made together, a dance of mirrors..." She was talking purely to herself, or to her imagined reflection.

"Eleanor?"

She made no response to Bale's call. Instead, her sister's name became fixed on her lips, repeated over and over.

"Eliza, Eliza, Eliza." Again, adding to it: "Eliza. Eliza Kinkaid."

Bale shouted at her. "Stop that!"

Eleanor let the word grow. Louder, more insistent. "Eliza. Eliza. Elizabeth." Her dance ceased at last, leaving only the word in play. She was emboldened by the name, the more she repeated it. "Eliza, Eliza, Eliza, Eliza!"

Bale put his hands to his ears, pressing tightly, but the name could still be heard.

Eliza. Eliza. Eliza. Eliza. Elizabeth. Eliza Kinkaid. Eliza. Eliza. Eliza. Eliza. Eliza. Elizabeth Kinkaid. Eliza. Eliza. Elizabeth. Eliza...

Behind her, the vast white curtain that stretched across the stage billowed; beyond that, the grey mists swirled at twilight's edge.

Eliza. Eliza. Elizabeth. Eliza...

Nyquist clambered up onto the stage. He could see that the situation was worsening. He'd let it go too far. He grabbed at her, saying, "Leave it now, Eleanor." But she wouldn't stop. The chant continued.

Eliza. Eliza. Eliza. Elizabeth. Eliza Kinkaid. Eliza. Eliza. Eliza.

The houselights doubled her shadow on the screen.

Bale had followed Nyquist. He pleaded with her. "Eleanor. Please stop it." He made to grab at her, to stop the words coming from her lips. She pulled away.

Eleanor cried out, "Leave me alone! You took her from me!"

Bale kept coming forward, Nyquist also.

In a blind panic, she backed into the curtain, trying to escape them both. The curtain bulged around her, enveloping her body in its folds.

"She's close. I can feel her! She's... she's calling to me!"

Bale made one last effort. But Eleanor spun wildly about and now the curtain had her completely. She could no longer be seen, only the folds of white cloth that still retained her shape. And then Nyquist heard a tearing sound as the cloth pulled loose from its supports above and fluttered like a dying phantom towards the stage floor.

Bale cried out in wordless pain.

"I'll get her," said Nyquist. Yet they both looked to where the wall of mist could be plainly seen, occupying the rear of the stage. There was no sign of Eleanor.

Bale whispered, "Where is she?"

"I don't know."

And then Nyquist saw her. Eleanor's body was draped in the fog as she stood right on the very edge of Dusk itself. Behind her two figures were glimpsed, each with faces hidden by masks of smoke.

He stepped towards her. "Eleanor. Don't be stupid. Come away."

He could sense the long cold fingers of twilight pulling at his flesh, and he felt he was being embraced by half-known things. He could go no further.

The two masked figures had vanished.

Bale came up close to him. He called out, "Eleanor. Please. Don't go. Let me explain. Come back to me. Come back!"

His final call was to no avail. The grey mist wrapped itself around Eleanor's body, embracing her softly, as a lover's shadow might. Nyquist took another step forward. The dusk worked its spell and the wall of fog moved forward and back like a slow tide.

The girl was taken by the mist.

Seeing this, Bale rushed forward, crying out, "Eleanor! Where are you? Eleanor?" Nyquist grabbed him by the shoulders, but the other man slipped forward, away, into the fog. Nyquist followed; he had no choice. It was all going wrong. He reached out again, keeping a good hold this time. "Bale! Don't be stupid."

The fog wrapped them together, the two men.

"It's too late."

"No!"

They struggled with each other briefly, but there was no fight left in Bale. Nyquist released him, letting him fall to the floor. The man's body felt weightless. "She'll die in there," Bale said, his voice choking with torment and then breaking up entirely, the words no longer making any kind of sense, only crying, weeping.

Nyquist left him there. He felt the mist all around, in whispers. The stage glowed with a deep silvery light, conjuring a strange music. Splinters of noise, melodic phrases, lost voices. He moved forward, across the blurred threshold, further, deeper. His skin crawled with a sudden coldness, and then a warmth. Acceptance: he could think of no other word for the feeling. It was time. The mist accepted him. A few steps took him across the backstage area. He found an open doorway and walked through into a mist-strewn corridor, and from there to another doorway, which led outside onto a patch of ground behind the theatre.

Dead flowers, the stench of rotten leaves.

Cobwebs strung with dew.

Weeds. Brambles. A great mass of them like a net, clutching at his feet.

It was too late.

There was no sign or hope of human life, not here.

But Nyquist carried on moving forward slowly, feeling the mist curl and weave, taking on his shape, closing around him.

Enfolding, caressing.

Cold damp air against his face.

All around the light was a dense silver, or grey. He could see no further than the tip of his outstretched hand.

The sudden shriek of a bird.

Fear was pricking at him, and he turned, and turned again and again, trying to place himself. The theatre had already vanished from his sight.

Which direction should he go, which way?

One more step, another. One more...

He was lost.

Moonlight. The fog. His body.

One more step.

His body, the fog. Where did one end, the other begin?

Already lost.

Moon. Fog. Flesh. All one, all one substance.

Lost, lost...

Another step.

PART THREE
DUSK

GUIDE BOOK:
FORBIDDEN PATHWAYS

PRECINCT ZERO is that mysterious tract of land existing between Dayzone and Nocturna.

It has no official name, and no exact limits on the map.

Most people call it Dusk.

The edges cannot be determined, or fixed.

The moon in her different guises is the lonely forgotten empress of this realm of fog and sorrow, alongside Hesperus, also known as Venus or the evening star.

Travellers should be aware that Dusk is considered to be strictly off limits. Only the city's trains are allowed to cross the region.

It is a danger zone, another world, with different rules, different physical properties.

People get lost in there, never to return.

For there are many pathways leading in, only a few leading out, and those few well-hidden and ever changing.

At its worst, the region steals, and hurts, and destroys.

It is that moment of time and space where nothing is certain, where the senses and the heart are caught halfway between darkness and light. There are stories told of demons and bizarre creatures, shadowless men and faceless women. Of ghosts and lost memories.

Nobody knows the truth.

All is nebulous, uncertain, fragile. From one side of the city the daylight melts away, dissolving, becoming new and strange. From the other side, night's tears are falling one by one into the mists of twilight.

In this way both day and night slowly begin to lose themselves.

Here, where the fog closes in...

UNDER A VIOLET MOON

All movements forward or back, to the left or the right, all led to the same place, to the mist, the endlessly slow-moving dreamlike play of the mist, which encased Nyquist in a new skin with every step taken. His eyes watered from irritation, and his throat ached. Yet he called out the girl's name: "Eleanor? Eleanor? Are you there? Eleanor?" But there was no reply, only his own words trapped in the thick grey air.

He moved on until a woman's voice was heard from close by, speaking softly, sighing almost. Nyquist could not tell what was being said, but he spun around and shouted again. "Eleanor? Is that you?" The voice quietened, and then came back into earshot, slightly louder than at first and from a different bearing. He listened intently, trying to pinpoint the exact location. But no, it was not possible, and now other voices – male and female, adult and child – joined in the hubbub, a choir of fragmented words and phrases, a few of which could just about be heard:

… Release me… which way… hungry… Matilda, please…he is crying… I can't see you… too cold… I can feel you still… why won't he stop crying?… the buildings are made of… help me… falling too far… Matilda?… I can't remember… made of ice, they are melting… falling…

please… let me go…

Recalling the stories he had learned over the years, Nyquist thought of these voices as all the hidden fears of the city, all the pleas of the mind to be released from the possibilities of pain and doubt and to be brought back to life. And now shapes were put to the sounds, dark writhing phantoms in the sombre landscape. Nyquist could take it no longer. He put his hands to his face and temples, trying to cover both his eyes and his ears at the same time. It did him little good. He could still hear, and still see. He cried out and his words of fear took flight from his mouth like a panicked bird of black and grey plumage. Still the eerie figures danced around him. He shouted out loud, "Stay away from me! Keep away!" It was no use. There was no substance to these visions, no flesh and blood capable of movement; only voices, only shadows; ideas, feelings, dreams, nightmares. They swirled and blurred around him.

Nyquist stumbled forward and then started to run.

The voices would not stop. Now pale red-eyed faces loomed at him, and white ghostly hands fluttered at his sides, clinging to his clothing and his hair.

Madly he ran on through the mist, across dry weed-licked ground, twisting this way and that, losing his footing and righting himself again, and on; he ran on until he was exhausted, until the noises and the shapes faded away into the slow breeze and the fog, and only then did he come to a standstill, his body heaving, his lungs desperate for clean air. His clothes clung to him in a cold sweat. And he stayed like that, just standing there for a good long moment until at last he gained some control, until his heart slowed and the flashes of red and yellow light faded from behind his eyelids.

The ground was paved beneath his feet.

By some weird chaotic navigation, he had managed

to find a road. Nyquist followed this given direction for a while. He had already lost all sense of time passing; he might have been inside the dusk for a few minutes, or a few hours. Certainly, the episode in the shadow theatre played like a memory from days and nights before.

Now he stopped. Another figure had appeared just ahead on the road, a darker shape in the foglight. It was not the girl. This person was taller, bulkier. The figure waited, unmoving, in silence. Nyquist approached cautiously. It was a man, or else some creature or spirit that had taken on a man's appearance. He was dressed in a black greatcoat, which was entirely buttoned up, from the ground-skirting hem to the high collar and neck. His hair was white and cropped short and only one of his eyes, the left, was visible; the other was hidden behind a watchmaker's *loupe* or eyeglass which the squeezed muscles of the cheek and brow held in place. The stranger regarded Nyquist for a moment, and then flicked open a large pocket watch. He asked, "Do you know what time it is?" Nyquist pressed at his own watch. The dial lit up brightly in green, but the atmosphere had seeped into the workings, so that the area between the glass and the dial was filled with the silvery mist. The numbers could not be seen, nor could the hands.

This was dusk time.

Nyquist shook his head. "No."

The man smiled. "It's nearly seven minutes past seven. Almost, not quite, coming up on, close to. Nearly. Does that make any kind of sense to you?"

"Yes. I understand that."

"Go on your way then. This road will take you there."

"I don't know where I'm going."

"Just follow the road."

The mist enveloped the stranger as though some unseen realm had taken him away. Nyquist was alone once more. He felt strange, disturbed at the core: were these events and people real, or figments of his twilit mind? Had he wished the timekeeper into being for his own comfort? Was he going mad?

For a moment he felt that his skull was as fogbound as his wristwatch.

But he walked on, keeping to the road as directed.

His clothes caught on the thorns of a flowerless shrub, and a wave of tiredness crept up on him. He could hardly keep his eyes open, and his feet dragged across the tarmac. No, it was more than tiredness, more unnerving than that; he felt he was both asleep and awake, simultaneously.

In the distance he saw the broken flickering lamplight of Hesperus sparkling through the fog like a glint of precious metal. The building that held her was a towering black shape in the mist, nothing more, all of its windows dark. Only the star-shaped neon sign held out hope as it burned from the skyscraper's peak. Who was maintaining it, who was polishing it? He told a fairy tale to himself of a renegade bulb monkey lost in the mist, feverously working at the neon, doing all they could to keep this star alight. It was enough, it was evidence of human life, and Nyquist felt his energy coming back.

Further on. Further. Keep moving...

An increasing number of cars were parked by the roadside, their doors open, their windscreens shattered. So many abandoned vehicles, abandoned stories. He followed the curve of the road. A few houses and shops were seen. One car he passed was covered in rust all over, and the interior was packed with sand; it trickled from a tiny gap at the top of a side window. The vehicle looked as though it had lain underwater for a long, long time; yet there was no water around here, only the bare ground, the weeds, the thorns, the shadowed buildings, and the mist, the endlessly curling and smothering mist.

And then his skin tingled.

He saw a low building at the side of the road, which turned out to be the remains of a transport café. The windows were broken, the door creaked open on its hinges. The painted sign told him that the place was called Darla's Rendezvous.

His mother's name. Darla.

She had spoken to him once as they sat by the fire in the living room of their home, of opening just such an establishment, with exactly that trade name. It was a dream of hers, a treasured escape from her part-time sewing work.

A dream only, never fulfilled.

And Nyquist knew then for certain that Dusk was a region not of the real world, but one conjured from his own inner landscape; or a land which modelled itself on his thoughts, his memories. Knowing this, he dared to look inside the café, through the half-open doorway. All was dark within, empty, inhabited only by shadows. And then something moved in a corner, a person sitting at a table. A woman, it looked like...

Nyquist's heart clenched.

It was a tailor's dummy, of female shape, dressed in a gown of blue and green.

His mother's favourite colours.

He reeled away from the door, stumbled back, tried to calm himself.

It was useless. This place did not lead to calmness.

He hurried on and soon reached a patch of open land. The ground was filled with old timepieces, some of which were broken, their workings on view, while others were still intact. A dull, muffled ticking sound was heard from all around. The fog ahead was flickering with orange light. He moved closer to the source and saw a grandfather clock on fire, the flames rising from the wooden casing. It didn't surprise him in the least, and he knew that the fire would never go out. He stared at the clockface. The time was five past seven.

He looked at his wristwatch. The dial had cleared of mist and the hands were clearly visible. They showed the exact same time: five minutes past seven. And he knew it would always be that time, no matter how far and wide he roamed this place, it would always be so until the moment of Eleanor's death arrived, only then would the clocks move forward one more minute, and then one more...

Beyond the firelight, a thread of gold moved and twinkled in the far distance. Nyquist realised it was a locomotive making its lonely way through Dusk from Night to Day or from Day to Night, he could not tell which. But he was suddenly, intensely envious of those aboard, sitting in their lighted carriage, reading magazines or chatting to their neighbours. They were going home, or to work, or to play, or to meet the man or woman who might become their future spouse. They might have children together, and bring them up safely, half in the lighted areas, half in the dark, fully balanced human beings with their whole lives ahead of them...

He stopped moving. Dead still.

It was pointless. Doubt took him over.

He was lost and alone in a place that cared nothing for him, that offered only fantasies and pathetic symbols drawn from his own nightmares.

The girl was long gone, taken by this realm for its own ends.

Was she dead already, or injured, or suffering in torture?

Only the thought of Eleanor drove him on. It was all he had. One reason. He would either save her, or kill her.

He picked up the road once more and followed it, as it wound between fields of dry grass. The dusk was silent now but for the soft call of owls, their dark and dusty smudges floating low above the ground. A few yellow moths fluttered about Nyquist's face. Again he saw the blue star of the evening, Hesperus, peeping into view above the fog banks. It might have been the same neon sign, or a different one, a sister star. How could he tell? He had lost all sense of orientation. Further on he came across a grand piano half buried in the soil. Hundreds of slimy, bulbous frogs were jumping around the piano's legs. Some of them had found their way inside the open lid of the instrument, where their croaking calls reverberated against the strings, making a new kind of music: beautiful, experimental, primitive. He pressed at a few of the black and white keys: E, D sharp, E, D sharp, E, B, D, C, A. The now familiar tune of "Für Elise" played out under his fingertips, although where such musical ability came from, he could not say. As he looked round, he saw other musical instruments in the field beyond – guitars, violins, trumpets, double basses, tubas, the bones of a xylophone – and he couldn't help imagining a ghostly ensemble playing for the lost souls of Dayzone and Nocturna.

Nyquist kept moving until he came to a small hamlet. The outlying streets were empty of life except for a dazzling white horse that walked alongside him for a while. Mist streamed around its warm, muscled body. And closer to the centre, he witnessed a gathering of spirits around the old village green, men and women clothed in the colours of twilight, who cried at the steps of a marble war memorial with its list of carved names, and were too pained to even notice Nyquist's presence. Somewhere far off in the mist a lone trumpeter played "The Last Post". The melody tugged at his heart, as it always did. One poor woman passed close by him. Her face was entirely featureless but for a crimson-lipped mouth. No eyes, no ears or nose, only this red maw opening and closing and babbling forth in some unknown language. Again, Nyquist felt he was seeing scraps torn loose from the subconscious of the city, bizarre remnants and offshoots of people's dreams and fears about themselves, and the days and nights yet to come, imagined here, brought into some pitiful version of life.

He walked on, leaving the hamlet behind.

The paving stones were crumbling beneath his feet, being eaten away by decay. The road was merging with the earth and the roots. A purple glow tinged the air. Many more of the yellow moths were flitting about as the mist started to thin. The landscape was changing. A little further on he saw before him a vast field of golden flowers that swayed in a gentle breeze. A few remaining drifts of fog moved with them, but mostly the flowers were fully exposed beneath the glow of the moon, a very different moon than the one visible from the Dayzone fogline. This giant orb was violet-coloured and hung low in the sky above the fields. The moths came here in their thousands, each wing the exact same luminous colour as the petals over which they fluttered, so it looked as though the flowers themselves were taking to the air. A number of human figures walked amongst the moonflowers. They moved with the slow dazed shuffle of sleepwalkers.

Nyquist stepped into the field, his every movement disturbing the flowers and raising clouds of orange seeds that dazzled and floated around him. The moths flew around his face; he could feel their wing beats against his brow and his cheeks, his lips, his eyes, his hair. He passed near to one of the fieldworkers. This was a ravaged man, his features so eaten away that only his eyes remained, each orb coloured entirely black.

Nyquist thought of the blind fiddler who had acted as a guide in his journey; had that musician in some way escaped from Dusk?

Yet the worker could see, at least a little, enough to do his work. He bent down and groped around until he managed to pull a large oval seedpod from one of the plants. He placed this in a canvas bag strapped around his shoulder. Then he turned his nightshaded eyes towards Nyquist. It was such a terrible stare, such an example of broken and lost humanity that Nyquist wanted to move away in fear. But a black liquor fell from each of the worker's eyes, down the cheeks to the broken, useless lips. He wiped at it feebly with a thin-fingered hand stained orange at the tips. Nyquist felt compassion; he reached in his pocket for his handkerchief and used it to wipe at the black substance dripping from the worker's eyes, whatever it might be. The worker flinched at the touch but then grew calm. The linen moved back and forth until the face was clean, or as clean as it could be in such a place. The black eyes blinked, the bare remains of the mouth crinkled at the edges. A trace of humanity remained, beneath the terrible process that had turned him into a slave. Nyquist pressed the handkerchief into the worker's grateful hands and moved on through the dusk blossoms. A few yards on he saw a second worker approaching, but with a more purposeful step. No, not a worker, a guard. This man's face was masked in smoke, and he carried a baton or club in his hands. Nyquist reacted quickly: he lowered himself to the rich black earth and started to crawl along between the tall stems of the plants. He kept moving in this way for as long as he dared and then he stopped and pressed his entire body flat on the ground.

He drew in a long breath and held it.

And waited.

The guard moved nearer, thrashing at the stems with his baton.

Nyquist willed his body into silence, and stillness.

A torch beam illuminated the adjacent stems, and the baton took off the heads of some flowers close by. The guard's passage disturbed the shadowy enclosed world for a moment longer, and then moved on.

Nyquist lay where he was, and then rolled over so he was facing upwards. The scent of the flowers was overwhelmingly sweet and cloying. The orange seeds were sticking to his face. He was reminded of the kia drug; it was the same colouring, the exact same perfume. And he realised that taking the drug actually carried the user into the dusklands, just for a tiny amount of time and only inside their heads, but enough to give them a peek of everything they wanted. Or feared. Paradise or hell, one glimpse at a time.

The fields of twilight closed around him.

His father had led the way, and the little boy had watched, and learned.

And followed.

Like this, Johnny. One step, another. You see? One more…

And now here he was, fully grown…

Nyquist looked up at the swarms of yellow moths as they fluttered by, and the artificial moon above them. He heard music, a soft lulling music as the many petals, leaves and stalks gently whispered against each other in the ether of twilight. All of these sights and sounds and aromas were a spell he was caught within, and he could not move his body for a good while, not until the blind worker had walked on to another part of the field.

Now he started to crawl along, keeping to his hands and knees, until he reached the edge of the field, where he got to his feet carefully. He was safe, alone once more. But he felt wretched. It was all he could do to look ahead, to see where the road continued. He set off walking. Progress was slow, his pace barely in time with his half-drawn breaths. Away from the violet moon's dominion, the drifts of fog moved in again, thicker than before, reducing his sight all around. The ground beneath his feet was veiled, and what little he could see was covered over by weeds and fallen leaves. The road markings were no longer visible, and he would have walked on blindly, unceasingly, perhaps turning in ever-increasing circles, if a dim light had not suddenly appeared before him. He was drawn towards this beacon, his only landmark, and a little further on the fog parted to reveal a neon sign in the shape of a white five-pointed star. It turned repeatedly on its pole through a half circle and then back again. Nyquist walked under its soft glow, into the light and back out again. There was a large building ahead, its form emerging slowly from the mist. Three people were walking up the steps toward the main doorway, where they stopped for a moment under a pale lamp. Two of them were indistinct shapes; the third was a young woman.

It looked very much like Eleanor Bale.

BROKEN CRYSTALS

Nyquist hurried towards the building, keeping to the shadows. He watched from a niche in the wall as the young woman disappeared through the hotel's doorway, followed by the two men. He was close enough now to see their faces of smoke, their nervous stances. The sight still filled him with fear and anger and he stopped for a moment, catching his breath. His eyes were burning. He rubbed at them, before walking on.

The Silver Star Hotel was only two storeys high, but covered a large area of ground. It had obviously been a fine establishment, before the dusk had overrun this part of the city. Now the frontage was dirty and crumbling and pitted, and the windows were smashed or missing entirely. A tattered flag hung down from a pole. A black car with shaded windows was parked in the forecourt, a few yards down from the main entrance. Nyquist recognised the vehicle from when he'd been attacked in Cotton Springs cemetery. Wisps of fog wrapped themselves around his face, across his features as they creased into rage.

And then he realised that he wasn't alone.

A few chairs and hammocks were set out on the hotel's terrace. Thick tangles of weeds grew up from the decking. An old couple were sitting beneath a sunshade at a table, looking for all the world as though they were on holiday, enjoying their gin and tonics and gazing out over the fields of mist. Both of their faces were covered by masks, each in the shape of a clock, both showing the same time. Five past seven.

There were still two minutes to go...

The residents turned to stare at him.

He stared back.

One of them, the woman, raised her glass and saluted him.

Nyquist entered the hotel. He looked around the foyer but there was no sign of Eleanor or the two shadow men. The mist had partially made its way inside, enough to blur the edges of the shabby furniture and the broken display cabinets. The receptionist was a woman in a blue uniform that was torn in places and marked with dirt. Her face carried scars, each one a brave sign of her time in Dusk.

"Would you like a room, sir?" The receptionist spoke soothingly, but her smile looked like a crack in a porcelain mask, one more disfigurement.

Nyquist couldn't bring himself to answer.

"Sir? May I help you?"

He kept staring at her. "Help me?" he said. It was either a question or a statement.

"I'm sorry?" She looked back at him with her vacant staring eyes; two uncomprehending beings reflecting upon each other.

Again the receptionist asked if he would like a room and somehow or other he managed a reply, a nod of the head, a single word: "Yes."

"Very good. Can I take your name, please?"

"My name?"

"If you would, sir."

"Nyquist. John Henry Nyquist."

"Ah yes, Mr Nyquist. We've been expecting you."

"You have?"

"Yes. We've put you in room–"

He banged his fist down on the counter. "I don't want a room!"

The receptionist flinched slightly. Her complexion reddened around the scars.

"I don't want a room," Nyquist said again, quietly this time, trying to keep in control. He looked around the foyer, hoping to find something, anything, that he could focus on, that would make him feel a part of this world. But there was nothing, nothing useful. All was strange. There was an ornate clock on the wall above the elevator doors but he hardly needed to read its dial. From somewhere in the distance, from another room or corridor, he could hear a bell tolling.

He turned back to the desk, saying, "Tell me, what happened to the young woman, the teenager who came in a few minutes ago?"

"I'm afraid..." The receptionist smiled again. "I don't know what you mean."

"She came inside, I watched her. She's called Eleanor Bale."

The woman studied a ledger. "There's no one of that name..."

"What about Eleanor Kinkaid?"

"We have an Elizabeth Kinkaid staying with us."

"What?"

"She's one of our long-term residents. She came in a few minutes ago, with her two guardians. Perhaps you meant her?"

"Let me see that."

Nyquist turned the ledger round so he could read the entry: *Room 225 – Elizabeth Kinkaid*. The words and the numbers danced in his sight. What could it mean? Was it Eleanor he'd seen, or Eliza?

"Give me the key for this room," he said.

The receptionist hesitated. "Both keys have been given out."

"Both keys?"

"Yes sir. The first was taken by Mr Kinkaid, Elizabeth's father. He always carried it with him, and would often visit that particular room. Unfortunately…"

"Yes?"

"He hasn't brought it back. In fact, we haven't seen Mr Kinkaid for a while now. Some of us are getting rather worried about his absence."

Nyquist recalled the hotel key that Detective Gardner had shown him, the one the police had found on Kinkaid's body. Room 225.

"What about the second key?" he asked.

"The girl's grandmother has that one."

"Her grandmother?"

"That's correct. Aisha Kinkaid."

Nyquist knew he was nearing the mystery's centre.

"Is there a master key?"

"The manager had one. I'm afraid, however–"

"Where is he?"

"He's dead, sir. Long dead."

The foyer drifted with smoke and echoes of footfalls. Ghostly voices called from room to room.

"Would sir like anything else?"

"No. No, thank you…"

"Very good. Enjoy your stay with us."

"I'm not staying."

Nyquist turned away. He would visit room 225, and see if Eleanor was there. But the receptionist called after him, "Oh sir…"

"Yes?"

"Elizabeth's grandmother went into the lounge bar. I thought you'd like to know."

He followed directions along a corridor and into the bar area. The place was deserted, but faint music could be heard coming through a pair of closed doors. These opened out onto a small ballroom. And even here the mist had penetrated, its ribbons of grey drifting slowly along in time with the music that came from some invisible, spectral orchestra. Nyquist listened closely: it sounded like an old recording, complete with scratches and the sound of the needle turning in the groove. A few lamps, three or four at most, shone down from the ceiling, their beams moving in lazy arcs and colouring the air: pale yellow, burnt orange, a dying scarlet. A giant chandelier had broken loose from its central fixture and fallen to the floor below. It looked to Nyquist's eye like a crashed spaceship, governed by an alien technology based on light and colour. Hundreds of candles had been set around the vast mound of broken crystals and smashed bulbs, each one aflame. He bent down to pick one of the crystals; it sparkled and glinted in his hand as the rays of light from overhead crossed the floor, back and forth, back and forth. The effect was hypnotic.

He managed at last to draw his gaze away from the crystal's depths and to look across to the far side of the ballroom where an old woman could be seen. She was dancing alone to the music, her body swaying on the spot. The two shadow men stood one to each side, their arms crossed over their chests. Nyquist walked up to the old lady, but she seemed to be unaware of him. One hand held a wine glass from which she would sip now and again. Her eyes were closed, her skin ravaged by life's claws, her cratered cheeks wet with tears. Her hair, a web of grey silk, reached at least a yard from skull to tip, hanging down around her face, shoulders, and below the waist; in this way she was carrying her own ready-prepared shroud. For, from all the evidence on view, the old lady was not long for this earth. She looked to be more than a hundred years old.

"Aisha?"

Still she danced.

"Aisha Kinkaid?"

Now she turned her head and opened her eyes at last. "Oh. Hello... Mr..."

"Nyquist."

Her eyes shone yellow in the dim light. "Ah yes. Of course. The private investigator." Alarmingly, whenever she spoke, filaments of mist rose from her mouth.

"Where's Eleanor?"

She stopped moving, with the feel of an automaton coming to a halt as her mechanism wound down. "Why, you rude, rude man. Are you still pursuing her?" Her voice was low and gravelly, as severely damaged by time as her flesh and blood was. And her teeth, when he glimpsed them, were quite black.

Nyquist spoke quickly. "She's in danger."

"Indeed she is. How well informed you are–"

"Let me have the key! To room 225."

"And why should I do that?"

"I believe you're holding Eleanor captive there."

She stared at him without speaking.

Nyquist held his fury in check, as far as he could. He said, "I'll do whatever it takes to stop you from hurting her."

The two guardians moved closer, the masks of fog shifting on their faces. But Aisha dismissed them with a simple wave of the hand and they both left the ballroom immediately under her orders. She took another sip of the dark red liquid in her glass. Her eyes, old as they were, and bloodshot where they weren't yellowed, twinkled disarmingly. And the mist rose from her mouth as she spoke.

"What a sad little dance we have performed, the two of

us, around and around like puny marionettes."

Nyquist grabbed her roughly, he couldn't help himself.

The wine glass fell to the parquet floor and shattered.

He pulled her to him, her body crackling like a basket of twigs.

"Tell me where she is!"

He was shaking the poor woman half to death, his frustration burning through his body in a current. But still she didn't answer, and he realised that he was doing more harm than good. He stopped the action but still held on tight to her brittle arms.

She spoke, her voice drowsy, fog-veiled. "Please... you're hurting me."

Nyquist looked into her eyes; they were more than halfway lidded, weighed down with sorrow or life itself or drifting memories, or all three combined.

"Unhand me, young man."

He did so. For a moment he thought she was going to fall but she found her balance, and her slippered heels crunched over the shards of glass on the floor as she led him to a side alcove under a ruby-red lamp. They sat down opposite each other across a small circular table. "You must forgive my manners," she said. "It has been a while since a gentleman has called on me." Each and every word was accompanied by a different pattern of mist.

Nyquist decided on a reasoned approach. "Why do you want Eleanor so much? Can't you let her stay in Dayzone, or Nocturna? It's where she belongs."

"Sadly, that cannot be."

"Why not?"

She tilted her head to one side as she listened to the music. It sounded far off, indistinct, performed in another time and place.

"Mrs Kinkaid. Answer me..."

"A ritual must take place." She looked at him as from

the depths of a pit. "Eleanor has to die, I'm afraid. It really
is that simple."

Nyquist gripped the tabletop in his anger.

She smiled. "My granddaughter Elizabeth was always a
sickly child. Perhaps you've heard?" He nodded, allowing
her to carry on. "My son Dominic brought her back into
Dusk. Only here, in these realms..." She gestured about
her. "Only here could the girl hope to survive. But of
course, he was not only saving her, he was bringing her
home. She belongs here."

She reached into a sequined handbag that rested on the
seat beside her and took out a white silk handkerchief.
With this she wiped at her eyes, trying to hold back from
crying.

It did little good. Her voice cracked as she spoke.

"Oh, her dear little face! She was as pale as a dying
moon, I swear, and her breath could hardly be felt.
Why, even her shadow was listless. I could not bear it.
I could not bear it at all, to see her like that. I took her
into my arms, calling her name softly. *Eliza. Lovely, sweet
Eliza...*" Now the tears escaped, one single droplet from
each eye. They trickled slowly from crevice to crevice on
her wrinkled face. Her hands reached out involuntarily,
worked by some electrical spasm. "Yet it wasn't enough.
It simply wasn't enough, not as she grew older, and more
in need of sustenance. And believe me, Mr Nyquist, we
have tried every possible means, to allow Eliza's survival.
You see how it is, we are a strange family. We live for one
purpose only."

"And what is that?"

"To bring the dusk into being."

She breathed out, allowing him to see the mist as it
travelled from her body. It formed in a cloud and then
dispersed around her in grey, threadlike, ever-searching
strands, each one curling, drifting, dancing, adding its

presence to the mist and fog that already floated around the ballroom. Her eyes clouded over as she told her story:

"For years and years and years and years and further, untold, wearisome, wretched years I have lived and breathed, and with every breath added to the dusk, from my first gasps as a baby, to my last, which cannot be that far away now. And my adopted son's only true task in life was to provide me with a female heir to carry on my work. I attended the coming together of Dominic Kinkaid and Catherine Bale, their bond of flesh, the sacred rite, and I worked my spells over their heaving flesh and sent the mist into her body. And so it was done: the child of dusk created."

Nyquist tried to concentrate; the air of the ballroom was too heavy, too sick with the old woman's vaporous energies.

"Alas, an intruder entered the womb as well. Her twin. Her sister. You see, I hadn't planned for that. The intruder sucked half or more of the life from poor Eliza."

Now he felt the urge to put his two hands tight around her neck and break her dried-out, fragile body into dust. But she spoke on and delivered the verdict as a judge might, at the end of a court case:

"And so it is, that Eleanor has to die, in order that Eliza might live."

Nyquist stood up. Without pause he grabbed the edge of the table with both hands and pulled it from the alcove with such force that it broke away from his grip. It hit the ballroom floor with a clatter and spun away until it came to rest against the fallen chandelier. The lights sparkled a thousand different hues and the crystals shivered and chimed like the workings of a vast timepiece. The old lady remained as she was throughout all this, perched on her red velvet seat, unmoving. Nyquist reached over and picked up her bag. He searched the contents and found the key to room 225 among them.

She said, "You won't find her, Mr Nyquist. I have hidden your dear Eleanor away, far away..."

And upon saying this, Aisha Kinkaid faded from his sight.

He stared at the empty seat, at the mist that quickly took her place.

Time froze.

He tried to move his hands forward, but he couldn't manage it.

Even his lungs had stopped drawing breath. His heart was no longer beating.

Suspended...

And then she reappeared in the same place, seated in the same position, saying, "Yes, she's safe. I have checked on her, on them both."

He breathed again, and felt the surge of life quicken once more in his body. The shock trembled him. He gasped.

"They're together, Mr Nyquist, the two sisters. They are preparing for the end."

"Where... where did you go?"

Aisha smiled. "As you move through space, so I can move through time."

His mind clicked back into motion. He worked it out. "She's on a different timeline?"

"That's right. One that you could never reach, and that she can never leave."

Nyquist considered: here was a person who far outstripped Patrick Bale's control of time, who manipulated it as an artist mixed paint on a canvas.

He said, "It's you. You're Quicksilver."

She nodded. "Yes, I was the very first perpetrator, and then later my son Dominic took over. I taught him the art of stealing time. Of course, after he died, I had to revert to my old ways." Aisha shuddered. "Only a short while ago I ventured into night and took a life."

Nyquist recalled the news he had heard on the streets of Nocturna. "That was you? You killed a man?"

"I'm afraid so." She shivered. "It very nearly destroyed me, to leave the dusklands."

Nyquist remembered the shadow man's words: *Quicksilver awaits you.* Finally, that promised meeting was taking place.

"But why?" he asked. "Why are you killing people?"

She dismissed the question. "Go! Go now. Find Eleanor, if you can. But know this, that no matter what you do, she will still give up her life."

"That's not going to happen."

"I believe it will. By your hand, or mine."

He turned away across the dance floor.

Aisha Kinkaid called after him. "Only one thing matters, Mr Nyquist. Not myself, not my son Dominic, and not Eleanor. Only Eliza. Through her the dusk will live and grow and take over your precious city…"

At last he was out of earshot. He hurried back to reception – the desk was now empty – and walked on until he reached the elevators. He ascended in the tiny car up to the floor above where he followed the arrows towards his destination. His mind was troubled, but this was what he had to do.

By your hand, or mine… Did that mean that Aisha Kinkaid had knowledge of his own predicted role in Eleanor's death?

Well no matter. Now it would end, one way or another.

The corridor ran around a large rectangular inner courtyard. Looking over the balcony he saw a swimming pool filled with fog rather than water, and a number of people sitting at a long table, each person working to strip and empty the seed pods of the kia flower. Bright orange seeds floated up to his level; Nyquist watched them sparkle in the trapped mist.

A little further along the corridor he came to room 225.

He was about to knock at the door when he paused.

He realised that he still had a choice, even now: he could still walk away, and keep on walking, hoping that he could forever outpace the feelings inside. But how far would he have to go? How many miles? And how many hours would have to pass? And even then, would he ever escape his destiny? Was it even a possibility?

But if he stayed, if he faced Eleanor, if he confronted the demon, whatever it turned out to be, he might yet defeat it. He might not have to kill her. He could force himself to be a good man, not a murderous man. Yes, he could do that.

A good man...

But Nyquist felt his fingers curling round to press into his palms, hard enough for his nails to draw blood. He glanced at his watch: it was still five past seven. The second hand was shivering, held in place by some spell, yet desperate to move on. And he felt the cruel mechanism of his own life at work, clicking away, his heart made of cogs and springs.

He knocked on the door.

There was no answer. He tried again with the same result. So he took the key and placed it in the lock and turned it, and the door opened.

It was dark inside. He found the light switch and clicked it on.

A perfectly normal hotel room was revealed. A double bed, expertly made up. A small desk, two chairs, a wardrobe. A bedside telephone. A clock on the wall, a mirror below it. Floral prints on the wall, a small drinks cabinet. The walls and bed linen in various shades of grey. It was all vaguely familiar from somewhere. He went to the window and looked out. Room 225 was situated at the rear of the building, looking down onto an empty street with a small cinema across the way. The cinema's neon sign shone on his face.

He turned back to the room.

This was it, exactly, down to the last detail.

This was the place he had seen in the drug vision, the room where he would force the last breaths from the helpless, suffering body of Eleanor Bale.

UNKNOWN AND CRUEL

He moved over to the mirror and stared at himself. Above his head, the wall clock hovered between one second and the next.

Those eyes.

He had seen them before, in the vision. The same look about them: cruel, selfish and cold. He couldn't bear it.

The hands closed on the soft grey pillow, holding it down across the face of...

Nyquist turned away from his own reflection, his own thoughts.

He looked around the hotel room, searching for a clue, a sign, anything that would help him understand the circumstances that held him. A photograph album on the desk caught his attention. He leafed through the pages, taking in one image after another. The first few showed a baby in swaddling clothes; later photographs revealed a girl of some three or four years, even then bearing a likeness to Eleanor, around the eyes and mouth especially. But it wasn't Eleanor. There was too much sadness in the expression; a sadness born not of daylight, and not of darkness, but of this godforsaken realm between. Even at this young age the girl had lived too strange a life, that was evident. Nyquist turned one photograph over to reveal a name: *Elizabeth, age 4*. Here she was, the missing part of the puzzle. All subsequent photographs showed the same girl, the earlier shots taken within the dusklands, her face and figure surrounded by the mists or bathed in moonlight, whilst all the later images showed the child sitting alone in this room, or in rooms similar to this one. Nyquist pictured the child being kept here, locked in against her will, for whatever purpose fate had in store for her. Until she reached the appointed age...

The final photograph showed Elizabeth Kinkaid at the age of twelve.

The resemblance to Eleanor was now complete. And she was now outside once more, released from captivity. Her mouth was open and a thin trail of mist came from her lips. The dusk came from her, she bore it into life, one breath at a time. Yet she still looked distraught, her skin stretched on the bones, pitted with marks. She was still suffering from the illness that threatened both her, and the dusk's continuance. And now Nyquist understood a little of Aisha Kinkaid's needs: this world, *her* world, whatever it might be, had to be kept alive by any means necessary.

And that meant Eleanor Kinkaid had to die.

She had stolen too much of her sister's energy from the womb.

Eleanor was seen as a parasite. It was that simple.

Nyquist cursed his own part in all this. He'd broken the girl out of the Aeon Institute, released her back onto the path that would lead to her death. And now he waited for her in this room, as tightly bound here as Eliza had ever been. He waited for the clock to start ticking again, to release those final two minutes on their countdown towards seven minutes past the hour.

What would happen then?

Had he been cast as the murderer all along, the agency of Eleanor's death? Perhaps Aisha had brought him here by her powers, through the drug, through her spell and charms.

It made sense. It made a terrible, horrific sense.

But still, he wasn't sure…

And he vowed there and then to never harm the girl, to never touch her, to allow her to live on. He would kick the future in the teeth, he would break the future in two.

The neon sign's light cast his shadow across the wall. He started to pace, to stalk the room like a caged animal, worrying at his confines. The mirror glimmered with his passing image but he would not look at himself. His hands itched at the palms and were slick with sweat and dried blood. His mind raced ahead of his body, seeking answers. There were none. Only the bad feelings crawling through him like a disease. It all hinged on the hidden events, yes, he knew that. Those stolen few minutes from the room on the edge of twilight, when Dominic Kinkaid had been killed. And as he thought of this, the mist almost cleared from his mind's eye and he saw himself once again in that room of death, moving towards the bed as Kinkaid screamed…

He screamed!

This was an unknown fact, a lost memory, until now. Kinkaid had screamed at the end; a suicide victim wouldn't do that, would they? Wouldn't they more willingly accept their fate? So that means… that meant that Kinkaid didn't slash his own throat. He was murdered. But whose hand was on the knife? Nyquist's or the girl's? He screwed his eyes shut to focus on the mental picture, the memories. But the mist closed over the scene as surely as a curtain at the end of a play.

He lay down on the bed a while and rested. Speckles of orange dust, the potent seeds of the kia plant, drifted around the room, across his field of vision. He was tired, his body drained of all energy, but he would not sleep. Not yet. Not until this was done, not until all the events had played out to their end. His mind flitted over the various details of the case as the seeds settled on him, setting his skin to tingle. His eyes closed and once again he was walking through the field of dusk flowers, beneath the electric violet moon. A dark object of some kind could be seen ahead, only slightly visible within the swaying stems and petals.

It was a gravestone.

The whole field glowed with an eerie light. Nyquist parted the stems in order to read the inscription on the stone, its letters clean and well defined, freshly carved. There were no dates, no acknowledgement of birth and death, only these words:

HERE LIES ELEANOR BALE

KILLED IN HER YOUTH

BY HANDS UNKNOWN

AND CRUEL

He touched at the lettering with his fingertips, tracing the girl's name. A mound of earth was clearly visible, stretching away from the stone. The flowers had not yet blossomed over the grave. Nyquist knelt down to dig into the soil. His bare hands brought up several objects, one after the other: a postcard of a beach scene; a shadow puppet; a piece of paper with a telephone number on it; a page torn from a travelogue; two vials filled with orange liquid. a photograph of a young man. He turned the photograph over and saw the words *Angelcroft* and *Silhouette* written on the back. Nyquist could make no sense of these mysterious objects, beyond a vague feeling that he might have seen them before somewhere, or heard about them from a friend, or read about them in a novel that someone had lent him once, a book that was now lost, as all things eventually become lost. His body shivered with cold as a smear of cloud passed over the moon. Mist clung to the stone, partially obscuring the name of the girl. He was afraid. What had he done? What had he done wrong?

Nyquist woke up. He was lying on the hotel bed. His mouth was dry, his eyes flashed with strange colours.

Something had changed. He could not comprehend it at first, except that the room was dark now, the overhead light had been turned off. Did he do this? The curtains were drawn. Did he do these things? He could not remember. Nyquist remained still, very still, listening.

He became aware of another presence in the room.

He turned his head slightly, enough to see that a person was sitting on a chair in the corner, in the darkest part of the room. He could not see the person's eyes or even their face, not clearly, but he could sense that he was being watched, stared at, examined closely.

The clock on the wall started to tick.

A LESSON FROM THE SHADOWS

It seemed that sleep still had a partial hold on him. Nyquist made to get up from the bed but found that he could not easily move his body. His limbs were filled with earth. His head turned back and forth like a machine pretending to be alive.

The wall clock filled the room with its slowed-down mantra, each single tick taking an age to complete its movement.

The figure had not yet made a sound or a gesture.

Nyquist screwed up his eyes, seeking knowledge of the visitor, the person that shared this space with him. His vision readjusted slightly, letting the silhouette take on a blurred identity.

"Eleanor? Is that you?"

There was no reply.

"Eleanor?"

Finally, the figure spoke: "Yes. It's me." The voice, a whisper only.

"Oh, thank Apollo. I was scared that you…"

His voice trailed away. There was something different about the girl, he could not make it out. Again, he tried to move; again finding it difficult. His body was under some kind of binding spell, some weight placed upon him.

Eleanor asked quietly, "Tell me your name, please?"

"What?"

"Your name?"

"It's John. John Nyquist."

"John?"

"Yes. Nyquist. The private detective."

He managed to raise his arms, enough to allow his fingers to rub at his eyes. He could feel granules of sand lodged at each tear duct.

Eleanor must be confused, he thought; it was this place taking control, this room, the dusk itself, the various moons and the mist, the few remaining neon stars, all under Aisha's control.

"I feel strange, John. I really do. I can't…"

"What? What is it?"

"I can't seem to breathe properly."

"Eleanor?"

He had to get her out of here, back to the daylight. And with that thought he managed to gain some control over his body, to sit up on the bed. He carried on the movement, lifting himself to his feet. His legs felt weak and he almost collapsed. The spell worked like a personal gravity. Eleanor was moving her arms slowly back and forth, over and over, and his internal body clock was slowing in turn, following the rhythm.

The girl settled back once more into the shadows.

Nyquist could just about make her out there; he could see that she was still wearing the plain blue tunic given her at the Aeon Institute; he could hear the shallow breaths that she took, the spittle in her throat. It was too intimate a sound and his own mouth went dry in response. If only he could think clearly.

He looked around the room. A crack in the curtain let in a beam of light which fell just so across the face of the wall clock, as though placed there by some purposeful hand. The dial was blurred. A black jellylike substance was seeping from the bottom of the clock. Here was Time; Time itself, escaping from the confines of the instrument.

At last he got the clockface in focus: it was six minutes past seven.

Nyquist felt sick. "Let me..." His voice would not work properly. "Let me see you. I need to... I need to see you, your face."

Eleanor nodded. She spoke quietly, using strange words, and then he could move again. Nyquist steadied himself, before taking a few tentative steps.

"Please, John. Not too close."

The girl's voice was changing, growing weary.

And he remembered what Aisha Kinkaid had said to him about Eleanor being caught in a different time zone. What a tremendous effort the girl must be making, to show herself to him like this, to force herself into his world, at least partially. Yes, yes; that's why the clock was wounded. The two worlds were clawing at each other, to stay connected.

"Eleanor, are you all right?"

"It's this place, isn't it?" she replied. "This twilight. All the clocks ticking away, so slowly. Tick away, tick away." The voice quietened. "Tick, tick, ticking away. Oh..."

Nyquist had clicked on a bedside lamp, causing Eleanor to gasp.

"Is that hurting you?" he asked.

"A little."

Nyquist picked up the lamp by its base. He walked forward slowly, towards the girl. She leant back into the shadows. Nyquist followed her, holding the lamp out in front of him.

Now he saw the face, one half of which was turned away.

"Eleanor? Look at me."

She did so, and he was shocked by what he saw.

"Please don't think badly of me, Johnny. You don't mind me calling you that, I hope? Because we're friends, aren't we? Of course we are. John Nyquist. A fine name, for a fine man."

The face loomed directly into the lamplight, fully visible, and Nyquist understood completely. He knew the truth. All the hidden patterns of this long difficult case unfolded, all the riddles and tangles pulling themselves into shape. His hand trembled, causing the light to quiver as he made a study of the person before him.

The girl's skin was palely drawn, almost translucent. Within this setting the mouth was stark red and open, labouring to draw in breath. The eyes were the worst, for they contained no colour, none of the startling blue he had seen before in Eleanor's sight, and no whiteness at all; instead they were black, entirely black, glistening. Strands of mist trailed around her head like the filaments of a dream escaping from her skull. Strangest of all, the face quivered slightly, blurring at the edges. She opened her mouth and a wisp of grey fog escaped, curling away from her lips.

Nyquist watched in horror. He knew that this was Eleanor Bale in body only, a body taken over by the spirit of her sister, Eliza Kinkaid. Or rather, yes he saw it now: the two women were occupying the exact same place at slightly different times. Just a few seconds separated them, enough to allow this merging to take hold. Nyquist felt his skin crawl. The fear rose in him and he dropped the lamp. The shadows of the room rushed away from the light's sudden downward swing, finally settling once more in new shapes, new positions.

"Eleanor?"

He could hardly dare look at her, but he did, he had to. He tried to say her name a second time, knowing it was a lie or at least part of a lie. His voice froze, mid-word.

"Quiet now, Johnny. You're weak, weak and fatigued." The girl's face took on a more serious aspect. "When I was younger, so very much younger..." The words drifted away, unfinished, barely heard. She was moving in and out of his time, and the struggle to remain in sync took all her concentration.

It made him bring a hand up to his own face, checking for evidence of his own flesh and blood, his own bodily warmth. Even to look upon this woman seemed like a small act of dying. All evidence of Eleanor's youthful awkwardness had vanished, the flesh caressed all over by the sister's presence. The years spent here in twilight had taken their own toll upon Eliza, causing her to lose sense of what life might be, all youthful vitality to be drained away. Now she was the parasite. And the ravenous look in the blackened eyes told him that she would soon take Eleanor's life force as her own, completely. Yet Nyquist sensed that she was following orders given out by her grandmother. A part of her still clung in love to her twin.

She said, "You have to listen to me. Can you do that?"

It was Eliza speaking. Nyquist nodded. "Yes."

"When I was younger I lived alone, here in this room. They locked me away, my father and my grandmother. Oh, they fed me, and cleaned me, and tended to my sickness, and they said that they loved me, very much so, but I was alone. I lived in the confines of this room, very often in the dark by my own choosing, and mist grew within me. I could feel it. Just here, as I grew older. And here..." Her hands touched at her chest and belly. "Until the time came for the door to be opened. I walked out, into the fields of dusk, and I breathed. I breathed out. I *breathed* the mist." Again, she demonstrated her skill for him.

Nyquist could take no more. He brushed the mist from where it clung to his face and cried out, "Eleanor! Eleanor, if you're in there, speak to me. Speak!"

The darker sister sighed. "She can't hear you. Eleanor can't do much of anything just now."

"Let her go."

"I can't do that."

"Eliza, please..." It was the first time he had used the young woman's name.

"I can't help you, I'm afraid."

He pleaded with her. "What do you want?"

The face smiled. It was unnerving to see Eleanor's face and form like this, to hear her voice, and yet to see the hands moving in a stranger's manner, the expressions awkward on the flesh, and the choice of words and syntax so different from those he was used to hearing from her.

He repeated his question. "Eliza, what is it that you want?"

"Only what was stolen from me. My life, my strength."

"You're going to kill her?"

The jet black eyes blinked. The head tilted slightly. "My grandmother will carry out the ceremony. Eleanor's physical body will die. But even then, I believe my sister will live on inside me, in a way."

Nyquist leaned closer. "This isn't the answer, Eliza. Her life isn't yours to steal."

The girl shivered. "I should've destroyed her in the womb."

Seven words, plainly spoken.

And that was all he needed: a trigger.

Nyquist moved away.

The girl stood up from her seat, holding out a hand in warning.

He went to the wall and clicked the switch.

The room was flooded with light.

She howled.

He went back to her and said, "Eleanor? I know you can hear me."

He reached out and placed his hands on her shoulders, one on each side. The body flinched. Her face was close to his. Her eyes were so deep and so dark at this range, they reminded Nyquist of the state of midnight into which he had entered, the pool of blackness at the night's furthest edge. But now he could see that thin trails of mist rose even from the pupils, like tears turned to vapour.

He whispered, "Eleanor. I'm here. I'll take you back home."

She pulled away. The ghost in her eyes had seen something, something in Nyquist. Something terrible. Her voice faltered, she couldn't speak.

Nyquist felt this strange desire come over him, this urgent need to wrap his hands around the girl's neck, or to push her back roughly. Energy coursed through his body.

He glanced at the clock.

It was still six minutes past seven.

He could hear the ticking in his head.

In the mirror below the clock he caught a glimpse of his own face. One look told him the truth, that he was no longer in charge of his own being. He was a slave. His demeanour was changing, becoming more cruel, more determined and trapped in its course. Nyquist scarcely knew what was happening, but the feelings were too strong. His mouth opened, showing his teeth. His eyes were pinpricks, with no expression in them, none.

Less than a minute to go. Fifty-five seconds.

The hands of the clock moved on, slowly, so very slowly...

He turned back to the girl.

"What's wrong?" she said. "What's happening?" It was Eleanor's voice.

"It's time," he answered.

She took a step away from him, another. "Please. Nyquist. You're scaring me. Leave me alone." He followed her, his long stride easily covering the distance, and he reached out with one hand and pushed her down onto the bed.

She was terrified. "Keep away from me. Keep away!"

He fell on the bed with her, straddling her body. The girl was screaming. But Nyquist could hear only the surge of blood inside his own head, nothing else. His hand reached out without need of instruction, grabbing the nearest pillow. He brought it round in a preordained movement, following the rehearsed pattern to place it over her face. He pressed down, lightly at first. Eleanor cried out: no words, just a noise, a noise, a dreadful, appalling noise and then Nyquist cut off the voice completely, pushing the pillow down hard on the girl's face.

Pressing down, pressing.

Eleanor struggled.

The seconds ticked away. He pressed harder.

Her hands reached up to...

To stop him...

To...

Her hands...

Reaching...

Failing...

Falling...

There was little chance for her now. She had given in, willingly, desiring only an end to this pain and for stillness to take her at last, nothing more. Her final movements were tiny, her breathing slowed to nothingness, to silence. Nyquist was too strong for her. It was done now, done, and yet still he held the pillow in place, keeping it there, whilst his mind entered another state, another place, another time, floating free from his immediate surroundings, from his body. He saw the clock on the wall reading exactly seven minutes past seven.

It was time.

He was a child again, seeing his mother lying in the road, his father emerging from the car, crying out in horror at what he'd done: he'd killed her, his own wife, his darling wife! And Nyquist knew that his father had walked into the dusk out of guilt, only that, sheer guilt. There was no exploration, no hope of seeing her again; only the mist taking him away.

All these thoughts came to Nyquist as he knelt there on the bed.

He let his hands uncurl on the pillow, and to lift up, lift up, further, taking the pillow with them as he willed the girl, the beautiful young woman, all that life, that life to come, willing her to breathe again. To breathe.

Then he threw the pillow aside and pressed down on her chest.

Breathe again. Breathe for me.

Again.

There was no movement.

Breathe. Eleanor. Please won't you breathe! Breathe.

His lips came down to hers and he pinched her nose shut with one hand and he breathed for her. He breathed for the girl, again, again, and again, sobbing, his eyes brimming with tears as he breathed out, letting his own breath go inside of her, pure air, willing her to live, again, again, pressing down on her chest now, violently, urging the flesh, and then returning to her lips, to breathe there, to breathe for her and with her. Breathing as two persons sharing one body might breathe, until a scream came from her, not from her lips but from within, and a shadow moved away from her body, was torn from her, and Eleanor stirred beneath him then, the flesh, the blood, slowly, reluctantly, clinging on, loosening their grip on darkness, stronger now, more determined, her chest starting to rise, to rise and to fall in a broken rhythm and she was coughing, choking, and he held her there, that moment, another, one more, he held on tight until she was sobbing with him, in his arms and breathing at last. And he looked into her eyes, her lovely blue eyes, clear, untainted, the colour of the sky in daylight, in sunlight.

The parasite had vanished.

OF FOG AND SORROW

Nyquist led Eleanor out of the hotel room, into the corridor. She was weak still and had to be supported most of the way to the elevator. He pressed the button and the door opened. They stepped inside. The girl slumped down against the wall, sliding to the floor. Nyquist wanted to say something, but any words he could think of seemed inadequate.

The car started to descend.

"Come on." Nyquist reached down to grab the girl's arm. She came up slowly, without resistance. He held her tightly and said, "Can you remember what happened back there?"

The girl looked at him without replying.

Nyquist started, "I didn't mean to–"

The girl spat in his face.

He kept silent after that.

The elevator reached the ground floor. They walked out, making their way past the main desk. The receptionist had returned to her post and she called out to him, "Mr Nyquist? Are you leaving us so soon?" He ignored her, moved on to the front door and out, and down the steps. The clock-faced couple stared at them from their terrace, their dials both set in the lopsided frown of twenty-five past seven.

There was no sign of Aisha Kinkaid or her guardians, but he imagined they wouldn't be far behind, now he had taken Eleanor from them.

The mist folded over on itself, becoming more opaque. The hotel's revolving sign was barely visible, a diffuse silver neon glow behind a curtain of thick grey and black air. Nyquist hurried over to the shadow men's car, looking inside; there was no key in the ignition.

"This way."

He led Eleanor across the hotel's car park. The road ought to be here somewhere, but all he could see was overgrown vegetation and dirt.

"Where are we going?" the girl asked, her voice drawling.

"Home. Nocturna. Dayzone. Wherever."

"I'm not feeling too good."

"I know that. I'll get you to safety."

"No. I can't... I don't think I can... I can't seem to move..."

Nyquist felt the girl slipping away from his hold.

"Hang on."

She made no response, only to pull further away. But Nyquist was ready for her. He grabbed on tight to her wrist. She struggled for a moment and then fell into a faint. Eliza had taken something from her sister already, that was obvious, added to his own desperate treatment of her; Eleanor was badly damaged, in shock, exhausted.

He pulled her along anyway, he had to. But where to go? There was no direction here, and he knew he was far away from the borderlines of either Day or Night.

The fog moved around them, closing in, but he dragged her along, stumbling, keeping his feet somehow.

Voices called from all around, the painful cries of the lost, and dark shapes followed after him with every step. But there was a faint light ahead. He made for it, having no other option, taking Eleanor with him. The soft glow was emitted by yet another of the artificial moons of duskland; this time a large theatrical spotlight that shone down on an open-air auditorium: three rows of banked seats around the circle of a sunken pit, with a vast stage of white sand at its centre to form an amphitheatre. A series of wooden upright poles, perhaps a dozen of them, were set in the earth at regular intervals, forming an inner circle. Lights and flecks of colour glinted on each pole, reflected off the many shards of mirrored glass fixed to the wood. Pools of mist were captured here like tiny clouds in a hollow. The whole circle seemed to hum with some magical, electrical power. This was a charged space.

Nyquist and Eleanor stopped at the theatre's edge.

The seats were empty. But there was movement below, a figure walking slowly across the flat stage, from one area of sand to another. It was Eliza Kinkaid, a frail luminous figure in a simple white gown.

She was unaware of her tiny audience. And then Nyquist realised that they weren't the only onlookers: Aisha Kinkaid was sitting on the far side of the circle, her ancient form almost lost in the shadows.

Eliza's movement faltered on the sand. She was weak, Nyquist saw that now. Weak and ill and growing weaker even as he watched. She was in desperate need of sustenance.

Eleanor shivered at his side, as though in sympathy.

Nyquist watched, fascinated, as one area of the stage came to life, displaying a tableau of some kind. Figures moved within it, but not of flesh and blood; they seemed more like ghosts, or living shadows. Whatever they were, Eliza was energised by their presence. Quickly she made her way over to view them more clearly. Her body suddenly bent double and jerked violently, and then came back upright, renewed, standing tall. For a moment at least. But soon she weakened once more, almost immediately.

Another tableau came to life, and she headed over to it, desperately, driven by some kind of hunger, her feet dragging in the white sand.

Nyquist watched it all from the edge of the sunken area. He was focused too closely on the spectacle, not seeing until it was too late that Eleanor had started to move, to walk down the steps towards the stage. He was too late to stop her.

"Eleanor..." The theatre's atmosphere hushed his voice to a whisper.

In a daze she walked onto the flat white earth, joining her sister. There was still some bond between them, forged by Aisha's magic.

Nyquist followed warily.

As soon as he touched the white sand with his feet he knew he had entered a new time zone, unlike any he had experienced in his life, even stranger than the full dark of midnight; there, time had slowed to a dead stop; whereas here he stepped out of normal time entirely, into a new realm where the past and the present coexisted, caught in the same circle of illuminated earth. And he felt himself visited by all the other versions of himself, from boyhood, to maturity: they lived inside him in a chattering of voices and thoughts.

The moon dazzled his eyes.

Vaguely, through the noise of his own senses, he was aware of the three women in their different positions, only as blurs in the light, darker shapes in the mist-filled space: Aisha Kinkaid was still on the far bank of seats; Eleanor was standing close by Eliza, as yet another tableau came to life. They were both enthralled by what they saw there, in the shimmer. Nyquist was close enough himself now to see that these dreamlike visions were projected onto the stage, possibly from the mirrored uprights.

He watched the dream unfurl, his eyes wide.

It was a murder scene.

A young man staggered back as a knife entered his flesh. Around him stood a roomful of people, all of them shocked at the sight they were witnessing, unable to move to help their friend. A woman cried out in fear.

Dominic Kinkaid was the murderer, the wielder of the knife.

The whole episode lasted a few seconds only, and then repeated itself on some kind of endless loop.

Nyquist recognised the scene: he had read about it in the *Beacon Fire*, one of the recent Quicksilver killings. A man killed at his own birthday party, right in front of his guests, his friends and relatives, and yet not one person there present could recall a single detail of the fatal act. Nyquist was watching that murder take place, here in this pit of sand, amid fog and electric moonlight: the same murder, the lost moments of time, happening over and over and over again. And Eliza Kinkaid drank deeply of the sight, the spell, of whatever frightful energies the murder gave off.

The tableau darkened. And another took its place.

Eliza rushed over to it, her mouth spewing out animalistic grunts and mewlings. She was nothing more or less than a ravenous creature in search of food.

Nyquist and Eleanor followed her. Now they saw a small portion of a crowded market place. Fahrenheit Square. A young shopper, a woman, a kaleidoscope falling from her hand as Dominic Kinkaid stabbed her repeatedly. Her husband at her side, unable to do a single thing to help his wife, unable to save her.

Nyquist knew the victim's name was Jenny James. Again, he had read the news reports: her friends called her Jay Jay. By all accounts she was well-liked, with a bright future ahead of her. But now she fell to the ground, clutching the wound in her stomach. A little boy looked on, a little boy holding a lantern in the shape of a star. He watched as the victim died, just a few feet away from his wide-eyed gaze.

This episode took longer to play out, a minute and a half of captured agony.

Eliza screamed in delight. Her body convulsed.

Nyquist tried to clear his head, but the stage held him within its field of visions as other tableaux came to life, nine or ten of them, more even, each one the record of a terrible crime. And at last he understood – all of Quicksilver's stolen minutes of time ended up here, stored in this theatre, to be viewed over and over as needed. This is why the moments could not be remembered; they had been transported to this place. Dusk acted as the memory bank of pain and death, all gathered together for a teenage girl's pleasure. And by these deaths, to bring her life.

Nyquist stopped moving. He trembled and looked on in wonder as the room on the edge of twilight materialised only a few yards in front of him. He stepped closer, utterly spellbound. He was back there again, in the house on Angelcroft Lane, the upstairs bedroom. Fog streaming in through the window, Eleanor standing there, her father Dominic Kinkaid on the bed, the knife in his hand, this same knife he used in all his killings. Nyquist himself by the open doorway of the room, a moth batting against his face, yet watching, watching, as he now watched on the theatre stage, watching as a figure emerged from out of the mist, to grab the knife from Kinkaid's hand, to turn the knife on Kinkaid, slicing it fiercely across his neck, and then plunging it deep in the flesh.

The room howled. A mouth opening...

Blood. Blood, fog and screams.

Kinkaid's body in the death throes, his eyes lit with shock.

Eleanor crying out in despair. Nyquist frozen by the

doorway, a helpless spectator of these few stolen minutes of time.

Nyquist moving to help the victim.

Eleanor picking up the knife from the bed. Staring at the blade, the colours it held as they mingled, silver and red: the wonder of it in her gaze, the strangeness.

The murderer slipping away, back into the fog, vanishing.

The same person was at Nyquist's back now, speaking softly: "Of course, he had to be the next victim. Dominic knew that."

Nyquist turned to see Aisha Kinkaid standing a short distance away.

He said, "You killed him?"

She answered plainly, "I did. My son had to die for two reasons."

Nyquist didn't let her relish the tale. He took it upon himself, saying, "He turned against the idea, is that it? He didn't want Eleanor to die, he didn't want her to visit the dusk, just to save Eliza, or the fog, whatever it might be."

She merely stared back at him in response, and he knew he'd got it right.

The other reason was more obvious, and in its way, even crueler. "And who better to give life to a child than the father? He must have had so much life force to pass on, so much more than the random strangers you and he killed under the Quicksilver guise."

Now she spoke. "Yes. Precisely. But Eleanor is the real prize, the only true sacrificial lamb. Once she dies, Eliza will live into her old age." A knife appeared in Aisha's hand. "Her death will be staged here over and over, a fitting act of kindness from one sister to another."

By now the entire area was filled with thirty or so different murder scenes, going back through the decades, some with Aisha as the perpetrator; others, the more recent, with Dominic Kinkaid as the killer. And yet within this parade of evil, Eleanor was enthralled only by the spectacle of her father's death, captured and displayed repeatedly in the swirls of light and fog and sorrow. Her face was bereft of feelings, her eyes glazed. Eliza stood close by, the twins bound together in spirit.

Aisha smiled seeing this and she called out to the whole of Dusk, a wordless banshee-like cry that caused the swirls of fog to flit back and forth like startled creatures of the air.

Aieeeeeeeeeeeeeeeeeeeeeeeeeeeeeeee!

The cry was answered.

Nyquist turned in a circle. Figures were appearing around the edge of the theatre, many of them, all standing close together and looking down towards the stage. Some of them were guardians, wearing their masks of smoke; others were the black-eyed workers, trapped in their own spell; others were the guests he had seen at the Silver Star hotel.

The strange audience closed around the pit, trapping the figures within their gaze.

Aisha walked slowly towards Eleanor and Eliza, the knife ready.

"Let us begin."

Nyquist moved quickly, or as quickly as he could, fighting against the zone's closed circle of time. He grabbed Eleanor's arms, tried to pull her away. She wouldn't move, her eyes still transfixed by the sight of the tableau. He moved his hand back and forth in front of her face, saying her name. "Eleanor." She stirred and turned to look at him as Nyquist spoke urgently: "Aisha killed your father. Not me, not you. Not himself. Your grandmother did it!"

She nodded wearily. "Yes… I see that… I understand…"

Now she moved with him, towards the banks of seats. They climbed together to the edge of the pit but the guardians with their batons were there, the workers with their ravaged faces, the hotel guests with their clocks and seed pods.

Nyquist was knocked back. Eleanor stumbled with him.

He moved around the middle row of the seated area, seeking a way through.

There was none.

The circle closed even tighter as more workers and guardians arrived.

There was no way out.

Aisha called to them with her banshee wail.

The guardians led the way, descending to the highest levels of seats.

Eleanor clung to Nyquist. They fell back to the stage area, where Aisha waited with the knife held outstretched before her.

And then he saw it, a small piece of cloth clutched in a worker's hand. That was all, a small patch of blue and white linen scarcely visible in a clenched fist. Nyquist pictured the human eye design embroidered on the cloth.

"This way! Follow me."

He led Eleanor back up the steps. And the circle parted there, as the field worker he had helped broke ranks.

Nyquist moved towards the gap.

And then stumbled.

Fell back.

Something… what was wrong?

Something had happened. He was suddenly dizzy.

But there was no pain, no yet.

Only blood. The sight of it, red and startling. Blood on his hand where he pressed it against his side. His mind reeled. The circle whirled around him, a blur of shapes, a clash of voices, all the ghosts, all the victims crying out at once in their final moments of agony, forever repeated. The flash of the blade in the old woman's hand, caught under the spotlight.

Now the pain. Piercing through him.

Eleanor was at his side, in charge now, taking his hand

and pulling up him back up towards the break in the circle. They pushed through, forcing a gap, as the wordless dusk-ridden screech of Aisha sounded behind them, a wailing wound of a voice.

"Run, Nyquist!"

He ran. Following Eleanor's call, her orders, her shape darting ahead.

A thick cloud of fog closed around them.

And they ran on, further, becoming lost, knowing one direction only; away from the terrible screams of Aisha.

Blood on his skin, his clothes.

He didn't want to look at it, nor to think about it, only to keep moving.

All was fog and moonless skies and black earth and desolation.

The breath dry in his lungs, his throat, hard drawn.

The slow hissing sound of twilight.

His father's acoustic recordings of the dusk's edge: the same mysterious sound heard so often as the wax discs spun round. The young boy listening back to the discs later, on his own, hoping to hear the lost sound of his mother's voice in the…

No. Enough of that. Keep going!

No roads underfoot, no signs to follow. No maps, no knowledge.

They might well be going round in circles, but he had no time to think of such things.

There was only the need to keep moving, to escape.

They ran, the girl ahead, the wounded man behind.

Ghostly figures hovered in the mist.

Whispers of despair all around.

A guardian lurched at them, his face of swirling shadows split by a shriek of anger. He rammed into Nyquist and they both fell to the cold damp ground, where they rolled over, a tumble of fists and snarls, over as suddenly as it had begun when Eleanor howled and grunted and brought a large rock down hard on the back of the shadow man's head.

Nyquist staggered to his feet.

She dropped the bloodied rock. "Where are we?"

"I don't know."

They could see only a few feet all around.

Neither of them moved.

Now the dusk seemed entirely made of silence.

The fog touched at their faces, stung their eyes, got inside their mouths, their nostrils, travelling down into their bodies.

Nyquist felt weak, suddenly. Life was ebbing away. He wanted nothing more than to fall to the ground. He put his hand to his side and touched at the knife wound.

He grimaced with pain.

Eleanor looked at the wound for him. "Aisha did this. I saw her."

"Yes."

"We need to get help. Get you to hospital."

He laughed at this, he couldn't help it. "I think we're lost, Eleanor."

She looked at him and said gently, "Take my hand."

He did so.

She walked on slowly, at ease. Nyquist was entirely under her guide. They moved through the fog. Apparitions hovered beyond the corner of his vision, vanishing whenever he turned his head. He had to concentrate, keep looking ahead, moving ahead…

A terrible sound pierced the silvery grey air around them.

It was the sound of Aisha's voice, a shriek.

Nyquist froze, Eleanor with him.

Then they saw her.

The old woman appeared out of the fog. For a moment

she stared at them both, almost without seeing. Her ghastly yellow eyes were lost, held by other things, other people.

"Where is she?" she cried. "Have you seen her?"

Neither of them answered.

Aisha screamed again. "Eliza! Eliza! Come to me. Where are you?" And she moved off back into the fog, her cries, her sobs heard long after she had vanished: "Don't leave me, Eliza. Come back! Come back to me. Forgive me..."

And then the voice faded also.

Nyquist felt an overwhelming desire to stay where he was, to be accepted as part of the dusklands, to rest here forever. But Eleanor took his hand once more. She urged him on, even though his limbs were so tired they hardly supported him. The blood drained away. Each movement was painful. Many times he almost fell.

Step by step by step...

Eleanor was moving ahead of him, too quickly now, he couldn't keep up with her.

Nyquist tried to call out, but his voice was weak.

He was staggering now, almost falling.

The fog folded around Eleanor, taking her from him.

He was alone.

Alone...

Alone here in the enclosing fog.

And the loss of that one other true human presence almost stopped him.

He could barely move.

Yet he saw a light flickering at his eye's corner and turned his head in that direction. He heard music playing, quietly, distantly, a slow waltz-like theme.

The two young women were turning slowly in a moonlit circle of mist, holding each other carefully, gracefully, hand on shoulder, hand on waist, each on each, turning in this slow almost silent dance they had made for themselves, out of their own separate lives and needs and love and loss, dancing in the fog, two girls of eighteen years, one in blue and one in white, their faces identical, each one a perfect reflection of the other.

Twins.

Eleanor.

Elizabeth.

Flesh and fog.

And the fog danced around the flesh, the flesh within the fog, as one now, as one.

Nyquist watched. He watched until the music ended and the dance came to an end, and the two women parted and returned each to their own worlds.

Eleanor walked towards him.

He knew it was her by her blue tunic. And he knew straightaway that something had happened, something crazy, probably bad, something between the two of them, the two women, something he couldn't understand but he saw it in her eyes, once her eyes were close enough to be seen. In her eyes and in her stance and her movement, everything just too slow, too weary, too sluggish, as though she'd given something away of herself, a gift from one sister to another.

Their very own private magic.

And she was brave about it until the very last steps, when she fell into his arms.

There were no words, nothing to be said. Nothing that could be said. Only the journey that lay ahead. Nyquist had to carry on, helping the girl as he could, with the both of them wounded in their very different ways. That was all. It was all he could do. He would have to keep on like this, one small slow step at a time with his blood dripping to the ground, walking on together like this until eventually they would reach the limits of Dusk and cross over into Day or Night, whichever borderline they came to first, whichever direction they might be going in, yes, he would do that, however many hours it took, however many miles he would have to travel, he would bring Eleanor to safety, no matter what else happened. Or else die trying. And then she fell to the ground and lay there, moaning a little. He bent down and picked her up. He carried her in his arms one painful step after another. It was a pure fantasy, he knew that, a vision in his head. A goal. It was the task he had taken on, a goddamn task he had taken on a long time ago now, days ago, weeks ago, months ago, whenever it was when all this started, some time ago, and he *would* do it, he would keep moving on through the fog until he came to the very edge of himself, of his own physical limits, until he dropped, tired suddenly and drained of all strength, like this, with too much blood lost, until he fell like this to his knees in the soft dirt, like this, weighed down by his burden, like this, his legs bending under him and the girl sliding to the ground, slipping away from his hold.

Nyquist's eyes closed. A great wave of sadness moved through him, that he had come so far and failed even now, even in the final moments.

And even in the final moments...

A noise. He could hear a noise. A faraway sound, slowed down, like metal shivering against itself, like a wheel turning, or wheels turning, a number of them, demons crying out in the twilight for their hunger, for all the lost souls that have ended up here. Nyquist looked up, following the sound, giving in to it, and he saw the light moving across the land, coming closer. There it was. He picked Eleanor up once more and struggled to his feet with his last strength and together they set off, even more slowly this time, haltingly. His feet nearly tripped on the iron rails of the track but he kept on walking forward, stumbling. Towards the noise, towards the light that burned ever brighter now, cutting through the fog.

At last they stopped and waited. He could go no further.

Nyquist was standing directly on the rail track itself, on the wooden sleepers, waiting for the wagon to approach and the workers on board to recognise him as a fellow outcast; not a denizen of this wasted realm, but of theirs, another human being. And despite whatever he might look like, despite the wounds and the blood and the scars and the dirt and the haunted look in his eyes; despite all this he was the same as them, drawn from the same mould as the burnt-out cases that worked the maintenance wagons.

It was his only hope, this fragile connection.

The wagon came into view, slowing to a halt. The track workers were big ugly rough hewn specimens, the men and the women both. They stood impassively inside the protective cage, peering down silently at the sight that greeted them. Their features were grey-streaked from the smoke and the soot of the small engine that dragged them here.

One of them lifted a shotgun and pointed it forward.

The beam of a spotlight moved slowly across the fogbanks, coming to rest finally upon these two people, upon Nyquist and the girl, this strange and pitiful couple.

Into the dusk I have wandered, in the pale fog I have fallen and become lost, both lost and found.

And the wire door of the cage swung open.

EPILOGUE
DAYZONE

CRAWLING AT THE EDGES

The time crash – the third to hit the city – affected most of the central areas of Dayzone, many of the outlying districts, and at least half of the precincts of Nocturna. Measured on the council's official timeline, the event lasted only seventy-nine seconds. Seventy-nine seconds during which eighteen people died, mainly in road and rail accidents, while many others were physically injured and even more suffered from mental disorders. Symptoms included disorientation, nausea, dizziness and feelings of being "lost in a void". Chronopsychologists had long been predicting such an occurrence, concerned that the city's overabundance of time would one day reach a critical level, collapsing in on itself.

One citizen described the effect of suddenly being thrust from one timeline to another, without warning: "I felt like I was caught in a hurricane, pulled into the air and set down in another place: or in this case, another time. I blinked, and at least two hours had gone by, just like that! It was frightening. Even now I can't look at my wristwatch without seeing the hands jumping around like crazy." Many others described similar effects. The streets were filled with screams and howls of pain; people were sobbing, many wandered in a daze as though lost, or blind, or caught in a bubble, unable to escape. Some people walked almost in slow motion, others sped past in a blur. In addition to these bodily effects a good number of businesses closed down as their timelines collapsed, often beyond repair. Every piece of machinery dependent on a regular beat, on clockwork, on a pulse of any kind – all stopped, or malfunctioned. Fortunes were lost. The city's stock exchange fell into chaos. One expert explained that the merchant classes had actually invented time as we know it, back in the late middle ages, in order to synchronise their myriad business deals. In a very real sense, time is money: as one element fragmented, so did the other.

After the crash, groups of protesters marched through the streets, eventually meeting outside the Ariadne Centre, the central headquarters of Dayzone's most prominent timeline management company. Here, the people showed their anger by smashing windows and daubing slogans on the walls and hoardings. They shouted the name of the company's chief executive, Patrick Bale, demanding an explanation from him, and recompense for the fatalities, the injuries, the lost revenues. Bale did not make an appearance. In fact, he had not been seen inside the building for a good while, to the consternation of his staff. He was later arrested by police officers at his home in Darkness Falls on the charges of first-degree murder, the trafficking of illegal substances, and intent to cause grievous bodily harm. With him was his second-in-command, Margaret Pearce, who was also arrested. Bale's wife Catherine refused to provide him with an alibi for the murder of Karl Sumak, a drug dealer.

Soon enough the city's timelines returned to stability, and the citizens chose to forget the pain and discomfort they had felt during the crash. In fact, many new chronologies were introduced, under the guiding hand of Ariadne's new CEO, Oliver Henley, whose previous experience had been in the financial sector. "A fresh start," was promised. "We will never give up on our dream of a unique timescale for every single citizen!"

The official report on the crash uncovered an interesting anomaly: people suffering from the psychological condition known as chronostasis had been entirely unaffected by the effects of the upheaval, causing some experts to predict that the city's fate might well rest with such beings.

But that was not the strangest mystery.

Shortly after the seventy-nine seconds had passed, George Frederick Carlisle – a retired meteorologist of the precinct of Fade Away – ventured out to check his wind gauges and barometers. He stumbled across the body of a woman lying prone at the very edge of Dusk. Carlisle told a reporter for the *Beacon Fire* newspaper that the dead woman's flesh was "warm to the touch", indicating that she had died recently, perhaps during the time crash, although there is no way of knowing for sure. She had one hand outstretched in front of her, the long black fingernails digging into the soil as though for purchase. The other hand lay at her side and clutched within it was a knife. Traces of blood were found on the blade, and the knife was subsequently identified as the weapon used in the so-called Quicksilver murders. The woman's identity was never established, nor her role in that series of terrible crimes. Perhaps she had simply found the knife? Or perhaps she was the murderer herself, as unlikely as it might seem, given her age. For the dead woman was ancient: the pathologist estimated that she was more than a hundred years old.

George Carlisle described her as being "ravaged by life": her face sunken, her bones in view through the skin, her eyes yellow and almost hollow, her hair a mass of long, knotted, insect-infested rags. He thought that she'd been crawling along the ground, when she died from sheer exhaustion. Her heart gave out and time finally caught up with her. What she was crawling away from or indeed towards, we do not know.

The newspaper's report finished with an account of the old woman's final expression, etched on her face.

She was terrified.

ANOTHER SKY

He got to the coach station early. The ticket-office clock told him it was twenty-five to nine, less than half an hour before departure. He bought his ticket, changed his wristwatch to the station's time, and then went in search of the coffee bar.

Eleanor was already there.

He ordered a coffee at the counter and walked over to sit down opposite her, placing his suitcase on the floor beside his feet. For a moment they sat in silence. She nursed her drink, staring through the window at the coaches as they came and went. Arrivals. Departures. People waiting around, looking worried or sad or elated. Nyquist looked at her. Some days and nights had gone by, and she had changed in a way he could barely fathom. He knew she'd been in hospital, like he had, and her face could not hide the recent experiences; her eyes, especially. She was still weak from her act of kindness, that much was clear. And yet he had the feeling that something else was being hidden, some other pain.

He tried conversation. "I gave the police evidence against Bale and Pearce."

There was no response.

"I'm sure they'll be found guilty. They'll go to prison."

Eleanor remained silent.

"So then..." Nyquist stood up slowly. His midriff still burned when he made sudden movements. "I might as well get in the queue."

"No. Wait. Please. Sit down."

He did so, and now she spoke in a rush: "Patrick will get away with it. I know him. He'll fight his way out of the trouble, with his money and his greed and his power."

Nyquist spoke quietly: "He's a fallen man. Especially after the crash and the loss of his position. It'll be a struggle, it really will."

Eleanor tapped a spoon against her coffee cup. She was shivering even under the hot lamps fixed to the ceiling. The waitress brought Nyquist's own drink to the table.

"Did you have any trouble?" he asked. "In the crash, I mean."

"After what we've been through, that was nothing."

"True. True." He smiled. "Where are you living?"

"You remember Melissa? The maid?"

"I do. She helped me to find you."

"I've moved in with her."

Nyquist nodded at this. He said, "What about your mother? How is she?"

Eleanor shook her head slowly. "The same. For now."

Nyquist could still picture Catherine Bale in her room of clocks, forever trying to hold time at that one particular setting.

"She'll need your help," he said.

"Yes. I know."

Another moment of silence between them. But then she looked at him properly for the first time and asked, "What happened in there, John? In the dusk?"

"You can't remember?"

"Just running, running away, trying to get away from Aisha and then dancing with Eliza, with my sister. And then the fog. Then, nothing. Like I'd fallen into sleep."

Nyquist took a sip of his coffee. Casually, he said, "The fog took hold of you. You must've have become disoriented. It can happen."

"Oh, right."

"It's easy to get lost."

She gave him a look that he could hardly bear to receive, never mind give back. But he held the stare.

"What about Eliza, did she get away?"

"I think so," he answered. "She was under her grandmother's power, under a spell, but I believe she broke away at the end."

"But she's still in there, still in twilight?"

"Eleanor…"

"Yes?"

"You gave her life. A share of life. That's…"

She stared at him, her eyes slowly blinking.

"That's all you need to know."

She nodded. "You tried to kill me in that hotel room. I remember that."

It almost broke him to hear her say it, but then she smiled, just a trace at the corners of her mouth and she continued, "Don't worry. I'm still here, still breathing."

He let a moment pass. Then he said, "Eleanor, you asked to see me before I left."

"I just want… I just wanted to see you off."

She looked down at the table. He touched her hand across the food-stained surface, saying quietly, "Keep away from the dusk. Don't let the past get hold of you. Or the future. This is what counts, this moment. Each passing moment."

"And what about you?" she asked.

"Another city, some other starting point."

Now she looked up. "Doing what?"

"Doing the only thing I can do. Being a hardhearted,

knuckleheaded son of a bitch with no good chance in hell, but happy enough to help people for money."

Here she smiled, properly this time. "Will I see you again?"

He kept his eyes on her. "There's a part of me..." His voice faltered. "All the time I was in the dusk, even towards the end, I kept expecting to see my father, still alive, and that he'd recognise me and offer me something, some kind of love, I guess. Of course, such things don't happen. They shouldn't happen." He pushed his cup away. "What can I say? You have to get tough on yourself, you know? Be wary of the things that pull you back."

"By running away?"

"It doesn't feel like I'm running away, not this time."

They fell to silence once again. Nyquist looked through the window. "I think that's my coach."

"Right. You'd better..."

"Listen, Eleanor..."

"I can't..."

She was tearful. Nyquist felt his heart moving at the sight of it.

"Please," he said. "Don't."

"I'm not crying for you, don't worry."

"I'm guessing that."

One more moment. She wiped at her face. "You'd better go. Quickly please."

He stood, picking up his suitcase.

"Just keep on," he said. "Keep on."

Then he turned and walked out of the coffee bar. He didn't look back. He walked across the tarmac to where his coach waited. People were getting on already. He joined the queue. No, he didn't look back.

The coach left on time, on the dot, the exact second as stated, and travelled through the streets of Dayzone. This city of sparkle and glitter and life and dazzle and glamour and radiance and fire and neon-lit brilliance, and the twenty million clocks, and the countless billions of light bulbs, incandescent, luminous, as they flash and flicker with power and heat.

The most beautiful of all cities.

And now the lamps were less bright, and further apart. The city faded at the edges until only dark blue skies remained, dim skies, and then twilit skies. They were getting close to the border. Out there it was night. He rested his head against the seat back, as his fingertips remembered that last touch of her hand on the tabletop. A spark, a memory. And the look in her eyes, a slight darkening of the blue, a mistiness. And he wondered about the moment of exchange: when Eleanor had given something of herself to her sister, had the sister given anything back in return? A message, perhaps; something good to take out of dusk, to bring into the light.

The steward made an announcement, that the vehicle was now leaving the city, and was entering the country's standard time zone, normal time. Nyquist adjusted his watch, as did all the people around him. He looked out of the window at the night sky, the wide open sky, the moon and the pale wash of the galaxy's central hub, and the ever circling stars in their ancient patterns. And somewhere in the distance, below the horizon, waiting for him: the sun.

The coach travelled on.

ACKNOWLEDGMENTS

Lots of people have helped with this story. Chief among them are Vana and Michelle, who both offered much needed advice and kindness. The team at Angry Robot – especially Marc Gascoigne and Penny Reeve – worked their wonders, bringing the story to fruition, and into the public eye. Simon Spanton did a brilliant editing job. And a special mention to Tim Dedopulos, for bringing myself and Angry Robot together.

ABOUT THE AUTHOR

Jeff Noon is an award-winning British novelist, short story writer and playwright. He won the Arthur C Clarke Award for *Vurt*, the John W Campbell award for Best New Writer, a Tinniswood Award for innovation in radio drama and the Mobil prize for playwriting. He was trained in the visual arts, and was musically active on the punk scene before starting to write plays for the theatre. His work spans SF and fantasy genres, exploring the ever-changing borderzone between genre fiction and the avant-garde.

jeffnoon.weebly.com • twitter.com/jeffnoon